Attaining The Realms

The Mortal Scales Book 1
Autumn Cox

AHCworx

To the people in my life who helped me realize I had a story worth telling.

Contents

Prologue

Estian

T he queen tapped her foot impatiently as she waited for a knock on the door of her sitting room. Despite its spacious opulence, she still felt stifled. Three days, she'd waited. Three days since the general crossed through the Wildes from the Expanse.

The missive she'd received sat on the desk beside her. The desk was a great carved wooden affair that had been her father's—a gift to his daughter on her coronation. He'd been glad enough to be rid of the monstrosity, he'd insisted. Especially after he and her mother moved into the smaller royal apartments they'd claimed in a far western tower where the view was almost as breathtaking as the furniture her mother commissioned for the move.

Estian thus received, upon her queenship, the rather impressive desk full of papers and a role that, as of late, sat heavy on her narrow shoulders.

She tried to calm herself. Despite her current mood, her sitting room *was* rather pleasant. The desk, even in its grandeur, occupied only a portion of the space to one side of the chamber. Most of the floor was taken up by a comfortable set of well-padded chairs around a table formed of a perfectly circular disc of stone placed on a sturdy wooden base; it was thick and smooth, sparkling with the fine crystals from which it was carved. The table had been her mother's and always one of Estian's favorite pieces, so again she was gifted furniture though this had been upon reaching her majority. Her mother insisted the table previously belonged to the first king and had been left in a storage room during the splitting—long forgotten until it was uncovered, dusted off, and placed in her mother's sitting room some years before Estian was born.

The tea in its worked metal pitcher still steamed merrily, the moisture dancing in the soft breeze passing through from the open window casings. She'd thrown open those windows this morning, and taken a seat on the long, padded bench that overlooked the courtyard and the road beyond. When one of her ladies brought the tea, she'd made herself leave her perch, but the tea had curdled on her tongue as she received the morning's reports.

Still no word from the general, and yet more reports of her own people leaving without word.

Estian told herself that the second part was less important; that her people were free to travel as they would. She was their queen, not their warden, after all. The truth was, she wasn't sure if the two reports were related and worried that they were.

When a hollow, booming knock rattled the door, she launched from her chair, nearly tripping on her skirts, and grabbing onto the edge of her desk to steady herself.

"Come!" Her own voice rang in her ears, resonant and formal. Estian gripped the soft fabric of her skirts hard as she waited for the door to open. She'd dressed partially in haste, but also partially to soothe herself in case of more bad news. The dress was light and soft and hung in long draping folds from her shoulders to brush the tops of her bare feet. She'd never gained the knack that many in her court had, of wearing shoes—not even the delicate slippers some wore—preferring to keep her feet bare and clean, grounded to the land she stewarded. The fabric was smooth under her hands, like the surface of a rose petal, and her favorite color; that of the feathered fronds of long grass, pale green like the underside of a leaf. It made her smile despite herself, but the smile disappeared almost as soon as it came.

The man who entered was tall and lean, his usually clean and perfect uniform dusty and wrinkled from the road. "Your Majesty." He bowed deeply before turning to close the door behind himself. She allowed herself a moment to watch his back, straight and so seemingly strong, despite his obvious exhaustion. But there was no missing the signs. There was a tear in the upper sleeve of his black-on-black doublet; the seams of his gray stockings were askew, and the knees bagged with wear. Even the baldric that crossed his chest and back, a thick strap of black leather normally so well maintained that it practically gleamed, was as dull and travel worn as the rest of him.

She gave the barest nod that he failed to see, but she didn't say anything. Her heart raced and pounded in her chest, and Estian tried to swallow past the hard lump in her throat. Formalities first. She may hate the protocols around her station, but her father had told her before that in times of high pressure, she would appreciate their existence. Now, as she worked to gather herself, she grasped his meaning.

"General Faylin, please, come in and be welcome. I appreciate your swiftness in this matter. I have anxiously awaited your arrival for some days."

3

"Your Majesty, I assure you I returned as swiftly as I could." He stood at attention, watching her as she approached the circle of chairs and allowed herself a moment to sit and arrange her skirts before continuing.

"I believe you, general." She waved her hand in dismissal of his defensive tone. "Please, sit. Continue."

The general, at her instruction, perched himself at the very edge of one of the chairs across from her. He gripped his hands together in his lap and gazed down at them, gathering himself before bringing his gaze up to meet hers. "I wish to report my findings, regarding the mission to the Bastion of Night." He watched her, waiting. He, too, seemingly found solace in the ceremony.

Estian gave another stiff nod, forcing her hands to remain still in her lap. "Of course, general. Were you able to locate her upon your arrival?"

"Your Majesty, I am greatly vexed to say that sadly we were not. By the time we got close enough to capture her, she'd vanished. Not before utterly demoralizing the ranks, however. Many of those you sent with me have been taken down into the catacombs. May the Void cradle them and Danann grant swift healing. Some who have returned with me show no physical ailments, and yet..."

He pulled off one of his gloves and ran the bare hand through his wavy golden hair. She'd forgotten he'd sheared it short before leaving. It now hung about his head in damp clumps.

A deep sigh dragged itself from his mouth and moved through the room like a strong wind. His eyes flashed with lightning among storm clouds, a sign of great distress. There was more than one reason he was referred to as the Storm Lord by his warriors. At this moment, though, it was less about his power and more about his exhaustion. He gave a small shudder and shook his head, his eyes closing. Suddenly, he was only her younger brother, the small boy she'd cradled to her chest and soothed after he'd fallen from a tree.

Faylin fought to gather himself. Her heart went out to him, but they both knew this wasn't done. When she finally spoke, her voice was as gentle as she could make it. "Did you find anything?"

"Just this." From his belt pouch the general produced a small scroll, tied with a black ribbon. Spidery script was scrawled along one edge.

To her Royal Majesty, Queen Estian Boryas Murhai

Her fingers trembled as she tugged the end of the ribbon to loosen the bow.

My Dear Estian

I made sure your darling general would survive to get this letter to you. I am sure you know what wonderful care I am taking with your little wards. Truly, there is nothing like the sound of screaming mortals. Better yet, how easily they give themselves over, once they understand what I offer. Something you never could. How Gracious. How Kind. You would deny them that which I promise?

But know this, my sweet queen; if you try again to hunt me down like some pathetic animal, I swear by the Void itself that you will share their fate under my tender care. Ah, but since you cannot die, my most glorious sweetling, there will be no end to the blessing of your screams in my ears.

Estian shivered, and the letter fell to her lap. There was no signature, but she didn't need one. As soon as the paper hit her skirts, it burst into flame. The flash was quick, dissipating in a cloud of ash and smoke that left her coughing and gagging on the stench of burnt flesh. Only then did she see the general slumped in his seat.

He was now nothing more than a form made of black ash in an otherwise unburnt uniform. Of his body, his eyes were the only part that remained intact; a ring of white sclera around the pupil, the storm clouds clearing as they glazed over in death.

Her scream tore from her throat and tolled like a bell through the halls of the palace.

Chapter One

Christian

"Christian Alexander Johnson, get your sorry ass out of bed, *now*! You're gonna be late for school again!"

Chris groaned and rolled over, pulling his blanket with him as he curled up against the wall and away from his mother's obnoxious screech. How did she have such a harsh voice, even this early in the morning? It seemed unnatural.

"Get. Up." She nudged him roughly on the hip with her slipper-shod foot in time with her words. His leg blossomed with pain, and Chris groaned again, shifting onto his back and letting his arms flop out to his sides. He squinted up at his mother from his mattress on the floor. Her expression was angry and puckered, but he wasn't sure how much of that was him and how much was the hangover she was probably nursing.

"I'm up, ma." Chris rolled himself the rest of the way off the bed and popped up to his feet in one move. He snatched his belt and jeans from the floor, pulling them on over his boxers, then snagged a moss green tank top from another spot on the floor and pulled it over his head, tucking it in before latching the belt buckle.

It had unintentionally become a sort of continued uniform. These—and all the rest of his clothes—were compliments of New Horizons Reform School. They'd provided him with four pairs of solidly functional, standard colored and surprisingly comfortable jeans; something he could wear on the long hikes that the school heads referred to as rejuvenating walks or working around the main campus. They were even comfortable enough for hanging around the bunk room.

The shirts were all just as functional, simple, and unadorned. Mostly a lot of gray and green colored raglan sleeved baseball tees and close-fitting tank tops to wear under dress shirts for important events; two bleached bone white and two moss green, like the one he was wearing. The two dress shirts and pairs of slacks were hung up in his closet, which was otherwise empty save a couple dust balls in one corner.

Originally, he'd wondered if he was silly for asking to bring home all the clothes they'd given him for the year he was there, but when he'd gotten home only two months ago, he'd found everything in his room had either been thrown out or sold by his mother's last boyfriend. Not even his bed was spared. At least he'd been able to buy a lumpy mattress from his boss at the job where New Horizons placed him. It wasn't perfect, but it was better than the floor.

From the same pile where he'd pulled the tank, he grabbed a clean pair of socks, also standard issue from New Horizons, and pulled them on followed by clunky, well-worn hiking boots that were long since broken in and hugged his feet snuggly without sore spots or toe pinches. *New Horizons, how is it you took better care of me in one year than my mother has, my whole life?*

His mother grumbled something under her breath before walking out of the room. He wasn't sure if he was meant to hear what she said, so he did his best to ignore it. He pretended he hadn't just heard his own mother compliment something about his body. She must still be drunk. That was probably it.

"Don't forget to take your lunch today. I won't keep paying for that junk they feed you at school—" She stood in the hall, watching him as he limped out of his bedroom and into the bathroom.

"—and don't forget to pick your sister up from the sitter after school. And make sure she gets dinner since I'm gonna be gone. And do the dishes, for god's sake. I'm tired of cleaning up after you! God knows why I keep letting you back under my roof. And your laundry is *still* in the laundry room, so you better put it away before I get home." The tone of her voice told him exactly what would happen if he didn't put his clothes away, and he quietly seethed. If not for Sara, he would have been long gone and on his own, his mother be damned. *Put it away where, ma? You sold my damned dresser.*

"Yes, ma." Chris mumbled as his mother continued her tirade. None of this was new. Annoying? Yes. Infuriating? Absolutely, but it hadn't been new since he was Sara's age. Right about the time his dad died.

His mother followed him and stopped in the doorway as he leaned on the counter over the sink. He peered at his own face in the mirror, rough with stubble, then picked up his hairbrush with one hand and an electric razor with the other, going at his face from both angles.

His hair was sandy blond and hung around his head in shaggy strands, straw straight and absolutely impossible to style in any way he actually liked on himself. His eyes were honest blue, and even he could see how tired he looked as he studied himself. He ran the brush through his hair, which flopped right back into place as soon as the bristles released it. All the while, he ran the electric razor over his cheeks, then set the brush down so he could tilt his head up to shave under his chin and along his neck.

"What the hell happened to your neck?" His mother paused in her rant and took a step forward, reaching for him.

Chris leaned forward scrutinizing the skin now cleared of hair. There was a welt around his neck that looked an awful lot like rope burn. The moment the thought came, the pain in his hip flared, as if the welt on his neck and the pain in his hip were part of a matching set.

He dropped the razor onto the counter and moved to shut the door on his mother, carefully edging her out of the doorway and back into the hall as he mumbled something about needing to go to the bathroom. With the door closed, he leaned against it and undid his belt buckle and pulled the waist of his jeans open and looked down. Then he pushed them and his boxers down all together, catching them at his knees.

Huge bruises ran along the outsides and fronts of his legs from hip bone to just above his knees, stark and vibrant against his pale skin. His crotch throbbed and ached from the swelling in his legs. His knees were sore, and his leg muscles burned like they had been twisted and pulled. His back always ached a little since he did a fairly labor heavy job, stocking shelves and helping with inventory in a hardware store, but this wasn't at all the same; it was more like he'd been stretched too far. He lifted his shirt to find more small bruises that ran along the sides of his spine.

"What the fuck?" Chris goggled at the bruises covering his back and legs. His mother knocked on the door and he jumped, startled. Hurriedly, he pulled his pants back up and zipped them closed then reached over and flushed the toilet. He tucked his shirt back in and relatched his belt, then finished shaving and gave himself a final once over in the mirror before he pulled open the door and flipped off the light.

His mother was still standing just outside the door, her eyes narrowed as he passed her and walked into the front room. His backpack and coat sat neatly by the front door where he'd placed them. Chris pulled on the coat as he stepped over to the old sofa that sagged against one wall where the small shape of his sleeping sister was curled under a thread-bare quilt. He leaned down to kiss her gently on the top of her head.

"See you this afternoon, kiddo." Chris whispered the words softly against her head, and when he moved back, he could see one of her eyes open. A sleepy smile crossed her face, then her eyes closed, and she snuggled back down into the blanket.

"Bye, Ma. See you later." Without looking at her, he grabbed up his backpack and pulled the door open and then closed behind himself. He winced as he made his way down the steps of the house, dragging his bag over his shoulder while he crossed the small lawn and headed toward the school.

Harlequin

Harlequin Swanson sat at her kitchen table, looking over the last of her homework. She was struggling to focus on the words on the page, as her mind kept wandering back to the vague memories of a dream and the pain in her body.

The early morning light shining in through the kitchen window should have made the room feel bright and homey, but her nose was full of the smell of mildew and under that, the coppery hint of blood. She'd already checked the fridge and the trash can, though she was sure her dad took the trash out the night before. Nothing she could find explained the smell, and she wished she'd thought to put orange juice on the grocery list. In her experience, the scent of citrus could cut through almost anything.

Instead, she sat in the clean, white tiled kitchen, and tried to breathe through her mouth.

Her body ached. Every part of her felt raw, like she'd been rubbed with sandpaper from the inside out. She'd struggled to eat her breakfast—a small bowl of cold cereal that now sat like a brick in her churning stomach. She had vague memories of hands, a table that was more like a stone slab in a dark room, and the sure knowledge that she was going to die.

Her dad puttered in the living room, humming to himself. Even without being able to hear it clearly, she knew it would be the same song he always hummed. The song he and her mom danced to at their wedding. The song they'd danced to on their first date. She let out a breath she didn't know she'd been holding and tried to put a convincing smile on her face as she saw the swinging door start to push open.

"Hey, Dad. Before you ask, yes, I ate breakfast, and I made my lunch." She patted part of her backpack. "Do you have a second that you could come read this essay before I leave? I want to make sure I didn't miss anything."

"Sure thing Harl, but I'm sure you didn't. You got your mother's brains." Her dad smiled as he entered the room, pulling his tie straight. Harley gave him an appraising look. He always led off with a compliment when he was hoping to get one back.

His slacks were cleanly pressed, the creases down the legs crisp and sharp. The cool toned charcoal pants were balanced nicely by a pale, cornflower blue dress shirt and a tie of a dark gray with tiny navy-blue musical notes. The suit jacket draped over his arm matched the slacks, showing a pale blue pocket square with a gray edge that matched the tie. All of it was quite striking against his warm, olive complexion and the thick waves of chestnut brown hair that curled around his ears and at the top of the shirt collar.

Harley's eyebrows rose. He was rarely this dressed up since her mom passed. A closet full of designer suits upstairs gathered dust as he mourned a woman thirteen years gone. Harley shook her head and gave him the look his outfit deserved.

"Wow. Dad, you look great! Attending another big meeting today?" Harley gave him a real smile as she handed over her essay. She hoped the suit and the humming were a sign that today would be one of his good days. He didn't get many of those, despite her best efforts.

"What? Oh, no. Not a big one, anyway. I'm meeting a friend tonight after work, and one of the clients is coming in today to hear my pitch for the case. Do you still have tutoring, tonight?"

"Oh, right. It's Wednesday." When he eyed her, brow furrowed, she gave him a grin. "Then yes, tutoring, and since you're going out for dinner, I'll plan to fend for myself."

He gave her a skeptical look, eyes narrowed before he went back to reading. Harley busied herself with putting away the rest of her homework in her backpack, only her English folder left on the table.

When her dad reached the end of the essay, he offered the papers back, a warm smile lighting his features. "Harley, this is an incredibly good paper.

The only critique I have is to watch your punctuation. You may have gotten your brains from your mom, but those commas are all me."

Harley smiled as she took the paper from him and tucked it into its folder, then into her backpack with everything else.

She rose from her chair and straightened her skirt, patting it down around her legs before checking to make sure her simple button-up blouse was properly tucked in.

The self-imposed uniform started in elementary school—A simple pleated plaid skirt that hung down to her knees for modesty, and a pale cream or white blouse that buttoned up over a white undershirt and white bike shorts— mostly to help her dad who had no idea how to shop for a little girl. His mom, Harley's Grandma Doris, had been helpful but old fashioned. Though, if Harley was honest, she appreciated not having to think too hard about what to wear each day. Even if it brought the occasional rude or inappropriate comment. She could only be in charge of herself.

Today's skirt was a standard wool plaid with stripes of red, green, and brown over dark gray, and her blouse was a pale cream cotton jersey knit so soft and drapey it was almost more of a night shirt than a blouse. She noticed as she checked the neat knife pleats of her skirt that she'd dressed in garments her mom's mom, Nana Mary, gave her. Favorites in her closet that she reached for when she was most in need of a hug. A dark green cardigan hung on the back of the dining chair, and it, too, told Harley just how much she was seeking comfort, this morning. Afterall, it had belonged to Harley's mom.

Her thick, dark curls were pulled up into a high ponytail, though little wisps had pulled themselves loose around the edges of her hairline. It was the most she'd felt up to doing this morning, but she had to admit, she liked the clean look of it, and it kept her hair up and off her neck. It wasn't that she didn't like her hair; she loved it, most of the time. Mostly, it was that her dad insisted her hair was her mom's, too.

Sometimes she wondered if her dad maintained a mental checklist of what parts of her belonged to her long dead mom and what parts belonged to him, the still living parent. If he did, Harley was fairly certain one was much longer than the other, and not in his favor. She was also fairly sure there wouldn't be a column on that list for herself.

Harley squared her wire-framed glasses on her face and hid a sigh by leaning over to pick up her bag.

Her dad stopped her as she started to walk toward the door at the far side of the kitchen that would take her out to the garage. "Oh, hey, I forgot to tell you. Go ahead and take the car today. The office guys are carpooling, and my friend is picking me up after work." He gave her another warm smile, and she tried to tell herself she was only imagining the despair she saw in his eyes.

"Thanks, Dad. I hope you have a good day! I love you!" She gave him a kiss on the cheek then headed out to the garage.

Harley said a quiet grateful prayer as she got into the car that her dad hadn't noticed her discomfort. The last thing he needed was more stress in his life. The pain in her body and stomach would go away, and until it did, she'd ignore it. If her dad had a checklist, she'd started one of her own, and at the top of it were the secrets she kept.

Chapter Two

Christian

C hris walked the last block to school slowly. He'd made it over halfway there before he realized he'd forgotten to grab his lunch. His mother would give him no end of shit for it, but he wasn't about to turn around. The big brick structure that made up the main building of Northfield High School was already only 100 yards away, crouched like a giant red toad against the dark green of the lawn and filling his vision.

It seemed stupid to come today. He wished he could have skipped, but he'd made an agreement with his boss. The more he showed up for school, the better bonuses he got, and the boss wouldn't report him to New Horizons. Chris admitted to himself that it was a fair deal, and he needed the money, even if he'd been strong-armed into it.

Ahead of him, Jenta Rawlings was headed up the steps to the main doors. He couldn't help but follow her with his eyes. Dressed in tight black jeans with a studded black leather belt, and billowing black dress shirt that gave him flashes of a black corset top he'd seen her wear before. Her hair hung in one long braid down her back and exposed ears lined in silver hoop earrings and showed the snug spiked collar at her neck. The boots she wore came up over the jeans and buckled nearly up to her knees. He always wondered if those were as uncomfortable as they appeared, but she moved in them as easily as if she were barefoot. Hell, even her backpack was black and covered in those little silver screw-on spikes.

Chris let out a sigh. One of these days, he would actually talk to her. Or at least, he'd say more than just 'hi'. They'd had classes together a few times in the past and seen each other in the halls. Every time he'd noticed her, he'd wanted to approach her. Everything about her screamed for his attention, called out to him, and Chris knew somehow that in Jenta Rawlings, he might have a chance to find something big that he wanted, or maybe *needed* to understand.

Up until and through Sophomore year, whenever he'd seen her, he bolted. Not fear of her, so much as fear of what it might mean to let himself admit how he felt. She'd been different, then. Quiet, yes, and that hard shell was around her even then—that bit of protection she held against the world—but somehow softer than it was, now. The black clothes had only just started to appear in her wardrobe back then, and her hair had still been the pale reddish brown he remembered from Junior high. Then he'd been sent off for a year because his mother's flavor-of-the-day boyfriend decided he was being *defiant* and *disrespectful*. He didn't think they anticipated that New Horizons would actually do him good. But it meant that he was out of the loop at Northfield for a year, and a lot could change in that time.

When school started back up a month ago, he'd gotten to see just how much had changed, Jenta included. Dark, broody, focused, with an I-don't-give-a-shit attitude. The hair, the collar, everything studded with spikes. She'd not just made the shell around herself thicker but armed it with thorns so that anyone who tried to hurt her would be hurt right back.

17

He wasn't the only one who'd become defiant. And then there was the look she sometimes got, like she'd woken from a bad dream, to a worse reality.

"Chris! Yo, Chris!"

"Huh?" Chris pivoted to regard the guy jogging toward him. Josh had also attended New Horizons, and they'd both been pleasantly surprised to see each other on campus at the beginning of the school year, both of them now 18 and seniors. Josh dropped into step beside him, and Chris gave his friend a measuring look, noting the lines of tension around Josh's eyes and the way his hand gripped a little too tightly at his backpack strap. Josh showed all the same signs of pain and exhaustion he used to after one of Officer Reinhard's rejuvenating walks.

He was dressed in similar clothes to those Chris wore, more New Horizons wardrobe options on display. The only difference was that compared to Chris' plain drab green army-style jacket, Josh wore an old letterman's jacket with the black leather sleeves just a little too short for his arms. Chris knew if he checked the back, it would have Josh's dad's baseball team nickname, 'Homerun Howie' in embroidery wrapped around a baseball patch, to go with the big 'N' patch on the left breast for Northfield. Josh had never lettered in anything, any more than Chris had. Chris noted a bruise on the wrist Josh was using to grip his bag. Following the look, Josh frowned and pulled the sleeve of his jacket up to cover the bruise before looking back up.

"Did you hear, man?"

"Hear what?" Chris hefted his bag and picked up his pace.

"At least like ten different kids were rushed to the hospital this morning."

"Shit. Really?"

"Right? That Cheerleader, Sierra? Remember her?"

"Yeah. I remember her. Why?"

"She's in the ICU. It's all over social." He stopped walking and grabbed Chris by the arm to pull him around.

"What?" Chris eyed his friend. Josh's expression became serious.

"Dude... Uh, did you have any dreams last night? Like, you know, bad ones?" His voice came out kind of strangled and strange, and he broke eye contact quickly, turning his head to gaze back at the school.

Chris tried not to flinch, and the lie tumbled out of his mouth before he really thought about it. "I never remember my dreams, man. I worry when I *do* remember them. Why?"

Before either of them could speak, the five-minute bell went off. Class would be starting soon. They shared a look, then adjusted their bags and jogged towards the school.

Harlequin

Harley was parked, her hands gripping the steering wheel as she tried to breathe through a wave of cramps that left her nauseous. Maybe it was good there hadn't been any orange juice in the fridge.

She peered up at her friend Jess who stood next to the car, regarding her with worried eyes. Jess, like Harley, had a self-imposed uniform—A pair of classic-cut, button-fly jeans with a white t-shirt tucked in under a garish Hawaiian shirt that she always left unbuttoned, and a pair of plain black and white slip-on sneakers. She dressed like she'd just stepped out of a coming-of-age movie from the 1990s, and Harley knew at least a part of that was because Jess's mom loved the look, but her dad, an aggressively traditional businessman, *hated* it.

Harley opened the driver's side door, Jess stepping to one side so she could climb slowly out, her body moving stiffly.

Jessica Tran, Harley's research and study partner, continued to watch Harley skeptically but remained silent, simply putting out a hand to take Harley's backpack from her. When Harley hesitated, Jess wiggled her fingers a little in a "gimme" gesture. Harley laughed and handed her the bag, strap first, before turning to close up her car.

"I'm okay Jess. Just really bad cramps. Why are you waiting out in the parking lot?"

"Harley. You look like crap."

"Thanks, Jess. So kind of you to say so. And how are you today?" Jess huffed and shook her head, then laughed.

"Fine, fine. You still look like crap, but if you can joke about it, you're not dying."

"Har Har. Seriously though, what's up?" Harley nodded toward the school. They started walking almost in unison. Jess flipped one side of her thick, shining black hair over one shoulder in a practiced gesture and gave Harley some serious side eye before she answered.

"I've heard at least ten students were rushed to the hospital this morning after waking up sick, and at least three more were found dead in their beds." Harley gaped at her.

"Dead? How?"

"They don't know. Folks on the news were saying it could be some kind of toxic gas attack or terrorist strike."

Harley gave her the look that statement deserved.

Jess raised her hands in defense. "Listen, I know. I don't agree with it, either. None of the victims even live close to each other, and none of the symptoms seem to match up with any known bio chems. Also, some reports mentioned injuries."

"Not to mention, who on Earth would coordinate a terrorist attack on Green Bridge?"

"Right? We're like... Nowheresville, USA. Also-also, most of them were super young."

Harley furrowed her brows, her eyes narrowing at that. "Did the news report say *how* young?"

"Um, I don't recall if they mentioned specific ages, but a lot of them were high school or college students. Maybe a couple older. I think that's why they were saying it might have been targeted."

"What, that they were young?"

"No. Specifically, that they were students. They're wondering if the schools were the source."

"Wait, didn't you say they were all sleeping? Like, that they woke up sick?"

"Yeah. Like I said, it doesn't make any sense. I think they're totally grasping at anything to explain what's happening."

A sudden sense of urgency filled Harley. Her thoughts racing, she hurried toward the building. Just behind her, Jess followed, their footsteps loud in the nearly empty parking lot. The five-minute bell rang out and bounced against the walls of the main building.

Harley and Jess walked faster.

Chapter Three

Harlequin

T he Northfield High School Library was enormous by high school
library standards, especially for a small town in middle America.
However, this particular library also doubled as the main branch for the
entire town of Green Bridge, meaning that it not only got whatever fund-
ing the school superintendent threw at it, but also received subsidies from
the town and donations from wealthy patrons of the arts.

For Harley, that meant she was granted access to books she otherwise
might never have seen. Books that were part of collections gifted by de-
scendants of the town founders who carried those same collections with
them at great cost from the far reaches of Europe, the Middle East, Africa
and beyond.

She was currently surrounded by many of those dusty tomes. Some were
full of fairy tales; stories about evil witches and trolls and a world of magic—a place that ran parallel to the one full of fast cars and computers but
where unicorns romped in green meadows under iridescent skies. Some
were large coffee table hardbound types, full of paintings and sculptures,
writings, and treatises. She took notes in a journal with a clean, cramped
hand as she flipped through pages filled with stories and art from long

before she was born. She turned each page slowly, searching for anything she might have missed the first time she'd done this.

The research paper she'd written a year ago had started as a joke during a conversation with a member of a student led role-playing club. What if fairytales were real? A real place that humans just lost the knack of reaching? Or what if the ability to get there was taken away? What if only artists or believers could reach it, or maybe you could only reach it in your dreams? Were vivid dreams actually times where humans touched that other world? What about when someone woke up in pain after a nightmare? It had opened up a huge world of questions and drew her down a rabbit hole of research that she'd funded with class credits, but it had all been hypothetical.

"Harley? Can I talk to you for a second?"

Cadence Murphy's voice spooked her enough to make her jump in her chair. She looked up into a pair of bright green eyes. Had his eyes always been so serious and sad? Harley studied him for a moment, and he squirmed under her scrutiny.

Cadence, 'call-me-Cay', Murphy was no longer the wiry, almost delicate looking young boy she'd met in sixth grade, after his family moved to Green Bridge. His dad had just taken an administrative role at a small army base nearby, after returning from service abroad. Back then, Cadence had still worn horn-rimmed glasses, and braces to correct an aggressive overbite. His hands had always been long-fingered and surprisingly elegant, and Harley wondered if he still practiced piano, or if his dad finally beat that out of him, too.

Standing next to her in crisp jeans and expensive, all-white tennis shoes, Cay towered at something like 6'5", his shoulders broad and strapped with muscle giving his chest and torso that tapered V that athletes strove for, but very few actually achieved. The close-fitting tee he wore certainly helped emphasize the hard work. The shirt was a red so dark it was nearly black, tucked into the jeans. It was almost unfortunate that he also wore a letterman jacket, though that too fit his new persona perfectly. Captain of the football team, quarterback, leader of the popular kids.

Much like Jess, Cay also could have easily stepped out of a movie, though his might have been a little less PG, a little more PG-13. Not quite R-rated. Cay might have turned as red as his hair if anyone even suggested it. For all that he'd physically become everything his father wanted him to be, Harley wasn't sure Cadence, within himself, would ever be anything other than the skinny boy who played Mozart concertos for his mother and rescued his older sisters from the spiders in their bathroom.

Even so, the truth was, she wasn't sure if she *wanted* him to talk to her. They'd been friends for years—right up until the summer after Tenth grade, in fact. When he was still just gangly, awkward, nerdy Cadence Murphy. Then came the contacts, weights, and sports. Shortly after that, the braces finally came off. She didn't blame him. Cadence was a born leader, despite anything his dad might tell him. He was clever, kind, and empathetic nearly to a fault. The world of research wasn't the right fit for him, but he'd never begrudged her books, any more than she'd begrudged his need to be liked and accepted.

Then Becky Lindstadt came along. Captain of Northfield Highschool's Champion cheerleading squad. Blond-haired, blue-eyed, Becky who believed the world was her very own personal fairy tale, and Becky was the princess seeking her prince. Harley rarely would have accused anyone of having main character energy, but Becky surely did.

If Becky was the princess, Harley was the troll beneath the keep, and Cadence, Becky's current prince, certainly should not be seen talking to the troll.

Harley shook her head. She wasn't a troll, any more than Becky was a princess, and Cadence was just a guy who used to be her friend.

She gestured to the seat beside her. "What's up, Cay? Have a seat."

Cadence sat but didn't talk at first. He was looking at the contents of the table in front of them.

"So, I guessed right, then. You think this has something to do with the dreams, don't you?" When Harley didn't immediately answer, he gave her serious eye contact, searching her face. "You had it too; the dream." It wasn't a question. He nodded to himself, then asked, "Harley, what's happening?"

He reached out and touched one of the books lying open in front of her, moving aside the bookmark she'd used to obscure the painting beneath. After glancing at the picture, he made a face and put the bookmark back. Harley didn't really blame him.

The painting was an incredibly detailed scene straight out of a nightmare. A woman draped over a table while a gray, hairless creature the size of a German shepherd crouched over her. Blood stood out on its face and dripped from a set of gleaming, razor-sharp teeth that glinted ruby red. The realism of the painting was disturbing.

The footnote below referred to the creature as a goblin. It was thin and wiry with a diamond shaped head and wide dark eyes. It gripped the woman's arms with long, spider-like fingers, tipped with black talons that dimpled into her flesh. The woman's head lolled to one side, her eyes partially closed as if drowsing, but the creature stared straight at where the painter would have been.

Harley sighed and ran ink-stained fingers through her hair. At some point, she'd pulled her ponytail out, and her hair now fell around her shoulders in a frizzy tangle. Her head hurt less with her hair down, but she felt awkward and exposed. She scrubbed at her scalp, trying to ease a growing headache.

"I'm honestly not sure, Cay. I'm reading back through every book I used for that research paper plus some I never got to. If it's related, it's way deeper than I went last time."

"What do you mean? Deeper how?"

"Do you remember my theory?"

Cadence was silent a moment, pensive. "Yeah, a little, I think. That when we dream, sometimes we are able to go to another world, right? Not like another planet, but like... another dimension, almost?"

"Pretty much, yeah. We have all this history that implies that there are all these other creatures. Some call them the Hidden People, or fae, or elves, or whatever. But I've always thought that implies that we've interacted with them before, somehow. Not only in our dreams, but directly."

Cadence stayed quiet beside her, and she met his eyes. He blinked, then voiced the thought that she watched cross his face. "You think that means we *all* had the dream? All the kids who've been hurt?"

Harley nodded. "Yes. I also think that means this may not be the first time, Cay. Not just in history, but I mean, I don't think the people in our town were the first to be, for lack of a better word, attacked. I had Jess check, and towns all over the country have been seeing casualties for the last three months or so."

"Three *months*?" Cadence clapped a hand over his mouth and peeked toward the main library desk where the librarian sat, looking over at them.

She raised a finger to her lips in a shushing motion, raised one brow, then went back to what she was doing.

When Cadence turned back, he was blushing, but his voice was insistent, if only a little above a whisper. "Three months? Harley, that's crazy. How could or *would* you connect that many deaths?"

"I'm not talking *every* death. I'm talking about a pattern of targeted people. Most of them were in their late teens to early thirties. Artistic types, according to their families. Everyone just assumed it was drugs or in a couple cases, possibly suicide."

"I guess I kind of understand artistic types, since I know they used to be called 'the poets and dreamers', but why drugs or suicide?"

"The other thing many of the deaths we found have in common is a history of trauma, depression, and drug use."

He scanned back over the items on the table. "Okay. Okay, I see the logic there, but even so, again, why? Why now, and why so many all of a sudden?"

Harley shrugged and picked up her pencil, tapping it on the notepad in front of her. "My best guess? Something happened. Something big, like a dam bursting or like someone flinging open a door that was previously stuck mostly shut."

Harley frowned at the books in front of her but didn't really see them. With a stifled cry, she shoved the books away.

The librarian at the desk got up and glared at them, brow furrowed in disapproval and concern. Harley took a deep breath, let it out, and waved at the librarian, then rose and reached across the table to tidy the books she'd just pushed.

"Damn it, Cay." She grumbled as she worked. "I hate that I can't figure out what it is. I know what I saw. I'm sure it has something to do with these stories, but I don't know *how* I know, or how to prove it. I feel like whatever it is, it's sitting just outside my peripheral, and if I could turn my head fast enough, I'd see it, and I'd understand." She rested her elbows on the table and pushed her fingers back through her hair, resting her forehead against her palms. "God. All those people." She closed her eyes and sighed heavily. "I don't know what's happening, but I feel like I should. The answer is right there, staring me in the face, but I can't see it, and I hate it."

Cadence rested a hand on her shoulder, a gentle touch of his fingers against the softness of her shirt. Her skin jumped at his touch, and she peered at him through the fall of her hair.

Concern shone from his eyes. "It's gonna be alright, Harley. The answer is there, and we're going to find it."

She turned to look at him more fully, and he grabbed at his bag, pulling it up in front of him. "I'll help you. It'll be like old times." He gave that same lopsided grin she remembered from the first day they met, and despite her frustration, the thought made her smile in return. She shook her head and laughed a little before turning back to the books. A bittersweet mix of emotions she wasn't ready to think about flooded her, so she tucked them away and tried to focus.

"Just like old times, huh? Well, dig in, then. Tag pages that have anything to do with stories of children or young poets or artists who disappear after going to sleep. Or any reference to dreams. Also, look for anything about glowing figures not related to aliens. Unicorns, gnomes, leprechauns; you know, anything that seems even remotely fae."

She gestured to the stacks of books, many at least a half dozen volumes tall. Cadence gave a low whistle. Harley eyed him, raised a brow, then pivoted to Jess just as the other girl came back to the table. Jess gave Cadence a skeptical look as she set a new pile of books down and took the seat to Harley's left. Harley almost laughed at the level of stink-eye Jess was sending his way, but cleared her throat surreptitiously, instead.

Jess gave a huff, then met Harley's gaze. "I grabbed all the titles you mentioned, but are you sure we're going to find anything of use in these?" She pulled one massive book—the old fabric kind with gold-leaf letter-ing—from the pile and scrutinized it dubiously.

Harley shrugged. She plucked the book out of Jess's hand, checking the title and flipping through it before handing it back. "I honestly don't know, but it's worth a try. Jess, have you met Cadence Murphy?"

"Cadence Murphy? *The* Cadence Murphy?" Jess gave a little gasp, widening her eyes and putting her hands up to her cheeks in mock surprise. After a moment, she laughed, shook her head, and extended one hand across the table. When Cadence took the offered hand and gave it a shake, a smile spread across her face. "Glad to have you on the team, sport. Or should I call you Captain?" Her smile broadened into a grin, then faded. "Seriously, though, we can use all the help we can get."

Chapter Four

Christian

At first bell, Chris was carried along on a tide of other teens to the auditorium where the principal had called a general assembly only to notify them that classes were canceled for the day in light of the, as he called them, "tragic circumstances". They were all instructed to consider their fellow students, and that counselors would be available.

They were also given a stern speech about "if you see something, say something" regarding strange packages, people who didn't look like they should be on campus, or any weird smells or substances anywhere in town. Josh, understandably freaked out, opted to head home. Chris, knowing home meant having to face his mother before she left for work, chose to wander the halls. Hell, maybe he'd even spot some nefarious bad guy planting pipe bombs full of anthrax.

Ultimately, he ended up in the library. The city had just paid for a brand-new bank of computers, and his library card got him unlimited free internet that was a great deal more stable than the spotty stolen Wi-Fi signal he used on his phone at the house. Though, he reasoned with himself, could it really be *stolen* Wi-Fi if they hadn't password protected it?

The library was thick with the smell of old books, and dust motes danced in the light coming from the upper windows. Chris had to admit, for a tiny town like Green Bridge, the library was pretty impressive, even if most of his reading experience here was to browse the Nat Geos or to see what movies were available.

This time he made his way past the wooden wrap around front desk, giving the librarian a nod. She was new, and he could never remember her name. Ms. Taggard, the old librarian from his sophomore year, apparently retired while he was gone. This one had a face like she'd been eating sour grapes for a month. And that was when she was smiling.

To his right, the main area was taken up by big circular tables for group studies. At one of those tables, he spotted the unmistakable red hair of Cadence Murphy, the captain of their football team. Chris remembered him being a bit of a pipsqueak when he first started school in Green Bridge. Sophomore year of high school, he'd sprouted up past six feet tall, and when Chris saw him next, he was just suddenly a mountain of muscle with the head cheerleader hanging from his arm and a posse of other players following him around like baby ducks.

Harley Swanson sat next to him. She'd helped tutor Chris sophomore year when he was risking failing one of his math classes. She'd been nice, patient, and made him feel at least a bit less stupid as he'd struggled through sheets of algebraic equations and how to plot the x/y axes.

She'd always worn the same sort of traditional catholic girl uniform style outfit she wore today, but Chris could admit, at least to himself, that she wore it better now than she had, a couple years ago. Harley had always been one of those people who didn't seem to think about their appearance, and yet was always put together, but she'd definitely grown out of her baby phase. Chris tried not to think of her as anything other than his friend and tutor, but he couldn't deny she was pretty. She had a kind face with warm brown eyes that always twinkled with some unsaid joke, but not like she was laughing at him.

Chris was about 6' even, and Harley was a little shorter than him, so maybe 5'8", but the growth seemed recent and stretched her out in a way that instead of making her look gangly, left her looking like she fit her curves and shape better than when she was shorter. Like she hadn't known how to move in her own body until she'd gained the height. She moved with practiced care, and noticed everything, and everyone. It always left Chris feeling like Harley really saw the people she helped.

He was a little surprised to see the two of them sitting next to each other, surrounded by a disturbingly vast selection of books, all stacked up on the table. He had one class with Cadence—a history class focused on international history and current events—but nothing with Harley, which wasn't really surprising. Maybe Harley was tutoring Cadence like she'd tutored him, though what class *all* those books could be for, Chris didn't want to even think about.

Chris had only just settled into one of the rigid plastic chairs at one of the terminals when he heard someone making sounds like they were having a panic attack. He scanned the room, and spotted Jenta at another computer. Fuck, when had she gotten there? What he saw on the screen over her shoulder filled him with dread, and he shoved his chair back, nearly knocking it over as he rushed over to help.

He reached her just as Harley came over from the table, shadowed by Cadence. Chris got his hands under Jenta's arms and carefully moved her off her chair to the floor where she curled over on her side and started dry heaving.

Harley knelt down beside the other girl, brushing hair out of her face and speaking quietly. Cadence was already ushering away students who came forward to help. While Harley held Jenta's attention, Chris straightened and leaned over the computer to close the picture on the screen. He tried not to think about what he was seeing, but it was hard not to be captivated, even in horror.

The picture was dark, like it had been taken without a flash in a dimly lit room, so that the image was grainy, but there was just enough light to make out details. Hanging there against a wall was Jenta, mounted on a big wooden X made of thick timbers. She was tied at wrists and ankles and her back was to the room, but her face was caught in profile.

She appeared to be naked except for a pair of black or dark colored underwear. A feminine figure stood beside her, but the features were distorted so that Chris couldn't make out much more than the shape of the body. One arm was hidden behind Jenta's rigid form. In their other hand, the figure held a nasty looking whip with many tails. The tool and the hand that held it were soaked with what was probably blood, and more blood was running down Jenta's back.

Jenta's hair was pulled to one side to expose her back in one long line from just below her hairline down to the swell of her hips where the edge of the underwear started. Her eyes were squeezed closed, but her mouth was open wide in a silent scream.

Chris tried not to pay too much attention, tried not to let his eyes follow the lines and curves of her body, even grainy as it was within the picture. *Fuck, Chris. Knock it off.* Now was not the time or the place, he reminded himself as he closed the app. The screen cleared, he crouched back down next to Jenta but looked at Harley, eyebrows raised.

"Thanks for helping." Harley dropped her gaze to Jenta, her expression softening. She made a soothing sound and touched the other girl gently on the shoulder.

Chris shrugged uncomfortably. "No problem. I have some first aid training from... from my last school. Comes in handy, sometimes." He looked down at Jenta, lying curled on the floor. She was huddled around herself, her breathing coming in ragged gasps, but at least she'd stopped retching. He pulled off his jacket and laid it over her.

Cadence came back and squatted down near Harley, his posture easy, his forearms resting on his knees. "I cleared everybody out. The librarian says if we don't get her sitting up, she's going to call the nurse and have her taken to the hospital."

Before anyone could respond, Jenta made a soft sound. A quiet moan escaped her as she tried to roll over, winced, and returned to her side. "Could somebody please help me up?" Her voice was and a little hoarse.

Chris moved first, tucking his hands back beneath her arms so he could help her to a sitting position. He stayed crouched behind her, holding most of her weight as she took a moment to catch her breath. "When you're ready, we're going to stand up together, okay? I won't let you fall."

After a moment, she nodded, letting him take much of her weight while he helped her to her feet. As they straightened, Harley stepped forward and pulled Chris's jacket more firmly around Jenta's shoulders, then stepped back again.

Chris helped steady her, his arms holding her carefully but firmly as she tested her legs. Harley and Cadence waited, watching and clearly concerned.

"Are you alright? Should we call your mom?" Harley spoke quietly as she started to lay a hand on Jenta's shoulder. When the other girl flinched away, Harley dropped her hand back to her side. "I can give you a ride home instead, if you want."

"I'm fine. I just need to catch my breath. Thank you for helping me." Jenta's eyes flicked to Cadence, the look in them closing down. She stepped away from Chris who continued to watch for any sign of imbalance. He knew the signs of shock, and how it could affect someone, and he certainly wouldn't blame her for it—that picture had been horrifying. If she'd really suffered that kind of damage? Chris shook his head, trying to chase the image away.

"Thank you. Really, I'm fine." Her voice was cold and distant, almost back to normal. Despite her tone however, she still seemed tired, wounded.

Chris wanted to hold her, to tell her it was going to be okay. Instead, his own voice had died in his throat, and he started to notice the pain shooting through his hips and back. He tried twice to speak then cleared his throat before trying a third time. "No problem. She's right, though. You should go home. You may be in shock." He took a step back, trying to give her space.

Jenta studied him, then shifted her attention over to Harley. "I don't want my mom to worry."

Chris didn't understand the look they shared, but Harley appeared to make some decision, nodding. "Come on. We'll go to my house. Do you mind if Chris helps you to the car?"

Jenta glanced back at him, then asked, "Why?"

Chris flushed, and he started to open his mouth to say that was okay, but Harley held up a hand.

"Because I want to make sure you get out to the car safely, and I'm not strong enough to catch you."

Jenta swallowed visibly. Chris checked the floor, but thankfully the carpet appeared clean and dry. Good thing, too, since he was pretty sure the librarian might insist on her going to the hospital anyway, if she'd actually thrown up. Harley gestured for him to follow as she headed toward the door of the library but stopped a moment and as if having forgotten something.

Harley walked back to the study table and waved Cadence over. "I don't think I'll be back today. You should stay and keep looking. Text me in an hour, okay? Let me know what you find."

With that, she grabbed her backpack and a notebook laying on the table and headed to the door where she stopped and held it open, waiting. Chris reached to grab the edge of the door so both of the girls could exit ahead of him. Glancing back, he said a quiet thanks as he registered with surprise that the librarian was nowhere in sight.

Chris followed Harley and Jenta out of the library and toward exterior doors that led to the student parking lot. Harley set her pace to Jenta's, which was slow but steady, he was glad to see. By the time they made it out to the car, Jenta was moving better, and with more certainty. Chris wanted to punch the part of his brain that was disappointed about that.

Jenta insisted on getting her own door when they got to the car. She pulled Chris's jacket off and handed it to him, then opened the passenger's side door, climbed in, and closed it without really looking at anyone.

Harley went around to the driver's side and opened her door but regarded him over the top of the car. "Thanks for the escort."

Chris just nodded. "Sure. Is she gonna be okay? Do you want me to go with you?"

Harley studied him for so long he wanted to break eye contact but couldn't seem to. Her deep brown eyes held him pinned to the spot, and he fought the urge to duck his head, though he could already feel a flush coming into his cheeks. He wanted to scream at her, to tell her to hurry up and get Jenta to a hospital, or take her home, or something; anything to get her to stop scrutinizing him like that.

"She'll be okay, Chris. Did you have any nightmares last night?"

The question caught him off guard. He blinked and then really considered her. Her eyes were tired, but whose weren't? He thought he saw the same pain lines on her face that he'd seen on Josh's. Probably the same kind reflected on his own.

He shrugged and tilted his head to one side as he answered. "I don't remember all of it, but I know I was somewhere dark. Smokey." She surprised him with her response.

"Not like 'firepit at a barbeque' smokey, but more like 'torch-lit hallway in an old movie' sort of smokey, right?"

He gave her wide eyes. "Yeah. Exactly."

When she gave him a nod, he went on.

"I'm pretty sure I was on a table or a slab or something. It was cold, so maybe stone. I could hear screams coming from somewhere nearby. I—"

He stopped himself. He'd started to describe what they'd been doing to him but couldn't. He swallowed hard and looked away, unable to take the concern on her face.

After a moment, she spoke, her tone quiet, almost hesitant. "I also had a nightmare last night. Not exactly the same but similar. I think I might have been chained to a wall. I smelled mostly mildew, but I'm pretty sure I smelled blood, too. Something coppery, anyway. The taste of the air coated the back of my throat and I remember gagging. When I woke up this morning, my throat and my chest hurt, and I could still smell the mildew." Harley stopped, sighed, and shook her head. "I promise I'll take care of her, and if it turns out she needs a hospital, I'll make sure she gets there. Get my number from Cay. Shoot me a text, and I'll update you as soon as I can."

A knock on the passenger window startled them both, and Chris heard Jenta say something to Harley from within the car. Harley crouched down and said something back then straightened, gave him a nod, and climbed in. He heard the heavy thump of the driver's side door closing and stepped back toward the building and out of her way as she pulled out of the parking spot. From inside the car, she gave him another wave while Jenta huddled in the passenger's seat.

Chris watched the car pull off, his heart pounding in his chest.

Chapter Five

Jenta

Jenta sat on the edge of a bed with blue-on-blue sheets in a blue-on-blue room. It might almost have been overwhelming but was just saved by the choice of the colors, themselves. The bedsheets were a rich, dark navy with pale blue accents while the walls were a blue so powdery they might have been white if she didn't have the pure white door frame to compare them to. All the furniture was that grown-up version of princess chic, whitewashed and delicate. The room was tidy and organized and *friendly*, and definitely wasn't her style, but it seemed so very *right* for the girl who sat in the white-on-white computer chair, watching her.

When they'd arrived at her house, Harley offered her a drink like a good little hostess, but praise be, there was real soda in the fridge, though Harley insisted on getting her a cup and ice so now she sat holding a tall glass tumbler that tinkled merrily every time she took a sip.

Sitting in the bright bedroom on pristine sheets, Jenta wasn't entirely sure why she hadn't just had Harley take her home after all.

Harlequin Swanson, Grade-A superstar, Mathelete, Queen Tutor Extraordinaire. Jenta shook her head.

"Are you okay? Are you getting a headache or anything?"

Jenta stared up into those big, sincere brown eyes and nearly laughed, but not out of happiness. "No, I'm fine, thank you. I was just thinking I should have had you take me home. I'm sure you have better things to do than babysit the goth kid."

Harley seemed taken aback. She turned to study one of the many paintings that festooned the walls. "Well, I'm sure that would be true, if I were 'babysitting the goth kid,' but I thought I was sitting in my bedroom, spending some time with an old friend."

"Oh, is that what we are? Old friends?"

"Jenta, I—" Harley started to say, as she turned back from the painting.

Jenta put up a hand to stop her. "No, Harley. True is true. I spooked the fuck out of you, and I get that, but don't make this anything it isn't. I don't even blame you for being freaked out."

"I wasn't—"

"And now you have your group, and I have mine."

Harley sighed and lowered her gaze to her hands. Her fingers were twisted around each other in a gesture Jenta knew was her 'how do I phrase this?' pose.

Jenta shook her head. "Just say it, Harley. If we're 'old friends,' then you'd remember I don't care about pretty words."

Harley huffed, but said, "Do you know the rumors being spread about you by your boyfriend?"

It was Jenta's turn to be taken aback. "Jonathon says a lot of shit. He talks a big game, but I can handle myself."

Harley actually scoffed this time. "Can you, though? Jenta, I just saw you have a panic attack in the middle of the library. I think we both know something terrible happened to a lot of people last night—Including you,

40

if that picture was any indication—and I know you heard what I said to Chris. Did you dream, too?"

Jenta felt like she'd been slapped. She tried to let herself really see the girl sitting in the chair in front of her.

Five years had changed both of them more than she'd realized.

She and Harley had been as close to best friends as she'd ever had until they were thirteen. Both of them had lost a parent. Both of them were in therapy. Both of them trying their best to grow up in a world of kids who didn't know what grief was and parents who were so far on the different sides of the grief spectrum that it was almost laughable.

Where Harley's father never recovered from his wife's death, Jenta's mom moved on almost as soon as her father was in the ground. Jenta's physical scars from the accident were still pink and shiny, and the hospital bills weren't even fully paid off yet when she announced the engagement.

This Harley wasn't the Harley who ran away and threw up when she'd found Jenta cutting herself in the girl's bathroom of the junior high school. Then again, she wasn't the same Jenta. She'd found other ways to reach the silence, since that day. One of those things had been becoming an ace sub in a BDSM group where she'd ultimately met Jonathon.

When Jenta didn't say anything, the other girl continued, her tone softening. "How much of your panic attack was because your back still hurts?" Jenta swallowed the lump in her throat. She wouldn't cry, damn it. But she couldn't stand to see the concern in Harley's eyes any longer. She focused on one of the paintings, a smaller framed landscape that was hung beside Harley's closet door. It was a terrible choice. Next to that painting was the full-body mirror that hung on the back of the closet door, and she caught her own reflection—pale and shock-y, her eyes wide and haunted.

41

She dropped her gaze to her own hands, gripping the glass. "I said I'm okay." Jenta hated how much her voice gave away the lie.

Harley reached out, pressing a gentle touch of fingers against one of her hands. When she didn't flinch away, the touch became a grip, Harley's warm, solid hand holding her own. Hot tears pushed hard at her eyes.

Jenta sighed. "Fuck. You're right. I'm not okay. Jonathon's a shitbag. I tried to show him the damage this morning when it was still kinda fresh."

"Fresh? The feeling, or the wounds?"

"Kinda both, I guess. My back was pretty shredded when I woke up, but the later it got, the faster it all healed. It was really weird."

"Tell me about it?" Harley said, more a question than a statement.

Jenta finally met Harley's eyes. "You're right. I did hear what you told Chris. Fuck, Harley, of all the people, the one guy in the school who follows me like a lost puppy was not necessarily the hero I would have wished for in that moment."

"I know. But you can't begrudge his willingness."

"Oh, I can."

Harley raised a brow at that, and Jenta barked a little laugh. Even that little sound seemed to break some of the tension that had built over years of silence between them.

"Okay. I *can*, but I *won't*." She gave Harley a weak smile before continuing. "The room was gross. Dark, moldy. Do you know what a Saint Andrew's Cross is?"

"I know its biblical connotation, but I assume that's not the one you're implying?"

"No. It's a BDSM apparatus for suspending a sub during a scene. It's similar to the one from the bible, basically a big X with straps on all the

42

arms. The sub is hung on the crossed boards, with their arms and legs splayed out to the arms of the X."

As she described it, she studied Harley's face, waiting to see horror, disgust, some sign to point at and say, "See? You haven't changed. You're horrified by me". What she got instead was polite attention and a mild curiosity. *Fuck.*

Jenta made herself continue, but had to look away again. Avoiding the mirror, she focused instead on the wall behind Harley where there was a window through which she could see the upper branches of an ash tree, only just starting to show signs of the leaf change.

"In my dream, I was on one. It wasn't like the ones I've been on before, though."

"How so?"

"I mean, for starters, my old dom Soren, and the guy who made one for Jonathon really care about the quality of the wood they use. Everything is well cared for, padded, clean. The leather for the straps is regularly oiled, and the wrist straps have a pull-away pin. Hell, the wood is polished so even if it weren't being used, it could be left out as a decoration as long as you were good with people knowing you were into that shit."

"Is that like a safety feature?" Harley tilted her head consideringly. The question sounded sincere.

"What, the pull-away pins?" Jenta asked. Harley nodded.

Jenta thought about it, trying to figure out how to explain, then answered. "Yeah. Um, it's like a long bar that runs through the wood, holding the leather in place. If you pull it from one side, it will release the straps so you can get yourself out."

"Interesting. That's really clever."

"Yeah, safety is a huge part of the BDSM culture. Safety and consent."

"Okay, so how was the one in your dream different?"

"Safety and consent." Jenta's tone was flat, but bile rose up in her throat. Harley gave her a horrified look. "No pull away pin. No soft leather. The wood was rough and splintery. I remember feeling wood shove up under one of my nails. But it wasn't just that. I don't think there's a single safe-word I could have screamed that would have made that dream stop until she was ready to let me go."

"She. The woman from the picture."

"Yes."

"I'm sorry, Jenta."

Jenta scrutinized Harley, her brows furrowed. "Why? Why are you sorry? You weren't holding the cat-o-nine. Or do you mean the other stuff? Because you didn't make my dad die, either. You didn't make my mom forget about me in the rush of a new marriage and then a new baby. Hell, you didn't even run and tell anyone, after you found me in the bathroom. You were only running *from* me."

It was Harley's turn to drop her gaze to her lap. "I'm sorry you had to go through that. I'm sorry I left. I'm sorry I didn't understand how much you were hurting and that I left you anyway, even though I knew it would hurt you more. I remember what your mom was like, even then."

Jenta shook her head. "You have no idea. She's worse now. She had Jeremy right after... everything. The day you found me was the day after they threw a big gender reveal party. I stayed in my room the whole time, and nobody came to even say hi or check on me."

"I mean, both of our families proved to be pretty terrible at dealing with our grief. Like because we're children, we're supposed to just get over it immediately."

"Yeah, that shit about kids being resilient is crap. Anyway, it's pretty much been boy-mom-central at my house, ever since. I don't really blame Matt for loving it. He was only six when dad died, and he's only just starting to dislike the attention now that he's a teen. I'm like the spooky ghost in the house only I think my mom would like it better if I was an *actual* ghost. At least then she might have a chance of exorcizing me." Jenta tried to make it a joke but couldn't keep the disappointment out of her voice.

Harley didn't laugh, or even crack a smile. "I'm not going to keep apologizing, because I know that's not the point. I wish in retrospect I'd been able to be there for you. I know I can't undo my part, but I can try to be here, now, if you'll let me." They shared a long, silent moment. Jenta squeezed Harley's hand then took her own hand back, wrapping it around her glass.

Harley heaved deep sigh. "I'm not trying to change the subject, but you said something about trying to show Jonathon your back this morning. What do you mean, 'try'?"

Hot tears pushed at her eyes, again. "He freaked out on me."

"Why would he freak out on you?" Harley said, clearly confused.

"He accused me of playing with someone else. Oh, and he called me a pain slut and a drama queen." Jenta saw Harley was satisfactorily horrified by that. "Yeah. I was in pain and basically crying in his arms, but he went pretty much straight to assuming I must be fucking around on him. Like, dick, the only reason I'm fucking *at all* is because you wouldn't leave me alone about it."

"What?"

That one word brought Jenta up short. She didn't think she'd ever heard one word hold so much anger. Indignation spurred her, and she gave Harley her own angry look. "What do you mean, 'what?' I didn't want to have sex with him. I didn't instigate it. Any of it. Don't you believe me? Or is that the one rumor you *do* believe?"

Harley's hands came up in a placating gesture as she leaned back in her chair, her brows lifting in startlement. "Jenta, I didn't mean it like that. I mean, did he force you? Because that's seriously not okay."

"Oh." Jenta blinked, all the fury running out of her at once.

"You don't have to answer me. It's not any of my business. It's just, if he forced you, that's not the same thing at all as you being in a consensual sexual relationship with him. That's him taking advantage of a power dynamic to get something out of you that you otherwise wouldn't have given him. That's called assault at best. At worst—"

"I don't know that I really want to talk about it, right now." Jenta said, interrupting her.

Harley frowned at her, and Jenta saw disapproval in the look.

"Just... Not with everything else already happening, okay? But," Jenta smiled, "thank you. For caring." She paused, then said, "I really missed you."

"I missed you too, Jen."

They sat there for a time, surrounded by the quiet hum of the AC and Harley's computer. Finally, Harley broke the silence. Her voice was back to being soft, placating. Jenta wondered how much of that tone had been cultivated over so many years of dealing with her dad.

"What do you know about the fae?"

Jenta narrowed her eyes, considering. "Do you mean like fairy tales? Cinderella and her wicked stepmother?"

Harley laughed a little. "More like goblins and unicorns and pixies."

Jenta shrugged. "I don't know. Not a lot, I guess. You were always way more into that stuff than I was."

"Fair point. I wrote a paper last year for an AP bio class based on a bunch of research I did. I called it *Dreaming and the Hidden People*."

"Epic title. That could totally be a band name." Jenta grinned, and Harley smiled back.

"The point is, as far back as any written records go, and even before there were written records, we've had myths and legends of creatures like us but different. Terrifying and beautiful and also alien."

"What, like changelings?"

"Exactly, actually. There used to be folklore about monsters in the forest and superstitions about human babies being replaced for fae babies. Supposedly, those human babies would be taken to another place and raised among the fae, never to be seen again. Sadly, the supposed fae babies were rarely so lucky."

"Right, okay. So, we're talking hypotheticals. Like, 'what if' scenarios. Right?" Jenta couldn't hide the heavy amount of disbelief in her voice.

Harley leaned forward earnestly. "Jenta, I know this probably sounds ridiculous and super far-fetched, but what if what's happening with these nightmares is that people are ending up in *that* place instead of staying here? What if something over there has figured out how to, I don't know, grab hold of dreamers?"

Jenta gawked at the other girl, her drink forgotten. She opened her mouth, then closed it again. Finally, she responded. "You're right, Harley. That's pretty far-fetched."

Harley nodded slowly, her gaze dropping to the carpeted floor between them.

Jenta's stomach clenched hard. They were finally mending things after five years, and she was fucking it up. She wasn't really sure how to fix it, but she tried. "Okay, okay. Say that what's happening really is related to some shared nightmare, started by some mythological creature. Why? What does it gain from that? Why us? Hell, *how*?"

Harley's head came up, her voice excited. "That's what I was trying to figure out at the library, but I can't seem to find much of anything other than proximity that would say why so many of us had that nightmare last night."

Jenta studied her, considering. "Okay. Let's start there, then. What *do* we know about the victims you've identified?"

Harley took a second before answering, turning to her computer where she pulled up a spreadsheet. "I had Jess compile the info she found from the news articles in the library. She was going to list stuff about each person mentioned." Jenta sat patiently, as Harley's fingers *click-clack-click*ed across the keyboard.

"Still using that super loud typewriter style, I see."

Harley grinned over her shoulder. "You know it. Okay. Here we go. 'Those who woke up reported unexplainable injuries that occurred while they were sleeping.'"

48

"Right. We know that part. Us, too, right?"

"Yeah, I think so. I noticed Chris was limping. I didn't get a chance to ask Cay, but he was definitely moving stiffly. Both of them mentioned also having at least *a* if not *the same* dream, so I think we can solidly put that in the 'similarities' box."

"Okay. What next?"

"All the victims are fairly young. Jess's notes don't have any ages under eight years old and nobody over forty, but those seem to be the most extreme outliers. I'm seeing a lot of late high school, early college ages, here."

"Fuck, Harley. I don't know if we can count that as a similarity except that all students everywhere are fucking exhausted."

Harley spun the chair to look at her, confused.

Jenta's response was incredulous. "What? You can't tell me you ever feel like you get enough sleep. We wake up early, we're perpetually stressed out, and most of us stay up late, either to finish homework or because it's the only time we have to ourselves. Hell, between family, friends, school drama, *personal* drama, whatever, I don't know that I've seen a solid night's sleep in years."

"That's actually a really good point."

"Gee, thanks." Jenta said sarcastically.

Harley stuck her tongue out in a moment of pique then became pensive. She stared up at the ceiling. "Everything I'd found in my research before pointed at fae approaching people who were poetic, dreamers, artistic types. Like a muse drawn to the painter."

"Okay... so?"

"So, what if the combination of being tired, and being, for lack of a better term, a dreamer, means that when we sleep, we sleep more deeply? Closer to the edge of that invisible boundary separating us from that other place? When you're trying to bob for apples, you don't go for the ones that sink—"

"—You go for the ones closest to the surface." Jenta finished.

Harley nodded. "The last thing, and this is purely based on my own experience, is that I saw her."

"Her." Jenta said the word, but not like it was a question.

Harley answered, anyway. "Whoever that was in that picture you got. They were in my dream, too."

They shared a long look.

Gooseflesh raised up on Jenta's arms, and she shuddered. "Shit, Harley. Shit."

"Yeah." Harley sighed and came to sit on the bed next to her.

Jenta set the glass down on the nightstand beside the bed—The ice had melted, and she'd drank most of the soda, anyway—and scrubbed her face with both hands.

She said, "Okay."

"Okay?" Harley asked.

Jenta eyed Harley, beside her. "Say it really is what you're suggesting. That people really are being pulled over into this other place while dreaming. What do we do about it? Like, how do we stop it?"

"I don't know. I don't know if we *can* stop it. Maybe Chris and Cay will find something I missed or come across something new that can point us in some kind of direction. For now, that's the best I can hope for."

"What if we get dragged back into that place again, tonight? Is there any way to tell? Or maybe some way to wake ourselves up?"

"When I was doing my first research, one of the things I learned about dreams was that if you can make yourself aware that it's a dream, sometimes you can wake yourself up."

"Would that still work if we're being pulled somewhere else, though?"

"Honestly, Jen, I don't know. I'm kinda grasping at straws at this point. I wasn't exactly expecting a research paper I wrote because of a joke to turn into something that might solve a life-or-death situation."

"Harley."

Harley scowled at her, and Jenta saw real exhaustion peeking through the other girl's expression.

"Harley, this is a lot to take on to yourself. What if we take your theory to one of the teachers, tomorrow? Didn't you say you wrote it for an AP Bio class?"

"Yeah. Miss Winters."

"Okay, so, tomorrow morning, I'll meet you at the doors to the auditorium, and we can go see Miss Winters. Worst case scenario, she doesn't take us seriously, and we're no worse off, right? But you don't need to solve this alone. Hell, I know Cay was sitting with you most of the morning."

"He and Jess, yeah." Jenta made a face, and Harley laughed. "I know. She's not exactly your cup of tea, but she's clever, quick, and her leaps of logic would make a genius gazelle envious."

"I'm sorry, did you just say, 'a genius gazelle'?" Jenta laughed. "But see? You don't have to tackle this alone."

Harley leaned over and bumped Jenta's shoulder with her own. "Neither do you."

"What do you mean?" Jenta said, confused.

"What are you going to do about Jonathon?" Harley asked, one eyebrow raised.

Jenta's expression closed down. "I told you. I can handle him."

Harley studied her for so long, Jenta started to feel an angry flush rise in her cheeks. "By 'handle' him, what exactly are you planning?"

Jenta let out a bitter snort of laughter. "You said it yourself: he's been spreading rumors about me. I figured I'd just show people the truth. He confused softness for weakness, so I figure it's time I clear up the confusion."

"Jenta..."

"Oh, don't worry, Harley. I don't have to kill him to kill his reputation. And anyway, he's not worth jail time."

Chapter Six

Christian

"Hey, take a look at this." Chris pushed an open book across the table so Cadence could see the image depicted. The top of the left-hand page showed a woodcut from the 1600s: a woman with her bare back exposed and covered in dark lines. Her face in profile, eyes closed and mouth open in a scream.

It was almost identical to the picture Chris glimpsed on Jenta's computer screen. Standing next to the woman was a towering creature, part bird, part woman, and part indescribable horror. The monstrosity held a long whip in one clawed hand.

Beneath the wood cut print was written the title of the work. "The Lady Plays", translated from the original Latin. The piece was among a collection of wood cuts, paintings, and clay tablets done by an artist who also left behind a journal of mad ramblings. All the pieces within the collection showed scenes depicting fantastical beasts and creatures straight out of myth.

Chris watched Cadence as he studied the page, then met his eyes. "Do you think Harley has seen this one? More of the pictures from the collection are shown in this book, and the table of contents also listed excerpts from the journal."

Cadence glanced back at the image on the page and shuddered. He flipped to the table of contents, then to the pages with the journal translations. "The author of the journal calls her a 'timeless evil', terrifying and beautiful. That sounds about right."

"Yeah, but the guy who researched the journal refers to her as a folk legend used to frighten, get this, children and young people. Sound familiar?"

Cadence grabbed a sticky note from the stack in front of him and attached it to the page with the journal entry, then shut the book. Finally, he looked back up at Chris. "Good find. I don't know if Harley has seen this, but it's definitely not something I want to try to sum up. Come on. I think, between this and our notes, we've done as much damage as we could for today."

He stood and packed up his backpack, then slung it over his shoulder and grabbed up the book. Chris packed up his things then followed Cadence to the checkout counter where the other guy set the book down in front of him. While he pulled his library card from his wallet, the librarian standing behind the counter scowled down at the book and raised an eyebrow. Chris wondered if she would say something, but instead, she scanned the book and Cadence's library card with her little portable scanner and handed both back without comment.

As they left the library, Chris nearly bumped into Cadence when the other guy stopped right outside the doors. Peering around him, Chris saw Becky Lindstadt in the hall, her face tear-streaked and rage-filled. She'd very obviously been headed toward the library, but before Cadence could say anything, she huffed and spun on her heel, stomping off down the hall.

Chris heard Cadence let out a heavy sigh. He mumbled something Chris didn't catch, before raising his voice and speaking out loud.

"I'm breaking up with you, Becky." Cadence didn't speak loudly, didn't shout, but his voice carried down the hall and hit Becky like a blow between her shoulders.

Chris gaped at Cadence's back. He couldn't stand Becky; She was one of the most entitled, meanest people he'd ever seen. She was gorgeous and she knew it, and never let anyone else forget it—petit, but with long legs and ample breasts that she loved to show off to best effect with her low tops that never got her dress-coded. Even today she was wearing a pair of jeans that might as well have been sewn onto her for how tight they were, and a short-sleeved sweater in the purple, green, and white of Northfield High School, a V-neck dipping dangerously close to spilling her whole chest out. Her make-up was smudged from crying, but her hair was somehow still perfect, floating around her head like a blond helmet made of loose waves. She couldn't be more than 5'6", but her personality usually towered over even Cadence, and not in a good way.

Chris's mother was a bully, but only because she didn't know better, whereas Becky knew better, but didn't care—which somehow made it worse. Even so, after the day everyone had, a public breakup between two popular kids hadn't exactly been on his bingo card. Then again, he hadn't expected to spend the day sitting in the library with one of those people, reading about fairies either.

Cadence started walking forward slowly, and Chris flanked him, staying back and to one side of the broad-shouldered football player. They kept their pace slow, and Chris wondered if Cadence was waiting to see if Becky would turn and come flying back at them like a bat out of hell. His own shoulders tensed in anticipation.

They hadn't made it very far down the hall when she whirled to face them, but she didn't come running at Cadence. Instead, she stood seething, glaring absolute murder at them. Cadence took a deep breath and continued forward. As they drew closer, Chris started to hope she would just let them walk past, but as they came up beside her, she grabbed Cadence by the front of his shirt, pulling his face down close to hers, tilting her own face up and holding his gaze. She spoke softly, but the hall was still and silent, and Chris was close enough to hear her clearly.

"You think you can just *announce* that we're breaking up? How fucking dare you. If you break up with me, I will ruin you. You'll be the cold, heartless asshole who abandoned your girlfriend while her best friend is in the hospital. *You'll* be the monster, Cay. I'll make absolutely fucking *sure* of it." A tiny sneer pulled at the corner of her mouth for only a moment, then vanished. If Chris hadn't been looking, he would have sworn he'd imagined it.

In that moment, Chris was startled to realize just how tall and imposing Cadence actually was. He could have palmed Becky's face if he wanted, but instead, he was like a boulder in a field, unmoving. In comparison, Becky, normally so much larger than life, was just an angry toy poodle. Trying to stare down his indifferent stoicism caused her to shrink. Chris had to stop himself from snorting at the visual.

Cadence's response matched Becky's volume, but he sounded resigned, tired. He wasn't shouting, but he also didn't seem to be making an effort to speak quietly. "But she isn't your best friend, Becky. You don't even like Sierra. I'm not certain you *like* anyone. You sabotaged her audition for head cheerleader because you know she's better than you. Fuck, she's nicer, smarter, and more popular than you. She actually cares about people. Oh, but that's not what you hate about her, is it? You hate her because you think she's prettier than you. People may think I'm the monster for breaking up with you, but you and I both know you're the only monster here. A shallow, jealous, petty, bitter monster." Cadence was leaning forward a little by that last sentence, practically spitting his last words in Becky's face.

Becky's opened-handed slap caught Cadence full in the cheek, and Cadence's hands curl into fists at his sides. Chris almost stepped forward—He wasn't entirely sure he'd be strong enough to stop the much larger guy if he really went after her—but stopped when he registered that Cadence was speaking.

"You're a bitch, Becky. You may be popular, but you don't have any friends, and because of you, I've lost most of mine."

Cadence shot a glance Chris. Chris saw fury written on his features, but it didn't seem to be aimed at him. Then that wrath zeroed in on Becky. She paled a little but held her ground. Cadence subconsciously flexed his hands in and out of fists as he continued in that tired, resigned tone, but Chris heard an edge of heat in it, now. "I realized that today, and I don't want it anymore. I don't want you. Dating you isn't worth hating myself."

Wrenching his shirt out of Becky's grasp, Cadence brushed himself off and continued down the hall. Chris moved with him past Becky, keeping an eye on her as he passed. She was standing in the middle of the hall, mouth hanging open as she gaped at Cadence's back.

A few students were gathered at classroom doors and hallway intersections, watching. Cadence hadn't raised his voice, but he also hadn't been whispering, and many of them appeared almost as shocked as Becky. As if she could feel his eyes on her, Becky glared at Chris, fury turning to disgust. That same cruel sneer spread across her face as some thought occurred to her. She started laughing, but the tone was patronizing and disdainful.

"Oh my God, you're talking about that *freak*, Harlequin, aren't you? Don't tell me you're going to start dating *her*. You would leave *me* for *that*? I should have fucking known. You're pathetic, Cay. You are an absolute fucking waste of my time. I should have stayed with Kaleb. At least he was *fun*." Scorn and derision dripped from her words like acid.

Cadence's back stiffened, and Chris stepped to one side. It was one thing to intercede, another to stand in front of that boulder, if he decided to throw himself downhill. Cadence glowered at Becky from down the hall, and when he spoke, his voice was tight and furious, his body trembling with tension. "Who *haven't* you dated, Becky? Better yet, who haven't you *fucked*? When I told you 'no' that first time, you ran to Kaleb, and he told you no. Who did you try to hit up next? Mike? Steve? D'vonne? Oh, that's right. They all told you no, too. Do you know why that is? Because they all saw what I did: a soulless, callous bitch, with a libido instead of a heart. If all you want is a dick, they sell dildos, but I'll tell you what I wish I had, after the first time you assaulted me. If you need sex so much, maybe you should just go fuck yourself." Cadence spun on his heel and marched down the hall and out the door without stopping.

The hallway behind him was full of held breaths. Chris was stunned. Had that really just happened?

Becky's face had gone white, and she stammered as she watched Cadence go. She didn't call him a liar. She didn't try to defend herself. She just stood there, her mouth working like a landed fish.

Chris, after making sure she wasn't going to follow, hurried after Cadence and out of the building. He had to jog to catch up with the other guy outside the doors, then slowed to walk beside him, not sure what to say.

"Do you need a ride home?" Cadence said as they made their way toward the parking lot. He took long, angry strides, and Chris did his best to keep up as he considered the offer. He easily could have walked home, but his hips and legs hurt, and if he was honest, Cadence didn't look like he should be left alone, though he'd never say that out loud to the other guy.

Chris answered, trying to keep his voice light. "I mean, sure, if it's cool."

Cadence shot him a look that Chris couldn't quite read as he answered. "I don't really feel like going home, just now, and practice was canceled because of everything going on. I'm kinda surprised they let us stay in the school at all." All the anger was gone from his voice after his fight with Becky. Now, he just sounded tired.

As they headed toward the student parking lot, Chris stole glances at the guy walking next to him. An almost palpable storm cloud of emotion hovered over his head, and Chris wasn't sure what to say, so he kept quiet. He wasn't entirely certain how he would have handled it.

If Becky really had done what Cadence said—if she'd forced him, and isolated him from his friends, which Chris had no reason to doubt, based on everything he'd seen—Chris wasn't certain he would have dealt with it nearly so well. Shit, and now the whole school was going to know. Chris tried to keep the look of realization off his face, but he needn't have bothered. Cadence didn't seem to be paying attention to anything more than putting one foot in front of the other, as they approached a big black SUV sitting alone at the back of the lot.

As they got close to the car, Cadence pulled a set of keys out of his pocket and pressed a button, making the car give a loud chirp and flash its headlights. Chris checked his watch. It was already three o'clock. Later than he'd expected. He went around to the passenger side of the car, pulling it open as Cadence climbed in on the driver's side.

He let the silence stretch as he climbed into the passenger's seat before he finally figured out what he wanted to say. "Hey, man, I don't wanna pry, and you can tell me to fuck off, but are you okay?"

Cadence's hands white-knuckled the steering wheel. He glanced at Chris, then down at his hands. He took a deep breath, held it, then let it out slowly and relaxed his hands. "Yeah. I'm okay. I mean, I'm not, but I will be. I guess I kinda can't believe I did that. I've wanted to say a lot of things to her for a long time, but I hadn't thought that would be the first thing to come out."

Chris gave a snort, and Cadence glared at him, ready to be mad. Chris held up his hands in a placating gesture. "Dude, based on the look on her face, I don't think she was expecting it either."

"No." Cadence gave a bitter bark of a laugh. "No, I don't suppose she was."

Cadence sat and moved his hands back and forth over the steering wheel. The silence stretched in the car again, Chris searching for what else to say. Talking out feelings wasn't exactly his strong suit, though right now, he almost wished it was. Then maybe he'd have some idea of how to help.

"Fuck." The word slipped out of Cadence, resounding and profound. It broke the silence like a rock dropped in a pond.

"What?" Chris said. He peered at Cadence, his gut tightening and his hand reaching for the door as he wondered if it had been such a good idea to accept the offered ride home.

"I'm in love with Harley Swanson." Cadence dropped his head back against the headrest, laughing, though to Chris, the laughter had an edge of both bitterness and a little madness to it.

Chapter Seven

Harlequin

Harley was in a small clearing among a copse of trees. Dappled sunlight shone down through leaves dancing in a soft breeze. The ground was blanketed in clover and honeysuckle and the air was filled with the rich smell of warm earth and the hum of summer insects and birdsong.

From among the trees on the far side of the clearing, a woman stepped out, tall and graceful, her hair falling in shining red-gold waves down around her, like a living cape that reached nearly to her ankles. She wore a simple Grecian chiton that hung from her shoulders in rippling folds of sage green, gathered at her waist by a golden cord. Pale arms reached in welcome, and her smile was warm and kind. "I am coming, child. Seek me, and you shall find me. Danann be with you."

The dream shifted.

Harley lay face-up on a table in a dark, torchlit room. A huge hulking creature hunched over her, great black bulging eyes and a head like a particularly ugly ball of slime was apparently finding great joy in her small shrieks and yelps as it pinched and prodded at her with thick, calloused fingers. Her body ached all over, bruises already blossoming on her legs and arms.

Bound as she was, she couldn't move anything but her head, and she'd tried. Pulling at her wrists, then legs, and tossing her head back and forth in the hopes of loosening whatever held her to the table.

The creature laughed as she flailed and threatened to tie her to the wall by her neck. It had a thick, hissing laugh, tongue lolling and twisting like a snake behind its jagged teeth.

"Wha'cha fink o'dat, lil lass, aye? Thinkin' ye might 'ang yersef 'afore I's done, eh?"

Harley went still. If she could survive this, she told herself, then she would. She wouldn't get killed for a stupid mistake. She wasn't stupid, and she could get through this. She *would* get through this.

Out of the corner of her eye, she saw a flash of movement against the wall. As she tried to tilt her head enough in that direction, a dark gray, clawed hand caught her chin in long, spidery fingers and dragged her face back.

A second creature gazed down at her. This one had three pairs of long, spindly arms extending from a nearly skeletal torso. Two of those arms ended in something more like a squid's paddles, and two ended in three toed bird's feet complete with great black talons. She cried out before she could stop herself and the creature slapped her hard, making the bug-eyed creature next to it give that same, hissing laughter.

"Harley? Harley, is that you? Oh, please, no... Please, don't... No...." The voice was plaintive, pain filled. Jenta? No, that couldn't be. Why would Jenta be here? Harley tried hard to clear her head, but her ears were ringing, and her cheek stung.

The six-armed creature moved its face over hers, its foul breath making her gag. She tried to breathe through clenched teeth, but the rotten meat

63

smell threatened to overcome her, coating her nostrils and pouring down her throat.

"So's, the little miss be thinkin' she a lookie loo, eh? May'aps me's as a good man and find somethin's yer be doin' ta's keepin' occupied, eh?"

The voice scoured and stabbed at her like sandpaper and thistles. The creature sneered at her, large eyes with sickly yellow irises floating in a sea of black pupil and sclera. His? It called itself a "good man."

A thick, red, forked tongue shot out of its mouth and licked across her lips, leaving a trail of slime. Even through her closed lips, the slime tried to trickle down into her mouth. Harley gagged violently and threw her head to the side, spitting and trying to reach a hand close enough to swipe the stuff from her face. The goblin cackled. Then one of those long-fingered hands closed around her throat, choking her. Harley's whole body went rigid, and she squeezed her eyes shut, willing herself to wake up.

New voices reverberated against the stone walls.

Harley's eyes popped open. New dreamers. She wasn't just dreaming, she was *dreaming,* and the room was suddenly filled with more people who'd been dragged from their own safe sleep, their screams and shouts echoing and bouncing, but the ringing in her ears was gone, and her head was clear.

She could hear someone crying out for "Sara" from the direction of her feet. If she hadn't known better, she would have said it sounded like Chris.

She deliberately ignored the feel of the claws digging into her belly, and the fingers gripping her neck as she tried to focus on the other people in the room and more importantly, tried to wake up.

A strong, masculine voice suddenly boomed through the room, driving everything and everyone else to silence. "Get the fuck off of her, you sick fucking bastard! I'll tear you apart with my bare hands!"

The sound startled her, and Harley tried to look in the direction it came from: the far side of the room to her right. A young man was chained against the wall, but she could barely make him out in the gloom.

"Cay?"

Chapter Eight

Christian

Chris sat up gasping, thrust suddenly out of the nightmare. His heart pounded and he tried to catch his breath, gulping at the air as he blinked and tried to orient himself. It felt like he was seeing double. When he closed his eyes, he could still picture the dim room, bodies lining the walls. Some of them had long since stopped moving. Those were the ones the tall, elegant woman in black had touched. Her voice had been soft, cooing at them, though her words were indistinguishable. She'd studied Chris, given him a strange, soft smile, then passed him by and left the room.

He opened his eyes wide, staring around at his bedroom. He was awake; he was safe. Chris was pretty sure he'd only just missed being one of those still bodies on the wall. He wasn't certain why he'd been skipped, but he wasn't about to question it.

Sitting there catching his breath, he racked his brain for what had freed him from the nightmare. He'd been hanging there on the wall, and then something *shifted*. In the way of dreams, he was suddenly somewhere else, and he could hear Sara screaming his name.

His little sister was crying out for her big brother to save her.

That reality rushed down his spine like cold water, and Chris launched himself from the mattress and out of his bedroom, down the hall into Sara's room, stopping at the edge of her bed. He grabbed ahold of her blanket and yanked it off her. Sara lay curled on her side, her eyes tightly closed as if, even in her sleep, she was squeezing them shut. Her legs twitched, and little mewling whimpers escaped her lips.

Chris knelt beside the bed to put him eye level with her instead of towering over. He reached out one hand and lay it near her as he said her name. At his voice, her eyes popped open, and she gasped hard, then started to cough. The cough became a wail of such distress that it broke Chris's heart.

He moved up onto the bed and pulled her into his lap, hugging her to him and cradling her as he petted her hair. While he held her, he checked her back and legs for injuries. Seeing no visible marks, he clutched her to his chest, rocking her as she cried.

A moment later, his mother stumbled into the room, her face a drunken maelstrom. Her nightgown hung down off one shoulder, and Chris flushed angrily as he did his best not to yell at her to cover herself in front of her children.

"What the fuck do you think you're doing, you perverted son of a bitch? What are you doing to your little sister?!" His mother's voice was heavy with indignation and slurred with alcohol.

She lurched forward and tried to drag Sara out of his arms, but Sara's arms were wrapped around his neck, and she wouldn't let go. She instead started kicking at their mother, screaming at her. "Let me go! Don't touch me! Chrissy's good! I hate you! Let go!"

Sara clung to Chris, and he tried to calm her, but it was no use. His mother started screaming back, wordless and fury filled as she alternated between slapping at him and trying to grab at Sara's flailing legs.

Chris shouted at his mother to calm down and struggled to get Sara to stop flailing but couldn't seem to get either to listen. Between his pain and lack of sleep, he lost it.

"Shut up, Ma! Just shut the fuck up and listen for a second! Jesus! I may be a son of a bitch, but only because you're the one who gave birth to me! For fuck's sake! You're drunk as fuck, and you stumble in here screaming that *I'm* the one hurting her? Maybe fix your fucking nightgown and stop flashing us, and then you can talk to me about scarring your daughter." The room had gone silent. He was panting, gripping Sara to him. His mother loomed in front of him, her whole torso heaving with the force of her breath. Her expression sobered a little as she assessed herself, then blushed hard while she yanked the sleeve of her nightgown back up.

When he caught his breath enough, he lowered his voice and continued on. "I had a nightmare that something happened to Sara. I came in to check on her, but she was having a nightmare too, so I woke her up. She was crying because she had a scary dream."

Chris gave Sara a squeeze, then moved to let her set her feet on the bed. She didn't want to let go of him, so he gave her his hand before turning back to face their mother. His brain was spiky with anger that jabbed at the insides of his skull, and suddenly, the words wouldn't stay in the back of his mind, anymore. He had a flash of remembering Cadence with Becky earlier, and something snapped inside him. *If Cadence can face his monster, maybe I can, too.* Then the words were out of his mouth, and he could almost see them forming in the air, to float there between him and his mother.

"I'll never be good enough for you, will I? No matter what I do, I'm always wrong. Do you hate me that much? What did I ever do to you?" By the end, his voice was shaking and pitched, tears stinging the corners of his eyes.

His mother goggled at him like he'd grown a second head. Instead of answering, she stumbled out of the room and down the hall. The next thing he heard was the front door slamming closed. Shortly after that, he heard her car start and peel out of the driveway.

Chris collapsed to sit at the edge of the bed. Sara climbed into his lap, wrapping her arms around his neck and resting her head on her own arm. It was all suddenly too much. He held her close, rested his own head against the top of hers, and started to cry.

They both wept. Sara clung to him, and he stroked her hair gently, shushing her even as tears coursed down his face. They sat that way for a while until Sara finally wore herself out. Her breathing changed as she wept herself into a twilight sleep of exhaustion.

"Come on, kiddo. You can sleep in my room. I'll keep an eye on you. I promise."

She nodded against his shoulder, a yawn already escaping her as she curled up in his arms. He carried her into his room and laid her on the bed, pulling the blankets up around her and tucking her in as she snuggled against the pillow. Leaning down, he kissed her forehead, then walked over to the window.

The darkness outside felt oppressive, as if it would swallow him whole. He thought about calling Jenta, to see if she was okay. The alarm clock next to the bed read 2:34am, and he decided a call now would probably have her mom ready to kill him.

On top of that, her boyfriend was one of those angry, violent goth guys who always sneered at him when they saw him on campus. While Chris thought he could probably take any one of them by themselves, as a group they outnumbered him. He knew how to fight, but he also knew he couldn't take on more than two of those long legged, spike-wearing douchebags without taking more damage than he could soak. Something about not knowing how many it would take to beat him, but knowing how many there were. He snorted and shook his head, watching his shadowed reflection in the window match the sentiment.

Chris left the window with its hungry darkness and returned to the bed to find Sara already deeply asleep, hugging one of his old sweatshirts like a teddy bear. He lay down and snuggled in behind her. Chris wrapped his arm around her, holding her to him as he kissed the top of her head softly. Sara made a small noise, burrowing closer as she cuddled his sweatshirt to her chest.

A sigh left him, and he lay his head back down on his pillow while he tried to will himself back to sleep. Only a couple more hours. Then he'd be headed back to school. He wondered if class would resume as normal. Normal. Fuck. After everything that had happened in the last twenty-four hours, he didn't think anything would be normal, ever again. Not for him, anyway.

Harlequin

Harley lay in her bed, wondering if she would ever sleep again or if it had been worth the effort of waking. She knew her alarm was about to go off, and for the first time in a long time, she struggled to make herself get up. Her body ached, her nerves were raw, and her brain was on fire. Something kept pushing at her mind in the dream, telling her it would all be over if she just gave up control. Even in the midst of the pain and humiliation, that voice whispered that if she just let go and gave in, it would all end, and she could rest.

In the moment, it had sounded amazing. That pressure on her mind would go away. The pain in her body would go away. Maybe she might even feel the weight on her heart ease. The weight that had been there since her mother died, and her father broke down; around the time she'd taken on the mantle of responsibility in caring for both her child self and the father who could barely function without his wife. Would that stress and loneliness ease? The pressure of being everyone else's safe space while having no safe space of her own?

Harley took a deep breath and held it until her lungs burned and her body screamed at her for air. Her throat ached and she knew she probably had bruises that would be impossible to hide without something as drastic as a turtleneck. She could feel the individual pressure points of where the thing gripped her, the tips of its nails digging in just enough to make little punctures that left blood drops on her pillow.

She let the air out slowly through her mouth as she gazed up at the ceiling of her bedroom and wondered again if the fight was worth the effort. It was a moot question since the voice inside her would never let her leave her obligations behind. What would her father do without her?

She couldn't be her mother; her beautiful, perfect, dead mother who could do no wrong and had no faults.

Growing up, Harley's father made sure she knew her mother. The house was littered with pictures of her, and Harley heard her voice through recordings and home movies. He made sure Harley would never question how much he loved her mother, his sweet, beautiful, perfect Eva who wore the rose soap and long, flowing skirts covered in flowers. Eva with her rich, beautiful silken brown skin and halo of midnight black curls like the nimbus around an angel's face. She couldn't even be angry at him. Harley wasn't certain about love at first sight, but if there was such a thing as soulmates, her father had his ripped from his arms and never recovered.

No. Harley was not her mother, and never would be. She was barely *herself*, most days, and if she had to battle the pain in these dreams along with the pain in her heart, she wasn't sure letting go was the worst option being offered to her.

The alarm next to her bed gave an electronic hiss and then started blaring its morning song. Harley rolled over, smacking it with more force than she meant to. Making herself sit up and scoot to the side of the bed, she stared at the dark screen of her computer and the book sitting in front of it.

It had been strange to see Cadence standing at her door after so long, that awkward grin on his face as he handed her the book. She'd invited him in, but he'd declined, saying he needed to get home. She understood. There were probably still boundaries he wasn't ready to cross if he was going to keep up appearances. Standing on her porch handing her a book was one thing in a neighborhood of students who all attended the same high school, but coming inside?

She'd flipped through the book and saw the picture he and Chris had spotted. The Lady Plays. She'd seen other woodcuts from the same artist in other places. His art all appeared to depict the same subjects: unicorns, goblins, elves, strange creatures who were half human, half animal—like satyrs and bird people—even mice and rabbits walking on hind legs and wearing clothing. She found the journal entries fascinating. Many of them spoke of some sort of doorway or gate through which he'd passed and entered into another world, and thus the inspired art.

Harley stretched and yawned, then got up and went to her closet to pick out clothes. Much like her struggle with waking up, for the first time in a long time, she actually kind of hoped classes were canceled.

Chapter Nine

Christian

A pounding on the front door woke Chris from—thankfully dream-less—sleep. He sat up and scrubbed at his face with both hands then glanced over to see Sara still cuddled around his sweatshirt but also now wrapped almost entirely in the blankets.

"Little blanket hog." He said warmly and tousled her hair gently before climbing off the bed and padding barefoot to answer the door. The person standing on the porch wasn't at all who he expected.

"Cadence? Fuck, what time is it? Shit. Hang on a sec." He closed the door so he could pop the safety chain, then pulled it back open enough to let the other guy walk into the relative dark of the living room. When Cadence didn't look at him after entering, Chris followed his gaze.

The living room wasn't large, and most of it was taken up by the big sofa that slouched against one wall. It was probably as old as Chris was, and had been his grandparents', received in the estate after his grandmother passed a couple years ago. His mother had covered it in an old bed sheet, supposedly to protect the upholstery, but it sagged heavily in the middle, the springs compressed and the cushions in desperate need of replacing.

On the far wall across from the sofa sat a small entertainment center where his mother kept their tiny movie collection, a combination video player, and a handful of family photo albums. The TV was also from the estate. It was a tube TV but still in good condition and a larger screen than anything they could have otherwise afforded.

Just in front of the sagging, sheet covered sofa hunched an old, beat-up coffee table strewn with cigarette soft packs, a partially full ashtray, and a couple open beer cans. On the floor next to it, an empty gin bottle sat accusingly in plain view. Chris barked a bitter laugh.

"That was my mother's. She emptied it last night." Cadence finally looked at him, then, and even in the dim, Chris could see his bemusement.

"Damn. Are you okay? I know my dad can get a little, well, scary."

"Yeah, We're okay. Sara had a nightmare." Chris scrubbed his face with both hands again and dropped onto the couch, his forearms resting on his knees as he stared at the coffee table. "Fuck, man. We both did. I don't know how I pulled myself out of it."

"Where is your mom?" Cadence scanned the room, then came back at Chris.

Chris peered up at the ceiling, took a deep breath, then met Cadence's concern with his own flat resignation. "So, funny story. When I woke up from my nightmare, I went to check on Sara. She screamed when I woke her, and my mother came in and started yelling."

"What? Why?"

Chris blushed hard, and hesitated. "She accused me of molesting Sara."

There was a long silence before Cadence said, "Oh."

"Yeah. Sara was sitting in my lap when she came in, and she tried to grab her from me. Sara kicked her and told her she hated her."

"Jesus. Chris…"

"I know. It doesn't help that I lost my temper and said some shit, too. She stormed out after that and hasn't been back since. That was at like 2:30 this morning."

As Chris spoke, a blanket wrapped Sara came trundling out from his bedroom, her face puffy with sleep. She moved into the room and climbed up into Chris' lap, curling against his chest. He held her in his arms tenderly, brushing stray hairs from her face before turning back to Cadence.

"Normally my mother takes her to the sitter on her way to work in the morning, and her school bus picks her up from there. I don't want to just leave her here alone, but I don't have any way to get her to the sitter, or to school."

"Why don't we just drop her off on the way?"

Chris gaped him, incredulous. "You don't have to do that."

"I didn't say I did." Cadence crouched down in front of them, and Sara blinked sleepy eyes at him. "What do you say, Sara? Is it okay if your brother and I drop you off this morning?"

The impression Sara's focused gaze had on Cadence was obvious, his expression growing earnest as he gave her a warm, winning smile. Sara wasn't normally a fan of strangers, but when she'd met Cadence the day before, she'd taken to him almost immediately. Chris couldn't even really blame her. At least to himself, he could recognize that Cadence had a certain charm and wholesomeness—two things his sister didn't see a whole lot of from the men their mother brought home.

Finally, Sara nodded. Her voice came out small but clear. "Thank you." She addressed Chris, giving him serious eyes. "Miss Monica makes me breakfast, but Momma usually makes me lunch to take."

76

Chris smiled back. "I got it, Kiddo. Go get dressed and we'll put together lunch for you, okay?"

She gave him a surprisingly intense look. "You, too, Chrissy."

Chris peered at her, then laughed. "Me, too. Promise."

She pushed one of her arms out of the blanket, holding up a small chubby pinky finger, her expression solemn. After a moment, Chris raised his own pinky, tucked it around hers, and they moved their hands in unison, up, then down.

Sara's face split into a broad grin. She hopped down from his lap and bundled the blanket up around her, waddled down the hall to her room, and closed the door.

There were fewer cars in the student lot than the previous morning, and Chris and Cadence shared a look as Cadence guided the SUV into a spot close to the building.

"More students out. I bet that means we weren't the only ones who had the nightmare again." Cadence shook his head as he put the car in park and extracted his keys.

"Yeah, no doubt. Do you think we should try to find Harley?" Chris popped the button on his seatbelt but didn't open the door. He looked over at Cadence, having a moment to remember what the other guy said while they sat in the car, the previous afternoon. It felt weird to know something so personal about someone he'd only known in passing for so long.

"I mean, if she's here, she'll be back in the library, is my guess, but yeah. If they had the same nightmare we did…"

"…Then it's more than just coincidence. Okay. Jenta and I have the same first period, so what if we head that way, first?"

"Sure. See if we can spot Jenta, and all head to the library?"

"Exactly." Chris pulled the handle and pushed his door open, stepping out onto the pavement. His body ached from bad sleep, and he had claw marks running the length of his arms and chest, but thankfully, the soreness in his legs had mostly passed.

He grabbed his bag from the passenger's side floorboard then stepped back and pushed the door closed, feeling the scratches catch a little on the fabric of his shirt, a gray-on-gray raglan-sleeved baseball tee. He'd picked it to cover the worst of the scratches, but it itched and rubbed against the raised and tender wounds.

He shrugged his bag up onto his shoulders and followed Cadence through the doors and into the hushed interior, trading the hum of late summer bugs for the hiss of the fluorescent overhead lights.

They didn't have to go far to find Jenta, but it took them a moment to realize it was her. A group of students was circled around her and her boyfriend Jonathon, who was crouched on the floor, one hand cupping a bloody ear. As Chris and Cadence pushed through the crowd, Jenta stepped past Jonathon to reach her locker, one heavy, booted foot swinging forward and then back, connecting solidly with his hip and pushing him forward, so that he dropped nearly on his nose, only just catching himself with a hand.

"Shit." Cadence uttered as Jenta opened her locker with an unhurried air. The crowd of students was absolutely silent, and Chris saw one of

Jonathon's cronies run off toward the bathrooms. Maybe whatever had gotten into him and Cadence yesterday was catching.

"What the fuck, Jenta? What's gotten into you? I can't believe you just fucking did that. That was my favorite earing!" Jonathon pushed himself slowly to his feet, his face flushed as blood dripped from what had been a piercing.

Jenta shoved a final book into her backpack, zipped it closed, and shut her locker before turning to face her much taller boyfriend. Chris froze. This wasn't like what he'd seen with Cadence and Becky. Jonathon definitely towered over Jenta, but where Becky was a yappy poodle, Jenta was a furious cat, hackles up and claws out. Chris was pretty sure he was about to see Jonathon become her scratching post. She stepped away from her locker and glared up into Jonathon's red-faced fury without flinching.

In the silence, her words were clear. Again, Chris realized how much different this was from what he'd witnessed between Cadence and Becky, yesterday. That had been sudden, a fire caused by a lightning strike. This was a slow stoked forge fire, and these embers had just been doused with jet-fuel.

"What's gotten into me? Maybe realizing just how much of a piece of shit you are. Consider this my way of balancing the books between us for the damage you've spent the last year doing to me."

"What the fuck are you talking about? Jenta, you're fucking delusional. I didn't do anything you didn't ask me, hell, *beg* me for."

Fury rose up and choked Chris. Gaslighting and innuendo in the same statement? He started to step forward, but a hand gripped his shoulder. He glanced over, ready to be angry, but Cadence's look made him pause.

The other guy shook his head, and then tipped his chin toward the arguing pair.

Jenta continued as if Jonathon hadn't spoken. "You never gave a shit about me, but God forbid anyone question *your* reputation. You're *pathetic*. You're so desperate for people to think you're a real tough guy, a real *bad* mother fucker, but you're not." She jabbed her index finger into Jonathon's chest to punctuate her words. Each poke rocked him back a little, and Chris wondered if Jonathon might end up with a bruise there. "You're a sad," *poke*, "lying," *poke*, "fake." *Poke.*

Jonathon opened his mouth to respond, but Jenta took another step forward, driving her fingers into his chest. "Fucking say it. Deny it. Try to deny all the rumors you've been spreading about me."

Jonathon flinched and started to take a step back before looking around. Then his brows furrowed, and he glared down at her, forcing himself to stay where he was.

Cadence's hand still gripped Chris' shoulder, and Chris made himself wait. He had to admit, he was almost surprised that Jonathon hadn't already gotten physical with her, but Cadence was right. Jonathon wasn't angry. He was terrified.

Jenta, on the other hand, was locked in on Jonathon. Even when she gestured at the crowd, she never looked at them, her rage focused entirely on the guy in front of her. Everyone in the hall was holding their breath, just like they had with Cadence. Chis thought his heart might rip itself out of his chest. What was happening to all of them?

She was so close that she practically spat the words up into Jonathon's face as she finished. "I gave you control because I didn't *want* it; not because I thought you *deserved* it. I'd rather give you a swift, hard kick in the balls but even *that* is more of my attention than you deserve. Instead, I'm going to leave you aching, bleeding, and full of impotent rage. Maybe you'll learn the same thing I did."

Jenta started to turn away, but Jonathon finally found his voice, his chin rising as he tried to salvage some level of his dignity. "And what the fuck is that, bitch?"

Jenta regarded him, and Chris thought for a moment that she wouldn't answer him. She scanned the crowd, and her eyes settled on him for just a moment. Or had he imagined it? But then her focus was back on Jonathon. "Everyone lets you down, even if they promise they won't."

A stunned silence filled the hallway as Jenta walked away. The only sound was her boots against the floor as she moved through the gathered crowd.

Harlequin

Harley stopped just outside the door for Miss Winters' AP Bio classroom. She'd waited for Jenta by the auditorium doors as long as she could before her nerves got the best of her. She'd even tried to text, but so far, hadn't gotten anything in response.

The light was on inside the classroom, and the door was open, but Miss Winters wasn't sitting at the desk by the door. Harley almost chickened out as she stood looking in from the hall. This had seemed like such a better idea the previous evening. She shrugged in an effort to rid her shoulders of some tension, then entered the classroom.

"Miss Winters? Are you here?"

"Harley? Yes, I'm here. One moment." Harley heard the rustle of papers and the squeak of a chair from the small, shared office that joined Miss Winters's classroom to the one next to it. Miss Winters came through the other door, a look of concern on her usually smiling face. "Are you alright? Do you need to talk?"

Harley gave her a genuine smile. Miss Winters was one of those people who always made her feel seen. She was model thin and always wore elegant pastel pants suits in solid colors with flowery blouses. White-blond hair hung nearly stick-straight around a perfectly oval face with bright, pale blue eyes. Her skin was so light it was almost translucent.

The first time Harley had a class with her, Miss Winters told all the students that if they could come up with a joke she hadn't heard about how she matched her name, she would bring them cupcakes. As far as Harley knew, Miss Winters had never been married, so she couldn't even say it was coincidental.

"I'm alright, Miss Winters. But yes, I would like to talk to you."

"Of course. I'm sure you heard classes were canceled again today, but we of the staff who could offered to be here for all of you. So, I'm here for whatever you need. How can I help?" She ushered Harley over to her desk, then brought her own wheeled chair over and sat down.

Harley tucked her skirt under her legs and sat, twisting her fingers in her lap as she tried to figure out how to start. Miss Winters waited quietly, letting the silence stretch. Even so, Harley felt that same sense of urgency from the previous morning take hold of her, and her words came out in a rush.

"I think what's happening might be related to my research paper from last year."

82

Miss Winters, who had been leaning forward, hands clasped and arms resting on her knees, sat back in her chair, her eyebrows going up. "I'm... I'm sorry, Harley, I'm not certain what you mean?"

"The news reports. The hospitalizations? The *deaths*?"

"Oh." Miss Winters considered her for a time before responding. "Harley..." The older woman seemed to struggle for what to say for a moment, then continued. "I appreciate that you're trying to help figure out what's going on, and I think it's really honorable—"

Harley flushed, and her jaw clenched before she could help herself. "But you don't believe me."

"Harley." Miss Winters clicked her tongue. "I'm not certain what would have you thinking that writing a research paper about *dreams* would cause something to be happening to the town, but I want to assure you that I really don't think they are related. Moreover, while I can appreciate your concern, and I know you care deeply about your fellow students, I think it's important that we let the authorities investigate what's happening."

She leaned forward again, resting her hand on the desk in front of Harley. Her voice was gentle, but all Harley could hear was the tone of someone talking to a small child. "I really appreciate that you came to me, and I don't want you to think I'm dismissing your concern. I know that what's happening right now is really scary, but, Harley, it's scary in the real world. While your research paper *was* very interesting, and very well cited, I think we need to focus on the here and now answers to solve this, and that means letting the police do their job, right?"

Harley swallowed and focused on her hands in her lap before nodding. "Of course."

Miss Winters patted her on the shoulder. "I know, Harley. I've been going through all my past research, too, trying to see if I have anything that might help. But the truth is, you and I, we're just not equipped to fix this kind of issue, and that's okay. There are other ways you can help your fellow students, right? You're such a wonderful source of support and encouragement, and I know many of your classmates really look to you as a leader, and a friend. I definitely think that would be a really wonderful way you could help during... Well, during what's happening."

Harley inclined her head, while a weight like a brick landed solidly in the pit of her stomach. "Of course. Sure. No, you're right." She tried to swallow, her face growing hot. "Um, Jess was going to wait for me in the library. If you'll excuse me?"

"Of course, Harley." Miss Winters stood with her and walked her to the door, one hand resting on Harley's shoulder. She stopped them both just inside the doorway, leaning a little forward so Harley would meet her eyes. "Hey. It's going to be okay. Just focus on the things you can do to help, alright? And I'm here if you need anything."

Harley gave another half-hearted nod, then left the classroom before she said something she knew she'd regret.

Chapter Ten

Harlequin

When Harley finally found Jenta sitting curled up on the little sofa in the girl's bathroom closest to the library, she panicked and only *just* stopped herself from screaming. She flashed back to a memory from five years ago, of finding Jenta in her bathroom, crouched and shaking with the slim blade still in her bloody fingers. She thought she might throw up, or faint.

I will NOT *run again!*

Then Jenta beamed at her, her face tear-streaked but grinning in triumph. She launched herself from the sofa and threw her arms around Harley, practically bouncing with joy in her thick black boots, even as little hiccupping sobs bubbled out of her.

Jenta's voice shook with nerves as she told Harley what happened, her flipping between pride and horror, but Harley could tell she was still high on adrenaline.

When Jenta finished, Harley held her at arm's length, studying her face. "Jenta, I'm so incredibly proud of you, but also, are you okay?"

Jenta settled back on her heels with a huff and gave Harley a flat look. "Why do I get the feeling *I* should be asking *you* that?"

Harley explained how things went with Miss Winters. It was almost worth the frustration to see Jenta's angry incredulousness.

"You're kidding me."

"Nope. She practically patted me on the head and gave me a cookie before sending me off to bed."

"Damn, Harley. And she was the only teacher you thought might listen?"

Harley frowned at her own reflection in the mirror that hung over the sinks. "Pretty much. The one most likely to humor me, and give me the benefit of the doubt, anyway. Looks like we're on our own."

"Do you still want to go find Cadence and Chris?"

"Yeah. They deserve to be in on this, too. Especially after what they found."

Jenta's brows came up. "What they found?"

"Let's head to the library. I got a text from Cay this morning that he was going to pick Chris up—"

"Oh, right." Jenta blushed. "Um... I'm pretty sure I saw them in the crowd while I... This morning."

Harley laughed despite herself. "That could either be a really good or a really bad thing."

Jenta rolled her eyes. She grabbed her bag from the floor and hefted it over one shoulder.

They left the girls' bathroom and nearly ran into the guys, already headed toward the library doors. When Cadence started to speak, Harley held up her hand. She pulled her bag open, extracting the book and holding it up. "We need to talk."

"What a bitch." Chris said into the silence, after Harley explained about trying to tell Miss Winters what they'd been researching.

Harley shrugged, though again she felt a small spike of satisfaction at his ire. "I guess I kind of understand where she was coming from, and I don't even necessarily think she would be wrong, except that, well…"

"We've all seen the truth." Jenta spoke for Harley when she hesitated.

"Yes. In fact, Chris and Cay, I need to ask—did you guys *dream* again, last night?" She said 'dream' like it had more than just the normal meaning.

Cadence and Chris both nodded. "Not just us." Chris answered. "I think my sister may have been there last night. I had to wake her from a pretty bad nightmare."

"Oh, Chris, that's horrible. Is she okay?" Harley vaguely remembered a small girl child from when she'd tutored Chris previously.

"As much as she can be, I hope. Even so, I doubt I'd know how to help if she isn't."

"I think maybe we should focus on stopping this—whatever is happening—before we start worrying about fixing the damage it's doing." Cadence said.

Harley's eyes widened. "Cay."

Cadence met her look, but just shrugged a little. "Sorry. I don't mean to sound harsh; I just think we all may walk away with scars after this, but if we don't figure out what's happening and how to stop it, how many of us may not walk away at all?" Cadence shifted uncomfortably and gestured at the book sitting in the middle of the table. "Did you learn anything new?"

Harley's pulse sped up as she reached for the book. She licked her lips, her fingertips tingling as she pulled it open to an image she'd marked with a sticky note.

The piece took up most of the left page, a detailed painting of a tall, graceful-looking woman with red-blond hair cascading down to her knees. She stood barefoot next to a fountain, surrounded by a copse of trees, dressed in something like a Grecian toga or a chiton. *Just like my dream.*

The painting, like the rest of the art in the book, was from the 1600's, painted by the same man who had written the journal. The woman's face was serene and calm, painted at a three-quarter profile so that she appeared to be looking at something off to one side of the artist. Harley spun the book and pushed it back to the middle of the table, so the other three could see the painting. "According to the description in the book, she's the queen of a group of creatures called the Seelie sidhe."

Jenta raised an eyebrow. Chris swallowed audibly, and Cadence gave a low whistle.

"From what I can tell, she's basically the counterpart to the Dark Lady we've been seeing. But, and guys, this is where I need you to really think. I think I saw *her* in my dream last night, too." Harley tapped on the page, beside the serene face.

Jenta shook her head and sat back, crossing her arms, tucking her chin against her chest. Chris started to open his mouth but then closed it and got a thoughtful look as he continued to study the figure in the painting.

Cadence searched Harley's expression. "Saw her how? Where?" He asked.

"Before. It was more like a real dream. Not like she'd taken me somewhere, but more like she'd sent me a vision if that makes sense." Harley shrugged.

Cadence considered her comment, then answered, "Yeah, kinda. Like, the difference between seeing wind in the trees and standing outside on a windy day."

Harley smiled. "Exactly. It was like she was being extra careful to seem, I don't know, different from the other."

Cadence nodded and went back to assessing the painting.

"And I think she said something." Harley said, nervously.

They all looked up at her.

"Do you remember what it was?" Cadence said.

Harley shook her head. "Not exactly, but it was something like, 'I'm coming. Look for me, and you'll find me.' and then something about someone being with me."

"Maybe she meant us? Like maybe because we're all together?" Chris said but not like he believed it.

Harley shrugged. "I'm not certain. I feel like I was dragged from that dream with her right into the other dream. I only remembered the part with her when I was flipping back through the book this morning, and saw the painting again."

Chris shook his head and sat back. "I don't remember. If I *did* dream about her, I feel like I would, but I don't."

"Guys..." Cadence pointed at the book with a shaking hand.

The picture started to move and shift perspective. The trees swayed in an unfelt breeze, the grass and plants around the woman's bare feet bent and bowed their heads. The woman moved as if walking forward within the painting. Her dress shifted and flowed around her long legs, giving glimpses of pale, almost gold tinted skin. Her hand raised in a welcoming gesture, and then her head shifted to look directly at them. The words on the page below the painting cleared in smoky wisps, replaced by graceful flowing script.

Find me in the mirror's reflection. Seek light—know truth. Choice is yours.

Before any of them could react, the book pulled itself shut with a snap so sharp it practically bounced on the table. Startled, they gaped at each other.

"Please tell me I'm not the only one who saw that?" Chris said.

Jenta was shaking her head steadily back and forth, muttering "holy shit."

Harley and Cadence shared a long look.

"A mirror is a window into another world." Cadence said the words softly, but Harley was already nodding.

"The journal pages. That's what the artist, Adlard, said. The artist who painted that picture and did the woodcuts of the fae creatures." *And the Dark Lady*, she thought to herself, but didn't say it out loud after glancing at Jenta.

"Okay, but how do you find someone in a reflection? I mean, besides the usual, anyway." Chris was looking back and forth at Cadence and Harley. Jenta had gone silent, her head down and her arms still crossed over her chest.

"Hey kids, I'm sorry but I'm going to have to ask you all to head home."

Harley turned in her chair to find the principal approaching the table where they sat, flanked by a small group of police officers. Principal Wilkins was a tall, heavy-set man in his late fifties, with a balding head and a thick salt and pepper beard. He hadn't pushed up his glasses in a while, so as he approached, he was squinting at them through lenses just barely perched on his small round nose. He was nervously wringing his hands and kept glancing back at the officers walking just behind him as if he were the one who was in trouble.

"Principal Wilkins? Is everything alright?" Cadence swiveled in his own chair to look at the principle. Harley saw a brief expression of surprise cross his face, and he rose, putting his back to the table and leaning against it. Harley stood up next to him, catching Chris' eye and glancing down at the book, then moved so she could lean her butt against the table, giving a warm smile to the officer to Principal Wilkins's right. She hoped Chris would understand what she wanted.

The officer to Principal Wilkins' left narrowed his eyes and tried to look past Cadence at the table behind them, but Harley was fairly certain none of them had seen what was on the table or would have any reason to suspect they'd been doing anything other than sharing a book and talking about it. What else would they be doing in a library, of all places? *What if they're looking for suspicious activity?* She swallowed and pivoted her smile to the other officer. Thankfully, Principal Wilkins didn't seem to notice.

"Cadence Murphy, this is Officer Lancer, and Sheriff Gilbert. Gentlemen, this is Cadence Murphy." Principal Wilkins gave a proud smile as he clapped Cadence on the shoulder. "He's going to help us stay in the top running for state this year." The smile faded, and Principal Wilkins cleared his throat. "Well, yes, that is, once sports are restarted."

He made serious eye contact with Cadence, then peered at Harley. "Miss Swanson, it's good to see you, as well! Nice to know you're still trying to get your studies in, in the face of..." He shot a look at the sheriff and cleared his throat again. "Yes, well. As I mentioned, I'm going to have to ask you—all of you—to head home. The school will be closed for... for the rest of the week." The principal sounded like he'd started to say something else before correcting himself. Harley and Cadence shared a look, then turned back to the principal.

"Oh, wow. The rest of the week?" Harley put as much disappointment in her voice as she could manage. With her weight pressed against the table, she felt what she hoped was the book slowly sliding across its surface. She didn't dare check on what Jenta and Chris were doing behind them.

Principal Wilkins took her tone at its face and tried to offer consolation. "I understand. You've done amazing things in this library, so your teachers tell me. I promise, the time will go by in a flash, and you'll be back in here before you know it. In the meantime, I would be happy to coordinate for your father to come pick up one of the computers—"

The sheriff coughed loudly, and Principal Wilkins peered at him, then back at Harley. "After it's been security cleared, that is. But really, children, I am going to have to ask you to vacate the campus."

The table shifted behind her, and then Chris was stepping up next to Cadence on his far side.

"Hey, Officer Lancer. Sheriff. We'll clear out, no problem. Is there anything else we can do to help?" Harley had to stop herself from gaping at Chris. His demeanor was completely different. Strong, confident, with just a hint of obsequiousness.

"Christian Johnson. It's good to see you moving in such positive—" Harley heard Jenta's chair move, and she stepped up next to Harley "—circles." The Sheriff's tone deflated as soon as he saw the fourth member of their group. He shook his head and went back to focusing on Chris and Cadence.

Harley got the distinct impression that she and Jenta had just been summarily dismissed. "We appreciate the offer of cooperation. We'll keep in touch if we need anything from you kids, but for now, it's probably best if you do what your principal says. Officer Lancer, would you escort them to the exit, please?"

Officer Lancer gave a stiff nod, big hands resting on his utility belt as he stepped forward.

"You heard the sheriff, kids. Let's go ahead and clear out, now." His accent was Midwestern thick by way of Chicago, Harley guessed, and as he moved, his wavy, salt-and-pepper hair caught the light of the upper windows. He was nearly as tall as Cadence, so definitely over 6 ft, though his shoulders weren't as broad. He stretched his long arms out to either side to corral them and drive them like cattle toward the glass doors that led outside instead of to the wooden ones that would take them deeper into the school.

Past his arm, Harley could see the rest of the officers who'd followed the principal into the library splitting up and moving among the stacks. One round-bellied older officer went to stand next to the doors leading into the school.

The four of them let Officer Lancer usher them out the doors to leave them standing on the sun-drenched sidewalk. As soon as they were outside, he pulled the doors closed and flipped the security lock.

"Chris?" Harley voiced his name like a question, not sure how much to say out loud.

"Got it." Chris patted his backpack strap on his shoulder.

"What the fuck was that about, anyway?" Jenta faced the doors, hands on her hips.

Harley studied the doors. Officer Lancer was gone, his dark uniform presumably blending into the reflected trees on the glass. "My guess is that the police are still running with the theory that whatever is happening is some kind of biochemical or terrorist attack."

Jenta scoffed. "In Green Bridge?"

Cadence nodded. "Yeah, one of the guys on the football team is the son of one of Sheriff Gilbert's deputies. When I got here yesterday, he said he heard his dad on the phone with the sheriff, and that they might have to close down sites where the victims spent their time. I guess we have our answer."

"Okay, so now what?" Jenta said, an edge of irritation coloring her words. "Not that I thought we could solve this from the public library, but it was better than nothing. Where are we going to get a big mirror so we can make a magical phone call to an alien queen?"

"Jenta, she's not an alien. She's just..."

"Not human." Jenta finished. Harley sighed.

"The only big mirror my house has is in our bathroom." Chris said.

"Same." Cadence grumbled. "I mean, I have my own bathroom, but it's certainly not big enough for all four of us to hang out in. Not to mention, I can't fathom what my dad would say."

Harley took a breath, then said, "I offer my house. I've got most of the research cross referenced on my computer, I have a big mirror on the back of my closet that I think would probably work, and maybe we can come up with a more solid plan. My dad left for a business trip this morning, so I have the house to myself."

"Good, because there's no way my mom wouldn't ask an absolute shit-ton of questions if we went there. I'm down for Harley's place." Jenta moved to stand next to her.

Harley waited for a nod from Chris and Cadence, then continued.

"Okay. My place it is, then." She checked her watch. "It's noon now. I say we go, grab lunch, check in with your families if you need to, whatever, and regroup at my place around three?" They all agreed and as a group, headed toward the student parking lot, a much longer walk from this side of the building.

Harley tried to remind herself that these were people she knew, at least in passing, and that it couldn't be weird to have them at her house all at once. But it was weird enough before, and that had only been dreams. Dreams were always weird. Now they were wide awake.

Chapter Eleven

Harlequin

Harley sat in her living room, waiting for the others to arrive. The house was empty, but there was a strange weight of anticipation in the quiet. Under the ever-existent hum of the central air and the electronic buzz of the old table lamp beside her was *something*. A skin tingling, hair raising something that left her feeling jangly and on edge. As if she should be able to turn quickly and find someone—or some*thing*—standing just behind her.

The living room, like everything else in the house other than her bedroom, hadn't been changed much since her mother passed. Small blessing, her grandmother told her once, that Harley's mother had a taste for the timeless. The middle of the room was taken up by an enormous area rug covered in small pale flowers and green leaves and vines on which sat a long white sofa, a cherrywood-stained Shaker-style coffee table, and two large, overstuffed armchairs upholstered in fabric with white and blue stripes, set facing the sofa at angles. Behind the armchairs was, to Harley, the only thing that really showed the age of the space—A fake fireplace with shiny brass trim around the edges.

Across the room from the front door was the entrance to the kitchen which shared the wall with a long, low entertainment center. That was the one thing her father had finally given in and changed. He'd let Harley trade out the old entertainment center—a giant hulking monstrosity with fake wood, glass doors, and a classic tube style TV—for the new low cabinet style that better matched the coffee table and had room for a much larger flat screen.

Harley sat curled in one of the armchairs, her feet tucked up under her as she tried to read while she waited, but mostly she just kept looking at the stairs leading up to the second floor while she let her mind wander.

What if she was wrong about this whole thing? What if it was some shared hallucination, and really *was* being caused by some neurotoxin or something? How would they know? The police were going to be checking the school with a fine-toothed comb, and there really wasn't anything else they could do in the meantime, if it turned out to be something so mundane. Even with everything, most of what they'd seen so far could potentially be explained away by the influence of some kind of hallucinogen, but that wouldn't explain the injuries, right?

Harley had just checked the clock hanging over the kitchen door to see it tick over to 3:14 PM when she heard a knock at the front door. Standing, she went to open it and found Cadence and Chris standing there, arguing.

"... Damn it Cay, I don't have time to sit around babysitting each other. I have to find my sister!"

A knot formed in the pit of her stomach. "Did something happen to your sister?"

Her voice apparently surprised Chris and Cadence, who both jumped and spun to face her. Chris was panicked and angry, but Cadence appeared frustrated.

"We think *she* has Sara." Cadence didn't have to specify who 'she' was. "I'm trying to convince Chris that the only way we're going to get Sara back is as a team instead of him running off when he doesn't even know where to go."

"Oh, God. Chris, I'm so sorry."

Chris' stricken look started to crumble, and he raised his hands to scrub at his face.

"Come inside." Harley stepped back from the door, holding it wide so Cadence could guide Chris into the living room. She closed the door behind them, locked it, then leaned on it while she considered them both. She met Cadence's concerned eyes and led them to sit on the sofa. "Can you tell me what happened?"

Chris sat like a puppet with his strings cut. Cadence waited a moment, examining the other guy, then answered. "Sara, Chris's sister, was supposed to have school today, but hers was canceled, too, according to her sitter. She came and picked Sara back up when the school called her and was watching Sara when their mom showed up to get her."

Harley looked at him, confused. "Wait, I thought you said—"

"The sitter said their mom wasn't alone. She had, and I quote, 'a beautiful woman with her.' Apparently, Sara didn't seem happy to see her, but the sitter wasn't sure why, since the lady seemed *polite enough*." He said those last two words with a sardonic sneer. "I don't give a shit how polite someone is, if a kid doesn't want to go with them, why would you let them take her?"

Harley shook her head, still confused. "I still don't understand. How can you be sure it was her?"

Chris raised his head, his voice flat. "She had a doorbell camera. When I asked, she showed me the video."

The blood drained from Harley's face, and the knot in her stomach grew into a brick. "Why? And how? Up until now, she's only been coming at us in our dreams. How could she have come and been with your mom, to pick up Sara?"

Cadence put a hand on Chris' shoulder then shifted in his seat, and hesitated, before talking. "You said something yesterday when I came to the library. Do you remember?"

"I said I thought something happened, like some door was opened. Jess and I found what appeared to us to be a trickle of victims becoming a flood pretty much overnight, like a dam bursting."

"What if that's exactly what it was? Not a dam bursting but a door opening? A door that was only one direction before, and now it's open from both sides, and that's how she was able to come get Chris's mom, and sister?"

"Her name is Tonya. My Mother. Toni, to her friends. Not that she has a lot of those." Chris had to stop and swallow before continuing. "Why would she want my mother? Or Sara? I don't understand." Chris stared at Harley, the pain in his eyes ripping a hole in her heart.

"I'm sorry, Chris. I don't know. My best guess is that she's using them as a lure in the hopes you'll come to her and try to get them back."

"Yeah, well. It's working. I don't care what we have to do. If I have to throw myself headlong into whatever mirror you have, I'm going to get my sister back."

"Chris." The way Cadence said his name made Chris turn to meet his look. "*We're* going to get your sister back. There's no way you're going alone."

Harley started to say something when there was a soft knock on the front door. "That's probably Jenta." She stood and went to the entry.

After a moment, Jenta came in with her school backpack slung over one shoulder. "...Told my mom I was going to be here for a couple of days, just in case. I hope you don't mind..." Jenta saw Chris and Cadence, then turned back to Harley. "What happened?"

"Chris's sister, and possibly his mother, appear to have been taken." Harley said it as she moved past Jenta to sit back down in one of the armchairs.

Jenta widened her eyes. "Well, Shit. I guess that kind of answers that question, doesn't it?"

"What question?" Cadence asked.

Jenta shrugged and came to sit in the other armchair. "Whether or not this all was just one big, stupid, fucked up dream. I've had some pretty messed up nightmares, but I've never dreamed of *someone else's* sibling being kidnapped."

Harley gathered their attention to her. "I think it's time us dreamers try to make that phone call."

Chapter Twelve

Christian

C hris sat with his back against the wall next to the bedroom door, shooting surreptitious peeks at Jenta who also sat on the floor, leaned against the foot of the bed as she studied herself in the tall mirror hanging on the back of Harley's closet. He wasn't sure if she could see his eyes flicking toward her, but he couldn't seem to stop himself.

His heart hurt. He knew Sara must be terrified, and he couldn't be sure what part their mother had in her being taken, or if she was just as much a victim as his sister. His stomach was full of snakes, wiggling and twisting and making him nauseous as Harley and Cadence discussed what to do next. Suddenly he was eight years old, again, a bystander waiting for other people to decide what was going to happen to him, feeling like he had no say in his own life. And yet, having Jenta sitting near him both helped him breathe, and filled him with a different kind of dread.

He met Jenta's eyes in the mirror, but her expression was indecipherable. She looked away first, and he studied the side of her face in the mirror, like he would memorize her features. *You have to stop this, Chris. Get your shit together.*

Jenta spoke up, interrupting the back and forth. She sounded as grumpy as Chris felt, but he didn't think it was for his sake. "Okay. So, we've locked in on who's doing this. Great. Super. What do we do with that? How does that help? We don't know how to stop her. We can't even just not sleep since now she's able to come here directly."

Cadence sat in the desk chair by Harley's computer. He'd been reading Harley's notes but spun the chair around to address Jenta, sounding irritated. "That's exactly what we've just been discussing. Maybe if you weren't sitting there admiring yourself in the mirror, you would have caught that already."

"Cay. Enough." Harley gave Cadence a warning look, then responded. "It's possible that knowing the *why* might help us figure out *how* to stop her, but you're right. Knowing who she is and what she's doing is all well and good, but how *do* we stop her? How do we even get to her?" Harley moved her attention to the mirror, and again, Chris found himself meeting someone's contemplative gaze within the reflective surface. Harley continued, seemingly speaking directly to Chris's image in the glass.

"We have a lot of questions, but not a whole lot of answers."

"What did the book say about the Seelie queen? Seek her in the mirror's reflection, right?" Chris asked. Harley's reflection nodded.

"The journal pages mentioned fae using mirrors to talk to each other, and sometimes even using them like doorways or portals to somewhere else." She sat on the bed with the book in her lap, her fingers tapping absently on the closed hard cover.

Cadence came to sit on the edge of the bed by Harley's feet, staring over Jenta's shoulder so that they all viewed themselves in the mirror. "Did the guy write *how*?"

Harley's reflection shook her head. "If he did, it's not in the journal pages they included here."

The mirror rippled. As if its surface was liquid and a rock had been dropped in the middle, little concentric circles moved out and out until they hit the edges.

"Did that...?" Chris said.

"That! That's what I was looking at!" Jenta pointed and looked at each of them. "I wasn't just staring at myself in the mirror, Cay. I was trying to figure out if I'd really seen the ripples. Please tell me you all saw them."

Harley gaped at herself in the mirror. "Definitely."

"What's that smell?" Chris sniffed the air. He caught the musk of old leather, warm wood, and book dust—the scents that filled his grandma's attic where he'd lived until his mother took him back at twelve, to come help take care of Sara. Smells that meant love and safety, and happy memories of playing with his grandpa's old army gear or being snuggled up in a quilt pulled from his grandma's old hope chest while she read to him.

Jenta and Cadence spoke at the same time, their own heads tilted up as they drew deep breaths.

"It smells like my dad's old leather coat." Jenta's voice was soft with wonder.

"I smell my mom's perfume." Cadence opened his eyes and grinned.

Harley remained quiet. Her expression was sad, though she too was taking long, deep breaths.

"Where is it coming from?" Chris continued scenting the air, while he scanned the room. The bedroom door was closed beside him, and across the room, the large window that showed a view of the afternoon sky was closed. Even if it had been open, the limbs of the tall tree outside were only just barely moving, and that wouldn't explain how they were all smelling something different.

A sound rang through the room like the jingle of a small bell.

They all stood and approached the mirror. Another ripple spun out from the center, causing the reflection of the room to become foggy around the edges. The surface of the mirror shimmered and started to stretch and push outward, filling with that glittering fog until they were looking at themselves through a sparkly haze. Eventually, they could no longer see themselves in the pane at all. Instead, only the soft fog filled the glass.

With an almost audible pop, the surface tension holding the fog gave way, spilling it into the room so that it quickly covered the floor and climbed up along the walls. It was soft but thick, like the stuffing inside a teddy bear. Tendrils curled up around them, floating in the air and filling their lungs as they breathed. The room disappeared around them as the fog continued to thicken until they were only able to see each other, standing in the middle of the cloud. Each breath vibrated in their chests and their ears rang with the sound of tiny distant bells. Without discussion, they reached out and grasped each other's hands.

Out of the mist in front of them, a wrought iron lamp post coalesced. A glass lantern sat at the top of the post, its light warm and welcoming.

"Okay, I know the book said seek the light, but this is a little on the nose, right?" Cadence's voice sounded strange and hollow.

"I believe what it said was 'seek light, know truth. Choice is yours.'." Harley gestured with their held hands at the lamp post.

"She *did* say to look for her in the mirror's reflection..." Chris said skeptically.

"What if it's a new trick? What if now that *she's* opened the door..." Jenta's voice bounced and echoed around them, and yet still somehow conveyed her fear.

"I don't know. This doesn't really seem like her M.O., does it?" Chris met her anxious gaze, trying to sound reassuring.

Cadence cleared his throat. "Look. Worst case scenario, say it *is* her? Well, this time, we're fully clothed and fully awake, and maybe that will give us a better chance than she's expecting."

Harley gave one quick nod. "True. We won't know until we know." They gripped each other's hands tightly and walked into the mist.

Chapter Thirteen

Estian

T he four emerged from the mist like dreamers, pulling gently free from the bonds of sleep and letting go of each other's hands. They stretched and yawned, assessing their surroundings. One by one, each of them found her, adding the weight of their focus.

Estian waited, hands clasped in front of her. Her heart thumped in her chest, and she prayed again to Danann for strength and to grant her the words that would move the hearts of these mortals. She'd brought them to her favorite place: her private garden sanctuary. Hopefully, they found it as comforting as she did.

She wore a dress the color of new buds, gathered at the waist by a cloth-of-gold sash, intentional in its similarity to what she wore in the painting. She couldn't help but smile a little at the thought of the young mortal, Adlard, and how he'd come and begged an audience. A handsome and charming young man, kind and talented, and she, yet still a new queen then, only perhaps a few centuries into her reign, had been glad to stand for him.

The painting hung bright in her memory, rich with color and emotion. It had perfectly captured her garden in its sun-dappled splendor, and she only wished his miraculous paints could have depicted the fountain's tinkling music and the tittering joy of the birds that splashed among the upper tiers, sending droplets flying like surprised rain. Behind her, the tree branches curled around this small glade, embracing the soft ground with their leaf-covered arms. Truly, she'd been blessed by his presence, and by his art. Even more so, now, as she grasped the import of his work and how Danann had set it in the hands of these four.

She studied them, even as they considered her. Varied in appearance, and yet...

Two girls, two boys.

Both girls were of a height with each other, though one of them appeared to be wearing rather tall shoes, while the other wore something akin to the slippers her court enjoyed.

The one with thick dark curls, skin the color of the feathers on a sparrow's wing, and eyes that saw everything, her expression one of awe and curiosity mingled. The other a study in light and dark. Black hair that tumbled around her face like water on a moonless night, her face like alabaster, and just as stoic as the stone itself. They complimented and countered each other, but Estian could see the lines of love and friendship drawn between them, strung in the air like bright ribbons to her mind's eye.

The boys were more disparate. The one, his hair like leaves in fall, and eyes the color of pale emeralds, towering over the other three, as if he would protect them with his sheer presence. The other, shorter, smaller, but in some ways, more wild, more dangerous. Flaxen locks hung down over eyes the color of cornflowers.

All their faces different, but all holding the beauty and wonder of youth, and the passion and resolve that it entailed.

Estian stepped forward carefully and inclined her head. "Welcome, mortals. Harlequin, Jenta, welcome. Cadence, Christian, welcome. I am so pleased you came."

One of the girls, Harlequin, started to step forward but the one Estian knew to be Cadence reached a hand forward, taking her arm to stop her. Estian found the interaction fascinating. The burning embers of some strong emotion flared in their eyes as they gazed upon each other, and yet this hesitation between them. Then they both turned back to her.

Harlequin spoke, her voice soft but curious, as if she were speaking to a wild animal. Estian wondered if the effort was for her benefit, or simply the girl's own nature. "You're her, aren't you? The woman from the painting. You're the Queen of the Seelie sidhe."

Estian inclined her head again, allowing herself a small smile. "I am Estian Boryas Murhai, Daughter of the Dawn and Queen of the Seelie. I will admit, it is long since I had need to announce myself among those who did not know me. I wish us to be friends, though, so I would ask you simply to call me Estian."

Jenta stepped past Harlequin and Cadence, her back straight. Estian could hear fear in her voice, but a light of determination shone from her like a beacon. "No offense, Estian, but why should we trust you? You've given us no specific reason to believe you and traipsing through a fog bank to get here means we don't exactly know where we are."

Harlequin gaped at Jenta, uttering her name in horror. "Jenta... don't be rude! What are you doing?"

Jenta shrugged uncomfortably, but her tone was firm. "How do we know we can trust her? What if she's just another illusion? What if all of this is just poisoned cake?" She waved a hand around them, gesturing at the garden. To the far side of the fountain was a small sitting area, similar to the one in Estian's study. A grouping of chairs set around a low table placed on the grass on the leeward side of an ancient reaching oak that had stood in this place as long as Estian could remember. Its branches stretched out and out, providing wonderful shade and the music of the breeze as it caused the leaves above to dance and spin on their stems.

The last of their group, Christian moved up next to Jenta, putting a hand on her shoulder. Estian saw something flare between them, too, some connection she didn't understand. Both more and less than unrequited. He addressed the others. "Jenta has a point. We've seen a lot of weird shit in the last couple days." He blushed a little, turning his attention back to Estian. "My apologies, um, Estian. I don't mean any offense either."

Estian appraised them all, then gave a graceful, Gallic shrug. "Perhaps the apology owed is my own. I had forgotten. It has been an exceedingly long time since we have hosted mortals here, and the way of lore and legend has changed much in that time. Though I will also say that I am not used to having my authority questioned." Her voice hardened for a moment before she shifted her shoulders and made her way toward the circle of chairs, allowing herself the moment to find calm.

Estian let the silence stretch as she took one of the seats, arranging her skirts just so before continuing. "You are right, though. Right to be concerned." She twisted a little in her chair so she could regard them over an extended arm. "Would you join me? I ask only for a conversation. By the end, if you are not convinced of my sincerity, I shall open your way home, and you need never set foot in this place again."

The four practically huddled together, seeming almost afraid to get too far apart. Harlequin sighed in exasperation. "You guys, we were just trying to figure out how to get answers to our questions. I think our answers are sitting at that table."

"I agree with Harley." Cadence said, and Estian thought he sounded quite convincing, though Christian and Jenta both appeared to remain skeptical. "Not to mention, she just flat out said, if we don't agree, she'll send us home. If I remember right, according to the stories, they don't usually speak that clearly unless they mean it."

Estian couldn't help but raise her eyebrows at that. It was interesting to hear what of their tales had been kept true. Danann bless them, if they knew about honest words and promises kept, maybe this would be easier than she'd feared.

Jenta peered at her over Harlequin's shoulder, and Estian met her questioning gaze, unflinching. She schooled her face to stillness since she wasn't sure this particular mortal would appreciate the smile that kept tugging at her lips. It was like watching children learning a new game. Charming, in its earnest sincerity. She tried to speak to the question in those eyes, and not the thought it invoked in her.

"Part of her power is to inspire fear and create doubt. She rules a kingdom of darkness and chaos, of pain and blood." Estian paused, then shook her head slightly. "Please. Join me. Ask all the questions you wish. If I may, I will answer, and if I may not, then in that too, I pray you will find truth."

Jenta finally gave Harlequin a nod. Estian barely caught herself from letting out a sigh of relief.

The four moved nearly as one, as they approached the chairs. There was a short, dance-like shuffle as they selected their seats and again, Estian was struck by just how seriously they were taking things. She hoped it boded well for their decision, but it also saddened her to know these mortals should be set on such a dangerous path as the one she knew they faced.

Once they were seated, Estian spread her hands. "What would you ask of me? You may speak freely in this place. Know that nothing you say here will reach any but Danann and my own ears."

There was a long silence, while they all considered what to say, then Harlequin spoke nearly in a rush. "Who is the Dark Lady?"

Estian answered simply, "She is the Dark Queen, ruler of the Unseelie court."

Cadence leaned forward in his chair, and asked, "So, she's like you? Doesn't she have a name or anything, other than 'the Dark Queen'?"

Estian frowned a little. "I am not certain what you mean. We are each other's balance, she and I. To my knowledge, either she never had a name, or her name has been lost to time. Since just after the first king was banished, she alone has held the Unseelie throne, but even so, there is a long and winding history, both between the Seelie and Unseelie, as well as that of the fae in entirety. I would tell you at least some if you will hear it?"

"May we ask questions, as you tell us?" Cadence asked.

"Of course. The story of the fae is a conversation between the one who tells and the one who hears." Estian smiled softly, before continuing. "Thus, the origins of my people: In the beginning, there was only darkness, and Danann. To some, they are called Tengri, Theos, or K'uh, but to the sidhe, they are Danann. Danann is both God and Goddess. They are one, but also themselves and each other. They are all things, and nothing at all. God, Goddess. Danann."

"A lot of our religions start the same way." Harlequin said, though the comment seemed more to herself.

Estian nodded as she continued. "Light was created, and in the light, a universe was formed, as is the power of creation. Within the universe are many worlds like our own, and many unlike ours. In this world, Danann first created the immortals. Fae, we were called; Danann's oldest children. We were placed on the earth and given access to its power. This became our magic—powers of growth and beauty, destruction and death."

"Are you saying our planet is made of magic?" Jenta said skeptically. Harlequin gave her another hard look, but Estian held up one hand to forestall comment.

"Yes, and no. Danann's magic fills all things, but also, Danann's magic *creates* all things. So, these things both are and are not magic. It is possible for something to exist without access to the magic with which it was created. Your heart beats in your chest, your mind seeks meaning and to understand the universe around you, and yet, where do mortals go, when you are no longer within your human form? There is a point at which a world of understanding can still find its limits. Do you see?"

Jenta shrugged. "Kinda. You're saying that even if we can't necessarily wiggle our fingers and start a fire a yard away, life is its own kind of magic?"

Estian smiled warmly. "You put it very well, Jenta." Jenta smiled in return, seemingly in spite of herself.

"And so, the magic of life was laid upon the land, and with it, the access to that same magic was gifted to us, to be stewards of its use. But we were young, and proud, full of all the presumption that came with our naivete. We failed to heed the instructions given. Instead of using our gifts to steward the land, we used them to wage war on each other. What should have been most precious to us, we squandered. We thought we knew better than our creator. Like children tugging on a doll, we ignored the impact our struggle had on the thing over which we fought."

The four leaned forward in their chairs as Estian spun out her history for them. Harlequin's eyes were alight with curiosity, but to Estian's surprise, it was Christian who spoke.

"So, what happened? How come there aren't any fae in our world? Or," he blanched as he continued, "why *weren't* there any, until recently?"

"It is a fair question. It is said Danann saw that our behavior would lead not only to our own destruction, but to that of a precious world for which they had great plans. So there must be punishment for our audacity, and that was two-fold: First, we were separated from the world to be, placed here, in a realm of our own, our access to the magic of our forebears diminished in an effort to ensure that if we were to war amongst ourselves again, the damage wrought would be more so to our immortal bodies, than to the finite perfection of the land on which we live. Among those powers diminished was the power of creation. We may build what we see, we may mimic and reflect the world around us, but ultimately, we became the muse, left to pose for an absent artist.

"Second, and more important to my point was this—we were now placed as guardians of a new race. A mortal race. Your ancestors were being created, your Adam and Eve, if you will. They were placed separate from us in a realm of their own but that ran parallel to ours, so that we might watch over them."

Jenta's expression again grew skeptical. Estian tried to remind herself that this was the point of those they'd searched for, and that this skepticism was part of what was needed. "Yes, Jenta." Her tone came out more statement than question, but Jenta took the invitation for what it was.

"You seem to know a lot about us, so I'm sure you know I have two little brothers. How exactly would I be able to keep an eye on them if I'm in a different room, which is basically what you're saying?"

Estian allowed herself another small smile. "Again, well said. We were not set as guardians to protect you from anything within your own world, but to protect you from those among our own number who might, in their jealousy or anger at your favor in Danann's eyes, attempt to harm you. Moreover, this 'other room' as you put it, contains windows of sorts, so we are not entirely blind to your world."

"Mirrors!" Harley blurted, then clapped a hand over her mouth.

Estian smiled fully. "Even so."

"Okay, but seriously, though? The prisoners were set to guarding themselves?" Cadence said it sardonically, but Christian responded before Estian could.

"Actually, that can work really well. Not watching themselves; watching *each other*. At New Horizons, we knew that if one of us failed, we all failed, and if we helped each other, we could all succeed. The teachers were really good at letting us self-police for the majority part, and no one was above the laws we'd set for ourselves. It meant that only a handful of teachers could reliably work comfortably and safely with a larger group of guys."

"New Horizons? Isn't that the reform school? What were you doing there?" Cadence focused a scrutinizing gaze on Christian. Estian stilled herself and waited. She had not anticipated this possibility. That those selected might not be able to get along well enough to take the journey.

Christian met Cadence's scrutiny without flinching, and answered, his head up. "Yeah. It is. I was there because my mother's boyfriend of the time was a piece of shit. When I stepped in one night and stopped him from hitting her, he decided I needed an attitude adjustment, so he got her to sign the paperwork for me to be sent there."

"Is that where you were last year?" Jenta asked, and Estian sensed caution in her words.

Christian answered, without reservation. "Yeah. I don't think they actually expected it to be good for me. My guess is that he thought it would teach me not to talk back, but really it just taught me how to fight back the right way."

"So, your mom isn't with him anymore, then?" Cadence asked.

"Naw. I got that S.O.B. arrested for domestic violence, and he's doing three years because he was on probation when it happened. Never had to raise a hand to him." Cadence and Christian shared a knowing look.

Estian let out a quiet breath. "As young Christian says, it has worked well, this realm of ours. In the time since the splitting, we have self-governed. Us of the Seelie have focused on stewardship, cultivation and reparation of the lands upon which Danann lay their divine hands."

"What about the Unseelie? Are they basically the evil version of you? *She* certainly seems like it..." Harlequin said.

"Not evil, no. We are two sides of a coin balanced on its edge. But they are the dark to our light. The fear of the Sluagh to balance the Daoine muse. Joy and hate both may inspire song, and as you have seen, the artist may depict both sun and shadow upon the canvas. So it is that we fae, the dreamless immortals, are the inspiration for those who dream." Estian took a moment to catch all their eyes.

"Last, I must tell you this: Between these two realms, ours and yours, lies the Void. A wall of sorts, clear as glass but hard as obsidian. The Void is the place the mortal mind seeks in sleep and dream. A dream may at times touch our world, offer the dreamer glimpses of the magic of fae, but always before, the wall of the Void has provided protection for the unaware youngest from the envious eldest."

"So, if we're separated from you, how did you make a way for us to come here?" Harlequin asked.

Estian inclined her head. "It is another good question, Harlequin. Yes, the Void is a wall that separates us, but there have been times throughout our long history where a bridge has opened within the Void, allowing passage between the realms, but these were specific, purposeful, and heavily guarded. We know not how these bridges were opened, or why. You asked why there are no fae in your world, to which I will say, I am not certain there are not, but those bloodlines will have been long since watered down by their mingling with mortal blood, so they may perhaps be long lived, but otherwise, still mortal, themselves."

Cadence shook his head. "You're saying that we may have spent our lives walking along side people with fae blood, and just not known it? Would they know it?"

Estian shrugged. "Perhaps, or perhaps not. The point is this: even in consideration of the Void Bridges, those openings that span the space between the realms, there has never been a time before now that a mortal was brought to our realm unwilling or unwitting. Always before, it has been their decision; to come to us, a celebrated guest, welcome and cherished."

Estian bowed her head, feeling their eyes on her. She knew before she raised her head that they would be watching, but even so, she tried to keep her own hope out of her tone, and expression. This needed to be their choice if it had any chance of succeeding. She made herself meet their eyes as she spoke.

"This brings me to why I have asked you here. Something you four already seem to know. There is a power at work that is a danger to us all; A power that, if left unchecked, I believe may bring the end that Danann warned of. It is my hope that you can stop the Dark Queen."

Cadence

"Why us?" The words were out of Cadence's mouth before he could stop them. He scanned his friends. Jenta was pale and a bit green, as if she'd swallowed a bug. Harley appeared anxious, but not surprised. They knew what this would lead to. What other purpose would there be for them to try to get here, and get answers, except to try to stop the big bad that was hurting their friends?

Chris had his head down, studying his hands. Cadence brought his attention back to Estian who sat quietly considering him even as he surveyed his friends.

"Another fair question, to which a fair answer should be given, and I am sorry that I cannot, 'fore I receive your answer."

Cadence shook his head in disbelief. "Estian... Your Majesty, you're asking an awful lot of us, and regardless of our reason for coming, I'm also not stupid enough to think that just because I'm young and capable means I'm properly equipped to hunt down an immortal, *mythical* being and stop them from, what, global destruction?"

The queen peered at him, and he made himself sit still. When she spoke, her voice was soft and sincere, her eyes sad. "I know, and I am sorry. I promise you, once you have made your decision, I may answer this and truly, any other questions you may have. Please understand that I would not ask if I did not think you four were capable of doing this."

"Can't you just fight her, yourself? I mean, you have magic too, right?" Jenta asked sardonically. Cadence wasn't surprised to hear it had seeped back into her tone. He knew she and Harley had been friends for a long time before he'd moved to town, and that Harley, at least, cared deeply about Jenta, even though they hadn't talked in a long time. He could see why Harley liked her, but sometimes he wished Jenta wasn't so damned cynical.

Despite Jenta's sarcasm, Estian answered in earnest. "The answer to that is somewhat complicated. Yes, I do have magic of my own, and yes, I am strong enough that, had I the wish to see our realm reduced back to the ruins from which we have worked diligently to raise it, I believe I could defeat her. Eventually. But we are well matched, she and I. Truly a balance and check to each other's power, and so I fear what a battle between us would mean to our peoples."

"I mean, you're all immortals, though. You said pretty much all of fae are immortals, right? So why not just fight it out and rebuild like you did before? I guess I don't see why four humans would be the ones standing between this Dark Queen and the destruction of, what, *everything*?" Jenta had propped her forearms on her knees, her hands clasped in front of her as she leaned forward, her full attention on the queen.

Estian's expression went from sadness to disappointment before she schooled her face to stillness and met his eyes.

"Is this the feeling you all have?" Her voice held the sadness she tried to keep from her features.

Cadence glanced at Harley and Chris, before answering. "No. I don't feel that way. I knew why we were coming, and what our goal was, here. I see Jenta's point, that it seems strange an immortal in a world of magic would need us to intercede, but I believe you have a good reason. As you said, you and your people have been the ones *guarding* us against this kind of thing. I don't know why you need us now, but I came to help, and that's what I'm going to do."

"Same." Chris said, fiercely. "Not to mention that bitch has my sister."

Estian's eyes went wide. "Is this true? Has she taken Christian's sister?"

"And his mom." Cadence snarled. He couldn't help the anger in his voice, and hoped Estian knew it wasn't specifically at her, but tried to dial it back, regardless.

Even so, Estian was horrified. "I am sorry. I had thought I was working quickly enough that she would not find you before I did. When I learned she'd identified you as those we hoped to enlist in this, I thought she had not yet found a way to travel to you."

"You don't know how she's doing this either, do you?" Harley asked, more curious than accusing.

The queen shook her head. "No. some time ago, I felt a great shifting of power and tried to send a delegation to her. They..." If it was possible, the queen paled even more. "My people were returned to us in pieces."

Cadence gave a low whistle, and Chris uttered, "Shit."

Jenta sighed. Everyone focused on her, and she blushed but spoke into the silence. "Listen, I didn't say I *wouldn't* go, I just don't understand how four teens are going to stop the big bad dark. I mean, I'm in, because why the hell not? What else do I have going for me? I would just really love to know how exactly we're supposed to fight big magic, with big brains," she pointed at Harley, "big brawn," her finger moved to Cadence, "big brass," was Chris, "and big sass." her finger settled on herself.

"Wait, why am I 'big brass'?" Chris said, sounding a bit offended.

"Because it takes big fucking balls to swear in front of a queen." Jenta grinned at him.

Chris rolled his eyes but laughed.

Cadence wondered what Estian must be making of them. How long had it been since she'd been around mortals? He tried to read her expression but gave up quickly. Her ageless features were schooled to stillness, so whatever she was feeling was hidden behind what was probably a thousand years and more of practice in stoicism. She met his eyes, her own vibrant, sky-blue irises giving him no sign of what she thought of their banter until she smiled. It was warm and real, and Cadence's breath caught in this throat with the full impact of her beauty. He thought he could have fallen into those eyes.

Smack.

"Ow!" He rubbed his arm and glared at Harley who was massaging her own hand as she glowered at him.

"No ogling the queen, dummy."

The small clearing rang with the queen's laughter.

Harlequin

Estian's laughter echoed through the trees, sending birds to flight from the branches above their heads. As the glade quieted, Harley and Jenta shared a glance.

She understood Jenta's hesitation, and even her questioning whether they were fit for the task, but she also knew that, like her, Jenta had a voice in her head that would never let her walk away from this. A part of her that always felt a need to prove herself worthy. Harley knew that if either of them refused the queen's request, they would never forgive themselves, especially knowing that it might mean more lives lost.

"Queen Estian." Harley's voice rang with conviction, as she rose, and faced the queen squarely. Estian's eyes still shone with laughter, but her expression grew otherwise serious. "I want to help stop the Dark Queen."

Beside Harley, Cadence stood up. "Queen Estian, I also want to help stop the Dark Queen."

Chris stood slowly, taking a deep breath, and letting it out before turning to face the queen. "Queen Estian, I want to help stop the Dark Queen."

Harley thought Jenta might hesitate, might make them wait, or just get up and walk back to where they'd first entered the clearing, but she was close on Chris' heels, standing and turning immediately to face Estian.

"Queen Estian, I don't want to *help* stop the Dark Queen." Harley snapped her mouth shut around her response when Jenta shot her a look. "This isn't about *helping*. This is about doing. I will either stop the Dark Queen, or I will die trying."

Estian studied them all, meeting their eyes one by one ending on Jenta, before standing.

"I, Queen Estian Boryas Murhai of the Seelie, accept this offer of Aid. May Danann bless this quest."

Chapter Fourteen

Christian

C hris knew he should feel something more than anxious and scared. Every book his grandmother ever read him about adventures implied that those people were at least a *little* excited, even if it was only at the beginning.

The queen had shown them their first taste of magic—well, the first taste of magic other than creating a cloud for them to travel through dreams into another dimension—and it was... anticlimactic.

Upon announcing that the aid was offered and accepted, Estian decided it was time for them to share tea. Like a stage magician, she swept one arm grandly in front of her, and suddenly there was a hammered silver tea set and a grouping of delicate cups, bone white and painted with scrolling vines and tiny purple flowers. The tea pot—a tall fluted thing that made Chris think immediately of the old Alice in Wonderland cartoon—poured its contents carefully into each small cup, not a single drop of the liquid spilled.

Steam rose in twisting curls from the spout of the pot as the tea was poured. Once each cup was filled, a small stream of pure honey floated up and out of its jar and spun down into one of the cups before the cup, saucer and all, lifted into the air and came to rest with not even a clink on the queen's waiting palm.

They all watched, fascinated, as she took her first sip, but Estian apparently took it as due, giving a small wave of her hand after she set the cup back on her saucer. "Please, enjoy. Honeysuckle and mint, I believe you call them."

"So, does that mean you guys have the same plants we do back home?" Harley sat on the edge of her seat, dribbling honey into her cup before taking it in her hands.

The queen considered before answering. "Not all of them, no, and many of them we have different names for, as with any language. You will find, as you travel among us, that many will know the languages of mortals. I am not embarrassed to say that we find your kind quite fascinating."

"How so? I mean, I may be biased as a human, but I think we're pretty standard, right?" Cadence held his cup delicately between two fingers. The effect was ridiculous.

Chris couldn't help himself and laughed. "Dude, it's a teacup, not a baby bird."

Cadence contemplated the tiny cup, a blush rising in his cheeks. "I don't want to break it."

The queen cleared her throat delicately, and Chris laughed again as Cadence blushed harder.

"As you say, Cadence, to you, your fellows are what and who you have grown up knowing. Just as perhaps one of my people may find it strange that you might admire their otherness. It is akin to perhaps traveling to another land where the people and culture are so vastly different to your own that what they may find mundane, you find endlessly fascinating."

"You know, tourism." Chris said, then laughed.

From the trees on the far side of the fountain, Chris caught movement and then a tall man was emerging from among the branches, his brows furrowed with fury. Chris tapped Cadence's arm and they both moved to stand between the chairs and the man, whose eyes grew wide and then narrowed as he slowed, then stopped just out of arms reach.

Chris could tell immediately that the guy was some kind of military official, just from how he held himself. He wore close-fitting pants, though they might have been tights or leggings for all Chris knew, and a long open-sided tabard tied with a twisted cord of silver and black. His tabard bore a crest on the front, a roaring black bear in profile, silver and black on white. Over the top of the outfit was a short cape that was pinned over one shoulder, just covering the hilt of a sword in a sheath that hung down beside his left leg. His features were as dark and broody as the queen's were pale and lovely, and black hair was brushed back away from his austere, scowling face.

He glowered at them, nostrils flaring, but his words appeared to be for Estian. "Your Majesty, you did not tell me you were having... *guests*. I would have had an escort provided for you."

"Cristobal." Behind them, Chris heard the rustle of skirts and felt a light touch on one shoulder as Estian moved past them.

Whatever look she was giving him, the color drained out of the man's cheeks, his dark features going a bit green around the edges, but to his credit, he didn't look away or back down. "Your Majesty, as your general, it is my duty to protect you. How am I to do this when you are always galivanting off to Danann knows where? And now I find you entertaining without even so much as a single one of your ladies?"

"Cristobal."

"No, I will not hear this argument again, your majesty. Either I am to protect you, or I am not, and—"

"*Cristobal*. These are the guests I told you of. *The most important ones*."

Cristobal blinked, and his entire bearing changed. The fury faded like a scent on the breeze. Suddenly, he looked like butter wouldn't melt in his mouth. Chris wasn't fooled—he'd known men like this his whole life, and immediately, he hated that this was the person in charge of the queen's safety. Didn't she have anyone else?

"Your Majesty, my apologies. Had you but informed me, I would have gladly escorted you myself. Truly, I am only concerned for your safety. Surely you can understand that, after your brother—"

"Enough." The queen held up one hand, and Cristobal's mouth snapped shut.

Chris tried to tell himself it wasn't because she might have actually just used magic. They were definitely seeing quite a different side of this fae queen, and Chris wasn't entirely certain it was a bad side. The general's expression was a study in indignation, but he stayed quiet.

Jenta and Harley came to stand with them behind the queen, Cristobal following them with furious eyes. He didn't seem particularly impressed. Chris was suddenly glad their selection hadn't been up to Cristobal.

After what seemed a surprisingly long time, Cristobal returned his focus to Estian. He gave her a stiff bow from his waist, right arm crossed in front of his chest, his uniform cape falling down over his left shoulder. "Again, my Queen, my deepest apologies. I forgot myself—"

"Yes, you did. You may have taken my brother's position, Cristobal, but you are not my brother, nor will you speak to me thus, again. Am I understood?"

"Yes. My Queen." The words came out strangled.

"Good. You will return to the formal grounds and have rooms prepared. The royal guest suite in the east tower I believe will do nicely."

Cristobal's head came up a little, but he remained otherwise bent at the waist, and still didn't look at her.

"Yes, Cristobal?" Chris shuddered. If that had been his mother talking to him, he would have just gone right back into his room.

"Your Majesty, may I confirm that you speak of the suite of rooms in the same tower as my sister's, Your Majesty?"

"The very one, Cristobal. I'm sure it will be considered quite the honor to reside so close to our esteemed guests, and I know Lady Stephania would be overjoyed to know of it. I believe I shall have a word with her upon my return to the palace grounds."

"Of course, Your Majesty. As you will, Your Majesty." Cristobal stayed bowed, and Chris wondered how long he could hold that posture. It had to be something they practiced.

"What is it, general?"

"Your Majesty, may I send an escort for you and your... em. Guests?"

Estian scrutinized him for a long time. Chris thought after a while that she might be doing it on purpose. When she eventually spoke, her tone held a note of resignation. "You may. We will await them at the Arch of the Glade. Send Dia and Yiannis."

Cristobal straightened out of his bow, and Chris caught another expression from him. Disapproval. Chris surreptitiously flipped the bird at the man as Cristobal left the way he'd come.

Harlequin

Harley caught her breath at the view in front of them as they came out from among the trees. The castle climbed high and higher, impossibly tall. Bridges spanned the gaps at various points along the tallest towers. Tiny figures navigated their lengths, looking like spiders navigating the threads of a crystalline web.

Lower down, the structures appeared more natural, at least by comparison. The stone of the walls was smooth and perfect, catching and reflecting the rays of the afternoon sun into sparkling motes that danced in the air among the branches of nearby trees.

The palace appeared carved out of one enormous piece of quartz crystal, here and there showing veins of lighter or darker stone that wrapped and swirled around thick towers, bridges, and even some of the smaller outbuildings she could just see to one side of a large curtain wall that hugged the hill on which the palace perched.

They stopped at the base of that hill, at the head of a wide, smooth path that meandered gracefully up toward a grand archway.

Estian turned to them, her expression serious.

"You are about to meet two of those who will be traveling with you. I had intended for you to meet them first regardless, so perhaps it is best they provide us their company, now. Yiannis will be leading your party, and Dia is his second."

"Are you saying this as an introduction or as a warning?" Cadence said, and Harley could tell he was only half joking.

"I am not certain what you mean?" Estian didn't seem to respond to the pseudo humor in his tone, and Cadence's slight smile disappeared.

"Are you preemptively introducing them to us, or warning us because they're like Cristobal?"

Estian considered his question, then surveyed the rest of them. "I had not thought to tell you of Cristobal, as you will not be traveling with him. Would you have had me, as you say, warn you of him?"

Harley shrugged. "I guess it would have been nice to have a heads up."

Jenta snorted. "Yeah, it might have been nice to know that the Dark Lady and her goons won't be the only fae we might have to fight."

Estian blinked, the smallest of furrows forming between her brows. "You will not have to battle Cristobal. He is my general, and so is mine to fight from my place as queen. You may not owe me fealty, and I would ask no such thing of you, but I am responsible for my people—both their care and their admonishment."

Cadence was shaking his head, even as the queen spoke.

Harley saw two figures approaching from the top of the hill. "Cadence, explain or don't, but it looks like company is coming."

Cadence's gaze followed hers then returned to Estian. "We mean no disrespect, Your Majesty. We only mean that Cristobal seems pretty unhappy about our presence here, and we are worried he might not be the only one. We believe you, and have no reason to do otherwise, but as you pointed out, we are the strangers here. Just as you would consider your people's safety more than anything else, we are trying to consider ours."

The queen's face changed as Cadence spoke, growing speculative. As he finished, she dipped her chin, and Harley just barely caught what she said. "Yes. I suppose it is fair to say there may be some who are more worried by your presence than pleased by it." She finished her statement just as Dia and Yiannis approached, so that they ended up close enough that they also heard her words.

"Cristobal is, for all his bluff, a dutiful and well-appointed leader. He is not General Faylin, nor will he ever be—though he tries. For that, I must commend him. Dia, I count as a close boon companion from my youth. Yiannis has been among our court for some years, leaving his time of hermitage and isolation specifically to join the ranks of the Seelie court guard. I would trust them both with my life and do so now as I entrust them with your safety."

Harley, Cadence, Chris, and Jenta stepped back from her as she waved the two figures forward. "Diaphony, Yiannis, I would like you to meet Harlequin, Cadence, Christian, and Jenta. Aid in our quest has been offered and accepted."

Diaphony was almost as tall as the queen, with hair like rich red wine and eyes that burned orange, red, and ember black in skin that was a shade of soft orange-y pink that would have made a rose jealous. She gave a loud whoop and, in a rush, scooped up Estian and spun her around. She wore a pair of dark, nearly black loose-fitting trousers that were gathered at the shin by thick cords and at the waist by a wide black sash. A long burgundy tunic with loose bell sleeves hung nearly to her knees but with slits up the sides to her waist so it flared out as she whirled.

Yiannis regarded them, stoically. He was even taller than Cay, maybe almost seven feet tall, but the height fit him so well that the idea of him being smaller was simply impossible. Harley thought at first that his skin was also milky pale, like his queen. But as the sun caught along one cheek, she realized that his skin wasn't just pale, but fully iridescent, like a fish's scales. His hair, cut nearly as short as Cay's except for one long braid that hung over his shoulder and down to mingle in the folds of his skirt, was nearly black in the shade, but in the sun, it was a mix of greens and blues so dark they could have been pulled straight out of the depths of the ocean. His eyes were a rich blue green, only a few shades lighter than his hair. He wore a long skirt the color of iris petals that moved around his long, long legs implying the fabric was much lighter than it looked, and a simple cream-colored peasant shirt, cinched with a simple leather belt from which hung a small, sheathed knife.

Both of them had beautiful, elegantly androgenous features like the queen's, but Dia's perpetual smile softened hers, where Yiannis' face had been shaped by long years of contemplation, so that while he still showed the same ageless perfection of the women, his gaze held an inexplicable weight.

He gave them an elegant bow, then straightened. His voice was low and smooth like deep water. "Welcome, Danann's youngest, to the Fae Realm."

Chapter Fifteen

Christian

Once again, they sat sipping tea while they waited. Chris itched to get up and do something. Thankfully, none of the others commented when he stood and started pacing. The tall redheaded warrior, Dia, didn't seem to have such qualms, though thankfully, she didn't address him directly. Not that he had anything against her specifically, but the longer all this talking and waiting went on, the more he felt like he might scream and go tearing off into the wilderness, escort or no.

The sitting room was spacious, and Chris took full advantage. He'd counted thirty angry strides from the hall door to the far wall where the draperies were open, exposing a wide bank of windows that let in the late afternoon sun. The windows were also open, allowing a soft breeze, and the view overlooked an impressive swath of palace grounds including a walking path through a riot of flowering bushes strewn here and there with benches, and a well-manicured hedge maze.

The sitting room had high ceilings with spanning support beams of some pale glittering stone that came together in the center of the room, pinned in the middle by a delicate looking light fixture. Chris wasn't sure if it could be called a chandelier, but in his head, that's what it was. It hung almost directly over the top of what Chris would have called a coffee table that had another of those hammered silver tea sets with the delicate little teacups, surrounded by padded armchairs, all placed just so for conversation. It made him think of those magazines full of houses no one actually lived in. Not anybody with kids, anyway.

To his left and right, there was a door on either wall. Glances through those doors gave glimpses of two spacious bedrooms with two beds each. Harley and Jenta claimed the room to the left of the bank of windows, where both of the beds were covered in their own gauzy canopy, and a carpet covered in a mosaic of flowering vines took up a good amount of the rest of the floorspace. Chris and Cadence had already stowed their things in the other room where their own beds sat on a similar carpet of interwoven grape vines. Each of the beds was paired with a comfortable looking armchair, and a small table beside it. The sitting room and two expansive bedrooms were nearly the size of his whole house, back home.

The sitting room floor was also covered in colorful carpets, these ones woven with geometric patterns that made him think of those really expensive oriental rugs. They muffled his steps as he paced, and it made him want to stomp his feet harder.

"Is your friend well?" Dia asked casually as if Chris couldn't hear her. She reclined on one of the, admittedly elegant, chairs, a tiny plate balanced in her hand as she lifted her teacup to take a sip.

Yiannis leaned against the wall near the door to the hall, arms crossed and his chin resting on his chest, but his eyes followed Chris as he paced.

"He's just anxious to get going." Cadence said guardedly.

"Of course he is. As I imagine you all are. I think if Yiannis had his way, we would have left as soon as the queen told us you'd agreed, but as Essie said—" Yiannis cleared his throat and Dia laughed. "Fine, fine. Pan's pipes, Yiannis, you're as bad as my father. As *Queen Estian* said, there are certain observances that must be made. The court would never forgive her if she welcomed not just mortals, but those who have come *questing*, and did not allow the court a fete to call Danann's blessings on the journey."

"A fate? Like the future? What, are we going to sit around and have our fortunes told before we leave?" Even Jenta's normally at least mildly funny version of sarcasm grated on Chris's frayed nerves. He knew before she answered that Harley would be the one to pipe up, and he wasn't wrong.

"Not F-A-T-E. A fete. F-E-T-E. It's like a party. She's saying that part of the court's protocol is that they want to give us like, well, basically a sendoff celebration to wish us well, right?"

Dia's voice held humor like another voice might hold sorrow. Maybe it was just Chris' anxiety about his sister, but that laughing, happy tone made him want to yell at her. "Yes, very much so. Please have no fear." She gestured with the delicate cup in her hand as she continued, "You will come down, make an appearance. There will be toasts, eating, and always dancing, and then at some point, those of us in the escort will announce our good eves in light of the morning's travel. At which point we will return you to your rooms. Tomorrow, once you have broken your fast, simply step out into the hall. I will ensure there is someone waiting to guide you to the map room."

Chris didn't slow in his pacing but focused on Dia as he pivoted. "The map room? Why do we need that? I thought you all were coming with us?"

Dia's brows furrowed, but it was Yiannis who answered. "Yes. We will be with you, but if by some chance we are separated, you must know where you are going, and the places along the way where you might find solace, and perhaps wait for us." Chris continued his lap, and when he spun on his heel for another, Yiannis was considering him solemnly. "You are anxious to leave. Far more so than your friends. Your mind buzzes like a hive that has been doused in water. Whatever it is that troubles you, Christian, Danann is with you, as are we."

Chris shook his head. "You sound like one of those old guys in a kung fu movie."

Yiannis raised his chin to look at Chris directly. "And you sound like recalcitrant child."

Cadence stood and rounded his seat so he could lean against the back of it. "Chris." He said Chris's name like he had at Harley's house, that balance of commiseration and command. Chris whirled to face him, his hands curling into fists. Cadence raised one eyebrow but continued, his tone neutral. "Picking fights with the people who are supposed to keep us safe to get to her won't get her back any faster."

Cadence was talking to him in that tone you use for someone who might become violent at any moment. He was trying to keep Chris's attention on himself. *So that if I attack someone, it will be him, since he knows he can take me.* That thought made Chris take a beat, but Cadence continued. "If you want to pick a fight, we can step outside and go a few rounds. I know you're worried about Sara, but this is going to take as long as it takes, and you tearing yourself apart about it won't make it go any faster, either."

Dia moved to sit on the edge of her seat. "Who is this 'Sara'?"

"Chris's sister. The Dark Lady came and took her while we were at school." Harley said it quietly, but he couldn't help himself from glaring at her.

Yiannis pushed away from the wall and came to stand in front of him, and Chris made himself look up to meet those deep-sea eyes. He wasn't sure what he was expecting to find, but what he saw was compassion. Yiannis placed one graceful hand on Chris's shoulder and held his gaze as he spoke. "I am sorry that you must travel with this weight on your heart."

Chris blinked away sudden tears and bowed his head. At length, he said, "I'm really worried about her."

"Not only understandable, but commendable." Dia's words were sincere, no sign of her earlier, jovial tone.

Yiannis continued. "We will travel as quickly as we may for safety's sake, and we shall reunite you with your sister. I have faith. I ask that you try to be patient with our people, and grant forbearance to our queen. She balances two great needs in the palms of her hands and must always weigh one against the other. That she has informed the court they will get this night only, I have no doubt is due in large part because she also wishes us to be away on our journey as soon as possible."

"So, if she hadn't rushed it, there would be more than just this dinner or whatever?" Jenta sounded almost horrified.

The laughter was back in Dia's voice when she answered. "You truly do not know much about the fae, do you? All things are a reason to celebrate here. Had you come for a less, shall we say, time-sensitive journey, there may have perhaps been a week of feasting. Those from small and great distances around the palace would come, and a grand market might be opened in the square outside the walls to allow for trade during the feasting, and for gifts to be brought to Queen Estian herself as well as various of her dignitaries. Do you not have these things? Surely, you must have celebrations, rites of passage, and such?"

"We do." Harley and Jenta both said.

As they started to tell Dia about things like birthdays and bar mitzvahs, and big celebrity events thrown every year, Yiannis led Chris to one side of the room. Chris made himself look again into those strange, sad eyes as the tall warrior spoke. "Have patience for this one eve, young Christian. Have faith. Danann is with your sister, and she is not forgotten." Chris nodded but couldn't speak. He tried to swallow the lump in his throat. Yiannis' voice was quiet and kind, and even in the midst of his frustration, Chris had to admit it was reassuring to know that someone like Yiannis would be traveling with them.

He went and sat in one of the chairs. He could admit to himself, even if he wouldn't say it out loud, the chair *was* comfortable. The fabric was silken soft under his fingers, and the padding was like sitting on a cloud. Hell, in a world made of magic, the chair might actually be padded with clouds.

Harlequin

Dia and Yiannis led them through the halls of the palace to a set of towering double doors that appeared hewn from one enormous tree, the wood polished so it shown in the light. The doors were already opened wide to admit them into the antechamber of a grand throne room. They were suddenly surrounded by floors and pillars of white marble with veins of gold and lapis blue. Deep blue, green, and gold patterned carpets ran just in front of their feet, down the room to the wide dais.

Among the pillars were a host of graceful figures in all the colors of the rainbow. They were radiant and striking, their clothing matching or complimenting hair and skin as varied as the figures themselves. All stood tall and thin, their faces elegant and androgynously beautiful with high cheekbones and eyes that glowed in the relative dim of the evening.

One sidhe wore a vibrant, purple dress that matched her eyes—which were the color of lilacs in bloom—and brought out the golden tones in her skin. Another leaned against one of the marble pillars, hair the color of marigolds over skin like burnt umber—a brown so rich and saturated he nearly glowed. His eyes, vibrant green like cat's, surveyed them while they made their way down the carpet to stand at the foot of the dais. Some wore their hair in relatively modern styles or carefully coiffed up-dos but most, both masculine and feminine, had hair down to waists or sometimes even to their knees, flowing in rippling tresses or plaited in ornate styles that hung around their shoulders and down their backs.

Atop the dais Estian stood in front of her throne with Cristobal at her shoulder.

The queen spread her arms wide, her gaze taking in the entire room before settling on the four, a smile spreading across her face. Her voice rang with authority and pride as she spoke. "On behalf of the Seelie Kingdom we welcome you, Cadence, Harlequin, Christian, and Jenta, of the Mortal Clans. On this, the eve of a grave undertaking to which you have offered aid, we honor you. Let us dine together in companionship that we might send you in joy."

Tables were brought out and laid with a feast. Trays and plates were carried by small winged fae or levitated and set out by curtsying creatures a little shorter than Jenta with soft looking brown fur and kind, wrinkled faces. Their noses were wide and flat, and their eyes were deep-set and dark. Their smiles were warm and broad, making the wrinkles in their faces deepen dramatically, but they moved with the same lithe grace as the much taller sidhe.

The four found themselves ushered forward by a small group of sidhe who drew them up the dais steps to the table where Estian sat and gestured for them to join her. Cristobal stood behind them, to one side of the throne, his eyes hard and cold as he glared out at the room and largely ignored them. As she passed him, Harley saw that what she originally thought was short, slicked back hair was actually pulled into one long cable of braid that hung down his back, the end of it reaching all the way to his calves. How long must it take to grow hair that long? *With my luck, I'd just end up sitting on it all the time.*

A small group of musicians was ushered in and to one side of the room, their instruments strange looking and only vaguely similar to any Harley had seen before. Two of them appeared to be stringed, one player pluck-ing hers like a guitar with long, graceful fingers while the other player, a willowy sidhe with wide, merry eyes, gave Harley a wink as they tucked their instrument up under their chin and drew across it with a bow, like a violin. Another held a hand drum with shallow sides and a big round surface that he tapped quickly with a strange, hooked stick. The last player got the others started with what Harley at first thought was a baton, only to realize it was some kind of flute, long and thin, but with a sound like a bird call.

As the musicians started to play, many of those present moved out onto the floor, gliding in graceful lines and circles with increasingly complex patterns.

The queen gestured to the table before them, now laden with food and pitchers, some steaming, and some covered in condensation. "Please, eat.

You are my hearth guests this night." She smiled warmly at them, grasping the hands of Jenta and Harley who sat closest to her. "I'm so grateful for you all. Tomorrow, before your leave-taking, we will speak more, and I will do my best to answer the question you posed, today. For tonight, I ask that you simply allow my people to rejoice, to raise your names to Danann, and to set a hopeful tone for your travels ahead."

She let go their hands and gave her attention over to the musicians and dancers. Behind her head, Harley shared a look with Jenta before turning to her own plate. She did her best to ignore Cristobal who hovered behind them, but his presence was like a wet blanket, threatening to drip all over their dinner.

Chapter Sixteen

Christian

C hris woke in a panic, the sound of his sister's cries ringing in his ears. He sat up and scanned his surroundings, trying to remember where he was. The room was almost perfectly square, with a door to the far wall on his right, and tall arched windows on the opposite wall, their drapes still partially closed so that the room was wrapped in suffuse predawn light. There was one other bed in the room, it's headboard placed against the opposite wall from his own so that as he sat up, he could see a form covered with blankets. *It's Cay.* Chris heaved a sigh of relief.

The windows behind the drapes were open, filling the room with a soft breeze and the smell of a garden in bloom. He could even hear the chirping of birds outside. Chris allowed himself a moment to simply appreciate this feeling and did his best not to let it be soured by self-disgust. It was the first time in a long time he hadn't woken to the sound of his mother yelling at him, and the nightmare was already dimming in the face of the fresh air, a soft mattress and warm blankets. They would be leaving soon enough, and rushing might just get him killed instead of getting his sister out of this alive and safe.

Cadence sat up slowly, looking around him. He spotted Chris and gave him a nod, then continued his assessment of the room. Chris wondered if Cadence was also trying to remember where they were.

Chris pulled the blanket off his legs and scooted to the side of the bed. His bag was sitting on the chair nearby, untouched from how he'd left it the night before. He reached for it and pulled out a change of clothes— a fresh pair of jeans, a green on gray baseball tee, and the underclothes to go with— then dressed quickly in the chill morning air. Too late, he realized he probably just could have gone and closed the windows. He folded up yesterday's clothes and stowed them, then zipped the bag closed and slung it over one shoulder. By the time he was done, Cadence was ready and standing by the door.

They entered the sitting room where the windows were still shut, but the drapes were open to let in the morning light. The door to the girls' room was closed, and Chris and Cadence both heard a knock at the main door. Cadence raised his brows, and Chris shrugged.

"Come in." Cadence said, his voice firm.

The door opened, apparently on its own. A long side table floated in and settled against the wall near a round table with four chairs, already set for breakfast. Had that table been there the night before? Chris couldn't remember, now. The side table was followed by a parade of plates and dishes and baskets covered with clean white cloths, all of which glided through the air as if on invisible ice. Last were a couple of wide-mouthed pitchers, beaded with condensation, and a small figure that padded in on soft bare feet, head bowed and hair hanging down around their shoulders in long shaggy waves. The smells of food filled the room, and Chris's stomach rumbled.

Chris and Cadence approached the round table which sat in a small alcove, lined with more windows.

"I'm pretty sure this wasn't here, yesterday." Cadence said, and Chris grunted.

"I was just thinking that."

They both picked up plates and went to the long side table. The little fae placed the last dish and stepped quickly to one side, watching Chris and Cadence nervously as they approached. Chris wondered if they'd ever seen humans before. Large liquid-brown eyes peered up at him from a soft round face with full lips and a long beak-like nose that hooked sharply at the tip. The eyes were set deep under a wide, heavy brow ridge. Their skin was nut brown, a slightly lighter shade than the long hair, and a small yet thick matronly body hid under a dress that hung like a sack from broad shoulders. The dress was covered in little pockets, a couple of which bulged, and Chris saw scraps of fabric hanging out of a couple, covered in neat stitching.

Chris gaped at how much food was set out for just the four of them. There was something like bacon and what might be eggs with bits of something in it that smelled sweet and spicy at the same time. A bowl of particularly lumpy oatmeal had flecks in it that might have been nuts or fruit. There was even a small pot beside the oatmeal that was probably honey, and Chris wondered again what kinds of bees they might have here?

He took some of the meat and the eggs and a massive biscuit that, he decided, smelled like Christmas. There was a whole stack of those, and the aroma was strong enough to make his mouth water. The roll was softer than it looked and left crumbly little flakes on the tips of his fingers that melted on his tongue like butter. There was also a basket of regular looking bread rolls, so he grabbed one of those, too.

Satisfied with his selection, he carried his plate past the little fae, gave a small nod and said a quiet, "This all looks amazing. Thank you".

The creature started to smile, but winced then met his eyes for just a moment. The look spoke volumes. It was a look his grandmother gave him once, after he and his grandpa went out hunting and came back tracking mud on her nice clean floors. "Aye." Was all they said and gave one stiff nod.

"Oh-kay." Chris mumbled to himself as he went back to the round table tucked into the alcove. Jenta and Harley came out of their room and grabbed their plates, then headed over where the food was laid out, talking quietly.

He noticed Jenta was dressed differently than he was used to seeing her, and it took him a moment to figure out how. Instead of her usual all black, she was in a pair of jeans that had once been black but were now a dingy dark gray. They were also so lose they were almost baggy. Her top was a long-sleeved black poet's shirt with ruffles at the collar and wrists. Her hair was braided back from her face, and she wasn't wearing any makeup. Only the toes of her buckled boots peeking out from under her jeans were familiar.

Noticing her made him notice Harley, mostly because he didn't think he'd ever seen her wearing pants. Harley wore a pair of cargo pants, of all things, in a dark olive green, with a pair of stout hiking boots, and a tucked in long sleeved t-shirt that fit her snuggly enough that he found Cadence very studiously focused on his food, except when he was stealing tiny peeks at her while she was distracted with picking out her breakfast.

"I don't think the phrase 'thank you' means the same to them as it does to us." Harley's words brought Chris back, and he blushed as he realized he'd been staring.

"What do you mean?" Cadence paused in the middle of a bite of his food. He had a small bowl of oatmeal with a pool of honey gathering in the hole his spoon left and a plate in front of him similar to Chris' own—Christmas biscuit and all.

Harley came back from the side table, her plate largely taken up with strange looking fruit and another small bowl of oatmeal. "I remember reading that the fae take their oaths very seriously, so saying 'thank you' is like implying that you expected them not to keep their promise, and you're pleasantly surprised they did." She glanced back at the creature beside the table, one of the small scraps of fabric in their hand as a needle and thread moved in and out by themselves.

"Like that used car dealer in town. 'Come on down to Big Man Dan's. If I don't have the lowest prices in town, I'll eat my hat!' There's no way that guy has ever eaten his hat." Cadence said with mock seriousness.

"I think it's more like, 'of course I took out the trash. You asked me to, and I said I'd do it.'" She focused back on her food. Picking up her fork, she took a bite of the fruit.

"Like when my mother acts surprised that I put away my laundry, after I explicitly said already that I was going to do it?" Chris tried to look toward the creature without turning his head.

The fae stood stoically, two glass cloches floating above and behind them like pet bubbles. He was fairly sure they understood every word being said, but said nothing.

Jenta came and sat between Chris and Harley and set down a bowl half full of oatmeal with a small drizzle of honey zigzagged over the top and a plate that held the smallest of the Christmas biscuits and a few bright yellow berries. She picked up one of the berries and contemplated it, then placed the fruit in her mouth and chewed it, closing her eyes as her jaw slowed. "This tastes like the freshest, ripest strawberry I've ever eaten. This is delicious."

The fae grunted, but then smiled. Chris, Cadence, and Harley admired the transaction.

"Fascinating." Harley said absently as she took a bite of her own fruit.

Cadence cleared his throat. "So. We're here. We've agreed to go on this quest to stop whatever is going on." He set down his own spoon and steepled his fingers in front of him, his brow furrowed. "I was thinking about it last night, and I don't think we should go into this with the expectation of a fight. At least, not right away."

"What are you talking about? I'm not going to walk in there and just lay myself down on one of the slabs if that's what you mean." Chris said.

"No, it's not, but she has to know we're coming. Hell, by taking your mom and sister, she practically laid down a gauntlet for us."

"I think she made sure we saw each other in the last dream, and I think she made sure we all saw her, too." Harley used her spoon to punctuate her statement.

"Coach always says our team's first goal is to psych out the competition. I think that's what she's trying to do: demoralize us, scare us into bad plays. What if she's trying to goad us into going straight for her instead of trying to fix what she broke?" Cadence took a bite of food, and Jenta picked up the biscuit in her hands, leaning back in her chair as she tore off little pieces and popped them in her mouth.

Chris chewed on a piece of meat, thinking. He made a satisfied sound that felt awkward, tried to ignore the blush coming up into his cheeks and deliberately didn't look back at the fae. He heard a satisfied grunt from behind him, and new steam started rising up off his eggs.

After a moment, Harley spoke. "The queen mentioned something called the Void. She said it acts basically like a wall, right?"

"Right. Clear as glass, strong as obsidian, and it runs between the two realms." Cadence said, nodding.

"Okay, so going on the theory we had in the first place, here's what I'm thinking. The queen says humans already touch the Void when we dream. I was thinking about something Jenta and I talked about, which is that the more tired you are, maybe the deeper into the void you sink, or the closer you get to the fae side. So, what if the same thing goes for people who are especially creative or more connected to their creative side? That would mean that if you're someone who is, say, doing a lot of creative stuff, but also making yourself tired with all the work, the combination would maybe put you the absolute closest to the fae side of the wall when you're asleep."

Jenta popped another piece of biscuit in her mouth, chewed, swallowed, and said, "So, if she started out being able to reach people only when they were dreaming, she had to wait for someone to go to sleep, and also to get close to where she could grab them?"

Harley pointed at Jenta with her spoon. "Right. I think the door opening, or whatever it was that happened a couple days ago, was her finally

146

breaking the hole open on both sides. That would also explain how she was able to come to our side physically."

Cadence had taken a huge bite of oatmeal. He set his spoon in his bowl and swallowed the bite, then sat back. "It sounds like what we need to do first is learn what we can about the Void and how it works. When a dam breaks, you don't attack the water, you try and shore up the stone."

A clearing throat spun them in their chairs to look at the fae. The creature initially shrank back a bit but then shook their head, focused on Jenta, and spoke, their accent thick with some ancient brogue. "You four speak of things I've not known, but you speak of them loudly. We brownies, we know. Not all our folk are as ancient as the sidhe, though we're born of this earth just as surely. Young blood burns hotter and yearns for a freedom they think they do nae have, confusing safety for prison, no matter how comfortable. A gilded cage is still a cage."

Jenta stared at the brownie, confusion clear on her face. "I'm not sure I understand what you mean. Are we in danger or something? Do you think there's going to be a war?"

The brownie waved thick fingered hands and gave a huff. "Nay, nay. None so far as that. Only that in battle, there are always three sides."

"Yours, mine, and ours?" Jenta said doubtfully. Again, the brownie shook their head.

"Theirs, ours, and mine." Cadence said it into the silence, and the brownie pointed at him, then tapped the side of their nose.

"Are you saying there are people here who may not agree with or support our quest?" Harley said.

"Aye."

"...But they won't outright defy the queen unless she proves to be on the losing side. That is, if we fail." Harley finished the thought, sounding a little dejected.

"Hey, we have people like that in our world, too. People who aren't on anyone's side but their own." Cadence said.

The brownie nodded, relaxing as a small smile spread across their face. "Aye. Tis true of many. Fear is a powerful ruler. I see in your eyes; you each have known its touch. We brownies, we know. My advice— 'ere you face the dark, learn to rule your fear, lest it be done for ye." The brownie blinked. Without another word, they left the room, the glass cloches floating after them.

"Learn to rule our fear before someone rules it for us. Well, that was ominous." Cadence tried to laugh a little, but it sounded forced.

"Not wrong, though, I think. Especially knowing even a portion of what—who—we're up against." Harley frowned at her empty plate, looking vaguely ill.

Chris rose and gathered their attention. "I think it's time we get going."

No one argued.

Chapter Seventeen

Harlequin

The tiny, winged fae waiting for them in the hall introduced herself as Poppy Blossom. She fluttered at eye level on bright butterfly wings, a living doll the size of Harley's hand with a laugh that sounded like tinkling chimes. Poppy Blossom guided them out of the tower and down into the body of the palace to a room with half a dozen sidhe as well as the queen's general, Cristobal.

A giant table took up the center of the floor, with a map spread out and held down with small weights. The four teens came in quietly and found spaces to stand at the table, listening as Cristobal described what they were seeing.

"It will take you at least three days to reach Comhaontu, which sits on the verge of a great wood, called the Wildes." He pointed at a small dot tucked in against a semicircle of jagged tree marks that bordered the lands denoted as belonging to the Seelie. The Wildes ran in a long band, hugging the edge of the Seelie kingdom far to the east.

"Her Majesty will be sending you with a boon gift in the hopes you may be able to barter for a guide at Comhaontu, through to the Expanse. If Danann is with you, you may be able to travel through largely unmolested." Cristobal moved down the table, pointing at a thin, barely visible line on the map. Whoever had drawn it appeared to change their mind multiple times about how the road through the Wildes actually ran.

Tucked down in the southeastern corner of the map was a small section that was blacked out. Tiny, cramped writing along the map's margin appeared hastily written, but Harley couldn't tell what it said.

Chris, standing closest to that section of the map, pointed at the writing and the blacked-out area. "Let me guess, this is where we have to go?"

Cristobal blanched and then flushed, his pale cheeks turning an angry pink. "No. We have no maps of *her* lands. You will follow this trail, here." He gestured to a portion of the map with repeatedly erased and redrawn lines that continued vaguely east. "Once you clear the Wildes, you will continue east for two days and two nights as you cross the Expanse. On the morning of the third day, you should reach Dark's doorstep and cross into her lands. It is my understanding that the Bastion of Night is not far from there."

"What's with all the re-drawn lines?" Cadence asked.

Cristobal gave an exasperated sigh and his answer dripped with condescension. "That is the Expanse. As clan territories change, so must the roads between, on which one may pass."

"Well, gosh, Mr. General sir, but if that big black spooky spot isn't where we're going, why does it look like that?" Jenta said in her most Jenta-like tone. Harley had to stop herself from looking over at the other girl. *Don't needle him, Jenta. We need to* win *points with these guys, not* lose *them...*

Cristobal glowered at Jenta as if he might not answer her, one eyebrow raised as he glared down his nose at her. Finally, he gave a huff and pointed at the dark splotch at the bottom of the map, "That, young mortal, is the

Guardian's Sepulcher. You will, in fact, do everything you can not to go there. Not even the Darkness herself is safe in those lands. You will find nothing there but your own swift death."

Chris's eyebrows went up and he moved his hand away as if even the map itself might be dangerous in that spot. "Well, that's certainly succinct. Duly noted, we'll stay away from the big black splotch with the ominous name."

Cadence tapped his finger on one of the territories that made up the Expanse. "You said these are the territories of other fae. Do you think they would be able or willing to help us? Should we approach them?"

Cristobal and two of the warriors made snorting noises. Harley took a moment to consider them. The two were quite similar, and, she saw, had a resemblance to Cristobal, as well.

Like Cristobal, these two had thick, dark eyebrows that shaded their smokey gray eyes, but where Cristobal came off as angry, both of them looked broody. Their features could have been pulled from any high fashion magazine. Like many of the sidhe Harley saw the night before, their features were more androgynous, with long straight noses, those same high cheekbones, and clean jaws. Could none of the sidhe grow a beard?

Even their clothing complimented each other. Both wore dark colored pants that fit close but not snuggly, and plain white tunics with laces at the chest and pinned cuffs under coats covered by tiny stone scales. On the taller, broad-shouldered warrior, those scales were dark, nearly black and glinted with purple highlights. Obsidian, maybe? The shorter, thinner warrior's coat scales were a deep saturated green with strange yellow flecks that practically crackled.

151

"You will be traveling with the most powerful sidhe in this realm. What could one of the lesser fae possibly offer you in help that you will not already have at your disposal?" Cristobal gestured at the warriors standing in the room, and Harley took the invitation to look at the others standing around the table.

Yiannis leaned against one whitewashed stone wall, his posture similar to how he'd placed himself near the door in their sitting room the night before. Harley was beginning to wonder if it was his version of a soldier's "at ease" pose—looking relaxed and inattentive while actually seeing much more than it seemed.

He wore something similar to what Dia had worn the day before, but his pants were a green so saturated it was nearly black, while his own long tunic hung nearly to his knees in draping folds of vibrant blue and gold embroidery. He wore a simple sword belt that doubled as a way to cinch the fabric of his shirt around his trim waist, and again that small dagger hung just in front of a sheathed rapier. On his wrists were a pair of matching bracers, laced with leather cords and impressed with repeating waves like those she'd seen in old Chinese paintings. When he noticed her looking at him, he gave a small nod, but otherwise didn't move.

Dia stood beside the table toward the northern edge of the map. Unlike the night before, she was stiff and upright in a set of finely articulated studded leather armor, stained a color only a little darker red than her hair which hung at the base of her neck in a thick club, leaving her face bare, and her eyes shining like tamped embers.

Two of the warriors standing at the table wore matching surcoats that hung down to their knees over black pants and boots. The surcoats were so

152

thickly covered in thread of gold embroidery that at first, she didn't realize the fabric underneath was white.

Besides their clothing, their features were also nearly identical, but one of them was just a little taller, with a slightly more masculine face—The jaw just a little wider, the cheekbones not as high and soft—and sad eyes the color of dark honey. That one's surcoat was repeating patterns of alternating wolves and lions, surrounded by flowery embellishments. The other's jaw was narrower, more pointed, with high dramatic cheekbones and eyes that blazed golden out of their sun-kissed tan face. Their surcoat was the lion's head over and over, separated by sets of crossed blades. Harley guessed they were siblings at least, but very possibly twins.

The golden eyed warrior met her gaze, one eyebrow raising and a small sneer pulling at the corner of her thin lips as Cristobal started speaking again.

"If not for her Majesty, I would have already led a squadron to remove that monster from her putrid nest and dragged her back here. I know that her Majesty does what she believes is best for our people, but do not misjudge me. I send my people with you because I believe in our queen. You will travel with my warriors, and you will stay out of their way. You will do as you're told, and when the time comes, you will do what you must, I'm sure. They will then return you back, safe as babes in swaddling, and you'll be deposited back to your own realm. Am I understood?"

Without waiting for a response, Cristobal grabbed up his shoulder cape from a peg on the wall behind him and practically stormed out of the room. The warriors in stone scale coats followed him, their footfalls loud and echoing in the hall. Harley watched them leave, wondering if Cristobal was one of those the brownie had been trying to warn them about.

Dia cleared her throat. "Aoife, Leif, this is Cadence, Harlequin, Christian, and Jenta." She gestured toward the two sidhe in their golden surcoats. "Aoife and Leif will be part of your escort, as I'm sure you guessed."

Aoife studied them, and Harley knew immediately that Jenta and Aoife would either get along *really* well or *really* badly. Harley initially thought the look Aoife gave her was targeted, but that vague impression of sneering derision didn't leave as she scanned each of the others.

Leif, on the other hand... everything about him screamed "I'm just following orders". Harley didn't think she'd ever met anyone in her life whose personality seemed entirely comprised of obeisance and resignation like his. No wonder, she thought, if Aoife's personality was as big as it already seemed. Some emotion flitted through his eyes. If she hadn't known better, she would have thought it was fear.

"As for Cristobal, I will not tell you to disregard him, but I would ask you to grant him forbearance. He is not only the queen's general but also her cousin. The queen's previous general, General Faylin, was also her younger brother. He was killed by the one we hunt." Dia's tone was more formal than the previous afternoon, so it took Harley a moment to realize what she'd just said.

Cadence leaned his hands against the table, but his focus was on Dia. "How? The queen told us yesterday that you are all immortal. I was under the impression that means you, you know, can't die?"

Dia inclined her head, sadly. "It should not have been possible. At most, he should only have been severed, but his body was destroyed, so if his spirit remains, there is nothing for it to heal and return to."

Harley swallowed hard. "His body was... *destroyed*?"

Dia gave her another sad nod. "Apparently, it was something to do with a missive *she* sent. Suffice it to say, it left many shaken."

"What, like poisoned paper?" Jenta said, and Cadence stepped back from the table, surreptitiously rubbing his hands together. He gave an awkward little laugh, then shoved his hands in his pockets.

"Spelled, at least." Dia said and continued. "The queen wishes us not to speak of it, and if I am honest, I am loath to consider the ramifications too deeply. Suffice to say, General Cristobal is anxious for an opportunity at retribution and has blinded himself to anything else, but the queen has denied his request to be a member of your escort. It rankles him."

Aoife scoffed. "You give him too much credit, Dia. Cristobal thinks himself the only one strong enough to defeat her, and that all else is pomp and waste. Let us not fool ourselves, first among his most notable traits is pride. You four, I believe you are mad, and if I were the queen, I would bundle you up and send you back to your mothers' skirts."

"I guess it's a good thing you're not the queen, then, huh?" Chris said, grumpily.

Aoife continued as if he hadn't spoken. "You are not only mortal, but you are also untried." She said 'mortal' like it was an illness, and 'untried' was an unforgivable crime, but then barked a laugh and smacked the back of one hand against Leif's chest. Out of her eyesight, Harley saw him glance down at his chest and the hand that had smacked it, moving only his eyes, and she thought his lips pursed minutely, but he remained silent. "Well. Never mind that, I suppose. I have already said my piece to the general, and you all seem to have made your decisions. You are aware, I suppose, that it is not merely the Darkness you face?"

"Aoife..." Dia said the name like a warning, but Harley met Aoife's eyes evenly as Aoife sauntered around the table to stand in front of her. She towered over Harley and scowled down at her, arms crossed.

Harley sighed and shook her head. She couldn't understand what was happening, but she answered the question honestly. "We know she's got minions. We've seen the creatures that are helping her, and that we'll probably have to fight them, too. We didn't come here with the expectation of an easy trip."

"We also know she's the queen of her own court, so most likely there will be other fae helping her—even if we haven't seen them specifically." Jenta leaned straight-armed against the table next to Harley, looking around her at the warrior.

Cadence stepped up on Harley's left, and even though he was nearly of a height with her, her attitude of smug pride made her seem bigger, somehow. Cadence didn't hesitate as he stepped up, saying, "Regardless of what you may think of us, we aren't walking into this blind. We know this isn't going to be a walk in the park. We may be young and 'untried' as you put it—" Aoife scoffed but Cadence continued, "—but we aren't stupid."

Harley spoke, trying her hardest to sound confident and sure. She had a moment to be grateful for all those debate club meetings. "I get the general is angry, but he isn't the one who asked us here. The queen chose us whether you like it or not, and you're right—we *did* make our choice. I'd say that makes us one step ahead of you guys, actually."

Aoife blinked, appearing honestly confused. "Ahead? How so?"

"You didn't choose to go on this journey. You were assigned. We *offered*. If anything, we may know even better than you what we're up against because we've *seen* it. Hell, all four of us have been *in* those dungeons, prisoners of the one we are going after, and that gives us insight that you guys don't have access to." Harley took a step forward, face tilted up at an uncomfortable angle so she could meet those golden eyes. "We are walking into sure danger. We know we may not come back from this. But regardless, we'll do everything we can to succeed."

Jenta spoke from behind Harley, and even without looking, Harley could see the sardonic smile that was probably playing across her friends lips, and a mischievous twinkle in her hazel eyes. "You know, Aoife, if you're scared or whatever, we can petition the queen for you. Or you can just drop us off at the edge of the Wildes, and we'll make our own way from there. We get it. This is scary, and maybe we aren't the only *untried* members of this party?" Aoife's expression changed as rage infused her features, a hot flush suffusing her cheeks. Her eyes narrowed as she glared at Jenta over Harley's shoulder. Harley tensed and fought not to step back as she waited for Aoife to yell or launch herself forward.

The tall warrior stood fuming for a moment, then the rage fled as quickly as it came, and she barked a laugh. "I have never refused an assignation, and I will not start now. We'll travel with you because our queen said so, *and* because I doubt you would make it a day on your own past the bounds of our lands, let alone make it all the way across them. Dia may be determined to like you, but I have only one goal: to keep you all alive long enough to get to where you're going. But know this—I swear by Danann and the Holy Grove that if you do anything to endanger us unnecessarily, I will find out how easily that mortal blood of yours spills." She leaned in toward them for a moment then spun on her heel and left the same way the general had gone. Leif sighed, shrugged, then followed her.

"Well." Dia said into the silence. "That went better than I expected."

"*Better*?" Cadence said incredulously.

Dia shrugged. "Aoife is very... mercurial, but she's good in a fight, and I've never once questioned her loyalty to the queen. I'm sure she'll come around once we get on the road, and where Aoife goes, Leif will follow."

"What about you both? Do you also think we're a bunch of stupid kids throwing ourselves at something better handled by the adults?" Jenta asked, looking back and forth at Dia and Yiannis.

Yiannis raised his head and met her eyes. "No. Danann is wise, and I see their hand on you all. I believe my fellows are blinded by their fear, but I have faith." At the last word, he smiled, his features softening. "It has been an exceptionally long time since mortals traveled our lands. I think it would be good for many of our number to be reminded that a short life does not immediately make for a weaker constitution."

"I agree." Dia said, her expression sincere. "I think Cristobal and Aoife are underestimating you, and I look forward to seeing you prove them wrong." She smiled warmly, then started moving the weights off the map. "We should go. We must still visit the armory, and the queen told Cristobal that you were to see her before we leave." Once the map was cleared, she rolled it tightly and tucked it into a case that she slung over one shoulder. With a final gesture at all of them, she led the way out of the room.

Chapter Eighteen

Harlequin

The armory turned out to be one long room with a door at either end. Along one wall were weapons racks and tables where swords, axes, and bows were hung up in rows. Two barrels sitting in a corner held a selection of staves and spears, and a number of sword belts and baldrics were hung up from pegs. The opposite wall was taken up by armor stands, and one shelf that ran the length of the room, full of helmets.

Harley marveled at the belts, not really knowing how to pick one. They were a multitude of colors and covered in tool work patterns of animals and vines and even just knots or lines. One belt caught her eye, hanging on a peg by itself on the wall. She pointed at it, just out of reach, and called for Dia.

"What's this one? Why's it separated?"

Dia stepped up next to her and pulled the belt off its peg, her hands moving deftly as she showed Harley the buckle which was shaped like the head of a dragon in profile, eating the tail end of the belt. Dia moved one hand to the back of the buckle, and it made a soft click. She held the now open belt out to Harley, showing her the small hook plate at the back where the belt end could be attached or released when pressed.

"It is called Fire's Bite. It was made to honor one of our legendary mounts who was lost in one of the great battles."

"How do you lose a dragon?" Cadence asked from over Harley's shoulder.

"I only know that the story says he was there, and then his rider was falling from the sky." She gestured again with the belt, encouraging Harley to take it. "I believe it would suit you well."

Harley took it from her, pulling the leather around her waist and pushing the buckle closed with another click. While she adjusted it on her hips, Dia tilted her head and scanned the others, before returning her attention to Harley.

"Are mortals no longer given any sort of weapons training as part of your childhood lessons?"

Harley touched the belt, admiring it, then looked up at Dia. "Not really. We can sign up for stuff if we want to, but I never did." She tried the buckle, opening and closing it a couple times.

"Don't let Harley fool you, Dia. She may not necessarily know any fighting, but she makes up for it in what she knows about almost everything else." Cadence was holding an unstrung bow in his hand, nearly as long as she was tall.

Harley peered at the bow, then made herself meet Cadence's sincere gaze. "Cay, that's not the same thing. She's talking about us being able to defend ourselves, and it's a valid question because I can't." She rolled her shoulders a little, self-consciously.

Cadence didn't drop the subject. "Harl, don't discount knowledge as a viable weapon." He stepped forward and rested a hand on her shoulder as she met his eyes. "We need to use everything we have. Anyway, who knows?

Maybe being here will be like in the movies, and you'll learn Jiu Jitsu during a montage." He grinned and despite herself, Harley smiled back.

Dia considered the bow in Cadence's hand. "Do you know the use of that?"

It was Cadence's turn to shrug. He held up the bow for Dia's inspection. It was, like so many of the other weapons Harley saw, crafted with seeming attention to every little detail. It had a rounded grip in the middle and arced off to either side, the tips curving back on themselves, and showing little groves where, presumably, the string would sit, when the bow was strung.

Dia took it from Cadence and hefted it as he spoke. "I just started taking lessons last summer. I'm no expert, but I hit the target more often than not. I figured this would be a good opportunity for real world practice. If that's okay, at least?"

Dia grinned. "Only if I may critique you when you miss."

Cadence grimaced. "Do I have a choice?"

The grin became a full-throated laugh. "Absolutely not. Come, let us get you a case and some spare strings." Dia gave Harley a warm smile then drew Cadence away to a nearby table with a shallow drawer and a shelf full of leather bow cases.

Harley smiled to herself as they left, then made her own way over to a table full of sheathed daggers and belt knives.

Christian

Chris and Jenta stood just inside the door through which they'd entered, watching the exchange between Harley, Cadence, and Dia. Chris was again impressed by Cadence's confidence. Even knowing how he felt about

Harley, Cadence didn't hesitate to talk to her. Hell, not even just talk, but actively encourage and support her. The thought made him glance at Jenta who was standing next to another table full of daggers and large knives, seemingly frozen. She had a look of vague horror or maybe fear, and she was gripping her own hands so hard her knuckles were white. He cleared his throat softly, and she startled as if she'd either forgotten or maybe not realized he was there.

"Hey. Jenta, you okay?"

She swallowed hard and hesitated before answering. "Yeah. Um. I just don't think any of this stuff is for me."

Chris glanced back down at the table. It was maybe five or so feet long, but only about two feet deep and covered in sheathed blades of all sizes, from small daggers with blades no longer than his thumb to long knives that could have been machetes, but with cross guarded hilts. Chris had been looking at one of the latter but sheathed it and set it back down when he'd noticed Jenta's initial distress. Returning his attention to her, he saw tears welling up at the edges of her eyes, and panic knotted up in his guts. The defiance and bravado of not even an hour ago in the map room was just suddenly gone. This wasn't the tough skinned badass Jenta he was used to.

He kept his voice low, and he tried to make it sound encouraging. "Hey, listen. You can do this. I can teach you some stuff I learned from my grandpa if you want. Just don't get stuck on what you can't do, okay?"

"That's not..." She started and then stopped. One big tear started running down her cheek and she blushed "I'm not a predator, Chris. I'm prey."

"Bullshit." Chris startled himself with the anger in his tone. Was this how Jonathon convinced her to stay with him as long as she had? Convinced her she was prey? Well, she'd proved him wrong when she'd left him bleeding and stunned in the hall, so why was she second guessing herself now?

Chris was furious all over again for all the rumors he'd heard being spread about her when he got back. Furious at the school for not trying to put a stop to it, furious at Jonathon, for being such an absolute piece of shit, but mostly furious at himself for not talking to her or confronting Jonathon and his little bootlicker cronies. What would Cadence have done in his place? Cadence wouldn't have let it stand.

Chris placed a hand on Jenta's shoulder and guided her to the table, but he couldn't help the heat in his voice. "That's bullshit, Jenta, and you know it. Absolute bullshit. Did that asshole, Jonathon tell you that?"

Jenta's face went blank, and she tried to pull away. "You're hurting me."

Chris pulled his hand away as if she'd burned him. He took a deep breath and let it out, trying to think of how to say what he wanted to. This wasn't going the way he'd hoped it would. He tried again, struggling to bring that encouragement back into his tone, but he wasn't sure if it worked.

"Jenta, of all the words I would use to describe you, the word 'prey' is not one of them. Just because you don't know how to use a weapon doesn't make you prey."

She stared at him, her expression closing down. He rushed on. This definitely wasn't going how he'd envisioned.

"As far as I'm concerned, the moment you agreed to come here, you proved you aren't prey. Prey doesn't stand up and fight—prey runs. Caring and being afraid don't make you weak, any more than being a bully makes someone strong."

Her eyes bored into his skull and Chris couldn't look away. He didn't understand what that look meant, but when he reached out this time, she didn't flinch away. He wrapped his fingers around one of her wrists and drew up her hand, so it was palm up between them. She was pliant under his touch. He reached behind him, grabbing one of the sheathed blades off the table and setting it in her upturned hand.

It was a dagger in a leather sheath that made him think of her the moment he saw it. The leather of the sheath was midnight black with simple but elegant tool work. The hilt was wrapped in the same heavy black leather, banded and sculpted into the knotted body of a cat with a small stone in the pommel like a cat's eye, bright gold-green with one thin black line of imperfection down its center.

He let go of her hand, but she didn't drop the blade, instead taking it in both hands so she could draw it from its sheath. Chris tensed, but didn't move, otherwise. The dagger was double edged, slim, and maybe five inches from the low-profile cross guard to the tip. After a moment, she re-sheathed it, but continued to stare at it, sitting in her hands. Chris tried not to let her see how he relaxed as she housed the blade back in its snug leather case.

Chris tapped the sheath lightly with one finger. "This is a really good all-purpose blade to keep on your belt, for anything from cutting the odd vine to slicing steak. It's light enough that you won't really notice the weight, but still enough to get the job done. That said, if you want something heavier, I'd say pick a single-edged blade instead, since once you get past this size, the double-edged blades start to feel more like a short sword than a long knife. Does that make sense?" Jenta nodded, but still wouldn't look at him.

"Do you want something heavier?" He asked.

Jenta gave it real thought, hefting the blade in her hand. She ran her fingers back over the cat set into the hilt. "No. I like this one. Thank you."

He opened his mouth to say something, but then she slapped him. The crack of it rang through the room.

"Don't touch me again." Her voice was quiet, her tone flat. Taking the knife with her, she moved past him toward where he'd last seen Harley.

Chris stood very still. His face stung and his ear was ringing. His fingers were tingling from where he'd touched her. His whole body was thrumming like a plucked string. What the fuck just happened? How had that all gone so wrong?

"Are you okay?" Chris, startled, spun to see Cadence standing next to him. He was still holding that huge bow, strung now with something that shone more like wire than string.

Chris shrugged, not really sure how to answer. He peered at the table full of knives but didn't really see them as he tried to rewind the last twenty minutes to find where he'd fucked up. He picked up the blade he'd been looking at previously to give himself something to do with his hands as he answered.

"Yeah. Maybe. I don't know. I didn't expect..." Chris shrugged again, trying to work the tension out of his shoulders. "I guess it doesn't matter. Did you get what you need?"

Cadence considered him for a moment, then hefted the bow and twisted a little to show a long leather case hanging from his shoulder, then patted the leather belt that rode low on his waist, complete with a horn hilted hunting knife tucked into a hardened leather sheath. Bless him, Chris thought, for letting the subject change without comment. "For a given level, yeah. Too bad we can't challenge her to a spelling bee or a game of tag football."

Chris barked a laugh. "Dude, if you were able to do either, I'd be useless, regardless."

He turned his attention back to the blade he was holding. It was long and gently curved, single-edged with a sharp thick hook toward the tip opposite the edge. The blade was a bit longer than his forearm with a hilt wrapped in the same rich dark brown leather as the sheath, and a cross guard like the tips of antlers that hooked down away from the hilt. Both the sheath and the flat of the blade had knot patterns worked into the shapes of antlers while the pommel was a doe's head, ears folded down and small brown stones for eyes. The belt he'd already picked was covered in running deer, and the buckle was a pair of stylized interwoven antlers, ingeniously shaped so one of the antler points was the pin that held the belt closed. He put it on and practiced drawing the blade a couple times, shifting everything around until it felt comfortable.

Chris found Dia regarding him, mild surprise turning into a pleased grin. She nodded with approval.

"Fine choice. Harlequin said mortal youths are not trained to weapons as we are, but you seem to know your way around one well enough."

Chris examined the blade in his hand, then gave her his own proud smile. "Yeah. I guess you're right." He sheathed the blade easily and patted the belt.

Both of the guys hefted their respective weaponry, and Dia handed Cadence a quiver, bristling with arrows.

"To the queen?" She asked them both, with a raised eyebrow.

"To the queen." They said in unison and followed her out of the armory.

Chapter Nineteen

Estian

E stian sat conversing with Harlequin and Jenta as Christian and Cadence were ushered into the sitting room. With a small secret smile, she handed the belt back to Harlequin and inclined her head to the two young mortals. "Welcome and well met, Christian. Cadence. Were you also able to avail yourselves of our arsenal?"

With almost identical grins, Chris and Cadence gave stiff, awkward bows. Estian laughed and clapped her hands as they straightened.

Cadence held up a bow case, and a quiver of arrows before setting them against the wall near the door. "Your Majesty, we were quite successful. We apologize for our delay."

Estian smiled warmly as she waved away his apology. "Of course, you are immediately forgiven. Please come join us. I am sure Dia mentioned that I would speak with you before your departure."

She gestured for them to sit. "When we spoke yesterday, you asked me a question that, at the time, I did not answer. I would answer it now. Do you remember?"

Jenta met her gaze and answered. "We asked why you picked us."

Estian smiled and rested a hand on the girl's knee. "Yes. It was a pertinent question, and I am grateful you allowed me the time to consider how best to explain my answer to you. Will you hear it?"

"Depends. Can we still ask questions while you're telling us?" Cadence grinned.

Estian returned his smile and inclined her head. "Of course. This story, too, is a conversation between the one who tells and the ones who listen." She took a moment, unnecessarily smoothing her skirts again as she determined where to start.

"I made reference yesterday to wars that led to the splitting. Know that this is not because ours are particularly violent people, but immortality can be a dull thing—especially for the young and impulsive. I do not seek forgiveness for my forebears, nor do I agree with their waste of the fae or the land we steward for the sake of bloody entertainment. I will not even claim that the violent thirst was only drawn from those of the Unseelie, though certainly, the Dark Queen's allies, the gobkin, are inherently violent. Theirs is a race made for war, battle, strength."

Harlequin blanched. "We've seen some of those, already."

"I look forward to seeing one when I'm not chained to a table." Christian said darkly.

Estian sighed. "I am sorry I could not protect you from the hurt caused you at her, or their, hands. I know it is a small consolation to know that the majority of those you will meet will most likely not harm you. Sadder news, though, is that many of those same will be unlikely to help you, either. As I am sure you have found of your own people, fae are, by and large, a capricious lot, and we have been left to our own devices for perhaps a bit too long."

She sat back in her chair, resting her hands in her lap as she considered each of the four. "But to my point. The Dark Queen has ruled for as far back as any can remember. The Seelie throne is both a position and, in some ways, a trophy. I fought and won to hold the seat of queen. But the Dark Queen has simply always been. When I took my place here, I sent a delegation to her to request a meeting. In consideration of the lands over which we rule, she and I made a treaty of sorts." Estian held up one hand, marking off fingers. "We would not outright attack each other nor send our armies or allies against each other directly. We would respect the boundaries set by Danann which parceled our lands, and we sidhe would allow the lesser kingdoms to select their allegiances without interference and respect those decisions without retaliation. We would respect the delineations of stewardship laid out by Danann at the splitting."

"Wow... She just agreed to all that?" Cadence said.

"As I said, Cadence, she is not evil. In fact, I found at the time when I met her that she was quite logical, and fair thinking, if a bit, well, intimidating. Despite what it may seem, even in all she has done, the Dark Queen has not broken any of these precepts. She has trod the line of our truce as if it were a rope strung between poles."

"Are you saying you think we *shouldn't* fight her?" Jenta asked.

"I am saying that I believe there is something more happening than I am able to see. However, Danann is wise and, outside of time as they are, can see the weaving of the tapestry far more clearly than we who make up its threads. We were given, at the time of the splitting of the realms, warnings, and a prophecy of sorts."

Estian met each of their curious expressions, as she continued. "And so, the answer to your question. The warning—that the dark would not accept a place of balance forever and would eventually attempt to rise and overpower the light, to claim dominion over all the worlds within its reach. The prophecy—that when night threatened to swallow the world again, it would be Danann's youngest children who would have the power to overcome the dark."

"By what power, though? We don't have any magic." Jenta's tone was plaintive and Estian gave her a sympathetic look.

"By their willing choice to welcome the dawn."

"I don't know what that means." Jenta shook her head, and Estian surveyed the others, her heart sinking as they gazed back at her, confused.

Estian sighed. She couldn't keep the disappointment out of her tone as she spoke. "Oh. We had hoped you would. The only other piece of knowledge I have from that same history is this: the answer lies between the will of Danann and the choice of mortals."

They sat in silence, and Estian's heart ached for them. She wished the scholars had been able to find more than the little snips and tidbits she'd gleaned, something she could give as proof that they would succeed.

On the wall above her desk, a small bell rang, and she clicked her tongue. "Time escapes us, and your departure draws close. I must know, did you meet your escort? You were to be introduced to them in the map room."

The four shared a look, and a wave of foreboding washed through Estian.

"Well, you introduced us to Yiannis and Dia yesterday, and this morning, we met Aoife and Leif."

Jenta made a face. "We sure did."

Estian waited, but she didn't expound. "There should have been six, but you mention only four. Were Faustus and Ximeno not there?"

Harley and Chris both shook their heads, and Jenta appeared to be glaring down at her hands, but it was Cadence who answered.

"They left. General Cristobal showed us the map, and when he left, two of the escort did too." There was an edge of anger in his voice as he continued. "Dia told us he's angry because you refused his request to be part of our escort. Those two that left seemed pretty solidly on his side."

"I had worried you didn't mention them because Cristobal decided to deny them their positions. They are his sons and including them in your escort should have been seen as a great honor."

"No offense, Your Majesty, but it definitely didn't seem like Cristobal was feeling very honored, this morning." Christian said the words softly, and Estian gave him a sad smile.

"If Cristobal were not my general, I would let him go to slake the need for revenge that rules him, but I cannot. When I sent my brother... Faylin's instructions had been clear. He was to bring her here so that we could have a trial. A *fair* trial, overseen by all those who rule the various clans and kingdoms of our realm." Estian stopped and closed her mouth around a sob. *Oh Faylin. Who could have known just how terribly I would fail you?*

"Oh, Estian, I'm so very sorry." Harlequin extended a hand and rested it on hers.

Estian drew in a breath that caught in her throat. Tears slid down her cheeks as she gave a bitter laugh. "I had thought myself so very clever in the idea, as it nicely danced along the same line she has been using. Had I known..." Estian shook her head to clear it of the thought. "Do not misunderstand me. I did not only select Faustus and Ximeno for their lineage. Both of them are powerful in both their magic and their martial skills, but I worry that their temperaments may be wrong for this journey.

I still have a hope that Yiannis will be a tempering force, but I am sorry that you will have to reap the consequences of my decision. Perhaps it will be that once you are away from the palace, and Cristobal's influence, you shall see their more convivial selves exposed."

A bell outside the windows tolled loudly, and Estian looked toward them, then back to the four. "A few things I will say before you depart—I have ensured that you will be well-provisioned. Even now, my people prepare your mounts, fine steeds from my own stable to speed your travel. To that same end, I wish to give you this advice—our world is both like and unlike yours. Many things you see may seem mundane. However, looks can often be deceiving. Trust your instincts and learn what you can from your escort. I will pray for your swift, safe travels and for your great success. I do not know the exact path that Danann lays for you, but I have faith."

Cadence and Christian shared a look, and Estian somehow didn't think she would like what they were about to say.

Cadence cleared his throat and stared down at the carpet. "Your Majesty, I wouldn't ask this, except that, as you pointed out, we are going into a land that isn't ours." He raised his eyes to meet hers, and she saw the sadness, there. Cadence was also not happy to ask this question. "Is there any way to kill an immortal?"

"No." Estian's immediate answer brought Cadence's brows down, but she held up a hand. "There is no way to permanently kill a fae so that they cannot eventually be returned among the living. However," She hesitated. She would have saved her people from having this information shared if she could but looking into the eyes of the mortals before her, she realized it was far too late. "We can be severed from our bodies. The separation of spirit from body that means even after the body heals, without intervention, the spirit will remain free, untethered. You would perhaps call them ghosts."

"Is it something we can do, or does it take magic?" Cadence pressed.

Estian held his gaze, but inside, she felt her brother's ghost. *It should not have been possible, Faylin. I would not do this, had I choice.* "The truth is, you four are the best weapon against the fae. Through your veins runs mortal blood. With a single drop, an object can be blessed or cursed. A dagger blooded by a mortal may sever even one of the high courts, no matter our magic, and a blade once so touched will forever hold its magic."

Cadence was nodding, but the other three had bowed their heads, so that the room grew silent.

"I know that this is not an easy quest on which you embark." Estian said. "But I truly believe that Danann is with you and will guide your feet. Despite this task being the reason, I am glad Danann has brought you to me."

Estian rose, and the four stood with her. She smiled warmly and extended her hands to them. "Come. Your journey beckons, and thus, history."

Chapter Twenty

Harlequin

Outside the doors of the queen's sitting room, they were met by their warrior entourage. The queen led them all to the main hall of the palace and through a set of tall wooden doors similar to those into the throne room, but these opened out into a sprawling, manicured garden full of blooming bushes and grand shade trees. A wide stone path led through the center of the garden to a towering archway and a courtyard paved with pale stone slabs. Ringing the courtyard were low outbuildings, a stable and, by the sound of it, a blacksmith.

The outer curtain walls rose over everything like shining white arms. Past the outer gates, Harley could see more buildings lining the sides of the road that ran in three directions out from the palace gate, centered on a broad central square with a fountain at least twelve feet tall that spouted water from the mouths of three giant golden fish into a basin so wide and deep she probably could have taken a swim in it. How many fairytales and adventure stories had been inspired by this sight? Or had the stories inspired the fae to build this in homage?

In the center of the courtyard, two groups of liveried stable hands waited with their horses. Six of them stood to one side, each holding the reins of a single grand steed covered in tack and gear that matched their rider; from the one who's saddle blanket was covered in crashing waves that immediately made Harley think of Yiannis, to the two enormous warhorses, one with crackling lightning on its gear, the other covered in stylized scales or stones.

The other group was guiding four more mounts and two pack horses weighed down with supplies. These mounts were all different, and Harley had to wonder if they'd been picked specifically with each of them in mind. If so, dare she hope that meant they guessed she'd never learned to ride?

Yiannis and Dia moved forward to speak with the stable hands, then Yiannis returned alone, giving the queen a deep bow. "My Queen, we await your word."

Harley shared a look with Jenta, and they made their way forward to give their goodbyes to the queen.

"Your Majesty, your hospitality has been more than we possibly could have expected or asked for. I promise we'll do our best." Harley said the words around a lump in her throat.

Estian placed a hand on each of their shoulders and smiled down at them. "I have no doubt, Harlequin. Travel safely, and when you can, return to us."

Harley just nodded, swallowing, and bowing her head.

They made their way over to the stable hands holding the four borrowed mounts. Harley frowned at them skeptically, but Jenta laughed and patted her on the shoulder.

"Don't worry. Riding a horse is like riding a bike. Sort of. Okay, not really."

Harley shot her a look, and Jenta laughed, startling a small flock of birds that lit into the air, circled twice, then flew east.

Yiannis clapped his hands once, his voice ringing across the courtyard. "A blessing. Danann guides us. Warriors, see to your mounts." He took his own instruction and went to retrieve the reins of the leggy gelding with bright eyes and a coat the color of fall leaves wearing the saddle blanket covered in crashing waves. The horse nudged Yiannis's shoulder and nickered softly. Yiannis rubbed the gelding's nose and appeared to whisper something to him. Harley tried to feel glad that she'd guessed right about the horse being his, but all she could really feel was trepidation. *What was I thinking?*

Jenta turned to her, and Harley flushed a bright red. "What?" The word came out a bit grumpier than she'd intended it, but she felt jangly and nervous in a way she hadn't in a long time. She wasn't sure how to feel about looking at perhaps a week or more of riding a horse when she'd never so much as sat on one.

Jenta put her hands up, placating. "Nothing. I was just going to offer to help."

Harley shook her head. "What if we have Estian open up a gate, and I can just go get my car?" She knew even before she said it that it wasn't going to happen, but her thudding heart was screaming at her to find any other way to get where they were going. Sure, conceptually she knew plenty about horses. She'd read about them, knew about the assorted colors, and how a draft horse might differ from a thoroughbred, even understood the basics of how to identify a gelding from a mare. But being around, let alone *on*, one of the giant beasts was… daunting.

The sound of approaching boots revealed itself to be Yiannis, leading his gelding. When Harley looked at him, his reaction told her that the panic might have been more obvious than she intended.

"We were uncertain of your experience with riding, though we had faith. May I?" Jenta gave him a 'go ahead' gesture and walked over to Cadence and Chris.

Yiannis looped the reins of the young gelding through his belt and gestured to one of the stable hands who gave him the reins to a graceful-looking gray dappled mare with beautiful warm brown eyes. He led Harley and the mare to a mounting block set off to one side of the courtyard, his own horse walking behind them slowly, snuffling at the ground behind his rider.

Without speaking, he showed Harley where to put her foot, how to step up and into the stirrup, then swing her leg up and over and settle into the saddle. After a couple tries, her foot slid into place and suddenly she was astride. She gave out a cry of glee, only to find the other three already mounted.

"Let me guess, while I was busy studying dreams, all of you were getting riding lessons?"

"Equine therapy." Jenta shrugged and grinned at her. Hers was a skittish looking buckskin with a focused look to him.

"I worked in a stable to get Sara some riding lessons. She changed her mind, so I used them for myself." Chris leaned over, patting the neck of his mount, a mare so black she had blue highlights, except for one white sock that came up to just below the knee of her front left hoof. The mare took a couple shy steps, and he corrected her easily, hands set comfortably on the pommel of his saddle.

Cadence guided his horse over to where Harley still sat hers near the mounting block. His was slightly smaller than Chris's, another gelding like Yiannis's but with a coat so deep red he looked like he'd been dipped in blood. Cadence patted him in much the same way Chris had patted his, flat handed on the side of the neck.

"Remember that aunt I have who lives out in the country? My cousin decided she wanted a pony, and my aunt insisted that any of us who came out to visit had to learn how to ride. I feel bad for the poor pony, though. She spends most of her time either stuck in her stall or being ridden by screaming kids." He showed Harley how to hold her reins and how to use them and her knees to direct her horse. The dappled mare was as gentle as her eyes promised and responded easily.

Yiannis waited near the mounting block. Once Harley made one full circuit around the courtyard and stopped back at the mounting block, he nodded to himself and clapped again.

"Warriors, mount up."

They mounted effortlessly, accompanied only by the jingling of their horses' tack. Yiannis led them to the open main gates at the far side of the courtyard and halted the party, turning them to look back at the queen who waited with her coterie at the head of the path leading out from the garden.

Harley tried to imagine what it might look like from a distance. How bizarre and juxtaposed must they seem compared to the finery of their escort?

The queen stepped forward, and her voice filled the open air, sending more birds to wing their way up into the sky and away. "May your path be smooth, your way clear. May you go in love and return in victory. Go forth and may Danann travel with you."

Each of the warriors raised a hand to the queen in salute while Harley and Jenta waved. Then Yiannis rose one hand high in the air, spinning it in a circle. The warriors drew their mounts around, and Harley did her best to do likewise, as a passage opened down the middle of the group to allow Yiannis to take the lead out the gates. Harley gazed up at the arch high above her head as they passed through and out into the large square with its cascading fountain.

Behind them, the palace walls loomed, shining brightly in the morning sun, the gate open and welcoming, and the courtyard beyond bustling with renewed activity.

For a short while, they rode in silence, until they cleared the last of the buildings and onto open road, then Jenta spoke up. "So, is there a marching song we need to learn? Oh, or do you guys juggle and break out instruments to entertain yourselves? Or do we just ride for a while in awkward silence? Just so I know what to plan for."

Christian

They'd been riding for a couple hours when Dia let her horse slow so that she could ride among them. Chris rode next to Cadence with Harley and Jenta in front of them, and Dia opted to nestle her mount, a sleek black and white stallion with long fetlocks and bells braided into his mane, smack dab in the middle of the group.

"Yiannis asked me to come and let you know of the plans for the coming days. We are not entirely pleased, either of us, with the minimal discussion we were able to have while reviewing the map this morning."

Chris peered toward the front of their group where Yiannis rode. Behind them, Aoife, and Leif held their rear guard while Faustus and Ximeno had already taken off into the broad grasslands beyond the town that sprawled for a quarter mile or so outside the palace walls. "Is there only this one road?" he asked.

"Yes." Dia responded. "These first days will be fairly easy. The road we currently travel is called Traveler's Way, and crosses the entirety of the Seelie lands, west to east."

"So, in all the grass around here, there are no other villages or towns or anything, besides what's on this road?" Harley asked, carefully turning only her head. Chris tried not to laugh. Harley, who had always impressed him with her knowledge and capabilities, legitimately seemed more than a little afraid of the gentle mare on which she rode.

Dia shook her head a little. "I do not mean there are no other roads *at all*, only that this is the main road that travels easterly, straight from the palace, and we shall not need to divert along any others. You will see other tracks and paths to either side of Traveler's Way, as we go."

"Cristobal said it would take three days just to cross the Seelie lands. Was he exaggerating?" Cadence asked, his voice holding an edge of frustration when he said Cristobal's name.

Dia either didn't hear it or focused on responding to the question instead of the tone. "For our general's faults," Dia said pointedly, "he is very good at gauging the timing of a thing, and there is a limit to how fast we may pass along Traveler's Way, so most likely, three days to reach

Comhaontu is fairly accurate. On a journey we may be, but we are sidhe and as the stewards of this land, we must remain visible and available to our people. So Yiannis will set our pace to ensure we have proper lodging each night, both for ourselves, and so that the people may make note of our presence."

"What about the Wildes? How long does it take to cross those?" Cadence asked.

"It will largely depend on whether or not we can get a guide once we reach Comhaontu, and what kind of weather we have once we get there." Dia shrugged, a little uncomfortably. "The Wildes is named not only for the creatures that live within it but also because of the forest itself. It will find ways to delay you until it tires of you or until you convince it you are more risk than reward."

"What happens if it gets tired of us?" Jenta asked, nervously.

"Sometimes, it will simply release you. Sometimes, it decides that it is hungry."

"Hungry. Great." Jenta shared a look with Harley, and both of them laughed nervously.

"So, how do we keep the forest from finding us interesting? Roll in mud? Tie sticks to our arms and pretend to be trees?" Cadence asked, giving Chris a grin.

Chris did a 'dang it!' gesture with his arm, snapping his fingers. "Too bad I left my camos back in my house. Oh, or better yet, a ghillie suit!"

He laughed, but Dia continued in a serious tone. "I am not certain what a 'ghillie suit' is. Is that some kind of armor? Regardless, I do not believe those things would likely do you any good."

"Just us? Wouldn't it want you all, too?" Harley asked and started to turn, but her horse started to turn with her. She faced back forward and dragged at the reins as if she were fighting a bucking stallion instead of a placid mare.

They all marked Harley's struggle for a moment then Dia answered, and her voice sounded a bit strangled. Chris wondered if it was worry or that she was trying not to laugh. Even Cadence had a hand over his mouth and his head down. "It will be able to sense your humanity, the moment we draw close. It has been an awfully long time since mortals traveled the Wildes, which is why we hope to find a guide."

"Are the guides also sidhe?" Jenta asked.

Dia scoffed. "No, the guides are most definitely not sidhe. They are fae who have traveled through the forest and often also have kinship with the land itself. They come from those who dwell within the Wildes or from the clans that live close to the edge of the expanse."

"They sound like park rangers." Cadence said, and Dia gave him a quizzical glance. "They're part guide, part steward of the forest in which they work, so they not only walk the trails and help hikers they find, but they also help care for the local wildlife, protect against forest fires, that sort of thing. A lot of them take turns living in the forests they watch over, or at least really close by so they can be on site quickly." Chris said.

Dia tilted her head slightly in thought, then answered. "Yes. That sounds similar. Most of those I've known have been of the Dryade clan led by their Queen, Eithne. Their territory abuts the Wildes far to the north, and their clan folk often travel within the bounds of the forest, guiding lost travelers."

"Dryade clan? Dryads are fae that have a connection to trees, right?" Harley said without looking back.

"True words, Harlequin. There are many that can be called fae, but none so close to the elements of the earth as the Nymphish clans. Most of them stay close within the bounds of their territories, or will find quiet, out of the way places that suit their needs and affinities. The Dryade clan is the most outgoing of all of them, perhaps because trees grow almost everywhere, and where there are trees, they will gladly reside."

"What's the Expanse like?" Cadence asked.

"Yiannis might be better equipped to answer that question. Of all of us, he is the only one who has traveled the whole of our realm, including to have passed the borders into Dark's domain. He has informed me he plans to speak with you all this evening."

Dia started to ride forward but Cadence stopped her and asked, "Dia, why do you call the Unseelie the Dark? Estian kept referring to her as the Dark Queen, and I get that we called her the Dark Lady, but that was mostly because she wears all black, but you all don't seem to call Estian the Light Queen, or the Light instead of the Seelie."

Dia didn't answer at first. when she eventually did, her tone was considering, and a little hesitant. "I think perhaps we have simply always called them that. They are the Unseelie, the Sluagh. Much of their number are made up of those creatures who prefer the night, live in the dark, hide among the shadows, and shrink away from the day. Even their queen is a creature of night. I have heard her referred to as 'The darkness and the monsters within it'. It is rumored that when Essie—That is, Queen Estian—sent a delegation upon becoming the Seelie queen, they were met and instructed only to enter during hours between dusk and dawn and refused audience if they attempted to come at any other time."

"Okay, but I don't think anybody in the Seelie court called you guys the light, and even Estian only ever referred to you guys as the Seelie." Cadence said.

"Also, I would just like to note, does her only wanting to be met at night mean the Dark Queen is a vampire or something?" Chris added, putting a heavy dose of snark into his tone.

Dia shrugged a little and tilted her head as she considered. "We do not think of ourselves as the light, though I suppose it is an apt description of our queen's and thus most of our powers. Perhaps we have too long been influenced by our own stories, but I will not deny my bias. Our people are as bright and vibrant and wonderous as the Dark's people are grim, broody, and dangerous. And as far as vampires, I know this word, though I've never known any of our number to actually feed on the blood of others as your stories imply. No, she may not feast upon you as perhaps you mean, but she *can* feed on the fear and terror of those she tortures. She can gain power from her victims, which is part of what makes her so very dangerous."

Dia nodded to herself and without waiting for any further questions, she urged her horse forward and settled back into pace alongside Yiannis.

Chris and Cadence had a moment of shared horror.

Jenta

The day wore on peacefully, and Jenta found herself surveying the land they passed. Dia had been right—she spotted the occasional track or narrow path, but all of them were thinner and less pronounced.

Birds and insects rustled in the long grass to either side of the road, and occasionally one would startle into flight as they rode past. One small flock of birds were similar to robins—they had the same dusty brown-gray wings and bright orange-red bellies. She noticed another flock that reminded her of the little black birds they had at home. Others barely looked like birds at all.

At one point, they came across a small pond to the right of the road, wreathed in reeds and other water grasses and fed from a small creek that trickled in from the field beyond. Amid those tall stalks Jenta spotted a bird with legs so long they were almost the same height again as the bird's body and neck together. The bird's bill was longer than a heron's, and the bird had a huge, rainbow hued plume that stuck out from the back of its head and fanned out like a peacock's tail in miniature. She laughed, and the thing glowered at her with eyes that were entirely too self-aware. Her laughter stopped immediately, and she turned away, wondering if it could use that long, pointy beak for more than spearing fish.

Later, she saw a bunch of tittering birds up in the branches of a sprawling oak, its arms reaching out across the road and over the fields around it. The birds had such vibrant yellow and blue feathers that at first, Jenta thought they were parrots. Then one tilted its head, peering down at her. It had a face like a rabbit, slightly squashed with a tiny split above its buck teeth. Instead of a nose, the birds had two small holes and a sort of spike that stuck out of the middle of their face. Harley was just as fascinated when Jenta pointed them out to her.

"What do you suppose they eat?" Harley said, looking up above them. The birds peered at them, chattering amongst themselves and gathering or hopping among the branches in little changing groups.

"I don't know. I mean, with teeth like that, maybe leaves? What do rabbits eat?" Jenta said, glancing up, then back at Harley.

"Rabbits are obligate herbivores, so you might not be wrong, or at least not far off." Harley met her gaze and shrugged then returned her attention to the road. Jenta had to admit she was impressed with how quickly Harley was already picking up riding, but she wondered how much of that credit should go to the sweet gray mare. Yiannis had picked the perfect horse for her friend, whether he knew it or not—but she had a feeling he probably did.

She tried to ignore Chris riding behind her. She could feel his eyes on her, and it made her shoulder blades itch. She owed him an apology, but she was also furious. Everything had gone so wrong, so quickly. She could tell he'd just been trying to help, but it all went downhill the moment he'd touched her. Maybe she could ask Harley.

Flashes of her history with Jonathon flooded her every time she tried to think on it and reminded her that she was woefully inexperienced in how to express herself with people. She continued to stare out at the fields as they rode, wondering what her life had become.

Chapter Twenty-One

Christian

F ireflies were dancing in the fields to either side of the road, and in front of them, a warm glow on the horizon revealed itself to be a sprawling town. Posts lining the lanes held lanterns hung on arms sticking out over the passers-by. Chris thought at first that the lanterns had light bulbs inside, then realized they were tiny winged fae. Their wings shone brightly, sending glittering dust drifting on the cool evening air. The delicate, doll-sized bodies glowed with a warm light, like overgrown fireflies.

The lanterns were much larger than he'd originally thought, hanging over their heads like big parrot cages with one massive, hinged door on the front. One of the little creatures was reading a book, while another appeared to be sewing, scraps of fabric set about them and a tiny needle glowing in their hand. There was even one sleeping on a little pallet laid out at the bottom of their lantern, their gossamer wings drifting slowly open then closed above them, shedding more of the glowing dust.

Fae moved through the streets and in and out of buildings, doors of houses open and delicious smells filling the air. Many of them had ears drawn out to points, making him think of the pictures of elves he'd seen. Some had feathers instead of hair, beak-like noses, and thin lips. A short, narrow shouldered little man with long, sharply pointed ears, an angular face with a little goatee, and wispy white hair that sat on his head like a cotton ball, wore a large vest hung about with different kinds of telescopes and spy glasses. He stood next to a wheeled cart hung with various objects made of glass and metal.

Yiannis guided them down a narrow alley that ran alongside a squat two-story building. Chris studied the front of the building as they passed. The sign hanging over the door was the old wooden kind with a picture instead of a name painted on it, showing an armored figure sitting at the base of a tree.

Aoife rode up behind him and glanced at the sign. "A Knight's Rest." She chuckled. "That joke only works in your language. Old Miles never seemed to care much, though." Aoife continued to nudge her mount past them into the alley where she dismounted and guided her horse forward.

Yiannis, Dia, and Faustus were talking quietly with a stable hand as Chris led his horse into the small yard. Amid the bustle of so many horses and riders, the young-looking stable lad shouted for another attendant who went running up a short set of wooden stairs and through a door at the back of the inn.

By the time the attendant brought out the innkeeper, Chris had already handed off his horse. He waited with Cadence, Harley, and Jenta, surrounded by their sidhe companions as the short, stout man waddled toward them, wiping his hands on a pristine white apron that stretched around his thick belly. He wasn't so much fat as he was one big block of muscle, and the apron covered him from shoulders to nearly his shins, showing just the bottoms of heavy trousers— ending at the tips of thick-soled boots—and the sleeves of a shirt rolled up to show massive forearms covered in thick dark red hair.

The innkeeper had an enormous beard that lay across his chest like a second shirt over the top of the apron. His face was broad and worn, his nose wide and bulbous and his eyes shadowed by bushy eyebrows the same bright shade of red as the strands that ran through the gray of his beard. *He's a dwarf!* Chris almost grinned. The only thing missing was a big steel helmet and a double-headed ax.

"Yiannis!" The stout man boomed, a large meaty hand with thick fingers ending in clean, blunt clipped nails reached out to grasp the tall sidhe's own hand while he gripped Yiannis' forearm with the other, his stubby fingers just barely reaching halfway around the taller man's arm. They shook hands, grinning at each other.

The conversation that followed between them was swift, spoken in another language until Yiannis said something that caused the innkeeper to clap his mouth shut, giving Yiannis a long, incredulous blink. He studied the rest of them, looking them over, then grinned broadly and switched to a heavily accented English.

"Ah, Welcome! Welcome! Yiannis tells me ye're from—" Yiannis cleared his throat loudly, and the innkeeper jumped, startled, then continued. "Ehm, yes, from the far side of the kingdom, that is. And ye were long on the road, this day. I am Brathlrig Millstone, but ye may call me Miles."

Miles gave them another considering look, making sure they understood him then continued. "Ah but come! Come! Warm food and good ale wait." He glanced again at Yiannis, who gave him a nod, then led them up a short set of stairs and through a thick wooden door into a bright, whitewashed hallway.

They all trooped through the back of the inn until they reached a hall with swinging doors to the left that led to a common room, and a doorway on the right that opened into a private dining room into which Miles guided them.

A heavy table made of some dark polished wood filled the center of the room, and a matching sideboard was pushed up against the far wall, its top lined with decorative mugs and small kegs marked with little carved labels Chris couldn't read. The smell of beeswax hung strong in the air, and two tall candles sat in the middle of the table, placed just so around a small flower arrangement in a clay pitcher, the flames dancing merrily in the wind made by their entrance. More sconces hung on the walls, lit with more candles, giving the room a warm, welcoming glow.

The four of them were instructed to take the seats with their backs to the wall with the sideboard, while Yiannis took a seat at the head of the table and gestured for Dia to take the seat at the other end. The other four sidhe took their cue and picked spots across the table. Aoife claimed the spot next to Yiannis and pointed at the chair next to her for Leif. Ximeno and Faustus did something that might have been rock-paper-scissors and when it appeared Ximeno lost, based on his grumpy sigh, and headshake, he took the seat next to Leif and Faustus, grinning, took the spot next to Dia.

Once they were all settled, Miles inclined his head to Yiannis and left through a far door on the same wall as the one through which they'd entered. He returned in short order, leading a small group of fae. Chris watched, fascinated. They were all delicate looking, with feathers instead of hair and angular, bird-like faces. They smiled as they entered, carrying steaming bowls, mugs with thick foamy tops, and a couple trays covered in clean white cloth.

Chris had one of the steaming bowls and a mug set in front of him, and one of the cloth-covered trays was placed in the center of their side of the table, the smell of fresh bread wafting from it. Chris licked his lips as one of the servers set his bowl in front of him, and they looked at each other. A blush rushed up into his cheeks, and the smiling fae gave him a wink, then let out a high, tittering laugh when he blushed more.

Their places set, Miles clapped his big hands together, and shooed the servers out of the room, then made as if to follow. At the door, he stopped and gave Yiannis a nod, his face suddenly serious. He waited a beat, scanning the room, then left, pulling it closed behind him with an audible *click*.

"Eat. Tomorrow will be tougher riding, and longer, and we must talk. There are things the queen could not tell you, but we must now discuss." Yiannis raised his mug and held it aloft. "To Danann, and to Queen Estian."

Chris raised his mug and repeated the words, then peered at everyone else. Each of the sidhe took a long swig. Cadence took a sip, then grinned and took a longer drink. Harley took a sip from hers, gave wide eyes, then set it on the table. He brought his attention back to his own cup, the foam on top was fizzing away to reveal hints of the amber liquid beneath. Ale, Miles had said. Chris set the mug down without tasting it and focused on the bowl in front of him instead.

It was a thick stew in a heavy brown gravy. He picked up the wooden spoon the pretty bird woman had set beside his bowl, and took a bite, then smiled. The stew was exactly right, the meat tender and the vegetables tasting just close enough to those he knew from home that he didn't hesitate after that first bite. Yiannis pulled aside the cloth from the tray in front of them to show a big round loaf, thickly sliced.

The day hadn't been cold, but it also hadn't been particularly warm, and the stew immediately made him feel warm down to his toes. The room quieted except for the sound of spoons in bowls and the lifting and setting down of mugs.

Chris was using a piece of bread to wipe the last of the stew from his bowl when Yiannis cleared his throat.

"Today went well, and I am pleased with our progress. However, I am mindful that a group of strangers accompanied by the queen's warriors may draw attention we do not want. Tomorrow, when we approach each settlement, scouts, you will skirt the edges and meet us on the other side." He took a moment and tapped his spoon on the edge of his bowl, thinking. "A rainstorm follows us. I will ask Miles about obtaining cloaks for you four."

"Speaking of weather, Dia told us we should ask you about the Expanse." Cadence said.

Yiannis glanced at Dia then back to Cadence. "I suppose that is a fair suggestion for her to make. What would you like to know?"

"I mean, what are they like? Are they like what we passed today?" Cadence asked, gesturing vaguely with one hand.

"Some are, yes. Some are not at all like any lands I have ever seen anywhere else."

"Like what?" Harley asked.

"To begin, the land and the clans who have claimed it have grown to mimic each other. As Cristobal pointed out on the map, we will strive to pass along the edges between territories where I believe these changes will be less obvious. It is my hope that as with the Wildes, we may obtain a guide. There is an outpost of elves who live on the far side of Merchants Road, the path which should be our best route through the Wildes. Last time I traveled this way, I had friends who resided there."

"How can you tell who lives in each territory?" Chris asked. He picked up another piece of bread and ripped off the crust to chew on.

"There are ways to identify the clans, based on how the land has changed for them. Unfortunately, it has been some time since I traversed the boundaries, but unless they have changed, we should be passing by five clan lands—three of them to the north and two to the south." Yiannis picked up his mug and took a long drink, then stared down into its depths.

"Leif and I came by way of the Expanse on a trip for our parents only perhaps a couple hundred years or so ago." Aoife said as she lifted a bite of stew to her mouth. It was almost impressive, how much smugness she could put in such a small statement.

Cadence, who had been taking a drink of his own, sputtered and set down his mug. "A couple *hundred?*"

"They *are* immortal, Cay." Jenta said, and Chris winced. They hadn't talked all day, since the incident in the armory, and every time he thought of it, he thought he might throw up.

Cadence shook his head, and his tone still held a note of incredulity. "Right. Right. Sorry. Please continue."

Aoife had that little smirk back on her face. After their incident in the map room, she'd mostly ignored them, and Chris was pretty okay with that.

"To the north, the lands are made up of waterways and marshlands, claimed by three of the Nymphish clans. Just along the edge of the Wildes are claimed by the Napaea. The Naiade and the Hydriade both live further out into the expanse, where the land slopes down into a watery valley with a vast lake." She stopped and took another drink of ale, as Yiannis nodded.

"Yes. I do not think they were in that order when last I was that way, but those three clans have always lived close to each other. Did the land still rise up to the south of their claim?" He asked.

Leif gave a non-committal grunt, and Chris had to remind himself that the sidhe *could* speak. He'd heard Leif and Aoife talking quietly with each other earlier in the day, otherwise Chris would have been convinced that the big blond was mute.

Aoife shot her brother a look, then continued. "Yes. Also, closer in toward the Wildes near the elven outpost is an immense wildflower forest. A group of demi- and winged fae have claimed that, though I would not call them a clan. Perhaps more of a swarm."

"Okay, so what's the last territory?" Cadence asked.

Aoife shrugged. "A Blessing of unicorns had a glade there, but they were hoping to beseech the land to move southwest, due to an encroaching clan of goblins with a mound to the southeast. So, it is most likely one or the other of those."

Chris and Cadence considered each other for a moment, and Cadence leaned over to him.

"Do you want to ask or should I?" Cadence asked quietly.

Chris answered honestly, keeping his own voice low. "You're leading the convo just fine, cap'n. Go for it."

Cadence met his gaze and held it. "You're okay with that?"

"What, you leading? Fuck yeah, man. Means less things I have to think about." Chris chuckled, and Cadence gave a weak smile.

"Fair enough." He straightened in his seat and pushed his bowl forward and out of his way, then leaned his arms against the table as he focused his attention on Yiannis. "What can you tell us about the Void?"

Yiannis gave a slow blink. "I am not certain what you mean." He said, but his tone implied otherwise.

Cadence apparently caught the hesitancy in his statement. "Yes, you do. Estian mentioned that sometimes bridges could open in the Void, but that no one knows what makes them. Everything we've heard and seen makes us think that maybe the Dark Queen found some way to open one of these things, or maybe break a hole through the wall. If Estian was able to bridge the gap through the Void to bring us through, would the Dark Queen be able to do the same thing? If she broke it, or found a way to damage the Void, should we try to fix it, first? Or could fighting her fix it?"

Yiannis regarded Cadence, his face expressionless, but Chris thought he might as well be screaming for Cay to shut up. "Aoife, Faustus, go check that our rooms are ready. Leif, Ximeno, go check the horses. Ensure they have been fed and curried. Dia—"

"No. I will stay."

Yiannis gave her a look that probably would have killed Chris, but Dia just gave Yiannis a hard stare right back. "I am your second. The queen may have given you instructions, but I have my own, and I will stay."

Yiannis practically snarled at her, the first real emotion Chris had seen on the ageless warrior. He made a gesture, and the other four rose from their seats and left without comment. Aoife was so angry her face became dark red, but Leif seemed almost glad. Faustus and Ximeno must regularly eat sour fruit because Chris couldn't tell any difference in their disgruntled expressions.

Once they were gone, Yiannis went to the hallway door. Instead of pulling the door closed though, he actually propped it all the way open then stepped back into the room held one of his hands up, the flat of his palm facing out toward the doorway. Chris felt a tingling rush like he'd been dipped in icy water. Beside him, Cadence gave a shudder. He didn't see anything different when he looked directly at the doorway, but like with the mirror in Harley's room, there was a constant rippling when looking out of the corner of his eye, like the surface of a pond.

"What did you just do?" Cadence asked. He was rubbing his arms up and down as if he had goosebumps.

"The sound in this room will now be muffled. It will not stop someone from hearing us if they are determined, but it will make the listening harder, and one of us will most likely have seen them long since." Yiannis turned to Dia, his expression softening. "You are right, Diaphony, that I was given instructions by the queen. Instructions that I agree with. While I understand your insistence to stay, I would save you this knowledge. Would that these young humans had not even asked, but I must do as I must, and now, so must you." He took a deep breath, shook himself, then took one of the vacated seats across the table from the four.

"As you know, the Void was created at the time of the splitting. A wall, it is, but also a world, and as such, it has its own inhabitants. Moreover, what good is a wall, without a guard? The Void is no different, and within resides the Keeper. The Keeper has free roam of its domain and acts as the last line of defense between the realms as well as to protect the Void itself from attack. The Void is, as its name implies, endless and open. And yet, the Keeper can be anywhere within it nearly instantaneously."

"What *is* the Keeper?" Harley asked.

"It is... Difficult to explain." Yiannis said hesitantly.

"You say that like you've seen it." Cadence said.

Yiannis didn't respond to Cadence's statement as he continued. "As I expressed to the queen, my concern is that in order for the Dark Queen to breach the Void, something must have happened to the Keeper."

"Like what?" Jenta asked.

Yiannis placed his fingers on the table, denoting specific spots with an invisible line between them. "The Void has what could best be described as anchor points that attach it to each of the realms. In times past, I believe the Void Bridges have formed at those anchor points. Otherwise, there has never been a way for the fae to reach, let alone pass through the Void from our side."

"Void Bridges. Like gates that opened in the wall, so you could travel from one side to the other?" Cadence asked.

"Even so." Yiannis nodded. "All of this is only conjecture, however. Our histories speak of the splitting and the creation of the Void, but nowhere are the Void Bridges mentioned."

"Regardless of conjecture, if you can't access the Void from this side, what would the Void Bridges have to do with this?" Cadence pushed.

Yiannis leaned his arms on the table as he spoke. "The anchor points of the Void are both a blessing and a curse. They are necessary, to keep the void in place, but they are also weak points in the wall. If the Dark Queen located or gained access to an anchor point in the fae realm, while it might take her quite a bit of magic, it would then simply be a matter of time before she could potentially wear away the wall until she is able to make herself, for lack of a better term, a hole into the Void where there was not one."

"So, what? You think she broke a hole through the wall and like... Hurt the Keeper?" Chris leaned back in his chair, crossing his arms.

Yiannis tilted his head and considered Chris's words. "I believe it may be so. As Cadence mentioned, our queen was able to open a way for you four to pass through, yes, but it was very specifically targeted, and required that you accept her invitation in order for her magic to complete the bridge. Void Bridges that appeared in the past always required willing and conscious choice, by the one passing through them, implying that the Keeper was aware, and allowed their passage. However, you all have seen what the Dark Queen is doing for yourselves. She is not asking permission, and yet, she has not been stopped."

Harley leaned forward, excited. "We were talking about that, this morning." She glanced at Chris. "Remember when we were talking over breakfast?"

Chris gave her a nod, and Harley continued, addressing Yiannis. "I did this extensive research paper a year ago, and I found things that made me think that sometimes when humans dream, we sort of," she moved her hand in a wiping movement, "*brush* the fae realm with our minds."

Yiannis sat back, interested. "I do not think you are wrong."

Harley gestured to Jenta. "Jenta pointed out that one thing a lot of the victims have in common is that people being taken are all at a time in their lives when they're thinking a lot about their future. They're doing a lot of learning, and most likely a lot of *dreaming*. But these same people are often also really tired from everything going on in their lives. I suggested this morning that the deeper the person sleeps, and the more creative they are, the closer they naturally may be pulled to the fae side of the wall."

Yiannis was nodding. "Yes, Harlequin, I think perhaps you are right. It is my belief that she had already started breaking the hole through our side of the Void, but that for a time, she could only pull through those who drifted closest to the hole she'd already made."

"Okay, but again, you talked about the Keeper. Why didn't it stop her?" Cadence asked.

Yiannis gave Cadence a small smile. "The queen selected well, with you four. The Keeper is both *of* the Void and *is* the Void, and thus is truly immortal within its domain. As long as that in-between realm exists, so the Keeper will exist, meaning it cannot be killed. However, if the Void can be damaged, perhaps it is, too, that the Keeper may be trapped. I believe that the Dark Queen has found some way to do exactly that."

"Could the Keeper be, I don't know, working with her, maybe?" Jenta asked, but Yiannis was already shaking his head.

"No. The Keeper has no allies, no alliances, no allegiances. The Keeper's task is singular and specific, and their nature is true. No, I believe that if the Dark Queen has access to the Void, it is because she has done something to them."

"Is there a way to get to the Keeper? To check and see if they're okay?" Harley asked.

Yiannis let out a slow breath, but his attention went back to Dia. "Yes, there is technically a way to reach the keeper, though I hesitate to use it. You asked about it in the map room, and Cristobal was not wrong, despite that I believe he has never seen the place, personally."

Harley goggled at him. "Do you mean the Guardian's Sepulture? That big black spot that was scribbled out on the map?"

Yiannis gave a small, bitter smile. "The very same. Most only know it as a place of great danger, where many have gone, but have never returned. In truth, it is the one and only access to the Void from the fae side, but it is also heavily guarded, by some of the most vicious, dangerous, violent, and powerful creatures of the fae. They hold no side and grant no oaths. They are the Keeper's alone to command."

"How would you know this, Yiannis?" Dia's voice was low and held none of her normal joviality. Yiannis met her questioning eyes, but Cadence interrupted before he could speak further.

"Wait, you said realm, and earlier, you called it a 'world'. I thought the Void is just a wall?"

Yiannis didn't answer right away. He seemed to be weighing and measuring each of them, and Chris made himself sit still under those considering eyes. He answered Cadence's question, but his attention was on Dia as he spoke. "It is a place that the fae truly cannot go, so most are not aware that it is a realm of its own, but the Void does have another name. One that has little meaning to the fae, which is part of why it is not used."

Chris noticed that all four of them were now leaning forward on the table, watching Yiannis, but he kept his eyes on Dia who met his gaze, unflinching. "Our histories sometimes refer to it as the Realm of Dreams."

Silence filled the room and the only thing that told Chris the oxygen hadn't been sucked out of it was that the candle flames still flickered and danced merrily.

When Cadence spoke, his voice was quiet, but the edge of fury in it was clear. "The Realm of *Dreams*. People started dying in their sleep. People *like us* being dragged through in their *dreams*. Are you fucking kidding me? You *think* this *might* have something to do with the Void? How are we only just having this conversation? Has anyone tried to get access to the Keeper, or even thought to check any of these anchor points? What the fuck have you guys even been *doing*, all this time?" Cadence was practically yelling by the time he stopped. He threw his hands up in the air then threw himself back in his seat, glaring at Yiannis, who's expression had gone almost blank.

"Waiting for you." Yiannis' voice was like being thrown in a mountain lake. His gaze was fierce as he met Cadence's glare, but his voice was almost dangerously calm. "We had to wait for mortals."

"*Why?*" The question came out angry, petulant, but again, Yiannis ignored Cadence's tone while answering his question.

"Fae do not dream. We can bridge the Void with our magic, but we cannot enter it. We are the things of dreams. We are the muses, the fantasies, the inspiration. We are Danann's eldest children, and our role has always been clear: to protect and inspire the hearts of mortals, whose passion, drive, and short lives push you to create, to invent, to *dream*." Yiannis left his chair and started to pace.

"Queen Estian has stood witness to the suffering of your people, her heart breaking, knowing there was nothing she could do to move against the Dark Queen directly. Their truce was useless, and her own words, her own oath, held her as tightly as any chains."

Cadence opened his mouth to say something, but Yiannis held up a hand and shook his head.

"In your world, it has only been perhaps days that you have known of the Dark Queen. Did you know that she has been taking people since before you were born? Only recently, did we learn of the vastness of the reach she has gained. Or did the queen perhaps mention that time runs differently in Fae? No? Well here, it has been hundreds of years. Hundreds. And in all that time, Queen Estian has sought to find the answer to Danann's warning."

Yiannis glared at the walls as he paced, and his words burned in the air around them. "All this time, the queen and her scholars have spent in study, searching in desperation to find four mortals at the cusp between the intuition of childhood and the fortitude of adulthood. Four mortals who knew the pain of despair but contained hearts full of compassion still. Four mortals touched by the divine, who would shine to us like beacons among the darkening clouds."

Yiannis stopped pacing, and rested his palms against the table, leaning forward. Waves crashed in his eyes. His hair, short as it was, flowed around his head as if he'd been submerged in water, and that one long tail that lay against his shoulder trailed across the table like the tail of some deep-sea leviathan. Magic crackled and rippled under his skin, and Chris saw Dia out of the corner of his eye, scooting her chair back a little as if readying herself.

Yiannis pointed at her without looking and she stilled, but not like she was happy about it. His words fell like rocks in water, sending ripples in the air. To Cadence's credit, despite having all that power focused on him, he didn't flinch, but it seemed to Chris that most of the anger had already drained out of Cadence before Yiannis finished.

"Still, we could not *make* you come. You had to *choose*. Danann's will, mortal's choice. I knew when you were born. I felt the call of your mortal magic. That is when I—" He bowed his head and his power drained out of him a little before his head came up. "When I left my exile and returned to the Seelie court to claim my place in the guard. But imagine, young human.

Hundreds of years spent haunted by the screams and cries of the mortals you cherish, that you desperately wish to protect, but who you cannot save. Every waking moment, those cries echo in Estian's ears, and she dares not close her eyes for the visions. Her only respite is knowing that they *will* die, granting them the rest she cannot. Truly, a desperate form of hope."

"We didn't know, Yiannis. How could we?" Harley's voice was soft, apologetic.

Heartsickness gripped Chris. Bad enough that the bitch had his sister… He shook his head, but Yiannis was speaking, again, his voice tired. "You are right. And I do not blame you, but you cannot ask me not to feel this anger." Yiannis straightened and met their eyes, his chin raising. "That is all I will say tonight. It is late, and we have far to travel in the morning." He went to the far door and gave a patterned knock then went back to the hall door where he did that same push-out gesture with one hand.

Chris watched him at first, then looked at the others. Cadence's gaze as it followed Yiannis was unreadable. Harley and Jenta both sat with their heads down, looking like they were focused on something in their laps. Dia also studied Yiannis, but tears glittered at the corners of her eyes. Had she known about Estian's struggles? Chris thought she probably had. If his best friend was suffering, he'd do everything he could to share the burden.

In the silence, the second door opened, and Miles came through with one of the bird-like servers behind him. He gestured toward the table with its empty dishes then turned to Yiannis. "Rooms are ready. One for the lasses, one for the lads." Miles waved for them to follow him, and he moved out the hallway door past Yiannis. Chris wondered how much the stout little innkeeper had heard, and how much he already knew.

Harlequin

Harley and Jenta sat in the armchairs set to face the unlit fireplace tucked into the far corner of their room. A small table between them held a little clay pitcher of flowers, a miniature version to the one on their dining table, and behind them were two four-poster beds. They would have to share one bed, and Dia and Aoife would be sharing the other. The room was dark except for the soft light of a single, thin candle in a clay holder on a low chest of drawers that took up most of one wall. The flame was tall and relatively still, creating long shadows in all the corners of the room, and casting a somber, private mood over them.

They'd changed out of their dusty riding clothes and taken turns shaking them out the window, then hanging them up to air out. Harley was watching Jenta twist and pick at her own fingers, a gesture she knew all too well.

When Jenta finally spoke, it all came out in a breathless rush. "I want to apologize to Chris for slapping him, but I also feel like he owes me an apology, and I don't really know what to do about it."

"Okay. Why *did* you slap him?" Harley asked.

Jenta opened her mouth, then closed it again, before answering. "It's hard to explain."

Harley adjusted herself in the seat, tucking her legs beneath her and leaned against the padded arm. It wasn't as elegant or luxurious as the seats in the palace, but it was soft and deep enough for her to sit back in it, the arms coming up high, like she was being hugged. When Jenta didn't continue, Harley tilted her head to consider the other girl. "Is it to do with Jonathon?"

Jenta nodded and went back to picking her fingers. "Kinda, yeah. Chris wasn't exactly wrong about that. You know I've always had a bit of a fascination with..." She gestured at her arms.

It was Harley's turn to nod, even though Jenta wasn't looking. "Yeah."

"So... shortly before I met Jonathon, my little brother, Matt, found me."

"Like I did?"

Jenta's expression saddened. "No. Not really, anyway. I guess you could say it was worse, in some ways, not as bad in others. Regardless, it really messed him up. So, when I met Jonathon, he decided I wasn't allowed to have knives without supervision anymore. Probably just another way to control me, but Harley, it worked. We went through my room and gathered up everything. He kept it all at his place, and I could practice with them if I was with him, but otherwise, I wasn't allowed to have even a butter knife if I was alone."

"Wow. Jenta, I can't imagine how scary and hard that must all have been." Harley said.

Jenta shrugged and curled up in her own chair, hugging her knees. "At first, yeah. I wasn't sure how to function without them initially, if that makes sense. But it got easier. It was the first time in a long time that I started to feel safe with myself. But today, standing there, all I could think was that if I let myself pick out a weapon, I wouldn't be safe anymore. Does that sound stupid?"

Harley frowned, thinking. "It's not stupid, Jen. You've come a long way in trying to heal by deliberately avoiding temptation. Then suddenly, you're shoved head long into a room full of it. I can't imagine how stressful that must have been."

"I know I've made a lot of progress, but it's always been while someone was there with me." Jenta's voice held something Harley wasn't used to hearing: fear.

Harley did her best to sound encouraging. "You've spent a lot of time desensitizing yourself to having weapons around you when around others, I get that. The good news is that you're not alone here, either. We're all here for you, okay?" She waited for Jenta to give a little nod before she continued. "But Jenta, only you can decide and keep deciding to see your progress."

Jenta let out a heavy sigh and slumped back in her chair. "I was afraid you'd say that. Hell, I even know you're right. I'm just really worried that Chris thinks I'm someone I'm not with this whole thing. He saw my fear this morning, but it was like he deliberately misunderstood it."

"How so?" Harley asked.

Jenta shrugged and shook her head. "Instead of asking *why* I was afraid, he just yelled at me, then treated me like I was a damsel in distress, and he would be my hero. I don't *need* a hero, and that he assumed I did, just made me mad."

"Okay, so a hero isn't what you need, but what about a friend? He's cared about you for a long time, Jenta. We've both seen that. I think maybe from the first moment he met you, he has been drawn to you."

Jenta stared into the dark fireplace, and Harley could just see one shining tear as it ran down her cheek before she wiped it away. "Yeah. Chris looks at me, and I know he can see the broken parts, but I don't think he sees any of my sharp edges. I let Jonathon break me down and rebuild me how he wanted, but it turns out he just wanted me broken. I don't want to hurt Chris or have him cut himself up trying to fix me. If he'd settle for being my friend, I think that would be okay, but I need to figure out how to fix myself before I can trust I won't slice anyone else up on my sharp edges. God, does that even make sense?"

Harley laughed a little bitterly, and Jenta raised her eyebrows. "Oh, it definitely makes sense. I'm not about to compare my pain to yours, but I definitely understand what you mean."

"Is it my turn to ask, 'how so'?" Jenta said and gave a half-hearted smile.

Harley smiled back a little. "I remember thinking the other morning that the only thing I had that was really mine were the secrets I've been keeping. I've spent my whole life having someone else given ownership for everything I am. Part of why I came is that I need to know I can do this. Not because someone else did it first, or because I was told to, or expected to, but because I chose to. My decision—just mine—and no one else's." Jenta was nodding, as Harley continued.

"So yeah, I get it. I need to take back all those bits of me that have been passed out to anyone *but* me." She barked a bitter laugh and shook her head. "The stupid thing is my mom has been dead since I was five. How can anything I am at eighteen belong to someone who's been gone thirteen years? I don't mean to be callous about it, and I *do* miss her, but sometimes I feel like my dad hasn't really existed since he lost her. Like he died in that hospital room with her, and all that's left is their ghosts haunting me."

They sat in silence for a long time. Jenta leaned forward and offered her hand, and Harley took it and gave it a squeeze, then gave her a sad smile, before speaking.

"By the way, as far as Chris is concerned, all you can do is be yourself. Whatever expectations he sets on you, you aren't obliged to live up to them. He seems like a good enough guy, but at the end of the day, the only expectations you should strive to live up to are your own."

"Any more than you're obliged to live up to your father's, or anyone else's, expectations but your own." Jenta's voice was soft, and sincere. They stared at each other in the quiet dark and didn't let go of each other's hands.

Chapter Twenty-Two

Christian

The stable yard was still heavily shadowed despite the dawn light shining into their room upstairs. Chris squinted up a couple times, wondering about the lanterns hanging on big metal pegs to light their work. One of the stable hands followed his gaze up to the lamps, and grinned.

He was small, standing only just up to Chris' shoulder and whip-thin, his face so narrow that when he grinned, his teeth seemed to take up more room than anything else. Chris thought he saw a hint of fangs.

The stable hand said, "Keine Sorge. Die Laternen brennen nicht." Then smiled and nodded.

Chris shrugged, having no idea what the little fae said. He smiled in return then went back to readying his horse but didn't look up again. In short order, the horses were saddled, bags settled, and riders mounted.

Miles waited at the top of the stairs leading into the inn, silhouetted by the light from the hall behind him. His face was in shadow, but his arms were crossed, and everything about his posture implied disapproval. While they led the horses out of their stalls, he and Yiannis were having a short, heated conversation, but the language was the same they'd spoken

the night before, and a night's sleep hadn't given Chris any more compre-
hension of it than he'd had previously.

Even so, despite Miles' seeming displeasure, he raised his hand in a wave
and shouted something to them as Yiannis led them out of the stable yard.
Chris waved, and Jenta and Harley both did the same. Cadence gave him
a boy scout salute which made Harley laugh.

There hadn't been a single moment for Chris to pull Jenta aside to
apologize, yesterday. He thought his skin might just twitch itself right off
him every time she looked his way as they'd saddled the horses. He wished
he'd just made himself go knock on her door last night to talk to her, but
Cadence pointed out that might or might not make things worse.

They made their way down the alley and out onto the main road, leaving him blinking in the bright morning sun already cresting the distant
landscape. The sun was a ball of molten gold in front of them, the streets
were already bustling, and Chris was suddenly struck by how normal it all
seemed.

There, a woman was arguing over the price of fish being displayed by
a man with thick, muscled arms. However, the woman had delicately
pointed teeth, whiskers, and cat's ears that stuck up and out from the sides
of her head, covered in the same creamy orange fur that showed on her face
and the backs of her hands. Gold earrings swayed and glinted along the
edges of those fine, nearly translucent pointed ears as she shook her head.

The fishmonger was completely, smoothly bald with long, thin earlobes
that pressed back to the sides of his head. His nose was uptilted, the point
almost flat against his face so that his nostrils flared when he breathed out,
but when he breathed in, tiny flaps covered them, and his ears flicked out
to the sides.

Chris gaped. When the man gestured to another of the fish on his stand, the webbing stretched between his fingers. Chris returned his attention the road in front of his horse, and hoped the guy hadn't seen him staring, but those had *definitely* been gills.

At another stall, a small man with a bright red chin beard who wore a green vest over a cream-colored puff sleeved shirt and brown trousers was standing behind a display of trinkets and jewelry in the shape of gold coins with an impression of the queen's face in profile. He was busy laying out a tray of small glass beads and buttons, each set with its own tiny four-leaf clover.

Ahead of them, a mother walked with her children to one side of the road. Two children scurried along behind her, and she carried the third. All of them had tawny, fur covered legs with hooves instead of feet, and tiny, delicate horns protruding from their foreheads. The only thing Chris could think to compare them to was Pan. Satyrs, maybe? He reminded himself to ask Harley later.

Despite them being the only people mounted, no one gave them much more than an initial glance. When they cleared the last of the buildings and out onto the empty road, there was almost a visceral pressure change. Chris's grandparents had lived in the country, and driving to town was always more like the houses just got closer and closer together until suddenly they were driving down Main Street, past the old ice cream parlor and the Mom and Pop Chicken Shop. Here, the community was all bundled up into one big bubble, and once it ended, it was just an open road ahead of them, with no other travelers.

Yiannis led them into a ground-eating canter that left them little focus for talking. Chris wondered how much of that was on purpose. Yiannis had been stoic all morning, but Chris couldn't tell how much was frustration—either at them or at himself—versus how much might be at Miles for whatever they'd discussed.

Aoife and Leif split off from the end of their group, ranging ahead and then out into the grasslands until Chris lost track of them. Faustus and Ximeno rode behind them, two looming shadows on their matching dun-colored chargers. Chris was duly impressed by the large, thick-necked beasts that towered and intimidated as much as their riders. For the riders themselves, the brothers beheld everything and everyone with hooded eyes, but at least those puckered scowls they'd worn all day yesterday seemed maybe a little less pinched.

Chris twisted in his saddle to look behind, and Ximeno gave him a bare hint of a smile, before he went back to surveying the surroundings.

Cadence

A bit after midday, Yiannis led them off the road and down a dirt track toward a large tree in the middle of a field. In the distance, Cadence could just make out the fluffy bodies of some grazing animals that might have been sheep. As they drew near to the tree, he saw that the grass there was already close cropped and cleared of detritus. An ancient stone wall ran near the tree, broken into sections with piles of rubble lining either side, and the gaps choked with grass. They dismounted under the shade of the tree, while Yiannis handed out something he called chew bread and hunks of a tangy, salty cheese for them to eat.

Cadence picked a spot along the old wall. While he ate, Dia set up a makeshift target further down along the top of the stones. She shot him a smile while she worked.

"When you are finished, string your bow."

"What? Why?" Cadence asked.

Dia rolled her eyes but gave him another smile. "How can I criticize your shots if I do not see them for myself?"

Cadence glanced at Yiannis, wondering if he would object. Instead, Yiannis gave him a raised eyebrow and quirked a smile. "As she says, lad. Better to know now than not at all. We're making suitable time, and the rain won't find us for another hour or so."

Cadence shrugged and finished his last bite of cheese, then headed over to his mount. He retrieved his bow and dug around in his saddlebag for his bracer and archer's glove, glad he'd thought to pack them. By the time he returned to Dia, she'd pushed five arrows, head down, into the loamy soil a fair distance away from the target, and had Cadence stand just behind the line they made.

Standing next to him, she pointed at the target, then gestured at his bow. "Draw, aim, and shoot as quickly as you are comfortable, but focus on accuracy. In a fight, it is hoped that the archer will always have someone between them and the enemy; both to distract, and to allow them time to adjust before firing. Otherwise, you should strive to have enough distance between yourself and your foe that you may lead your aim and land your shot, before they can fell you."

She gave him a nod then stepped back, and Cadence waited to make sure she was clear of him before drawing up the first arrow.

The strung bow was a little more than half his height, the wood perfectly hewn and tight as a wound spring. He nocked the arrow and raised up to aim at the target, only drawing part way as he adjusted his shot. Once he was satisfied with his aim, he drew back fully and loosed, reaching for the second arrow while the first was still in flight.

After that initial shot, the next four went more quickly, and the first arrow was the only one that didn't at least land a glancing hit. It went flying just over the edge of the target, landing somewhere in the grassy field beyond. The other four buried into wood or caught and tore the fabric in places before clattering down at the base of the wall.

None of them hit the center of the target, but each progressive shot got closer until the final arrow, still wobbling back and forth, buried itself into the sticks holding up the target fabric just below the center circle.

Cadence turned to Dia, a nervous but hopeful smile on his face.

"Well done! As you said, you hit more often than not." She came and clapped him on the shoulder, giving him a warm, pleased smile.

"And the criticism?" Cadence said, but his smile was genuine, now.

Dia inclined her head but returned his smile. "Fair enough. When you aimed first, you anticipated too much distance between you and the target, but you adjusted quickly. That means you second-guessed your first instinct. Remember, Danann gave you eyes so that you might see, and instinct so that you might learn to trust it."

She spoke as she approached the target, retrieving the arrows. "Overall, very good, and I wish we had more time for you to practice, but I think you will do well when and if you have need."

"Thanks. I really do appreciate your feedback."

"Of course. Now that we've seen what you can do, I recommend you keep your bow out, but unstrung, and keep your arrows handy. If we run into trouble, it is much faster to string a bow already out, than to fumble with the case *and* stringing." Dia stopped at the wall, instead of moving past it, and Cadence watched her. She was looking out into the field, one hand extended like Yiannis had, the night before.

"What are you doing?" Cadence said, suddenly nervous.

Dia smiled but didn't look at him. Her raised hand had swirling tattoos or markings on it that glowed and twisted against her skin. She flexed her fingers, and the arrow was suddenly flying through the air back toward her with a sound like two people whistling at two different pitches. Cadence ducked and covered his head only to watch the arrow come to a quick stop and land gently in her hand.

"Danann says our magic should be a joy as well as a tool." Dia turned to grin at him but seeing his nervous expression sobered her. "My apologies. I did not mean to frighten you."

Yiannis huffed from his spot near the tree. "Enough, Dia. We must be going. You could have gotten the arrow faster by simply walking to it."

Cadence headed back to his horse and unstrung his bow, while the rest of the group started standing up from where they'd been reclining.

Harley got to her feet, dusting herself off. For the second day in a row, she was wearing pants—a pair of jeans so faded with age that they were nearly white. It had been a really long time since he'd seen her in anything but her plaid skirts and blouses. Along with the jeans, she wore a plain white t-shirt tucked in, and that strange dragon belt was around her waist with a dagger that rode on her hip, only partially covered by an old red, yellow, and white flannel that hung open with the sleeves rolled up.

She was focused on Dia as they made their way to the horses, and he allowed himself a moment to study her in profile while she spoke. "So, is your magic like some kind of kinesis? Or like being able to manipulate sound waves?"

Harley approached her mare, giving him a smile before she set to checking the straps on her saddle like he'd showed her that morning. She was already getting better at riding, but he forced himself to let her try three times to lift her leg up to reach the stirrup. He waited for her to glance at him, again. Cadence knew Harley well enough to know that she needed to try something by herself first before she would accept help.

He stepped forward without saying anything and crouched, offering her a boost. She looked down at his hands, fingers laced together like a step, then at him. She rested her hand on his shoulder and for a moment, he thought she'd say something, but she just smiled wider, stepped into his waiting hands, and he boosted her up and into her saddle.

"Thank you." She said, her voice quiet and almost shy. He patted her horse's neck to give himself something to do while he schooled his face, then gave her a smile of his own.

"Of course." He went back to his own mount as Dia answered Harley's question. Had she been talking the whole time Cadence was helping Harley into her saddle? He hoped not, because if so, he hadn't heard a single word she'd said.

"I am not certain what this 'kinesis' is, but I have been able to play instruments with my powers, so perhaps it is as you say? According to my mother, I am very good at two things: making noise and giving headaches." Dia laughed, and her horse tossed his head, the sound of jingling bells making the rest of them join in on the laughter.

Chapter Twenty-Three

Cadence

They'd been riding for an hour or so when, just as Yiannis said, the rain started. It was a slow, steady drizzle that soaked through their clothes and caught in their hair, and created a haze over the surrounding landscape.

Dia rode back among them and handed out simple cloaks of stout wool that made Cadence think of his mother's favorite winter coat. *It will stay warm, even when it's wet, Cay. It'll hold in your body heat.* She'd made him a scarf out of wool yarn that she insisted he wear even when it wasn't cold enough for a scarf, but she wasn't wrong about the wool. The cloak was a welcome cover with a deep hood that he pulled up over his already damp hair.

Each of the others gladly pulled their own cloaks around their shoulders, Harley having to bring her gray mare to a halt to do so. Cadence stopped his own horse to wait for her, but that meant they fell to the back of the group, Ximeno and Faustus slowing their mounts so they could bridge the distance as Harley finally got the garment settled and pulled the hood up around her head, shoving her curls up under it and out of her face.

"Ready?" Cadence said, and Harley met his eyes, then blushed.

"Yes. sorry." She lifted her reins and nudged her mare forward, and Cadence stifled a grin. Her second day of riding and she was doing great, all things considered, but it was still like seeing a very determined child do something that required all their attention.

Once she was next to him, he heeled his own mount forward, and Faustus let them pass him. Ximeno, waiting a little ahead, did the same so that the brothers returned to their places as rear guard.

Cadence gave them both a nod and nearly bit his tongue around the 'thanks' he started to say.

As they made their way down the road among the trees, Cadence swore he heard movement in the leaves and underbrush, but every time he looked, he saw nothing. After about the third time, he met Faustus's gaze. The sidhe was just turning to look at him, his brows furrowed.

"Do you hear that?" Cadence asked him.

"Hear what?" Harley asked beside him, but he didn't answer, his attention focused on Faustus and his brother beside him. Aoife and Leif were supposed to be scouting—they'd traded with the brothers just before the rain started—but if it were them, wouldn't they just have announced themselves?

"Yes." Faustus said and addressed his brother. "Informeu a Yiannis. Miraré darrere i tornaré aviat. No els deixeu quedar enrere." He didn't wait for Ximeno to nod before wheeling his horse and riding back down the road the way they'd come.

Ximeno pivoted in his saddle, and Cadence caught nervous tension in the warrior's face.

"My brother will return. Ride forward. I must tell Yiannis." The words came out clipped, and Cadence didn't argue, nudging his horse faster as Harley followed suit while Ximeno passed them along the side of the road toward where Yiannis rode at the head of the column.

"What's going on?" Jenta asked as they caught up.

"Faustus and I both saw something in the trees. Faustus is going to check it out, and Ximeno went to tell Yiannis."

"What did you see?" Chris asked.

"I'm not sure." Cadence shrugged. "Could have just been animals in the underbrush, but it didn't seem like it."

"Cay, look." Harley pointed up ahead of them, where a handful of fae stood to either side of the road as if they'd coalesced out of the trees and rain.

Yiannis had drawn his horse to a stop, and Ximeno was riding back to rejoin them as they heard Yiannis address the strange fae. He raised his hand and spoke, but Cadence couldn't make out what he said. The fae ignored him, turning instead to address Dia. Their leader spoke loudly, and in English. Cadence's skin ran cold at the words.

"Diaphony Song Breaker, we know who you ward. Give them over and you're free to continue on."

Cadence squinted through the rain, trying to see who'd spoken. The voice was masculine and rang with the authority of someone accustomed to being obeyed. The figure towered over the fae who flanked him, and Cadence immediately thought, *sidhe*. He had to be, but he was covered in a cloak similar to the ones they all wore, and his features were lost within the shadow of his hood.

Dia nonchalantly assessed the fae arrayed before them. "Since you ask so kindly to take on the escort of my wards, how could I deny you?" She pressed one hand to her chest in feigned startlement before continuing. "Oh, but surely, I would know the name of the hero who wishes to relieve me of this *arduous* task?"

Cadence wished he could get closer. Yiannis's hood moved and Cadence thought he must have said something, but Dia gave a ringing laugh and shook her head.

"Ah, it will not do, I am afraid. I do not lead this retinue and am informed it is not my decision. You will need to take it up with Yiannis. However, I would still know you, who seem to know me by simple sight. Tell me, is it the horse that gives me away?" Dia leaned forward in her saddle and patted the neck of her black and white stallion who tossed his head, the bells in his mane ringing through the trees.

The one who'd spoken stepped closer and pushed his hood back, tilting his face up so that drops caught on his cheeks and in the hair that pulled loose of his hood. He was definitely a sidhe, no guessing. His hair was so pale blond, Cadence would have called it white, and the face that shone out from among the damp tresses was like paper, and almost as blank.

Beside him, three other fae moved when he did, but there were still perhaps five or so more who stayed back, their heads down and hoods obscuring their features. Cadence peered at them, trying to figure out if he recognized any of them either from the palace or from one of the communities they'd passed through.

Ximeno rode up to them, taking a spot to Harley's right. The warrior gave Cadence a nod, then returned his attention to the forest around them. Cadence followed suit, surveying the forest on his side. While the tableau ahead of them was happening, the rustling among the trees continued. Now he saw shapes flitting from trunk to trunk, drifting closer to the road. He grabbed for his bow, stringing it quickly. He'd never shot from a horse but wasn't sure he was going to have time to dismount.

"Ximeno?" He said, his voice a question.

"Yes," was the answer he got back. The word dropped like a stone in the middle of everything.

As if the interchange had been some signal, the forest around them was suddenly alive with more cloaked figures, many of them holding bows already nocked but not yet aimed.

"Shit!" Chris said with feeling, and Cadence swallowed hard. He didn't dare look away, but he heard Dia speaking. Some of the figures stopped just off the edge of the road while others circled wide behind them onto the path to cut off their chance to back track. Where the hell was Faustus? Hell, where were Aoife and Leif? *It's like showing up for a game only to find half the team is out sick and the other half are all new players.*

"Cillian Red-Hand. If this is your way of attempting to win my affections, you've been misguided. Your father already spoke with mine, and the answer was no." Dia sounded angry, her voice thrumming in the air with her magic, and the hair on Cadence's arms rose. He reached for the quiver of arrows hanging from his saddle, lamenting that he hadn't had a chance to blood any. One of the figures near him shook its hooded head. Cadence let his hand settle near the quiver but not quite touching the arrows. Yet.

"Our fathers still speak on our behalf, Dia, but that does not determine my own private actions. As I say, give us the mortals. We do not wish to fight you and yours, but we will if you force us."

"What exactly are you planning to do with them?" Dia snapped, but a hint of confusion had crept in.

"Do not fight us, Dia. We have you surrounded and far outnumbered," Cillian answered, his voice sounding so reasonable, so confident.

"Cillian, if you persist, my answer will never be yes," Dia said. "Again, I ask. Why are you doing this?"

Something large passed through the shadows back among the trees, and at first, Cadence wondered if it was more fae coming to surround them. Shit, did they have more coming? The strange group, most of them still cloaked and hooded, outnumbered their group nearly three to one already. If this came down to a fight, could the sidhe get them out? They weren't even two days out from the palace, and Cristobal had been pretty emphatic about them being safe this close to the seat of the Seelie throne.

"You will say yes if your father wills it, and he will once I have been granted what I was promised. The Dark Lady is kind. Far kinder than you, my lady love." Cillian's tone was sneering. Cadence didn't dare check, but he could imagine a stupid, smug smile in need of a solid punch to the nose.

"You are a fool. Regardless of what she offered, we both know the only promise the Darkness keeps is death." Dia said the words almost like a benediction.

"So much for diplomacy," Chris said.

Cadence finally saw what had been in the shadows among the trees. A bear? Seriously? Like they didn't have enough trouble. The thing was tall enough that its shoulders brushed the lower branches of one of the trees, putting it at nearly five feet tall while on all fours, Cadence guessed.

They were completely surrounded, and Cadence was pretty sure they were all going to die.

Instead of answering, Cillian made a gesture. Cadence threw himself out of his saddle, grabbing Harley's arm as he dropped to the ground so that he pulled her down with him. There was a clatter of arrows hitting a hard surface, and Cadence waved Harley down to huddle next to her horse while he made a quick scan. They were surrounded by a circular wall of stone, but it was already dropping back toward the ground. A rough ring of arrows lay around them, having bounced off the shield and dropped to the ground or ricocheted back among the trees. Cadence reached for his quiver, slung it over his shoulder, and nocked an arrow before he stepped from around his horse.

The air filled with shouts, some of which quickly became screams. Cadence tried to ignore them, using the distraction to draw, aim, and fire at a hooded figure standing maybe twenty yards away. The fae still held their bow, but an arrow hung limp in their other hand. Cadence's arrow flew true and buried itself deep into their body, which whirled, dislodging the hood to expose a bald, gray-skinned face with sharp pointed ears, huge black eyes, and a mouth full of sharp teeth. It screamed and threw down the bow, then ran at him, only to be tackled by an enormous blond wolf that pressed it to the ground and bit hard onto its head, sending blood spurting in arcs to splash on the road and out into the trees.

The wolf pulled up, ripping the goblin in half and shaking its long muzzle, sending the goblin's head tumbling out into the leaves, the body still twitching on the ground as it tried to stand back up. The wolf clawed at it, dislodging flesh and limbs with great nails like butcher's hooks, then appeared to get bored and ran to tackle another fae.

Ximeno had also dismounted and was flexing his hand out, sometimes pointing, sometimes crooking a finger in a hooking gesture, and where he pointed or moved his hand, a long line of crackling chain lightning danced and jumped between the fae among the trees, sending them twitching and crashing to the ground to thrash and buck as the damp air added to the damage being done. Each fae touched was dropped to the ground, bodies twitching and giving off a mix of steam and smoke. Somehow, despite passing close by them, the lightning never hit a single tree.

The huge bear he'd seen was, much like the wolf, barreling from one of their enemies to another, ripping them apart with paws the size of Cadence's chest, throwing its head back to let out a bellow that raised the hair on his arms all over again. Nearly all of the attackers appeared to be goblins. Cadence shuddered, remembering what those foul beasts had done to him in dreams.

Harley and Jenta were crouched between the horses, gripping each other's hands and scanning around them. Cadence nocked another arrow and moved a little further out into the road, aimed, and shot again at a wiry goblin who was trying to sneak up on Yiannis who sat atop his horse still, directing a giant ball of water around in the air.

The arrow caught the goblin in the meat of its raised arm, and it let out a gargling bellow, then threw itself backward among the trees just as Yiannis hung the water ball in the air with a fae he'd caught still in it. The fae in the bubble floated and flailed, their clothing and hair floating around them.

Yiannis swiveled in his saddle and thrust one hand toward the fleeing goblin. Fluid burst out in a cloud, as what must have been all the water in its body was ripped out of it. It never even had time to scream. Cadence thought he might throw up. The goblin collapsed to the ground and went still, and Yiannis pivoted in his saddle to look at something or someone else nearby.

Cadence stood transfixed. If one of their attackers came up and tried to stab him, he wasn't sure he would have noticed. *What the fuck did I just see? Who* are *these guys?*

Christian

Someone was screaming off to his left. In front of him was the goblin he'd just hacked into pieces. He'd had to, so it would stop trying to attack him. Even now, the head laying partially on the bloody stump of its neck glared at him and tried to snap at him with broken teeth.

"What the actual fuck?" Chris said as he scowled down at the thing. "I'd say 'why won't you die?' but I already know the answer. Damn. I will say though, you're not so scary once I have my *own* weapon." He knelt and scrubbed his blade on the goblin's clothes, and contemplated blooding his blade here and now. *Tonight, definitely.* He was glad he'd thought to check the armory for things like a polishing cloth and a whetstone before leaving.

"Well done." Chris raised his head to find Faustus approaching him. The warrior carried his own sword naked in his hand, and Chris swallowed hard as Faustus approached him, the tip of his long, curved blade dripping brackish ichor in a trail behind him.

Faustus stopped closer than Chris would have liked and studied him with hooded eyes. Then the tall warrior raised his blade and Chris flinched as he waited for the blow, but the sword swiped past and behind him to stab into the goblin's disembodied hand, pinning it into the ground right next to Chris's leg. The tip of the sword dug deep into the loamy soil, and the goblin's fingers wiggled a little, then stopped moving.

Chris was panting and dizzy. What had he been thinking? Why would Faustus attack *him*?

Faustus, straightening, met Chris's panicked eyes with his own steely resolve. "I am not my father."

With that, he yanked the blade back out of the ground and ran it across a rag he'd grabbed off the goblin's body to clear off the worst of the viscera, then sheathed it in one clean motion. He gave Chris a slight nod, then continued in the direction of the screaming. The direction where Chris knew Dia and Yiannis were. Chris wondered if the one screaming was that sidhe, Cillian.

"Couldn't happen to a nicer guy." Chris said to himself as he followed Faustus.

Harlequin

The ground was covered with blood and body parts. Harley had already thrown up twice, but her stomach still churned like she's swallowed a washing machine stuck on the spin cycle. It was only a small blessing that a lot of the "blood" was more of a sludgy black goop. Goblin blood.

She'd seen Cadence shoot at least five arrows, and all of them found their targets. None of his hits had stopped any of the fae, which she could tell he found frustrating, but he'd provided good distraction and, in some cases, a warning when the goblin he shot cried out.

How many of their attackers had been shredded to pieces by the twins in their animal forms?

Yiannis and Dia had caught three of the non-goblin members of the group and were currently interrogating them. Harley didn't even try to approach. She could hear the screaming from where she waited, gripping her horse's reins.

She was mostly just trying not to feel like a burden. With no weapon other than her little belt dagger and no specific fighting skills, she'd stayed huddled near her mare, tucked in among the horses while Chris and Cadence faced off with the enemy, right alongside the sidhe. Her only consolation was that Jenta was right there with her, both of them gripping the reins of their mounts and watching for attackers despite knowing there was nothing they could do if they *did* see one.

Apparently, they needn't have worried.

"You guys did the right thing, staying with the horses. That was... chaos." Cadence said, his voice trembling a little as he caught his breath. "Faustus spotted them in the trees and threw up a shield to protect us from that first round of arrows. Aoife and Leif were only just coming back from ahead to report that they'd seen people moving in the woods when they saw them already attacking us, but Yiannis is pretty pissed at them. Seems they waited to finish their full circuit before turning around."

"Did Aoife say why they didn't come back?" Jenta asked, putting a hint of emphasis on the word "say". Harley couldn't really blame her. Aoife so far hadn't given her much reason to believe in her reliability, regardless of Dia's insistence to the contrary.

"Yeah. She claimed at first that she thought they were just foragers, but it wasn't until she met back up with Leif at their halfway arc and he said he'd spotted goblins among them." Cadence said. "I'm not sure how he would have seen them if they all had their hoods up, but maybe they didn't before they came out to surround us?"

Harley narrowed her eyes and pursed her lips. "Maybe, but it seems unlikely, doesn't it?"

"Yeah." Cadence answered. "It does."

Harley shrugged uncomfortably, the frustration coming back all at once. "I think I may ask Chris to show me how to do some of that knife work he talked about."

"Harley... You don't have to." Cadence started to reach out to her, then dropped his hand when her look hardened.

"I know that, but I *want* to." She squared her shoulders and let out a breath. "If this happens again, I want to feel like I can help." Cadence opened his mouth, but Harley snapped, "By doing more than just holding the reins of a bunch of horses."

Cadence held up his hand in surrender. "Fair enough."

Harley sighed, looking at the ground as she tried to recollect her composure. "I'm sorry. This was a lot."

Cadence reached out again, and when she didn't flinch, he gave her an awkward side hug. "I know. And I wish I could say this will be a one off..."

Harley hugged him back a little. "I know. It won't be."

In the silence that followed, Harley realized that the screaming had stopped. They must have finished with the interrogation. Or so she hoped.

Yiannis approached them from among the horses, Dia behind him looking somehow furious and pleased at the same time.

"Is everyone well?" he asked, assessing each of them. Chris was coming up from their right, Ximeno behind him. Aoife and Leif rode out of the trees. Leif's head was down but Aoife's face was red with indignation. When Yiannis glowered at her, though, she ducked to avoid meeting his gaze.

"Yeah, we're okay." Cadence said. "Wet, and a little shaken. How much longer until we reach the next village?"

Yiannis let out a relieved sigh. "Yes. It will be good for all of us to have a hot meal and a warm bed after this afternoon's... activities." He said 'activities' like they'd been out hawking instead of fending off attackers trying to kill or capture them. All the sidhe were taking the attack in stride, as if it was barely of consequence. *Is that what it's like to be immortal?*

Maybe it was that the four of them had already faced their own deaths at the hand of the Dark Queen or that all four of them had come into this with the understanding of the danger involved, but Harley was still really impressed with her friends. None of them ran, and all of them were still standing. *Let's hear it for resilient children.* If she hadn't still felt a bit ill, she might have laughed.

Yiannis peered up into the sky where gray clouds still hung suspended, but the rain was slacking off. That said, the air was still heavy with mist that settled onto them like a cold sheet..

"I would say perhaps another two hours of riding will see us to our stop for the night. We are close to Büyük Ağaç, the home of a good and long-time friend." Yiannis gestured for them to mount and made for his own horse at the front of the line. "Come. All is well, and all will be well."

Chapter Twenty-Four

Harlequin

After two days in the saddle, Harley had to agree with Cay that it *was* getting easier, but a lot of it might have to do with her mare. Whether Yiannis had known or not, the horse was perfect for her. She wondered if he'd be offended if she thanked him. Nonetheless, she was relieved when they slowed at the edge of Büyük Ağaç just after sunset.

Dia told them the name meant Great Tree. Harley decided that the name didn't do the place enough justice.

In the waning light, the streetlamps shone like beacons in the misty air. The lanterns were lit with strange, wispy orbs that hovered and bobbed within their little glass enclosures.

Trees loomed up over them, vast and shadowed, their branches spanning hundreds of feet in either direction. Part of Büyük Ağaç *was* the trees, some of which had doors set into their trunks and small structures tucked in at the branch junctions or hanging down from the branches by thick ropes and vines.

Yiannis led them down to a street that was almost as wide as Traveler's Way, and up a small slope into a gated courtyard. Here, stable hands rushed out to take the reins of their mounts which were led off to a brightly lit stable. Harley could barely feel her legs, and as she slid from her saddle, she gave an involuntary grunt of discomfort. *Is this what playing sports is like? Everything hurts.* Was this what Cadence felt like, when playing football? She rubbed at her aching muscles and decided that if they got back, Cadence was getting a gift card for a massage for his birthday.

She handed off her reins to a small fae with a pointed, feline face wearing only loose trousers belted by a thick woven cord. His chest had a fine layer of gray fur, and his hands only contained three fingers and a thumb, each tipped with a set of retractable claws instead of nails. When he smiled, he flashed delicate fangs.

A booming voice echoed across the courtyard, and the fae grinned wider, then gave her a minute bow before trotting off with her horse following sedately behind. Harley found the rest of the party was already facing the trunk of an enormous tree, and the huge fae approaching them.

He was at least as tall as Yiannis but broad-shouldered and barrel-chested with legs like a bull, ending at hooves the size of hubcaps. His skin was a deep forest green and immense black ram's horns curled up out of his head then back to wrap around the tips of long, pointed ears. His hair was thick and dark, and a heavy beard hung down his chest in a multitude of braids adorned with small charms.

"Theortian Hianius Murhai! Xush kelibsiz, do'stim! Ah, sizni bu eski ko'zlar bilan ko'rgan ma'qul. Ammo qarang! Kimni olib keldingiz? Siz kutganlar shularmi? Men ularga qarayman!"

"Orman iyesi, Iltimos ingliz tilida gapiring. Allow me to introduce Cadence, Christian, Jenta, and Harlequin."

"Ah! Of course, my friend! Of course!" He stopped a few long steps in front of them and turned toward their group. Harley stood behind

Cadence and Chris, waiting, as kind, dark eyes moved over them, taking them all in. "And to you, welcome! Children of Adem, be welcome to my home. I am honored!"

He held a staff like a walking stick, thick and knobby with a glass orb the size of a bowling ball at the top that glowed with a warm green light. When he gave a sweeping bow with a flare of his cloak for emphasis, the staff bobbed toward them, and Harley could just make out a chestnut floating in the center of the orb.

The enormous fae straightened and adjusted his cloak back in place, revealing small animals huddled around his feet, hidden previously among the folds of fabric. Two broad snakes' heads sat just above his shoulders, regarding them, and small birds were perched along his horns like living ornaments.

Yiannis gestured towards the green man. "Mortals, this is Orman Iyesi. A longtime friend, and well in the making." A broad grin split his face as he addressed the towering fae. "Might we join you in repast? I could do with somewhat out of those casks you had last time I was about."

Orman threw his head back and laughed, a warm sound that set the birds in the trees around them to chirping. "Of course, my friend! Come, come! Be welcome in my home. Let us adjourn, and we will share in the breaking of bread, this night."

With a flourish of his massive cloak, Orman led them toward the trunk of a tree so large that the edges of it were lost among the smaller trees and outbuildings in the gloaming darkness.

Chris, walking behind her, gave a laugh and said "Great tree, huh? Maybe they should have called it "The biggest, most insane looking tree you've ever seen in your life."

"Naw. That would never fit on a signpost." Cadence said, grinning.

"You've obviously never seen the names of some of the towns in New Zealand." Harley replied.

"Or Iceland." Jenta added.

They laughed, and it felt strange but also a relief after the attack. Harley's smile slipped a little at the thought.

"Hey, you okay?" Cadence bumped her shoulder with his.

"Huh? Oh, yeah. Just… still processing today." Harley answered.

"Yeah. I don't think I ever expected to use archery the way I did, today." He ducked his head a little, embarrassed.

"Do you regret it?" Harley asked sincerely.

Cadence took a moment before responding. "No. No, I don't think I do."

"Good." Harley said and tucked her arm in his. Cadence smiled at her, and Harley couldn't help but smile back.

Christian

The doors leading into the great tree had to be at least three stories tall and were still dwarfed by the tree itself. He gazed up and up into the hollowed out tree trunk whose interior footprint was easily the size of a city block.

Growing up out of the middle of the floor was an old, gnarled yew tree. Its branches spread out wide and high but still didn't touch the inside walls of the outer trunk. Lanterns hung among the limbs of the yew like giant glass fireflies, and the ground beneath the branches was grassy and soft, laid out with rugs and blankets strewn with pillows.

Everywhere Orman Iyesi stepped, small flowers blossomed at his feet. His hooves, instead of leaving a deep imprint in the loam, sprouted small rings of blossoms and new shoots with bright green leaves and tightly furled buds. Small creatures frolicked around his legs and up into his cloak, ignored by the snakes on his shoulders.

They were ushered to the blankets and bid to sit, then served a meal made up mostly of vegetarian offerings. Most notable to him were a porridge that was warm and thick, dappled with nuts and dried fruit and sweetened with a spicy honey with little red and brown flecks, and a salad of fresh greens and sliced berries that burst when he bit into them, releasing a wave of juice. A small fae child came and offered Chris, Jenta, Harley, and Cadence a plate of grilled mushroom tops, drizzled with a green sauce that smelled sharp and sweet at the same time.

The four of them sat on their own blanket, brightly colored and soft under their hands. Orman and Yiannis sat on their own blanket not far away, speaking while everyone dined, though the green man occasionally shot glances toward them, as if he were inspecting something curious and wonderful. The sidhe warriors settled to the other side of the pair, seemingly determined to keep a reverent distance from the large horned man.

Dia came to their blanket and sat down with her own bowl of porridge.

"I thought I would come check on you all. This day's ride was obviously not as... pleasant as yesterday's. Are you all feeling well?"

"Are *you* okay, Dia?" Jenta asked sincerely.

Dia considered Jenta for a moment before answering, but ultimately gave a small nod. "I am. Cillian thought himself guaranteed to my favor simply due to his position in the court. I believe he expected my father to say yes without hesitation to his father's proposal, and when he did not..." Dia shook her head sadly. "I am sad he felt such desperation, but Cillian was never one to accept 'no' as a final answer, regardless of who was saying it, except perhaps from the queen, herself. He was promised power to influence my father, and assumed it was already his to call. Instead, what he has gained is the task of regrowing his limbs."

She appeared unphased by her own statement, but Harley paled and Chris, who had just stuck a spoon full of porridge into his mouth had to stop from spitting it out. Sadly, he also couldn't bring himself to swallow it.

Dia took another bite of her own porridge as if she hadn't just mentioned dismembering someone who was still alive to feel it. After a couple bites, she tapped her spoon on the edge of her bowl and asked, "Other than that, are you all well? I want to reiterate that we are safe, here. Orman Iyesi is a powerful ally, and while Büyük Ağaç is not Comhaontu, it is still considered a neutral place, and Orman takes the care of his guests very seriously."

Chris finally swallowed the porridge and mumbled, "M'mm guhwd," around a bite of mushroom.

Dia peered at him, then at Cadence. "Was that some new mortal language?"

Cadence toasted her with his bowl of salad. "Not technically, no. It was 'mouth-full-ese' for 'I'm good,' I think. I don't know about them, but that cloak definitely came in clutch for me."

Harley and Jenta were both nodding before he finished, and Chris finished swallowing just to talk over them as they all said "yes" and "yes" to his "sure, yeah."

Harley leaned forward and gazed past Dia to the blanket where Orman Iyesi had just started laughing, a jolly sound that filled the hollow tree and sent more birds to tittering. "Dia, who is he? I mean, besides an old friend of Yiannis's?"

Dia glanced behind her at the green man, and when she turned back, her expression was admiring. "Orman Iyesi is legendary, even among us. It is said that his power allows him to travel openly between the realms to any green, uninhabited place. He was once well known among mortals as one of Danann's liaisons. I did not know before today that this was where we would be staying or that Yiannis knew him."

"Will we all be staying in the same room, again?" Jenta asked. Harley gave her a funny look. Jenta shrugged and shot Harley a grin. "It's not my fault your feet are cold. I'd rather not wake up feeling like my legs are going to fall off."

Dia laughed, and Harley scowled. "No, you will have your own room, here. Rooms have been set aside for us, and when you are ready, simply find one of the small fae who live here, and they will guide you to a nest for the night."

Before any of them could respond, Dia raised back to her feet in one smooth motion and made her way over to the blanket where Yiannis and Orman had cracked a cask of something that was already giving Yiannis a rosy complexion and an irrepressible grin.

"She keeps doing that." Cadence grumbled.

"I'm sorry, did she just say 'nest?'" Harley said.

Aoife and Leif approached with Ximeno and Faustus close behind them, carrying a small cask of their own. Their cheeks were rosy, and like Yiannis, they couldn't seem to keep the smiles off their faces as they stopped at the edge of the blanket. Aoife dropped into an easy crouch on her heels in front of them. "Would any of you be interested in joining us for a bit of mead? It is good and sweet, and we've plenty." She gestured at Leif who hefted the little wooden barrel in his arms as if it were a child.

Harley and Cadence looked at each other, then at Chris and Jenta. Chris waved his hand before they could say anything. "Go. Drink, be merry."

Jenta appeared to study him, her expression unreadable, then she nodded at Harley. "Same for me. You kids have a good time, okay?"

Harley studied him, then Jenta, and Chris couldn't help feeling like he must be missing something, but then she was up, grabbing Cadence by the hand and dragging him to his feet to follow the four tall sidhe over to another blanket.

Suddenly, they were alone for the first time in two days. Chris sat cross-legged, his forearms resting on his knees as he regarded Jenta, wondering if he should say something, or just keep his mouth shut. Last time he'd opened it with good intentions, he'd just ended up eating his foot, boot and all.

Jenta cleared her throat, and said "You were pretty impressive, today. With that sword, I mean." Chris opened his mouth then closed it, not really sure how to respond. He tried to keep his expression neutral, but he must have failed, because Jenta's face flushed. "What? Why are you looking at me like that?" She said, defensively, and Chris's pulse sped up. *Say something, dummy! You're doing it, again!*

"I... Jenta... Fuck. I mean... Okay." Chris took a deep breath and sat up straight. Jenta tensed even as he shifted himself to focus more directly on her.

In the same moment, they opened their mouths and spoke.

"Look, I'm sorry."

"Chris, I owe you an apology."

Chris blinked. They stared at each other for a moment, then spoke over each other again.

He said, "*You* owe *me* an apology?" Just as she blurted, "Wait, why are *you* sorry?"

Chris barked a bitter laugh, and Jenta clapped a hand over her mouth, looking like she was ready to be angry. He held up his hands and caught her gaze.

"Jenta, I'm sorry. Both for the other morning, and because I didn't mean to laugh. It doesn't matter how good my intentions were when I was trying to help you, yesterday. I should have just asked if you wanted my help, instead of assuming you *needed* it. And I'm sorry if I hurt your shoulder. I'm not always great at... well..." He gestured between them.

Jenta let out her own surprised laughter. "What, people-ing? Yeah, me neither." She shook her head, and her smile faded as she continued. "Thank you, but I also owe you an apology. I know you were just trying to help. I reacted badly in the moment, but you were right. The voice I was hearing wasn't mine." She extended her hand out, offering it to him. "Truce?"

Chris smiled, took her hand, and shook it. "Truce."

"Good." Her face broke into a broad grin, and she leaned back on her hands. "Listen, I feel like we kinda got off on the wrong foot. Hi, I'm Jenta. I think we have some of our classes together. What's your name?"

Chris laughed, and the tightness in his chest eased. "Hey, Jenta. I'm Chris. Nice to meet you. You've got some solid style." Today's outfit was a little more classic Jenta, as far as he was concerned—Black jeans and a pair of well-worn black boots, a comfortable-looking black t-shirt over a mesh long sleeve shirt, and a plain black leather collar.

She glanced down at herself then grinned up at him. "Thanks. My mom hates it." And all of a sudden, they were both laughing, and the tension that had been knotted up between his shoulders for the last two days nearly disappeared.

As their laughter subsided, Chris surveyed their surroundings, causing Jenta to do the same. "So, Jenta, what do you make of all this?

"Honestly? I think it's fucking weird." They shared a moment of quiet consternation.

"I know we agreed to go of our own free will, and we knew shit could and most likely *would* get a bit weird, but I feel like I'm less impacted by the fight on the road than I am by where I am, right now. Maybe because I've had my share of violence, and at some point, that just kinda stops feeling different... But this? There's nothing like this, back home. We're sitting in a tree the size of the Sears tower." Chris leaned forward on his forearms, picking at the blanket.

Jenta scoffed. "Yeah. I think if you'd asked me about this shit a week ago, I would have asked what drugs you were on, and why you weren't sharing. But now, I just wish I'd read even half the books Harley has. Maybe then some of this stuff would make more sense."

"I keep trying to remind myself that it's real; that I'm not having some crazy fever dream." Chris frowned toward the big yew, but not really seeing it. "Not even just that, though."

"Worried about your sister?" Jenta asked, her voice gentle.

Chris blinked and flushed, and wondered if Jenta registered just how much she affected him. "Yeah. I just wish I knew what was happening to her, you know? Or if she's okay. I know we can't move any faster than we are, but the longer this takes, the more worried I am that what I'll get back won't be her."

He felt a soft touch on the back of his hand. Jenta was leaned forward, touching his hand with the tips of her fingers. The touch became a grip as she held his gaze with hers. "She'll be okay, Chris. We have to keep thinking that, no matter what. She'll be okay, and we'll get her back, okay? You just have to keep thinking happy thoughts."

She gave his hand a squeeze, then let go and leaned back on her hands.

Chris tried to give her a smile, but it turned out lopsided and weak. "Sure thing, Tink."

Jenta rolled her eyes but grinned back at him. "I think I'd rather be one of the lost boys."

Chris looked at her seriously, then at their surroundings again. "I'm pretty sure we already are."

Chapter Twenty-Five

Jenta

The room had quieted over the last hour. Jenta saw Ximeno and Faustus headed up the broad flight of stairs that wound around the inner wall of the great tree, and Harley and Cay were both gone, presumably also to find rooms. Yiannis and Orman Iyesi still sat on their blanket, talking quietly with their heads bent together.

Some of the fae who'd dined with them were curled up on the soft grass or leaned up against the trunk of the central tree, their heads lolling. The ache of exhaustion washed over her, and she spoke to Chris, still sitting on the blanket with her.

"I don't know about you, but I'm going to get some sleep." She rose, dusting herself off. To one side of the atrium, she spotted one of the fae standing near a doorway. He was small, maybe only up to her waist, and wore a strange sort of hat woven of reeds and grass with a tall crown and a wide brim that flopped about his shoulders. She made her way to him, catching his eye.

"Excuse me?" She said the words clearly but quietly, afraid to startle him. He had rabbit's feet poking out from the bottoms of his baggy trousers, his face was slightly pointed, his nose flat so that it almost blended into his fuzzy cheeks, and he had the tips of two long front teeth peeking out from between his thin lips. Everything about him said *skittish*.

"Hm? How'm'ep?" He looked up at her quizzically. His eyes were wide and round, cinnamon-colored pools with big, black pupils.

It took her a moment to figure out what he'd said. At least, she hoped it was what he said. She couldn't think of any other language that would sound like 'how may I help?' so she tried her luck. "Um... Could you show me where I can sleep?"

"Hm? Oh. Yep'mhm!" He gave one quick nod then a wave of a paw-like hand. When he turned, Jenta saw that the hat had no top, revealing a pair of long ears with tufted tips.

He took her up the same staircase Ximeno and Faustus had taken. The stairs were wide and deep, seemingly made for longer legs than hers, and the little fae took a couple hopping steps for every stair they cleared. He checked to make sure she was still following him at the first landing then led her out one of the archways onto a wide branch with a path worn into it. Just to her left outside the door, there was a tiny woven hut with a rope coming out of the top of it. The other end of the rope disappeared up into the darkness. The little fae pointed to the hut.

Jenta contemplated the little building skeptically. It was only just tall enough for her to stand in, and maybe only wide enough from side to side for her to sit down, but no way she would be able to lay down comfortably in the thing. Not to mention, there was no pillow or blanket or, in fact, *anything* in the tiny little building.

"Are you sure?" She asked, unable to keep the doubt out of her tone.

The little fae looked at her, then at the hut, then back at her. He smiled and pointed at the hut again. Jenta sighed, shrugged, and stepped into the tiny hut. He got in behind her, then reached up next to the inside of the door and pulled a string which rang a small bell mounted in the woven branches of the hut's roof.

The hut lurched and shifted, then started going up. The branch dropped away below them, and they rose up into the tree's canopy. When the little hut stopped, they were at a much smaller branch, though still incredibly wide. This branch had railings along one side, and when she stepped out after the little fae, she saw that there were large, woven baskets like covered birds' nests the size of cars all along the branch on either side. A couple had lights shining from within, including the one she was led to.

The door was really a curtain of vines, currently drawn to one side. The room within was small and circular—just tall enough for her to stand with hunched shoulders—with a bed piled up with blankets and pillows on one side and a little bench seat to the other. On the bench seat, she spotted her saddlebags. Hanging from the center of the room was a small glass ball filled with fireflies that was cradled up toward the ceiling in more woven branches.

The little fae pointed to a small stick hung on the wall, and then at the lantern. The stick had a little hook on one end, and she could just make out a loop on the upper portion of the ball. To turn off the light, all she needed to do was release the fireflies.

Jenta started to say, "thank you," then stopped herself. "This is wonderful. Just what I needed."

His thin mouth split into a grin, showing even more of those little buck teeth. He gave her a small wave and a little bow, and then he was gone, out the door and into the night.

Jenta was suddenly completely alone for the first time in days. She made sure the curtain was closed, changed into a big baggy tee-shirt that hung down to her knees, and curled up under the blankets. She could just reach the hooked stick from the bed, using it to pop the latch and let the top of the lantern swing open.

She was asleep before all the fireflies had flown away.

Jenta stood in one of the dungeon rooms, her heart racing. Screams and cries echoed in the distance, but this room was empty except for a small table.

She froze, waiting, but nothing happened. No pain came. No one hissed threats in her ears. No hands groped at her. Jenta inspected herself and found she was fully dressed, standing free without chains or ropes holding her. She tried to calm her pulse as she let herself really *see* where she was.

The walls were damp with mold, and only one lone torch guttered and hissed, giving off scant light. It hung from a ring on the wall to her left, the smoke curling up toward the ceiling and the flame dancing in a draft. The table in front of her was plain wood and sat on an otherwise bare stone floor. Placed just so on its surface were a tawse, a flog, a set of padded clips, a short riding crop, and a small, flat leather-bound case.

The table and all the things on it were filthy, blood-stained versions of the pristine ones that Jonathon kept in his collection. She suddenly had to know if the case had the same things inside, too. One hand reached out hesitantly to lift the lid up. A set of various sized blades glinted dully in the torchlight. The only clean thing in the room, the blades were all sharpened to a keen edge.

"Brand new in the package," she whispered to herself.

"Oh God. Who's there? Help me... Please, don't do this." The voice was broken and piteous, hoarse from screaming.

Jenta's head came up.

A Saint Andrew's Cross hung against the wall on the far side of the room, like the one she'd been strapped to in her first dream. This time, someone *else* was mounted to it. They were blindfolded but otherwise naked.

Jenta heard a whisper and felt a soft brush of breath against her cheek, but when she spun toward the shadows in the far side of the room to her right, no one was there. The voice caressed over her, raising gooseflesh along her skin and a shudder from her lips. *"He may be yours for eternity if you so wish it. My gift to you."*

Jenta turned back to the guy hanging from the Saint Andrew's cross. His back was crisscrossed with red raised welts and cuts that dribbled out small liquid garnets of blood when he moved. She hadn't let herself recognize him at first. She said his name, barely more than a whisper, but he heard her. "Jonathon."

"Jenta?"

Jenta sat bolt upright in the bed, her heart pounding in her ears. A wave of nausea hit her, and she rushed off the bed and through the curtain, tripping and measuring her height along the path. She moved her head and vomited off the side of the branch, her gaze swimming as she blinked away tears and goggled down at the drop below her.

She lay there, feeling the night wind brush across her back and whip through her hair. It was still mostly dark, but the predawn light was just touching these upper branches. *Fair enough*, she thought. She didn't know if she'd be able to go back to sleep if she tried.

Pushing herself up to all fours, she looked around, then got back to her feet using the small railing. She made her way back to her room and pulled the little cat dagger from its place at the bottom of her saddle bags. Gripping the sheathed weapon tightly in both hands, she curled up on the low bench, pushing herself hard against the woven wall, as if she could meld herself into the branches. She sat with the little cat dagger in her lap, and waited for the sun to come up.

Chapter Twenty-Six

Christian

The tree bustled with activity as they gathered in the courtyard. The sidhe present all appeared well rested and jovial, the smiles and easy manner from the night before clinging to even stoic Faustus. He hadn't seen Yiannis yet, and wondered how late he'd been up, talking with Orman.

Harley and Cadence came up to him, moving in companionable silence. Despite knowing they had all been drinking, there were no apparent signs of hangover like he usually saw from his mother.

Jenta led her buckskin out from the stables while he was still waiting for the stable hand who'd run off for his mount. How long had she been up to get to the stables before any of them even made it to the courtyard? She exuded exhaustion, her eyes hollow and shadowed. He started to make his way toward her, just as the stable hand appeared with his horse, followed closely by another leading Harley's and Cadence's. Even so, Chris started to walk toward her again when raised voices drew everyone's attention back to the great tree.

"I am truly sorry, my friend, but I cannot. You, of all, would know that it is not *my* will, but Tengri's that grants me dominion. I cannot use the gift of my stewardship in this manner." Orman and Yiannis were making their way across the courtyard. Yiannis looked disappointed to the edge of anger as Orman spoke. Chris surveyed them out of the corner of his eye as he checked over his mount.

"*Will* not, you mean." Yiannis' voice was a frustrated growl, the sound of waves crashing against a cliff face.

"Very well, Hianius. *Will* not." Orman sighed heavily and folded his hands in front of him, not responding to the anger in Yiannis' voice.

"Orman, Danann is in this journey. Surely, they would agree that using such a gift to reduce the time and distance between ourselves and our goal is good sense."

"So you say, and I say if Tengri is in the journey, then the full journey is the one you must make. Hianius, you have heard as I have spoken. I will not do this thing. You have had my sorrow; I shan't repeat it and make it a lie."

"Fine. Then we ride." Yiannis turned his back on Orman who watched him with sad eyes before directing his attention to Chris. Chris couldn't keep the concern out of his expression. Orman gave him a smile, though it didn't quite chase the sadness out of his eyes. He made his way to Chris and Cadence who waited by their horses.

"Ah! Youth is wasted on the young! Well, my thanks to you for joining us, and for alighting among my branches like birds of good omen." He clapped them each on the shoulder with large, thick-fingered hands. A multitude of birds perched and sang from his horns, and a group of tiny, winged fae sat on his shoulders, all waving happily in farewell.

Chris and Cadence grinned and swept slightly more practiced bows than the ones they'd given the queen. Orman's eyes lit up and he laughed, a rich sound that sent the fae launching from his shoulders to dance in the air around him, adding their laughter to his. Glittering dust drifted from their quickly beating wings, coating his dark hair in a fine sheen that glinted in the morning sun.

"Ah, Well done! Well done!" Orman clapped his hands.

Yiannis's voice cut through the air, a vein of anger still present. "Warriors, mount up. We ride."

"Ah, that will be you as well." Orman Iyesi's expression became serious though a happy twinkle still shone in his eyes "Ride well and come back for rest when your journey is through."

He stepped back, giving room for them to mount. Chris and Cadence pulled themselves up into their saddles and gave Orman a wave as they joined the rest of the group. Harley and Jenta were already mounted and talking quietly nearby, so rode with them behind the sidhe who were already falling in behind Yiannis at the courtyard gates.

Once outside Büyük Ağaç, the trees and underbrush swallowed them up in leaf-covered arms. The canopy of branches reached out over the road, and they moved through green, shifting light that danced in the air and speckled the ground. As with the previous day, Aoife and Leif took the first round of scouting, splitting off and disappearing into the trees around them. Their mounts picked such careful paths among the underbrush that the direction they'd gone was barely visible after they vanished among the green.

Faustus and Ximeno, in surprisingly good spirits, struck up a song between them made up of interwoven harmonies and a small hand drum Ximeno had pulled from his saddle bags.

Meanwhile, Yiannis rode ahead of them, his head down and his expression fierce. Dia tried to ride with him, but after he snapped at her for a third time, she let her horse drop back to ride among them like she'd done the first day, a worried look on her face. It was strange to see her frowning as her horse pranced in front of him, the bells in the horse's mane jingling like a parade pony.

Chris let his own horse drop back so he rode next to Ximeno, and pointed at the little drum. "Does it have a name?"

Ximeno looked at him, confused. "A name? It is a drum."

Chris shook his head. "No, sorry, I mean, what kind of drum is it?"

Ximeno laughed and offered it to him. "It is the drum kind of drum, young mortal. Would you try?"

Chris shrugged, then reached over for the instrument. It was maybe as wide as the span from the tip of his thumb to the tip of his pinky, if he stretched them to either side, with deep sides, and a hole to grip the edge without disrupting the stretched animal skin head.

Once he was holding it like he'd seen Ximeno do, the sidhe pointed at the drum, then held up his hand in a loose fist, with only his thumb and pinky a little extended. He wiggled his hand back and forth. "You see? Like this."

Chris held his hand in the same position, and once Ximeno gave him a nod of approval, he tried beating on the drum. It felt awkward, and his thumb kept brushing the edge, dampening the sound. He handed the drum back to Ximeno. "That's hard, dude."

"Noooo. Practice." Ximeno took the drum back and showed Chris how to hold it— his grip on the rim, and the angle of his wrist—then showed his hand movements. Then he handed the drum back to Chris.

"Try again."

Chris really let himself consider Ximeno. This wasn't the stoic, pinch-faced rider who'd left the palace with them. Just past him, Faustus was surveying the road ahead, but he wore a small smile and was humming quietly.

Chris shrugged and took back the drum, then held it up in his hand to show Ximeno.

"Move your thumb." Chris adjusted his hand a little, and Ximeno grinned. "Just so."

Chris held up his other hand in that strange loose position that made him think of a limp-wristed surfer's sign, and Ximeno gave him another small nod.

The sidhe held his own hands out, pretending he was holding his own drum, and put his playing hand into position, so Chris could match it. He started playing again and while it was still awkward, it was definitely easier, and he found his thumb wasn't bumping the edge anymore.

Shortly after they'd started, Aoife and Leif came riding back from their scouting. Chris tried to hand the drum back, but Ximeno pushed it at him, and just said "practice" with a grin before he rode off with his brother. Chris was starting to wonder if the quiet brothers simply didn't speak English as fluently as the other sidhe. Ximeno's speech was heavily accented, though with what language, Chris wasn't about to guess.

He grinned, and continued to play with the little drum as he rode. Meanwhile, Harley had been trying to get Dia to talk while Ximeno showed him the drum, and Chris pretended to be fully focused on how his fingers were working against the well-worn leather as he listened.

"Dia, please just tell us what happened. You're not the only ones on this journey." Harley said, exasperated.

Dia sighed, looking defeated. "You are right. Yiannis seems determined to keep you all ignorant, as if that will protect you from harm, but you are not babes in swaddling. As I said last night, one of Orman's greatest gifts from Danann is his ability to move to any uninhabited green space. Yiannis had hoped Orman would take us to the far side of the Expanse, perhaps even straight to the Bastion of Night. Orman refused him."

"Maybe Orman's power just doesn't work that way." Harley said, skeptically.

Dia was already shaking her head. "That is why Yiannis is angry. He knows Orman is capable of doing this thing."

"*Knows*? How?" Cadence said, fascinated.

"In the past, Orman Iyesi often ferried groups both large and small, mortal and immortal, to and from the Great Tree." Dia said, and she almost smiled, like she was thinking of some fond memory.

"Okay, so then why won't he take us, now?" Chris asked.

"He believes that part of your task *is* the journey, so says Danann, and Orman Iyesi will not gainsay the message he was given, for whatever that means."

"Oh. I guess I can't really begrudge him if he's going on what his faith says is right." Cadence said, though his tone belied the thought.

Dia grunted. "I suppose. Yiannis tried to argue that you are touched by Danann, and so how could Danann argue with something that helps you? But Orman does not see it that way."

"I don't know if I want to know what that means—that he says we're touched by Danann. Or do you think he was just trying to bluff to get Orman to take us?" Chris asked.

"Don't you remember what he said in the inn?" Cadence said. "They can see us. Not just 'us,'" and he picked at his clothes, "but *us*." He pointed at his head.

Chris shrugged uncomfortably.

Dia glanced at them. "It is not so simple a discussion as that, and it is not as if you glow with pixie dust, but the point remains: instead of being able to cut out three, perhaps four days' worth of travel, avoiding the dangers of the Wildes, and depositing us at her bastion with surprise in our favor, we must continue as we began."

Chapter Twenty-Seven

Harlequin

T he trees around them thinned out as they rode, and traffic along
Traveler's Way started to pick up. Yiannis drew them to one side so
that they rode in a nearly single file line, leaving a clear swath of hard packed
dirt for those coming from the opposite direction. Harley couldn't help
but wonder whether it was because of the rain stopping, or if it was that
people living closer to the Seelie palace just didn't move around as much.
Maybe they didn't need to. The town that hugged the palace walls and
the large community—Harley felt like it might have been too big to call
a village, but too small to call it something larger—where they'd stopped
that first night both seemed pretty self-sufficient, but the further out and
away they got, the smaller the groupings of buildings became, the more
agrarian their populous, and yet more frequent their appearances.

Regardless, every time she met a scrutinizing gaze, Harley's skin
twitched. She felt nervous and jumpy after the attack the previous day, and
the number of strangers they passed seemed to increase exponentially as
they continued along the road to Comhaontu.

Yiannis insisted that the scouts continue to circle around the settlements they passed. Despite Dia's attempt to point out the dangers, he seemed convinced that yesterday's attack was more about Cillian's poor decision making than it was about the actual likelihood of pursuers. He'd pointed out, too, that an ambush was surely unlikely near the edges of the villages where folk might come to aid them. Harley couldn't help but think he would have seen Dia's logic if he hadn't already been upset about Orman Iyesi's refusal.

Around mid-morning, the group was just coming up on a large hamlet and Yiannis sent the scouts off, while the rest of them continued on. Traveler's Way was deserted for the first time all morning with just the six of them on the road as they approached an overturned cart.

A man, the owner of the cart, Harley guessed, poked at a broken axle as they approached. He was big and broad shouldered, with thick goat legs and horns that stuck out over long folded ears to either side of his head. He had a tangled beard of dark brown hair that joined up with that on the top of his head to create a frizzy mane around a face like an old Billy goat, right down to the strange sideways slitted eyes, and his hands each only had two fingers and a thumb.

"Ho. Haail. Good Lords and Laaaasses, might an old faaarmer get a haaand o'help?" He pointed one of those knobby fingers at the axle, and said "Me aaaaxle is broke, seeee? I'd fiiiix it me'self, but not enough haaaaands." He held up his two hands and grinned, showing a row of long bottom teeth and one thick top ridge of gums. Harley just stopped herself from laughing. Every time he said a long vowel, he bleated like a sheep. *Or a goat.*

Yiannis dismounted, but gestured for Dia to stay with them. He approached the cart, while the farmer stepped aside, giving him a wide berth. Harley wondered if the farmer also noticed Yiannis exuding disgruntlement. "I assume you have a spare axle in your cart?" he said to the farmer as he passed him.

Something felt off about the scene, but Harley couldn't figure out what. Something seemed to be missing. Then it struck her. *Where is the horse, or something to pull the cart? Surely, he hadn't been pulling it, by himself.* There was nothing spilled out behind the cart. Harley opened her mouth to say something to Dia, then hesitated. Maybe he'd been coming from the little hamlet beyond, where he'd just sold off everything including his horse? He did look a bit worse for wear...

The farmer shot a fearful glance at the rest of them, wringing his big hands, then said, "Much thaaanks, good Lord. Ye maaaay be wantin' the heeeelp of yer second, though, aye?"

The moment the words were out of the farmer's mouth, his eyes went wide. As Yiannis spun toward him, he put his big hands in the air and backed himself toward the edge of the road.

From the field to their right, a loud call went up. A net was thrown over Harley's head and she was yanked from her saddle, too startled to scream. She heard Jenta's panicked yelp, and Cadence and Chris both shouted "Hey!" before Harley heard them also being dragged off their horses.

Harley's shoulder exploded with pain as she landed, and one of her hips might have gotten dislocated in the fall. She was dizzy and her glasses were knocked askew so she couldn't see much besides the dust being kicked up around her by the milling horses. All she could think was *please, God, don't let them step on me. Please, don't let me die here.*

The net holding her started moving, dragging her along the ground. Even with the thick ropes buffeting her from the rough ground, she could feel rocks and scree pulling at her clothing and tearing at her skin, her body being bounced and jounced along the hard-packed track. Her joints ached with every bump, and Harley let out little involuntary yelps as she thumped gracelessly, clearing the road and getting swallowed up by the tall grass of the field.

I am with you. Help comes.

Nearby, she could hear Jenta fighting to free herself. Harley tried to roll herself over but couldn't seem to get enough momentum. The net stopped for just a moment, and she threw herself over with as much force as she could get. To her other side, nearly within arm's reach, she saw another goat-man fae standing over Cadence, a pitchfork in his grip held ready to stab down.

"*CADENCE!*" She screamed his name just as the fork's prongs came rushing at him.

A spearhead jabbed forward, catching between the tool's tines. Then Leif was driving the spear shaft up and forward, stabbing it into the goat-man's chest, making him drop the pitchfork. Harley's hip flared and her vision went white as the thick wooden handle thudded against her leg, jarring the joint. Then she was moving again, as her net was dragged further off into the field.

"Help! Help me! Leif, Dia, Yiannis! Fuck!" The swear came out and startled Harley into her own silence, but it also gave her a moment of clarity. She was still being pulled across the ground, bumping against every rock and lump on the ground, but she wasn't moving fast. She rolled onto her back and used her free hand to draw the dagger from her belt, trying not to slit her own leg or side as she pulled it free. Her shoulder protested and her arm ached and fought her, but she was able to get a hold of the net and seat the blade against the rope.

The dagger, for all it wasn't very big, was incredibly sharp and made short work of the rough spun cords that made up the net, until it was open enough above her that she could push the ropes to either side, leaving her laying on the remains of it rather than being cocooned.

Harley tried to sit up, but whoever was dragging her started picking up speed. She had to be nearly halfway across the field, by now, and could hear more fighting behind her, back toward the road. *Get off the net, Harley. You can do this.* She tried to sheath the dagger, but it was no use. Instead, she held it up above her head in her good hand and, gathering as much of her strength as she could, threw herself to her left, using the momentum of her good leg and arm to keep herself rolling until she cleared her limbs free of the frayed ropes.

She came to a stop in cool dirt, surrounded by tall grass, and above her was nothing but a clear sky with big fluffy clouds. Harley lay for a moment, trying to catch her breath. Her entire left side was one big throbbing ache from shoulder to shin. She wondered if she'd be able to sit up, or if she should even try.

The decision was made for her. The grass near her head rustled, and then there was another goat-man peering down at her. Before she could let herself think about it, she swung her dagger, aiming for the goat-man's face. She closed her eyes at the last moment, but the goat-man screamed, and she felt resistance as the blade hit something solid. She yanked to pull it free and fell back. When she opened her eyes, the grass around her was moving again. The goat-man's bleating yell ended in a gurgle and then hands were on her, pulling her to her feet.

With a rush of adrenaline born of pain and fear, Harley lashed out again, but her arm was caught by a pale hand covered in swirling red lines, and Harley froze, looking up into Dia's eyes.

Harley's breath caught in her throat and the dagger fell from her hand as she collapsed into the warrior's arms.

Christian

"I don't understand. What did they hope to accomplish?" Cadence spoke through gritted teeth as he waited his turn for healing.

Chris stood next to him, flexing a hand that five minutes ago had a long gash running across the palm. The ghost of pain still tingled up his arm, but his hand was perfect. Even the hangnail he'd had when he woke up was healed.

For all that the goat-man by the cart had botched his part, the group of fae who tried to take them came disturbingly close to succeeding. They'd dragged Harley a significant distance into the field, where Faustus said he'd sensed a tunnel opening. She had some serious bruises on her left side, and she'd sliced herself with her own dagger while trying to draw it. Only adrenaline kept her from feeling the injury. She wouldn't even need stitches, now.

He gazed over his hand at Jenta who sat on the ground beside Harley, holding her hand while Yiannis healed her. Yiannis, who had again taken minimal injury, appeared appropriately chastened, looking horrified as he'd assessed their wounds. Chris wondered if maybe it was suddenly becoming real for Yiannis that the people he warded were *actually* mortal.

"I would say whatever it was, they almost accomplished it, if it hadn't been for you four fighting back. I do not think they expected that." Dia said, sounding a bit awed. "Tell me, was it the queen who told you about blooding your blades?"

"Yeah. We asked about it before we left." Cadence said, but his attention was focused largely on Harley. She'd just let out a sharp gasp and a stifled sob. Jenta helped her to sit up, and they hugged as Harley's shoulders shook with silent tears.

"Come, Cadence. I would see to your wounds." Yiannis said more as a request than a command. He couldn't really blame Yiannis for feeling shitty. He'd nearly gotten them killed, and now they were all having to face the consequences of assuming the safety of the Seelie kingdom. *Again.* Chris marveled at his hand one more time, then deliberately shoved it into his pocket.

"It has always intrigued me that mortal blood is the surest way to stop a fae." Aoife said, from where she sat on the tailgate of the cart; She and Leif had righted it so that they could move it off the road. Behind her, one of the goat-men was tied up and gagged, his eyes panic filled. "After the splitting, each of the kingdoms had kept a stockpile of just such for some time." She almost sounded disappointed at no longer having access to them.

She sat next to the goat-man, flexing hands that became massive cat paws complete with claws, then back, as easy as blinking. Apparently, Aoife and Leif were shapeshifters. She'd been the enormous bear they'd seen, while Leif had been the golden furred wolf. The two claimed quite a few of the bloody messes left beneath the trees on the road to Büyük Ağaç.

"I-I didn't mean to..." Harley said, her voice shaky and quiet. She seemed more upset that she was at fault for the severing of one of the goat-men, than she was at the actual outcome. Chris couldn't really blame her. Shock could do that.

Jenta patted her shoulder. "You did good. I'm proud of you. Progress is hard, and sometimes, so is fighting back." The two girls shared a look, then Jenta helped Harley to her feet, the both of them moving back toward the horses.

Cadence came over to Yiannis and put his back to the warrior. Yiannis tried to lift the fabric of the shirt from the skin, but the bloody shreds of cloth stuck to him, making him hiss and jerk away reflexively.

"My apologies, Cadence, but we will need to remove this. I am afraid it will not be salvageable." Yiannis said, plucking at a strand of the stained material. Cadence tried to shrug but stopped mid motion and bit hard at his lip, instead doing his best to hold still. Yiannis drew his tiny belt knife and used it to slice through the rest of the shirt back. Chris watched, fascinated, as the blade left wet edges on the fabric, which spread until parts of the tattered cloth were actually dripping pink water. Yiannis carefully extracted the soaked fabric from what was probably the worst case of road rash Chris could imagine, that went from Cadence's waist all the way up his back to his shoulders. Even saturated and dripping, Yiannis had to move slowly, using the flat of the blade in some places to draw up the cloth and ease it off of the wounds that lacerated Cadence's back.

"Damn." The word came out before Chris could catch it, and he met Cadence's pained glance with a commiserating wince of his own. Harley came back from the horses, followed by Jenta. She reached up gingerly and helped him pull the shirt the rest of the way off as Jenta stepped up and held up a cloak in front of him to give a bit of privacy. It was as if the girls had choreographed it, and the appreciation showed in Cadence's face just before his back arced hard. Faustus had stepped up next to Yiannis, the two of them working in tandem as Cadence gaped like a fish, his face toward the sky as his mouth worked open and closed. Chris was pretty sure he would be screaming if he had the breath for it.

Blood and rocks were drawn out of Cadence's back and dropped to the ground like spent bullet casings. For a moment, the air grew very hot, and Chris thought he might throw up. Then came that tingling wash over his skin, the feeling that always accompanied Yiannis's magic.

Cadence dropped slowly to his knees, but Chris could already see his back was healed, whole and hale, not even a drop of blood still showing on his skin.

Jenta and Harley wrapped the cloak around Cadence as he sat back on his heels, and Chris tried not to feel a little jealous. Jenta *had* been duly impressed with his wounds. He couldn't help that his healing simply hadn't been as impressive as the one just done on Cadence.

"Ximeno, report." Dia said, her voice tired.

Chris was honestly kind of surprised she hadn't done so earlier, but maybe it was because they'd all needed healing, first. This ambush had been much closer to successful than any of the sidhe might want to admit, and Yiannis wasn't the only one seeming chastened, though Dia's version of it suggested much more fury than anything.

"Now, Second?" Ximeno asked, glancing around at the rest of them, then back at Dia, whose expression darkened. They were all being very careful of each other. That was the first time Chris had heard one of the other sidhe specifically refer to her by her position instead of just by her name.

"Now, Ximeno." Dia's words held the undeniable note of command, and Ximeno bowed in acknowledgment.

Ximeno's report was fairly unsurprising. The four scouts had left off into the grasslands to circle around the hamlet. Aoife and Leif were ranging to the left, Faustus and Ximeno to the right, past a line of trees that blocked their view of the field where the attack took place. Ximeno heard Harley's cry for help, and they'd come riding. That was when Faustus found the tunnel entrance and they proceeded to dispatch a couple of the goat men, then continued back to the road to join the fight.

"What do you mean, a tunnel entrance? Why would that matter?" Jenta asked.

Faustus glanced at her, his expression shutting down like he didn't want her to see what he was thinking.

Ximeno answered the question as if Dia had been the one to ask, his attention still focused on her and Yiannis. "Our father was told previously of tunnels being used by some of the lesser fae closer to the kingdom's border, to carry..." Ximeno hesitated, and Chris only just caught that his gaze flicked to Yiannis then back to Dia.

"What, Ximeno?" Dia said, exasperated.

"Ehm. Father referred to it only as *product.*" Ximeno said, swallowing hard.

"It is not only we sidhe who learned to find enjoyment in the tactical pursuits." Leif said, then raised his hands in surrender when Aoife glared at him.

"Are you saying *we* would have been their product?" Harley said, the color draining out of her face.

Ximeno stared fixedly at Dia, but again seemed to be answering Harley's question. "It... Is possible that they did not want *all* of our wards..."

Chris felt the blood run out of his face, and Jenta and Harley seemed to be trying not to look at each other, while Cadence was angrily glaring around at everyone, as if trying to learn something from the decidedly stoic expressions that the sidhe had plastered onto their faces.

Yiannis cleared his throat. "Ximeno, Faustus, we will discuss this further, tonight. You will tell me what you know, or at least what your father has told you, of these tunnels." He paused, and his expression grew grim. "As well as the *products*."

According to Leif and Aoife, they had been only slightly closer, and heard the first of the yelling, so Leif returned to help. When asked why Aoife didn't return with him, Leif said she'd been approached by a group of fae asking for assistance, so she'd stayed to aid the locals.

"One of them fell into the Perairan Deras."

"What's the Perairan Deras?" Cadence asked.

Aoife gave a decidedly prissy sigh, Chris thought, then pointed in a vague direction across the opposite fields from those they'd been dragged through. "A river that runs from east to west, a bit north of here. None of the local folk are strong enough swimmers so they asked that I offer aid."

"Seriously?" Chris said, dubiously.

Aoife shifted her glower to him, but unlike Leif, Chris just stared at her. He'd gotten worse from his mother after one of her particularly rowdy benders, and certainly wasn't about to back down, now.

Dia glanced between the two of them, and Chris heard the tone of re-luctant agreement as she spoke. "I had not remembered how close the river runs to the Traveler's Way, this far east. You may not believe so, Christian, but Aoife and Leif's family line are all very powerful shapeshifters, and bear is not her only form."

"You have more than one?" Jenta blurted out, sounding surprised.

"Yes, I have more than *one*." Aoife sneered, sounding offended.

"Which did you use in the river, then?" Chris asked, but he couldn't keep the skepticism out of his voice.

"You are not in any way my superior, and I am not beholden to answer your questions." Aoife growled, crossing her arms, but after a surprisingly short time, she dropped her glare to the ground in front of her. If looks could catch fire, Chris thought, that would be some scorched earth.

Dia rolled her eyes and gave Aoife a look the other sidhe didn't see before responding to Chris. "One of her strongest forms is something akin to what I believe you would call an alligator."

"Oh." Chris considered Aoife for a moment, and though she seemed to sense him looking at her based on how she rolled her shoulders, she didn't raise her head. "That's pretty cool." he admitted.

The goat-men refused to answer or perhaps didn't know why the mortals were wanted. Even after Aoife—almost gleefully—started cutting them apart, they mostly just regressed to bleating. Dia ultimately called a stop to the "questioning", since they needed to get moving. Despite Yiannis's healing, all of them were tired, and they still had quite a bit of riding to do before they could stop for the night. They'd lost precious time with the fight, and Yiannis was anxious that they make sure they were within the walls of Comhaontu by no later than sunset.

One of their own pack horses was hitched up to draw the cart with its fixed axle and load of tied up goat-men to the hamlet's large central green. If there had been other fae among their attackers, none of them had been left in the fields to be retrieved. They left the cart, and Yiannis had a conversation with what Chris assumed was probably the person in charge, a stout-looking fae with skin that looked a lot like tree bark and hair that might have been sticks growing every which way out of their head, but who wore a clean and tidy dress with a pristine white apron tied around their waist.

As they continued on past the last of the houses—squat buildings with thatched rooves and neatly pointed stonework around their foundations—Chris was struck by just how quickly the four of them were adjusting, and wondered again how much of it was shock. Or was it that they'd all been through so much in their individual lives that nothing was phasing them, anymore?

So much for the first three days being the easiest and safest.

Chapter Twenty-Eight

Harlequin

Harley blinked. She'd nearly fallen asleep in her saddle. A quick scan of the group found Faustus and Ximeno riding directly behind her, their own horses keeping her mare to the group's pace. Harley opened her mouth to apologize, but instead, a jaw-cracking yawn left her blushing as the two brothers watched her with similar, chagrinned expressions.

Faustus heeled his horse forward, but Ximeno stayed where he was, just behind and to the left of her mount.

"You are well?" Faustus's voice was quiet, and Harley thought she heard genuine concern in his tone. Had Estian been right about them? In the last two days, the further they got from the Seelie palace, the more the two brothers drew free of their broody, sulky haughtiness, showing a keen awareness of the land around them, as well as a swift and endearing congeniality toward the four humans.

She fought another face stretching yawn as she answered. "I'm well, Faustus. I appreciate your concern. Are you... Are you and Ximeno okay?"

Jenta had told her how Faustus rode through the field to come help them only to have a pitchfork thrown at him by one of the fae hiding in the grass. One of the tines pierced his side, but instead of stopping, he'd ripped the thing from his own body and thrown it aside, only dismounting to free Chris from his net. Ximeno had taken an arrow to the shoulder from one of the attackers in the trees as he was riding away from the two goat-men he'd felled.

"We are well, yes. No need for healing." Faustus grabbed his waterskin from the pommel of his saddle, offering it to her. Harley looked at it, then met his earnest gaze.

"It's okay, Faustus, I have my own." She pointed at her waterskin, hanging from her saddle bags behind her.

He frowned and shook his head a little, then offered the waterskin again. "This will help, I think." Harley peered at him. It wasn't that she didn't trust him, so much... Was it? Maybe it *was* that she didn't trust him. Twice, now, they'd been attacked when the scouts were either distant or had deliberately left. Was it on purpose? Faustus and Ximeno were Cristobal's sons, and Cristobal wasn't exactly their biggest fan.

Harley shook her head, but when Faustus started to take the waterskin back, disappointed, Harley put out her hand for it. The gesture earned her a glad smile and he handed it to her. Harley opened the top and took a swig. With a little 'o' of pleased surprise, she took a longer drink then stoppered the waterskin and wiped her mouth with the back of her hand.

After inspecting the waterskin, she handed it back to Faustus, meeting his smile with one of her own. "That was very good. What's in it? Not just water, I assume?" It *was* good. She felt invigorated, as if she'd just gotten an hour's rest and a fresh cup of coffee.

"A..." Faustus searched for the word.

"A restorative." Ximeno answered from behind them.

"Yes. A restorative." Faustus said, the smile returning.

"Well, that was *some* restorative! Honestly. I feel much better, already." It was strange and kind of adorable that even though they were two ageless fae—and she had no way to gauge how many years they'd seen—they were as pleased as sons bringing their mother flowers in response to her words.

Faustus nodded, his face smoothing out, though his eyes were still alight with that same pleasure. He let his big horse drop back to ride alongside his brother. Harley took the cue, urging her mare forward to catch up with the group. She was still tired but not nearly as much, and the shock-y feeling of the last few hours was washed away in the tide of her drink from Faustus' waterskin.

"You good?" Jenta asked, as Harley caught up and matched pace with the other girls' horse.

"Me? Yeah. Just tired." Harley said and gave her a little smile.

Jenta smiled back, though it didn't quite reach her tired eyes. "I know what you mean. I can't wait until we stop for the night. Do you suppose we could get hot baths, in Comhaontu?"

Harley considered, then shrugged. "I don't know. Maybe? We can always ask."

Cadence

As the sun was setting, a great, green wall loomed up ahead out of the grasslands. The trees towered and wrapped around them as they drew closer, coming in from either side to flank the road. Cadence wondered if this was what it might be like to enter the Amazon. Unlike the trees surrounding Büyük Ağaç, these dripped with dangling vines, and the air was wet and heavy, and smelled like a greenhouse—a riotous mix of florals, rotting leaves and mossy, damp wood.

Comhaontu was tucked in among the trees, hanging like a big brown muddy bubble amid the greenery. It occurred to Cadence that this was the first walled village they'd seen. All the rest—even Büyük Ağaç—weren't really walled so much as just surrounded by trees at most. This was more like a fort, with actual wooden ramparts and watch towers that poked their heads up over the sharpened logs.

It was only maybe thirty feet between the walls and the ring of forest that pushed and reached for the thick hewn timbers. A set of towering wooden gates cut across the road, and thick posts were stuck deep into the muck to either side of the packed earth of Traveler's Way denoting the start of the wall. One side of the gate was already closed, the other only open wide enough for a single person to ride in at a time. Archers were poised along the ramparts; bows held but not drawn as they surveyed the last travelers of the day riding toward them.

The hairs at the back of Cadence's neck stood up, and gooseflesh ran down his arms, similar to when Yiannis cast that spell in the inn, and he wondered if they'd just crossed the edge of some kind of magic shield. Strangely, the feeling lined up almost perfectly with the edge of the trees.

Cadence waited in line as each of their group passed through the gate, his pulse speeding up as one by one, those ahead of him disappeared inside. He held his breath as Harley made her way through and didn't let it out until his own horse was crossing the muddy threshold. Sensing his nerves, the gelding gave a whinny and stamped his hooves, his head shaking against the reins.

Comhaontu's buildings, compared to the walls surrounding it, were rickety and rough looking. Most of them were balanced precariously on stilts, with small ladders or unrailed stairs leading up from wooden plank sidewalks to small porches with narrow awnings over the entry. What looked like the only actual *road* through Comhaontu stretched from the gate through which they'd entered, down the length of what was probably only a couple city blocks back home, to another gate in the opposite side of the wall, also made of metal wrapped wood.

Along the walls beside both gates were stairs leading up to the watch towers, and ramparts, giving good vantage of both inside and outside the village. The main road, as well as many of the walkways he could see running between the buildings, were all lit by torches, and compared to the lights and lanterns they'd seen in other places they'd passed through, these were downright prehistoric.

While most of the other buildings he saw were fairly small—only maybe one or two stories tall and not more than maybe a room's width across by that same length back—just in front of them across what was probably intended to be a main square was a much taller building, at least three stories of stone and mortar that was easily 100 feet across by maybe 30 feet from front to back, the front of it punctuated by glass paned windows all lit with candles. A set of ornate double doors at the center front of the building stood open.

Like someone had taken a government building and plopped it in the middle of a mud bog.

There were maybe twenty people standing around the square, besides their group. All appeared to have come out from the long building and waited in a rough semicircle around them. To their right and left were contingents of ten each; archers in boiled leather armor, bows ready and eyes sharp, watching everyone and everything.

Cadence spotted Harley, dismounted and holding the reins of her gray mare as she talked quietly with Jenta. In front of them, Chris was trying to peer over his mount, but Dia and Yiannis' mounts blocked the view of what was happening. They weren't the only riders entering Comhaontu, but those not in their party were steering their mounts around them and toward a well-lit stable to the far right side of the big stone building.

Cadence dismounted and led his horse over to Harley and Jenta. Chris was just ahead of them, still focused on whatever was happening at the head of the group. Cadence glanced at Harley, who shook her head a little.

"They don't want us to stop here." She said, sounding worried.

"What? Why?" Cadence said, unable to keep the disgruntlement out of his voice. He'd been healed, yes, but they were all tired, and he'd been looking forward to a hot meal and a warm bed.

"They want us to keep going, but Yiannis is refusing." Jenta answered.

Cadence frowned. "I thought this is supposed to be a haven town. Like there's a truce here or something." He went up on his toes to see over the milling horses.

There wasn't much to see in the torchlight. They should have had at least another hour of daylight left, but the trees ate at the light, leaving everything in shadowed gloom. Along with that, other than the hushed mumble of the people in the square, it was strangely silent, except for the crackle of the torches and the sound of their horses' hooves squelching and stamping on the damp ground.

Through all the other settlements they'd passed, big and small, there was the bustle of people moving, talking, *living*. Here, Cadence thought that even with the low buzz of the fae standing nearby, he could have heard a pin drop. It was as if the sound of the people, even standing only yards away, was only just loud enough to cover something hiding in the silence. Something that whispered and hummed *beneath* the silence. He bowed his head, trying to listen.

There. A sound like wind in trees, but not. The rustle of leaves, the soft whoosh of branches moving. A susurrus whisper, trying to tell him something. He thought he could almost make out words.

"Stop listening." Aoife startled him, her face close to his as she studied him.

"What?" He blinked at her.

"Stop. Listening." she punctuated her words with a hard finger, jabbing at his chest.

"Ow. Okay. Sorry." There appeared to be actual worry in her expression. "What is it?"

She scanned the dark forest that hovered and waited just outside the walls. "The trees are trying to call to you. Do not listen. If they cannot catch you, they cannot keep you." She pointed at Harley and Jenta. "That goes for you two, as well. Leif, Ximeno, stay with them. Faustus, with me."

Aoife handed Leif the reins to her coarser, a slim, creamy white stallion with fierce eyes. The horse nickered after her then nipped at Leif's own mount, a rangy chestnut roan mare. When the other horse didn't react, Aoife's horse chuffed and bent his neck to snuffle at the muddy ground.

Leif remained silent as his sister stormed away. Ximeno held the reins of his and his brother's horses—absolute units that made Cadence think of the big plow horses he'd seen in commercials, except these were the color of good butter—and shot Cadence a grin. Cadence smiled back at him.

Shouting brought Cadence around to find the largest man he'd ever seen. Based on the building behind him, Cadence thought the guy must be over ten feet tall. His shoulders were thick, and his arms roped with muscle. His hands were huge, but only had three fingers and a thumb, each finger banded with a twisted copper ring. One massive fist gripped the front of Yiannis' tunic, holding the sidhe warrior at least a foot up into the air. The other hand was pointed to the opposite gate from the one through which they'd entered.

"I said *leave*, sidhe!" The enormous man said 'sidhe' like it was a curse, but Yiannis never flinched.

"Wallbuilder Thornfist, set him down, please." The voice that spoke rang with authority. Another figure stepped out from around the huge man. His clothing was ornate, a thick cowled robe covered in vibrant embroidery, but under the finery, he was thin and frail looking. His head was bald except for a wisp of white around his ears and a long thin chin beard that hung down his chest, braided into one long strand.

The giant nodded at the old man, lowering his arm, and letting go his fingers at the same time, so that Yiannis was partially set, partially dropped to the ground.

Cadence started to move forward but Ximeno grabbed his shoulder. Cadence gave him wide eyes, but stayed where he was, his hands flexing, and muscles twitching with the effort. Instead, he asked "Who is that guy?"

"Which? The ogre or the elder?" Leif said from behind him.

Cadence tried not to gape. It was the first time Leif had directly spoken to him, since they'd left the palace. He had a flash of memory, Leif standing over him, his spear the only thing between Cadence and the goat-man's pitchfork. Hesitantly, he answered, "The elder." Leif called the enormous man an ogre. He would have to ask about that, later.

"He is who you think: the leader of Comhaontu." Leif said.

"He looks almost...Human." Cadence said, puzzled.

"You are not far wrong." Leif said, then raised his finger to his lips, and pointed back toward the tableau. Cadence dutifully focused his attention ahead, particularly on the elder who now stood at the ogre's elbow, glaring up at Yiannis.

The man wasn't just the village elder, he really *looked* old. Not just gray haired, but ancient. His skin, where it wasn't tight against his skull, was wrinkled with time, and Cadence could see a couple darker liver spots on the man's skull.

When the elder spoke again, his voice dripped with derision. "He is only doing as his queen bids. Are you not, Hianius? Oh, I *am* sorry, I suppose I should call you by your *human* name; Yiannis. You have been told by my people twice, and by your own rules, three times will make it the truth. You and yours are not welcome to stay within my walls. You will leave, and if the Wildes should take you, well, that will be as *fate* decides."

Cadence paled. This was definitely not going the way Yiannis or Dia told them it would.

"Lord Phythilian, do not do this. If not for me, then for those I ward. You endanger not only yourself but all the people over whom you rule." Yiannis's voice belied his request. He already knew the answer.

The elder scanned the crowd, his eyes settling on Cadence for a moment. Cadence flinched. Lord Phythilian's eyes were completely white. Even in the torch light, he couldn't see any other color in them, just a milky film. When those strange eyes left him and went back to Yiannis, Cadence let out a breath he didn't realize he'd been holding. He shook off Ximeno's hand and moved up next to Chris. Someone stepped up beside him. Expecting Ximeno, instead, he found Leif. The big blond gave him a curt nod, then returned his attention to their surroundings.

"No, *Yiannis*. I do not endanger my people with my choice. I know who you ward. Your little pet *mortals*. A fourth and final time, I say. Neither you, O fallen king, nor your mortal *mutts* may stay within my walls."

Harley and Jenta shifted nervously behind him, but Cadence was focused on Yiannis. *Do something*! He screamed it in his head at the sidhe warrior. Why weren't any of the sidhe fighting back? All of them were just standing around. Cadence didn't know what faced them if they spent the night outside the walls, but Yiannis did. Perhaps better than any of them, Yiannis knew, but he just stood there.

"Phythilian Surhain, you have chosen your fate, and that of your people. *She* may keep her promise *if* she wins, but it will not be the promise you expect. Regardless, I shall make an oath of my own." Yiannis gestured for them to mount.

There was pressure in Cadence's chest. He wasn't sure if it was something Yiannis was doing, or simply fear gripping his heart, but either way he made for his horse. All of them mounted and rode down the main road through the middle of Comhaontu. Eyes followed them from cracked doors and mostly shuttered windows as they passed among the buildings. If Comhaontu was quiet before, now that absence of sound felt nearly vacuous. Cadence swallowed hard under the weight of those watchers and tried not to throw up. The pressure in his chest grew as they drew closer to the far gate.

The old man followed them on foot, shadowed closely by the ogre—who now hefted a thick wooden cudgel on one shoulder—and a small contingent of archers in that same boiled leather armor, bows ready.

It seemed to take an eternity for them to travel to the far side of the ramshackle fort, though it probably wasn't more than a handful of minutes. There really *was* only the one main road, cut to either side by small alleys and toe paths. As they reached the far gate, Yiannis waved them through, making himself the last to exit through the wooden palisade.

Once they'd all gathered on the outside of the wall, Yiannis halted them with another gesture, then turned to face back through the gate, staring straight at Phythilian. When he spoke, his voice wasn't loud, but it echoed throughout the buildings, nonetheless. "This, I promise to you, Lord Phythilian Surhain, and to you, the people of Comhaontu; For three times spoken, three times truth. Accord is ended. Accord is ended. Accord is ended. Thus, three times spoken, three times true, and three days Danann grant you. Make your peace. Or grow gills."

A gasp ripped from Cadence's throat, echoed by his companions. The pressure in his chest built and rushed over him in another wave of gooseflesh as Yiannis threw up his hands and with them, Cadence sensed more than saw something like a giant hollow sphere form around the walls. It made him think of how he saw the ripples of air, in the doorway at the inn.

Holy shit. A giant glowing bubble coalesced around Comhaontu, nearly instantaneously. It wavered perpetually; a much larger version of the one Yiannis had wrapped around the fae in the woods, and much like that one, versus the shield at the inn, he didn't think this bubble was just to muffle sound.

Chapter Twenty-Nine

Christian

The forest swallowed them as they rode, until they could no longer see the reflected glow of the bubble on the trees around them or hear the muffled cries of those inside it. The darkness surrounding them was complete, and the only sounds were what Chris assumed—hoped—were night insects and birds.

"Holy Shit. Holy *Shit*. Yiannis, Holy shit, you just murdered an entire village!" Chris tried to push his horse forward, but Dia moved her mount to ride alongside him while Yiannis kept his silent position at their front, completely focused on the forest around them. Unless he had night vision, Chris wasn't certain Yiannis could see any more than the rest of them.

Behind them, he heard a noise that made him think of putting fizzy candy in soda—kind of a hissing hum, and then the area around them was filled with suffuse light. A glance down showed that all the rocks along their path were glowing faintly. They continued their slow ride, and the glow in the rocks followed them, fading behind even has it led the way on the road ahead. The light was more like a particularly powerful nightlight than a torch, but it was enough.

While Chris was distracted, Dia grabbed his reins to stop him from moving any further forward. Her voice was stern and lecturing. "They will not die, and they may leave. It is far kinder than the choice they have given us, which is no choice at all. In three days, Comhaontu will sink into the mud from which it was raised, but staying when that happens will be their choice. *They* have given *us* over to the forest and the night, knowing our chances. Knowing *your* chances. Yiannis has set the price of their decision to exile us and given them a new choice to weigh." Dia's voice filled up with fury as she spoke. Her eyes shone, and her hair glowed like banked embers in the night-dark forest, making shadows crackle and dance against the background underbrush.

Harley spoke quietly, her voice carefully neutral. "What did he mean, 'accord is ended?'"

Dia tried to split her attention between Harley and Chris as she answered. "Comhaontu was named by the half human, half fae who founded it. The word meant 'agreement' or 'accord' in his mother's language."

"Did the queen have some sort of agreement with them?" Jenta asked.

"Not specifically, no, but all in fae know it is a neutral place, between the two kingdoms. Those who live there must agree to live in accordance with the laws of Danann: safe passage, safe harbor, safe trade."

"So, did we violate one of those rules or something?" Jenta asked, even *her* bravado subdued.

Dia's answer was immediate, her fury rekindled. "No. We have done nothing. We were within our rights to request safe harbor for the night and safe passage in the morning. Had that pompous mud-head of a leader thought for a moment, we would have been granted safe trade as well, since as the queen's dignitaries, he would have known we carried a boon gift."

Harley shook her head a little, in disbelief. "Who was that guy, anyway? Why did he refer to Yiannis as a fallen king?"

Yiannis's back stiffened at that second question, but Dia was already talking. "That," she spat the word, "was Phythilian Surhain. He is the Great Great Grandson of the founder, Tadhg Surhainin, and his family line has ruled Comhaontu since its founding. But Phythilian never wed and has no kin."

"And that's bad, right?" Jenta asked.

Dia grimaced. "Yes. He has refused to continue his lineage, but also refuses to choose a successor for leadership of Comhaontu. He forces all who live within the walls to live the way of humans though he despises the mortal side of his ancestry. That is why you saw no winged or demi-fae—they are not allowed within the walls. Sidhe may abide but are not allowed, or truly even able, to use our powers within the walls to do much more than light a candle or wash a dish."

"So that's why you guys just took what that asshole was handing you." Cadence grumbled.

"I knew I felt something." Chris said. "That weird tingly sensation. I felt it at the inn, when Yiannis, you know... did his magic." He wiggled his fingers in the air.

"Yes. There is a shield of sorts around the whole of Comhaontu that was originally put in place by the founder and his father who was no lover of the sidhe."

Cadence rode up past Chris on his other side, dodging Dia to confront Yiannis. "What about the third question? Who are you, really, Yiannis? Or should we call you Theortian Hianius Murhai? Hianius. Yiannis."

"We must keep moving." was all Yiannis said, continuing to watch the forest.

"Very clever to find a name from our own world." Cadence's voice was patronizing. He heeled his horse forward to get out in front of Yiannis where he drew up his reins, blocking the road, as he glared at the tall warrior. Dia tried to ride forward, but Chris used his own horse to block her. Her glower, still crackling with her magic, made Chris swallow hard, but he didn't back down.

"Cadence, we do not have time for this. It is not safe here. I know that you would not endanger your friends." Chris didn't dare look away from Dia, but Yiannis's voice was quiet and flat in comparison to the frustration he heard in Cadence's.

"Right now, I feel like we're in more danger *with* you than without you. You have used every opportunity to remind us of our responsibility to our people, to our world, to *your* world, but Queen Estian talked about you like she didn't know you as anything other than a legend until you showed up, demanding a place in our escort. Why is that? Who are you? 'Fallen king' sounds an awful lot like you would be more likely to align yourself with *her*, so I'm going to ask again, and as you yourself said, three times makes truth. *Who are you?*"

The squeal of a horse brought everyone around. A creeping green tendril covered in thorns had snaked out from the shadows and wound around one of the legs of Leif's mount, pulling the horse as if trying to drag it back into the forest. The horse's eyes were wild, the trapped leg trying to pull free or kick, but failing to make contact.

Aoife drew her sword but hesitated to dismount, and her own stallion shied away from Leif's panicked mare, though Chris couldn't tell if that was because of or in spite of any urging from his rider. Leif shot her a look that spoke volumes, then pulled his own spear free of his back sheath and attempted to slash at the vine while trying to keep his mare from bolting.

Faustus dismounted, throwing his reins to his brother, and jogged forward, his own sword drawn. He extended his hand in front of him in that gesture they all used, and rocks wrenched themselves from the path and shot toward the thick limb, their sharp edges finding purchase within the soft flesh of the plant fibers. Chris thought the rocks might just shred the damned thing, but instead, they were sucked up within it. Already, thinner twisting runners were crawling along the ground and up onto the path, tiny leaf-topped ends weaving back and forth as if testing the air.

"Shit." Chris dismounted and ran after Faustus, drawing his own blade and holding it in front of him with his right hand, his left poised slightly behind. As he ran forward, a branch shot out at him from one side, and Chris swept down with the blade. The fine edge sliced straight through without slowing, and Chris never lost momentum.

Faustus's sword was a slightly larger version of the one Chris wielded: a single edged, gently curved blade that was making short work of the spiky rope currently holding Leif's horse. He took a chopping swing, and flexed his off-hand, making the stones still embedded within come flying out, ripping and tearing even as his blade sliced down, causing enough damage that, Chris was glad to see, the thorny bastard finally lost its grip on the mare's leg. It looked like the thing started to shift its aim, but Faustus drove his blade hard into the last part of the woody flesh still attached, and the segment of tendril that had started reaching toward him dropped to the ground, unmoving.

With her leg freed, Leif's horse tried to run, launching herself forward and nearly bucking her rider in her fright. Leif almost lost his seat and dropped his spear as he gripped the reins with both hands. Only a hard drag kept the mare from throwing herself out into the trees. Even so, she fought fiercely, her eyes rolling with fear as she screamed and bucked. Leif pulled her around by sheer force, but at least they were out of the range of their leafy attackers.

Chris scanned the rest of their group, worried more creepers or climbers might be coming out of the darkness, but strangely, the attack was focused in this one spot, for now. He turned his attention back to find Faustus was already surrounded by more writhing, slithering fingers. One shot out low to the ground, grabbing at a leg, while another was already wrapping itself around the wrist holding his sword.

Ximeno made a noise, but Chris waved him back. "I'll get him. Stay mounted."

Chris didn't wait for confirmation and moved in, stepping quickly and trying to keep his feet moving while he chopped and slashed his way along the path. As he worked his way closer, Faustus drew a belt knife with his right hand and sliced through the vine holding his left wrist. With an angry bellow, the big warrior swiped down with his sword again, slicing through three more thicker limbs that had started to wrap themselves around his torso.

Chris was able to get up next to him and together, they sliced through yet more of the foul things reaching for them but that hadn't yet gotten purchase. Chris put himself back-to-back with Faustus, and reached back with his left hand, grabbing the fabric of the warrior's coat. Doing his best to split his attention between the ground and the space in front of him,

Chris started quickly guiding them both back toward the horses. Part way back, he crouched and grabbed up Leif's spear, even though it meant he could no longer swing his sword effectively.

Once they drew up close to the waiting riders, Faustus spun on his heel, shoving Chris toward his black mare while Faustus jogged to his own great warhorse. More runners were making their way out of the forest along the sides of the path, just visible in the light of the glowing stones around their horse's feet. Leif had finally calmed his mare enough to draw up near Yiannis at the front of the group, but there was no time for Chris to take him his weapon. He sheathed his own blade and stuck the shaft of the spear through one of his saddlebag straps so he could mount.

As soon as Chris was astride, Yiannis called loudly, "Move!" No one argued. Yiannis led them at a quick trot down the path, just fast enough to keep them away from the grabby fuckers behind them, but not so fast they couldn't watch the ground ahead. Chris couldn't help but feel like the forest was herding them away from what should have been the safety of Comhaontu.

Leif had pulled a short spear from its sheath along the back of his saddlebags, and Aoife still had her sword out. She took a position along the side of the group behind Leif, who stayed up next to Yiannis instead of trying to double back along their column. Both of them were focused on the forest, slicing at any of the reaching tendrils that drew too close. Faustus and Ximeno held their spots at the back of the group doing the same, and Dia dropped back to ride to the opposite side of the path from Aoife, so that the four teens were held in the center of the group, out of the reach of their tenacious attackers. Even so, Chris drew his sword again shortly after they'd started forward.

Harley let out a yelp and Chris spun in his saddle just as something brushed at the top of her head. Another climber had dropped down from among the branches, the tip of it flicking and twitching like a snake's tongue. It didn't have time to do more than grab at her hair, but now that Chris was looking up, he could see more of the damned things dropping out of the night-dark trees.

Yiannis led them down a side trail which opened up to a small glade with a pond to one side. The trees crowded around them like curious onlookers, their branches reaching out to cover all but the very center of the glade through which the moon shone down like a great, blind eye. Yiannis stopped at the opening of the clearing and waved them past him.

"Ximeno, with me." Yiannis dismounted and barely waited for the rest of them to clear the edge of the trees before he was raising his hands. Above and around them, Chris caught the ripples of another bubble shield forming, spanning the width and breadth of the area beneath the trees, and arching high above their heads. Panic gripped him for a moment. It was too close to what they'd just seen Yiannis do to Comhaontu. *But he's in here* with *us.*

Ximeno dismounted and tossed his reins to Faustus, then ran to stand next to Yiannis, raising his own hands. The rippling air waivered for just a moment, and then there was a bright flash. Chris had to blink repeatedly, and when he was able to see again, the surface of the bubble was shot with crackling lines of lightning. Jagged streaks of light wove themselves across the dome above their heads.

Dia led them to the center of the glade. "Dismount and calm your steeds. If they spook, settle them immediately. Do *not* let them run off into the forest!"

Chris ended up next to Cadence, all of them trying to soothe their horses, even as they sent fearful glances at the entrance where Yiannis and Ximeno still waited, watching out into the forest.

A bundle of the nearly arm-thick tentacles wound themselves around each other, poised just outside the bubble as if watching the group. In a rush, the bundle threw itself straight into the shield. Chris tensed, and saw Cadence do the same beside him. There was another bright flash, a sharp hiss like water on a hot griddle, and then a keening whistle that retreated back among the trees and was gone.

There was no mark on the dome where the attack had slammed into the surface of Yiannis and Ximeno's combined magic—no damage or dent—but at the base of the shield, along the edge of the path where it became grass, lay the blistered and sizzling remains of a chunk of viscous green goo, and tiny leafy feelers still twitching and hissing as steam escaped them.

Everyone moved in silence. A weight sat over the glade as they worked to hobble the horses and set out their blankets. There was no wood for a fire, and not even the sidhe warriors were inclined to try looking past the borders of the magic shield. Instead, after they fed the horses from provisions in their bags, they sat down to a cold dinner of more cheese and bread.

They ate in silence for a time, listening to the sounds of nighttime in the Wildes. Amid the quiet, Yiannis finally spoke.

"I did not choose the name Yiannis out of convenience. My name is as true as my faith. Danann *is* gracious. They gave me a second chance, after I failed and nearly allowed my realm and people to be destroyed in my pride." He stopped, swallowed, and focused on Cadence, who returned his look stoically. "I was once Theortian Hianius Murhai, the first King of the fae. I failed my people and my Creator, and for that, I was punished—and rightly so. Danann cast me to the Void."

Chris gaped. Harley nodded, as if she'd expected this, but Jenta appeared as surprised as him. Cadence just watched Yiannis, his expression unreadable.

The other sidhe, however... Aoife hissed, her expression a mixture of fury and disgust. She threw down her food and rose, walking away from the group to the edge of the barrier that separated them from the whispering forest. Compared to her, the rest of them kept their composure at least a little better; Faustus and Ximeno bowed their heads, though they, too, set down their food, seemingly having lost their appetites. Dia stared him with a mix of awe and horror.

Of all of them, Leif gave the least amount of response. He'd watched his sister get up and walk away but seemed reluctant to follow, instead sitting on his own blanket regarding Yiannis with hooded eyes, only a slight frown of disapproval giving any indication of his mood.

Yiannis also watched Aoife walk away, his eyes tired, then gave Cadence his full attention. "I was its first and only official prisoner that I know of. Years, eons, epochs beyond reckoning. I sat and waited, accompanied by nothing but the Void and the Keeper, who paroled my prison, to ensure I did not attempt to escape. In that time, my only solace was that I was given a window of sorts—a one-way mirror, to watch the world as it was rebuilt in a new image."

"Wow." Chris said, unable to stop himself. "That sounds... shitty."

Yiannis smiled, in spite of himself. "I suppose. Truly, though, the Keeper need not have worried. Danann had given me the promise of an opportunity for redemption. A chance to walk among my people once again, though I knew Danann and I were in agreement that I would never again wear a crown. So, you see, the queen's is not the only salvation you carry in your veins along with your mortal blood. You carry mine as well. Thus, my release from the Void, my name, and my place among your escort."

"Is that how you knew about..." Cadence started to say, then hesitated. Even now, he was trying to be as circumspect as Yiannis, in consideration of their conversation at the inn. When Cadence continued, he seemed to be picking his words carefully. "The place you told us about?" He gave Yiannis serious eyes, as if to say, "you know the place I mean".

Yiannis exhaled, blowing the air through pursed lips. "Yes. It was how I was able to return, and how I know it is beyond dangerous for us to attempt to go there, if we can avoid it."

Cadence considered him for a very long time, and Yiannis for his part, sat stoic under that critical gaze. After a long pause, Cadence gave a bare nod. "I believe you."

Yiannis gave another sigh, this one full of relief. "I swear that I am no danger to you, any of you. As Dia said, the people of Comhaontu will not die, though they may wish they could. Three days hence, the village itself will have sunk below the mud and muck of the Wildes, swallowed back into the ground that has borne it. The people within are still fae, and so may either leave, or stay, but staying will mean they will be buried with their homes until such time as perhaps another comes and raises the buildings back to the surface. No one will be able to build in that spot. Accord is ended, and will not be, again."

"How could you do that?" Harley asked, horrified.

Yiannis opened his mouth, but it was Dia who spoke, the lecturing sternness returning. "Fae is not an easy place to live, and the laws of our land are sacrosanct. Queen Estian may not agree with Yiannis's decision, and opt to come free them, or command him to do so, but I would back his decision if she questioned me. They denied us the right of *all* Danann's laws, turning us out to face the Wildes, knowing our chances of survival in the night. You may think it or us cruel, but Phythilian knew what he was doing, and not a single resident gainsaid him. By their inaction, they showed implicit consent to their leader's choice."

"What about Phythilian? Why do you think he did it?" Chris asked.

Yiannis shrugged. "I believe Dia also guesses correctly regarding Phythilian. It may be that the combination of his immortal mind and aging body have finally driven him to desperation. I smelled the Dark's magic on him."

"Smelled it?" Jenta asked, startled.

"Yes. It burns in my nostrils, like fetid rot, though it did not always." Yiannis's tone was sad as he answered.

"I didn't smell anything. Are you sure it was not just the muck? Or perhaps Thornfist? Those Ogres can sometimes smell quite... ripe." Dia said, but not as if she thought it was funny.

Yiannis gave her a look, and she paled, then bowed her head. "I know what I smelled. Phythilian reeked of her magic as if he'd bathed in it, but whatever she promised him, I believe she will find a way to twist it so thoroughly he will pray for his death by the time she is done with him."

"You said her magic didn't always smell like that?" Harley asked. She'd obviously latched onto some idea, though Chris couldn't begin to guess what.

Yiannis regarded her as he considered her question. "No. Her magic, when first I had known her, smelled of petrichor, and night blooming flowers. Sweet, smoky, fleeting. Like Estian's, it was a fine perfume, though the likenesses ended there."

"You knew the Dark Queen before? How?" Jenta asked.

"I was the first king. I had subjects just as any monarch. She was one. Beautiful, clever, but also aloof and distant. Her power almost made it a prerequisite that she had few friends, even then. It did not surprise me when she was selected to rule the Unseelie."

"Estian said no one remembers her name. That she's just always ruled the Dark." Jenta said, her tone indecipherable.

Yiannis shook his head a little, the sadness back in his expression. "She is not wrong. At the time of the splitting, I was not yet in my right mind, and it took me some time to regain myself. By then, I had forgotten much of who I once was, and she had already thrown off the mantle of her previous self and was known only as the Dark Queen by any outside of her kingdom. There may be some in her court who remember her name still, but I fear that if they have not already stopped her, they either *can*not or *will* not."

They all sat silent. Chris had so many questions, but his brain was as muddy as the ground around Comhaontu, and suddenly, all he wanted was sleep.

Yiannis continued, his voice quiet, as if he were talking to himself. "Danann willing, we will survive this night. The magic should keep, and I

291

believe we set a solid enough example that we are not easy prey. Traveling the Wildes by day is dangerous enough."

He spoke a little louder, as he addressed them. "Everyone, stay within the bounds of the glade, bed down and get what sleep you may. Lastly, note these rules for the coming days." He ticked off three fingers as he spoke, "Eat no plants grown here; drink nothing that is not from your waterskin or from one of us; and have your weapons ready." He lowered his hands to his lap, and let the silence stretch for a moment as the import of his words set in. "I will make no promises that this will be easy, but I have faith." Then he stood up and walked away from the group toward the horses.

Dia frowned after Yiannis, concerned. "No one knew what had become of our first king. I am not certain how I feel about this knowing." After a moment, she looked back at the other warriors. "Leif, you and Aoife will have first watch. Once the moon clears the glade's eye, wake Faustus and myself—we will take second. Ximeno, we will wake you for third, and if Yiannis is not awake, wake him for third with you. Weapons ready, all of you." She met each of their fearful gazes in turn. "If you have to fight anything more than vines and you've not already, take my advice—blood your weapons."

Dia removed her belt and lay her sheathed sword next to her as she bedded down. Chris peered around at his friends, then shrugged, unhooking his own belt so he could set it next to his blanket, the hilt pointed toward him, and saw the others doing similar with their own weapons. Cadence had brought his quiver with him and sat tying small red ribbons of fabric torn from a shirt around the shafts of arrows. The last thing Chris heard as he fell asleep was the sound of the forest around them, and the crackle and hum of magic.

Chapter Thirty

Harlequin

Something was sitting on Harley's chest, and she could feel hot breath on her cheek. The breath smelled putrid, like rotten meat and dung, and she fought not to gag. She opened her eyes slowly, afraid of what she would see. Wide eyes met hers, two beady black pools that filled immediately with fear. The creature screamed, high and piteous, scrambling back off of her. Harley, confused, sat up.

The glade was different than when they'd fallen asleep. The little pond was gone, and there was no trail leading out through the trees. There were no horses, no sidhe warriors. No magic barrier, protecting them from the forest. Harley's and Jenta's beds lay on the ground, which was otherwise just a small grass clearing, surrounded by trees.

The creature was small and thin with arms like twigs, and tiny hands with long, boney fingers. It was wearing only a pair of dirty, old, tattered trousers held up by a crude leather belt. Spindly legs and rodent-like feet stuck out, grimy and caked with mud. It had a rat-like face, with thick black whiskers poking out from either side of a sharply pointed twitching nose, translucent round ears, and sickly gray skin.

Harley was too confused to scream. The thing stared at her in terror. It was pathetic looking, keening as it huddled against a tree trunk. Harley was almost offended, then couldn't help rolling her eyes at herself.

"Harley? Are you okay?" Jenta was just starting to sit up, and her voice was sleep fogged.

"Hey, Jenta..." Harley said, but didn't take her eyes off the creature.

Jenta caught the hesitancy in her tone, and Harley heard the rustle of leaves behind her, then, "What the hell is that?" Jenta came up beside her, helping Harley to her feet. They stood together, looking down at the strange rat-man.

For his part, the creature continued to cower away from them, pressing himself hard against the trunk of the tree at his back but making no effort to run away. Since he didn't seem to be attacking them, Harley took a moment to assess their surroundings, trusting Jenta to keep an eye on their visitor.

"I think we have bigger problems than Stewart Little, here."

Jenta eyed Harley, then the clearing. "Well, fuck. Where are we?"

Harley shrugged. "Your guess is as good as mine."

Harley turned back to the little creature. He'd started to slink off into the trees but stopped as soon as Harley's attention returned to him. She held her hands up, palms out, placating.

"Hey, little guy. Do you know where our friends went?" The creature flinched when she spoke.

"Harley, he may not even speak English." Jenta said skeptically.

Harley shrugged. "It's worth a try. You remember what Estian said. A lot of them get bored, and immortality is a really long time."

Jenta grunted. "Come on. We should get moving and see if we can find the guys."

Harley looked squarely at Jenta. "No offense, but how exactly do we do that? We don't even know where *we* are."

From her pocket, Jenta pulled out a small, round disc. At first, Harley thought it was a pocket watch.

"I've been checking it every once in a while, since we left the palace." Jenta held it up and showed Harley the face with its four cardinal directions, and the red and black hands wobbling back and forth.

Harley gawked. "Is that a *compass?*"

Jenta grinned at her. "We've been pretty consistently heading east toward the sunrise, and sunset has been at our back every night. Cristobal said we would travel east for around seven days to get to Dark's doorstep, so I just kept checking to see if the compass would deviate. Every time I've checked, it confirmed our direction, which means it works here."

"Holy crap! Jenta, that's brilliant!"

Jenta laughed, a startled sound that sent birds fluttering up in the trees. "Did you just swear? Wow. I didn't think it was *that* impressive."

Harley laughed and rolled her eyes. "Seriously, I never even thought of it."

Jenta gave her a wink, and said sarcastically, "Well, I guess it's a good thing *I* did, then, isn't it?"

"What do you suppose we should do about our visitor?" They both turned to look at him. He'd moved even further along the tree trunk, eyes darting hopefully toward the woods, but stopped moving again as soon as he felt their eyes.

Jenta crouched low with her hands on her knees, facing him. "I kinda feel bad for him. I mean, look at him, Harley. He looks terrified of us. Hey, little friend, can you understand me?"

The creature's eyes widened, but after a moment he gave the tiniest nod.

"Okay, cool. If we let you go, do you promise not to harm us or any of our friends?"

"I promisssssse." The words came out as a raspy hiss. Harley shuddered but couldn't really argue with Jenta's choice. He hadn't harmed them or even threatened them.

Jenta smiled and straightened. "Great. Good. Go on, then. We won't stop you." He started to scurry off behind the tree when Jenta spoke again, stopping him in his tracks, one foot poised in the air. "Oh, and if you're able, can you ask the forest to let us find our friends? We don't mean any harm—we just want to get out of here in one piece."

A grin split his narrow face, and he gave a tiny nod, then bolted, vanishing into the underbrush with only a rustle of leaves to show his path. Harley stifled a laugh. Sticking out of a hole in his pants was a long, wiry, hairless tail.

"Well, there's that sorted anyway. Now what?" Harley asked, as she stooped to roll up her blanket. Jenta did the same, then they took a moment to check the compass.

"Like I said, we've pretty much been heading east without fail, and if I remember right, every one of our landmarks was going to be to the east." Jenta said, pointing out the direction through the trees.

Harley stared out at the direction Jenta was pointing. "I think we'll have better luck finding the edge of the Expanse and getting our bearings from there. Didn't Yiannis say there was an outpost on the far side of the Wildes? Maybe we should aim to find that."

Jenta nodded. "Agreed."

Harley did a quick scan of the glade, to make sure they didn't leave anything behind. She checked her belt, where she'd re-attached the knife in its sheath just as Jenta was finishing her own inspection. They both straightened, and headed east out into the trees.

Christian

Aoife, Leif, Harley, and Jenta had vanished. Chris paced the clearing, his shoulders tense. Both of the twins' coarsers were missing, but there was no evidence of who had been the one—or ones—to take them. It also didn't explain how any of that had happened while there was someone else on watch. Unless they were in on it, too.

Dia and Faustus both agreed that Leif and Aoife woke them for their watch and then bedded down. Dia did a check of everyone's positions at that point, confirming all of them were present. Ximeno claimed he had done the same but had to look for Yiannis, who was dozing over by the small pond. Had they gone missing while Ximeno was looking for Yiannis? Or while someone was walking their rounds on the far side of the clearing?

Yiannis's first words to the rest of the warriors after the discovery was "armor up". Chris found himself again watching in fascination as magic was intermingled with what would otherwise have been utterly mundane.

Dia's armor was hardened leather dyed a dark red and covered in the same swirls and lines that covered her hands and arms. Yiannis wore what looked like some kind of scale mail of overlapping metallic fish scales, in various iridescent shades of blue and green, as if his hair and eyes had been spun out into some ultra-light metal and hammered into those neatly shaped plates. Faustus and Ximeno still wore those strange coats covered in stones, but Faustus had done something to them so that instead of just hanging loose against the fabric, they'd stretched and flattened into plates, which Ximeno charged so that wherever there would have been a gap, it was crisscrossed by laces of arcing electricity.

Just as Chris made for his horse, Cadence and Yiannis started arguing. Dia sighed and went to check on the other horses, and Faustus and Ximeno decided they would re-check the perimeter of the clearing for tracks or signs. No one wanted to talk about how they couldn't even figure out *when* any of the four disappeared. Chris shrugged, sighed, and returned to pacing.

"Are you fucking kidding me? They're *somewhere* in a forest you have *repeatedly* told us is deadly, and you want us to just *keep going*?" Cadence's face was so red it nearly matched his hair.

Yiannis was back to his stoic self, giving away nothing of what he might be feeling. "You ask if I am 'kidding' you, but I do not find this amusing either, Cadence." He sounded sincere, but Cadence shook his head.

"Damn it, Yiannis, what if they're hurt? What if they're trapped?" Cadence paused and his voice dropped, as it filled with panic. "What if *she* has them?!"

Yiannis waited quietly, his focus entirely on Cadence who stood, his chest heaving and his hands in fists at his sides as if he was resisting the urge to swing a fist at the taller man.

As Cadence's temper subsided, Yiannis spoke with quiet earnest. "You are right. They very well may be out in the forest somewhere. But it is *also* possible that all four of them are together in which case Harlequin and Jenta are as safe as we could hope, and I will believe that to be the case until I know otherwise."

"How can you *say* that?" Cadence snapped, but all the fire had dropped out of his voice, and he just sounded scared. Chris came to stand by him as Yiannis answered.

"If the forest took them, they are less likely to be hurt until it satisfies its curiosity with them. If we go in search of them, we are more likely to get ourselves lost than we are to find them." Yiannis gestured expansively with one hand. "The Wildes are vast, and much of it is impassable unless you grow wings."

"So, what do we do, then?" Chris asked.

Yiannis inclined his head to Chris. "As I mentioned before: there is a small outpost for guides on the far side of the trail. If we make it there, I believe we may find someone to help us directly or able to beseech the forest for aid. We have neither the provisions nor the experience to do anything else, but I swear to you that I will give anything within my power to ensure help is obtained to find them, once we reach the Expanse."

Cadence bowed his head and squeezed his eyes shut for a moment, then threw his head back and let out a roar of frustration that sent birds launching from the trees.

Yiannis rested a hand on his shoulder as he met Chris's worried look. "I understand. Come. the faster we leave, the faster we may return for them."

They turned together and made their way to the horses. Dia called for Faustus and Ximeno to mount up, and in short order, they were back on the track out of the glade.

Chapter Thirty-One

Harlequin

Harley's boots kept sinking down into the mossy loam and underbrush. The day had become warm, and she was so sweaty and foot sore that she almost missed her saddle soreness.

Ahead of her, Jenta stopped and dropped to a crouch. She stuck her arm out to one side, gesturing for Harley to do the same.

Harley matched the movement as well as she could, then scuttled forward.

"Do you hear that?" Jenta said in a bare whisper, and Harley started to shake her head, then stopped.

The forest was quiet except the normal animal noises: birds singing high up in the branches, the skittering of small animals on the forest floor rustling through the leaves. They'd even glimpsed a couple sets of large, luminescent eyes regarding them from hollow logs before disappearing into the shadows. She thought at first Jenta had just heard another one of those little skittering creatures in the underbrush, but then she heard it.

Splashing water... and voices.

Jenta checked her dagger, and Harley reflected on the conversation they'd had at the inn. When did Jenta start wearing the little cat dagger at her belt instead of keeping it hidden in the bottom of her saddlebags?

One of the voices started singing in a high contralto. It sounded like words, but in no language Harley knew. They stayed crouched and tried to move closer, doing their best to keep themselves covered by the underbrush.

Jenta

The forest opened into a clearing taken up almost entirely by a rocky pool. A wide stone shelf hung over the water on one side, creating a ledge on which a young woman sat, her back to them. Down in the pool itself, another young woman swam, her face uptilted to watch the one sitting on the ledge.

Harley and Jenta looked at each other. Jenta mouthed, "dryads?" at Harley, questioningly.

Harley thought for a moment, then shook her head and mouthed back, "naiads."

The singing stopped, and the two naiads focused their attention on the woods where the girls crouched beyond the tree line.

The naiad sitting on the ledge scented the air. "Ah. Ssse myrízo ánthrope."

Jenta shook her head at Harley, her lips forming the word "don't."

Harley frowned, and whispered, "They might be able to help us."

"Or they might *eat* us." Jenta whispered back.

It was Harley's turn to shake her head. "Worst case, we run." She straightened, and Jenta tried to grab her arm, but Harley took a step forward and pushed her way out of the bushes to stop at the edge of the clearing.

Jenta stayed crouched in the brush, her heart pounding.

"I'm sorry, but I don't know that language. My name is Harley. My friend and I are trying to make it to the other side of the forest."

The woman sitting on the ledge tilted her head to one side as she studied Harley.

"Oh, poor mortal. You ssssmell of fear and desssperation. Let ussss help you." The woman's voice was sibilant and a delicate, forked tongue flicked between her teeth when she spoke.

The hair on the back of Jenta's neck rose and she scuttled forward, hoping to reach for Harley to pull her back among the trees, but Harley was already moving closer toward the edge of the pond.

The woman sitting on the ledge drew herself up gracefully while the other swam to the edge of the water where Harley was standing, drawing herself up and out of the pool in one easy movement. Jenta couldn't see Harley's face, but her posture was wrong. It was like she wasn't fully in control of herself.

Jenta continued to watch from the trees, frozen and shaking as the two naiads approached her friend. Both were nude, their bodies glistening, the one still dripping with water. Their hair hung down around their shoulders like seaweed. Their skin was the color of a fish's belly, and the outsides of their thighs and arms glinted with iridescent scales.

Harley watched them come toward her like a mouse would watch a snake. One of the creatures reached up, running fingers across Harley's cheek, letting long claw-like nails trail along the skin of her neck.

"Sssso sweet. Sssoo young." The second naiad moved up to Harley's other side, playing her hands through Harley's hair, droplets of water catching in her curls. The first buried her clawed hand into the hair close to Harley's scalp, yanking her head to the side to expose the long delicate line of her neck.

Jenta flinched at the movement, but Harley still didn't fight. Her body jerked with the movement, and the woman on her other side wrapped supple arms around Harley, who sagged against her. She was like a puppet with all her strings cut, limp and pliant in their arms. Jenta screamed at herself in her head and tried to make herself move as the creatures cooed and caressed Harley, running sharp nails across the exposed skin of her arms, but she felt just as frozen as Harley seemed to be.

Jenta gripped the hilt of her dagger tightly. She heard a cat hiss, and a sharp pain sliced through her forearm. Shocked, she looked down. There, across her forearm just above her wrist, was a long scratch, as if from a cat. What had Dia said? *If you have to fight something more than a vine, blood your weapon.*

Blood welled up on her arm, and she drew the blade, sliding the flat of it along the cut. Her heart pounded as she stared down at the now bloody dagger.

Then she was running, throwing herself out from among the brush and into the clearing. She crossed the ground in long strides and used her momentum to drive the blade hard into the side of one of the naiads, just below where ribs would end on a human. She wasn't entirely certain about naiad anatomy, but she hoped where she stabbed wouldn't matter.

The creature crumpled almost immediately, its eyes wide and glazed. Mortal blood, indeed. Jenta shook her head and yanked the blade free, then spun to face the other naiad, but she was too late. The woman vanished into the water with barely a splash.

Jenta wiped the flat of the blade on her pants, sheathed it, and dropped to her knees next to her friend. Harley lay on the ground, her eyes wide and staring. Jenta panicked. *Oh God, please don't let her be dead...* She took one of Harley's hands in hers. The skin was cold and clammy, but she could feel a pulse at her wrist, strong and steady. Jenta tried to chafe Harley's hand and forearm with her own hands. She stared at Harley's torso, waiting for it to move.

After what felt like an eternity, Harley drew in a sudden sharp breath and let it out, but her eyes continued to stare up into the sky.

She patted Harley's cheek with one hand, calling her name. "Harley... Harley, please, come back. Harley, please come back. Oh God, Harley, please..." Tears welled in her eyes, hot and immediate. Harley was breathing and Jenta couldn't find any injuries on her, but the other girl kept staring with that glazed expression.

The crumpled body of the naiad lay on the ground at Harley's feet. The creature hadn't moved, hadn't blinked, and her companion appeared to be long gone. Jenta got to her feet and looked around. Other than the pond, there was nothing in the clearing. The rocky edge that ringed the water abutted right up against the tree line everywhere but the small grassy patch where Harley lay. She didn't dare stay there by the side of the water. That other naiad might come back—or worse, come back with company.

Tucking her hands under the other girl's armpits, Jenta gave a grunt and half lifted, half pulled Harley into the underbrush. Harley's head lolled to the side, her body a dead weight in Jenta's arms.

Once they were back within the trees and out of sight of the clearing, Jenta laid Harley down in the leaves. The forest around them was warm and humid, full of birdsong and the chittering of insects that echoed through the branches. The rich smell of turned leaves filled the air, so thick Jenta could almost taste it.

She checked Harley's hands again. They were still cool and clammy. Her face was pale, and her eyes gazed blindly up into the speckled green canopy. When was the last time she'd seen Harley blink? She didn't think she'd seen a single eyelash flutter since the attack. The tears pushed at her eyes again. She took their blankets and used them to cover Harley up to her neck, then sat on a fallen log nearby.

What had the naiads done? It *looked* like they'd only touched her, but what if their claws had some sort of neurotoxin? Jenta hadn't seen any cuts or scratches. What if they had poison in their skin like frogs? Jenta had no idea. Anger at Harley rose up in her throat like bile, and then she felt stupid for being angry just as suddenly. What if it had been her? Would Harley have killed for her? She didn't think Harley would have hesitated even a second to help her, but she wasn't violent, and it might have meant both their lives. Jenta peered back toward where she'd left the severed naiad, then shook her head.

"It doesn't matter, dummy. You did what you did, and it's done, now. Focus on getting Harley back, and you can have a moral crisis later, okay? Great. Now I'm talking to myself." In the silence after she'd spoken, she realized the forest had gone quiet. No birds, no chittering. She scanned the forest, afraid she would see the other naiad.

Jenta had always thought that unicorns were just horses with horns. Beautiful, in her imagination, with their pure white coats and delicate hooves, their horns long and spiraled. The animal stepping silently among the tree shadows was similar to that vision, but not merely that.

Everything about the creature was thinner and smaller, and shaped closer to something between a small horse and a large goat. Their neck was long but nearly straight, and their mane was more like a lion's, covering the neck in long flowing tresses of shining hair down to narrow shoulders. The delicate head was more pointed than a horse's and had a long chin beard of the same spun thread-of-silver hair as the mane and the tuft of hair that grew from the tip of its otherwise whip-like tail. The long spiral horn that stuck from the center of that delicate head glowed with reflected afternoon sunlight.

She held her breath as the unicorn approached. They ignored her, entirely focused on Harley who lay prone among the leaves. Jenta's hand moved to her dagger again, unsure. The naiads seemed so innocent at first, beautiful and ethereal. Yiannis warned them repeatedly about the dangers of the forest, but this was a unicorn. Surely, she could trust a unicorn, right? Then she saw movement at the unicorns' feet. A tiny rat-man face peeking out from behind one dainty, fetlocked hoof. He grinned and waved at her, and Jenta nearly sobbed in relief.

The unicorn stopped just out of reach of Harley, studying her with large, liquid eyes surrounded by fine lashes the color of moonlit snow. They peered down at the little rat-man, and something brushed past Jenta's mind, like a conversation in a memory. Then the unicorn turned their attention Jenta. Her breath caught in her throat, and her heart thumped hard in her chest. Once, twice. Then a kind, motherly voice rang through her mind.

They are looking for you. Thistle has led me, and I have found you, and that is well. I shall help your friend and take you to them. That, also, shall be well. Tengri wills it, and so Oddyn Gal obeys.

Jenta blinked, and it felt like it took a really long time. When she opened her eyes again, she found the unicorn had lowered herself to lay beside Harley, nuzzling her gently. Harley gave a great gasp and sat up, her chest heaving as if she'd been under water. Startled, Jenta fell off the back of the log and was scrambling to stand as the unicorn pushed herself back to her feet.

Jenta rushed to Harley and hugged her, tears sliding freely down her cheeks.

"Oh God, Harley, I was so scared." She drew back, holding the other girl by the shoulders and looking into her face.

Harley frowned back, confused. "Jenta, what are you talking about? Why am I laying in the leaves? Oh…" Without looking, Jenta knew Harley had spotted the unicorn. "Um, Jenta, did you know there's a unicorn watching us?"

Jenta laughed. "Yes, Harley, I'm aware there's a unicorn watching us." She sniffed hard and wiped at her eyes, then scooted back and crouched among the leaves. "Are you okay? Do you feel alright?"

Harley raised a hand as if to touch her head, but then dropped her hand to her lap. "I don't remember anything after we heard that splashing sound. What happened?"

Jenta hesitated, glancing behind her at the unicorn, but more so at the clearing beyond. She wondered if the body was still there. When she turned back, Harley was peering at her, brows furrowed slightly. "You... You fell. I think you bumped your head, but I couldn't get you to wake up."

Harley continued to peer at her, and Jenta wondered if the other girl had caught her hesitation. "What was the splashing sound?"

"Some big animal. I think it smelled us because it came running after us. You fell down, and it ran off." Jenta pointed vaguely back toward the clearing. "Are you sure you're okay?"

"I think so. A little foggy headed, maybe. I feel like I had a weird dream, but I can't remember it."

Jenta cleared her throat. "The, uh, unicorn said someone was looking for us." Harley and Jenta both turned to the unicorn. She tossed her head and stamped one small hoof, knocking loose leaves into the air. The little rat-man squeaked and scurried to one side.

Harley pointed, eyes wide. "Hey, is that—?"

"His name is Thistle, apparently. He brought her to help us get back to our friends." Jenta smiled. Harley smiled back then glanced down at Jenta's arm. Jenta extended the limb obediently so Harley could see it. "Just a scratch. I think it happened while we were running."

At Harley's skeptical look, Jenta felt another surge of anger and then sadness. She tried to look at the scratch through Harley's perspective, then sighed and shook her head. "Never mind. We should get going." She tried to keep her voice clear of emotion, but Harley flicked her eyes from Jenta's arm to her face anyway, then away and out into the trees.

"Sure. Yeah." Harley said, but Jenta heard the hesitation in her words.

She straightened, offered Harley a hand up, and together they shook out their blankets. By the time they finished rolling them up, their guide was already making her way through the undergrowth, hooves leaving no trace among debris that littered the forest floor.

Chapter Thirty-Two

Christian

The forest around them was green and alive with animal sounds. The insect buzz was especially loud, and all Chris could think about was those damned cicadas that spent like thirteen years underground then came up in swarms to cover cars and trees and then died. Except, other than the noise, he didn't see anything. He could *hear* all the sounds of a forest in full swing, and even through the thick canopy above, he could tell the sun was shining, bright and sweltering.

He'd stowed the cloak Dia gave him and stripped down to a tank top and still his arms and back dripped sweat as he rode. Cadence was no better off, both of them stuck in thick jeans that seemed to weigh down their legs. They rode in what probably could have passed for companionable silence, which was to say both of them were anxious, their nerves frayed, and neither of those feelings was helped by the sidhe riding fully armored but without a single drop of sweat on them, for all the world as if they were out for a pleasant morning ride on a cool fall day.

They rode as the four points of a square with Chris and Cadence in the middle through the verdant forest.

Despite the excitement of the night before—and other than the girls and the twins being missing—the morning was fairly uneventful. Once the big dome came down, they'd ridden back out to the main road. Dia informed them that, past the gates of Comhaontu, the road was referred to as Merchant's Route.

When asked why the name change, her response was fairly succinct. "Because merchants are the only folk brave or fool hearty enough to regularly travel through the Wildes."

In the light of day, the path through the forest was clear and wide, dotted here and there with tiny shoots where plants were trying to grow from beneath the rock-studded, hard-packed earth.

Ahead of them, the trees opened up and Chris thought initially that they'd reached a break in the forest. Instead, he was greeted by a clear pond, expansive and still, with a ring of reedy water plants that stuck out at various heights above the surface and along the shore. Chris's mouth was instantly dry, and more sweat broke out on his skin. The water was pristine and pure, and he could see all the way to the bottom where fish shadows flitted and dashed among rocks and plants.

Chris was suddenly walking toward the pond, though he didn't remember dismounting. The buzzing of the insects grew louder, like an approaching swarm. He tried to look around for them, but his eyes just kept being drawn back to that dazzling, beautiful water. His mouth felt full of sand, and he was drenched in sweat that soaked through his clothes. He felt sticky and disgusting and his whole body hurt from the heat as the insect noise grew and grew, filling his head with that insistent high-pitched droning.

He was inches from that perfect, cool water. He could *feel* it, as if a breeze were coming from the water itself—as crisp as wind coming down off a snow-covered mountain—and Chris actually shivered, even in the heat. He licked his dry lips with a swollen tongue. Cadence stopped beside him, and they grinned at each other.

Strong hands grabbed him by the shoulders.

Chris was fighting, fighting. Trying to get free, trying to get to the water.

"No! Please! Just a sip, please!" Chris kicked and screamed, fought the hands dragging him away from the water, while the buzzing became a clatter that grew and grew in his head, until his screaming was just part of the noise, and his skin was burning as if he'd been set on fire and the only way to put it out was the pond.

Cold water splashed over him, and Chris gasped, panting and blinking up into the tree canopy. He sat up, his hair dripping down in his face. Cadence was beside him, equally soaking, spluttering as if he'd just had a bucket of ice water dumped over his head.

More water splashed onto Chris's back, soaking him all the way down, and leaving him sitting in a muddy puddle, trying to remember how to breathe.

The buzzing in his head vanished, and in the vacuum of silence, sound slowly returned, filtered among the pounding of his heart in his ears.

"...you hear me? Nod if you can hear me." Dia crouched in front of him, giving him serious eyes. Chris nodded and tried to swallow past a thick, dry lump in his throat.

When he finally spoke, his voice sounded as if he'd been eating sandpaper. "I can hear you."

Dia let out a relieved sigh. "Thank Danann. You two were not responding to us at all. We were trying to turn around, and then you two just dismounted and were nearly at the water before we could stop you."

Chris stared past her to the pond, and bile surged up in his throat. The pristine, perfect, crystal-clear water was gone—or had never been there. Instead, the water was murky and brown, and as soon as he saw it, he could smell it. It was the stink of stagnant water back home, the kind of water that gave host to not just huge mosquitos, but also all kinds of diseases. The kind of water that you dumped out and didn't even let birds drink. "Dead water," his grandmother had called it. The reeds growing around the edges were moldy where they touched the water, their stems already rotting even as the plants grew up from the muck.

"Fuck... I almost swam in *that*!" Chris's skin raised with gooseflesh. Icy fear ran down his spine so hard his teeth started chattering.

Dia offered him her hand to help him stand, and then someone was placing his cloak over his shoulders. Chris started to protest, knowing his back was still covered in sweat-sticky mud from the ground, but he began shivering all over again as the tingle of magic washed over him from head to toe. The water and dirt sloughed off of him in great droplets that splatted to the ground like fat raindrops. He huddled in his now completely dry cloak, watching little rivulets dribble back toward the water's edge.

"Um..." Cadence said, and Chris followed his pointing finger out to the middle of the pond, which started to bubble. First, only one or two little pops, but it was quickly becoming a rolling boil.

"Run!" Dia shoved them toward their horses and followed suit. Chris nearly tripped on the edge of his cloak as he spun and lunged toward his mare. Even so, he caught sight of that boiling water rushing toward the shore before vaulting up into his saddle and heeling his horse away from the water's edge and back among the trees.

Chris started to turn his head, to look at whatever was making that high, angry screech as it launched itself at them from the water, but Faustus's shouted "Do not look!" was as good as a physical blow, and Chris snapped his attention forward, keeping his eyes on the ground between his horses' ears as they sped back the way they'd come.

Cadence

Cadence hurt *everywhere*. After a day of riding, dodging vines, and the chaos of their escape from the monster pond—a chase that went on for far too long before the creature finally gave up and disappeared off into the trees from where it had come—they'd found a small patch of open ground to try and get some sleep.

Try because Cadence was convinced he'd found every possible rock or root under his blankets. Not that he suspected he would have slept much, anyway. Every time he closed his eyes, all he could see was visions of different ways the forest might have already hurt or killed Harley. His chest tightened, and his eyes burned with unshed tears as he lay staring up at the dome of crackling shield over their heads and prayed. *God... or Danann, or whoever... Please take care of her. Please. If I don't make it out of this stupid forest alive, please just make sure Harley is safe.*

I am with you. Have faith.

Cadence sat up and scanned the trees. Even the night birds were silent except for the occasional rustle of the branches higher up. Nothing moved in the darkness beyond Yiannis's shield.

Ximeno sat on an upturned portion of log to one side of their makeshift camp. He met Cadence's confused expression with raised eyebrows. He started to stand, but Cadence waved his hands and shook his head, then pulled his blanket back up and lay back, then rolled on his side.

Eventually, his eyes slid closed, and sleep swallowed him.

Chapter Thirty-Three

Christian

"Okay, is it just me or are we going around in circles?" Cadence said in exasperation as they rounded another turn in the path only to find the same scene in front of them. To the left was a clearing with a big, lightning split tree trunk, the sky above clear of branches in a ring high above their heads to show scudding clouds among the blue. To the right, a wall of dead vines still showed the scorch marks from Ximeno's magic.

It was the third, or maybe fourth time they'd ridden around a bend in the forest to find themselves facing the split tree and the burnt vines, and that was *after* the first time, when they'd had the initial fight with, Chris reminded himself, an apparently sentient tree that lashed at them with branches and roots, while the vines on the other side of the path kept trying to strangle their horses.

"Naw, I'm sure the forest is probably full of groups just riding around, exploding trees with lightening for funzies. If we come across them, do you suppose it's golf rules if we want to pass? You know, ask them if we can play through, only, in this case, 'play' means 'fight plants that are trying to eat us'?" Chris asked, as he glanced at Cadence questioningly.

Cadence rolled his eyes. "I know you're joking, but I'd like it better if it was *actually* funny."

Chris feigned a pained look and pressed a hand to his chest. "You wound me."

Cadence gave him a look. "You know what I mean."

Ahead of them, Yiannis drew his horse to a stop and dismounted. He went to the burnt stump of tree, pressing a hand to it and bowing his head.

"What's he doing?" Chris asked Dia as they moved their horses up next to hers.

"Looking for water." Dia said distractedly, as she tried to pay attention to both Yiannis and the forest around them.

"Why?" Cadence asked. "We just filled our waterskins this morning. After yesterday, I don't think I would even want to take a bath in a clean tub let alone see that much water for a bit..."

"Aww, you're no fun, Cay. We could have probably tamed that thing, put a saddle on it. Maybe even hugged it and squeezed it and called it George." Chris said, giving Cadence a sardonic smile.

"Saddle sounds about right considering how big it sounded even just tromping back into the trees." Cadence said, considering.

"I would not encourage trying to ride a boobrie." Faustus said from behind them.

Chris gave wide eyes, as he tried not to laugh. "I'm sorry... Did you just say, a boobrie?"

Faustus gave a nod, his expression serious. "Yes."

Ximeno tilted his head, gazing at Chris curiously. "Do you have much experience with boobries?"

In his peripheral, Chris saw Cadence's eyes nearly pop out of his head with how hard he was trying not to laugh. Chris couldn't blame him. He knew he shouldn't be laughing, but he was too tired to be scared. He choked back the laugh that tried to bubble up in his throat and shook his head, answering the brothers' questioning looks.

"No, I can't say that I do." He said, trying to keep his tone even.

They took his answer on its face, nodding. "It is for the best, I think." Ximeno said. "They can be capricious, at best. At worst... Well."

Yiannis rejoined them, interrupting whatever conversation might have come next.

"This way. We will follow the water out of this damned forest if we have to." Yiannis grumbled, then drew his horse down a track Chris never would have seen if he hadn't been looking for it.

Harlequin

Harley sat in a big wooden tub with hot water up to her neck as she luxuriated in the feeling of being *clean*. Behind her, an elven woman sat, using a comb to carefully brush out her hair, working fingers and comb deftly through multiple days' worth of knots while Harley soaked and slowly melted into water that smelled like lilacs.

Her skin had already been scrubbed with coarse soup until it tingled, and her fingers were slowly turning prune-y as the water cooled around her.

"No falling asleep in the tub." Jenta said from a second big wooden basin, though her voice sounded just as sleepy as Harley felt. She heard the other girl's yawn follow almost immediately, and then her own yawn caught her, even as she laughed.

Oddyn Gal had led them out of the forest and straight into the arms of an outpost full of elves. They'd been immediately embraced and welcomed into low stone huts like long-lost family members.

The outpost sat on the far side of a hill past the road out of the Wildes, about three hours' walk from where they'd exited the tree line. Harley nearly cried when Gildred, the elven woman who'd offered them a place in her own incredibly charming cottage, came right away upon their arrival, bearing an armful of clothing for them, news of hot baths, and the comb she was now easing through Harley's damp curls.

The sound of sloshing and Jenta's good-natured grumbling made Harley smile, even as she opened her eyes to see another elven woman, Ingrid, already wrapping a swath of fluffy fabric around Jenta's shoulders and ushering her toward a curtained doorway out of the room where the bathing tubs stood. The only other things in the room were a huge, crackling fireplace where they boiled the water, a line of wooden pegs on one wall, all holding similar pieces of fabric to what Jenta had just been wrapped in, and two stools. Gildred sat on one, and Ingrid had been sitting on the other, giving Jenta's hair the same treatment Gildred was giving hers.

Harley felt a soft tap of the comb on her head and smiled up at Gildred.

The motherly elf smiled at her but said, "You'll be as wrinkled as a winter apple, soon. Come. We shall get you dressed, and then seek out word of your menfolk. I've heard Arne will be among those to retrieve them, and that's well. He's as fine a scout as any."

Harley took a moment while she rose from the water, closing her eyes and letting the warm humid air of the bathing room wrap around her. *Cay.*

Please be alright. Danann, if you can hear me, please take care of them. We have your journey to finish, and I don't know if I can do this without him.

I hear you, child.

Harley opened her eyes and studied the room. Other than Gildred, standing there holding a towel out for her, there was no one else. "Did you say something, Gildred?" Harley asked doubtfully.

"I? No. Though it is said that Danann sometimes answers those who call." Gildred gave her a comforting smile as she wrapped Harley in her own cozy towel.

"Hm." Harley said, more to herself, as she followed Gildred back out of the bathing room.

Chapter Thirty-Four

Christian

C hris ached to go faster.

Yiannis had mentioned that morning that if the forest continued to cooperate, they should reach the far side of it by nightfall. If this was the forest *cooperating*, Chris wondered what it would have been like otherwise.

They were rounding yet another bend in the road when Yiannis brought them to a stop with a raised hand. The trees blocked the view of what was ahead, and Chris scanned the forest to see if Yiannis had spotted something among the undergrowth. The forest was mostly quiet except for the usual sounds of birds and insects moving in the branches and the underbrush.

Cadence grabbed his arm and pointed at the path ahead of them. After a moment, Chris heard it—the distinctive sound of horses. Yiannis led them forward slowly, and all of them focused on the road ahead. From around the bend, three fae rode toward them, grins splitting their faces as soon as they laid eyes on the party. Relief spread across Yiannis's face, his shoulders relaxing as he returned their grins.

"Ho, Yiannis! Hail and well met, friend! We've been searching for you! Grandame Oddyn Gal said we would find you here, and sure as rain, there you are!" The front rider was dressed in forest greens and browns, his mount small and agile compared to the larger sidhe-bred ones. Rider and horse alike were slim and strong looking, and moved as if they were one.

The two riders that followed him wore similar attire: simple tunics and vests over loose trousers. All three riders had narrow faces, sharply angled chins and long pointed ears, and hair that hung over their shoulders in split braids decorated with charms and tiny bells. Bow cases hung on their backs and full quivers weighted one side of their belts to offset sheathed short swords.

"Hail, Wilhelm, Frode, Arne! Danann's eyes, but it is good to see you!" Yiannis urged his horse forward to meet the three riders. Chris and Cadence hung back while Faustus and Ximeno rode forward, gripping wrists and exchanging greetings as well. Finally, Yiannis waved them forward, gesturing to the three new fae.

"Cadence, Christian, let me introduce Wilhelm the Stout, Frode the Scribe, and Arne Fleet Shot. Wilhelm, Frode, Arne, these are Cadence and Christian." The three riders bowed from their saddles, then grinned at Chris and Cadence.

"Ah, the young mortals! Well met! Come! Grandame Oddyn Gal is waiting." With that, Wilhelm spun his mount in a tight circle, and made way back up the path.

With the riders leading them, the forest subsided its attacks. Though many of the grasping vines hovered at the edges of the path, it was more like they were watching the party pass—if vines with no discernable eyes could watch.

Then they were clearing the trees and entering rolling hills. In the distance, Chris could see the top of a great stone tower poking above the first rise. He stopped his horse for a moment and took a breath. Though they were still close to the forest, the air immediately became cooler, less humid.

Yiannis allowed them only a moment, then he and Wilhelm led them into a quick canter. Ahead, the tower rose up as if it had sprouted straight from the grass of the field in which it sat. The valley they entered was long and flat, running between two tall ridges and dipping down into a line of trees behind the buildings that made up the outpost. Low buildings made of the same big pale stones as the tower formed a rough semicircle with an open-sided stable taking up a long section on the far side. They headed toward the stable, Chris guiding his mount past the first line of buildings.

Just to the right of the open, grassy field that made up the stable yard was a set of squat little stone cottages. Figures were stepping out of one of them and Chris drew up on his reins just as Cadence launched himself from his saddle and ran, scooping one of them up in his arms and lifting her from the ground. Cadence buried his face in Harley's hair, and she laughed and hugged him back.

Chris dismounted and handed his horse over to a small woman with features similar to their guides, who gave him a shy smile and a curtsy before leading the horse away. Chris approached, seeing Jenta had also just exited the same cottage. He gingerly offered a hug, which she accepted awkwardly, then they stepped apart, both watching the spectacle.

Cadence was brushing a lock of hair from Harley's cheek, searching her eyes as if he would find some long-lost answer in them. "Are you okay?

God, Harley, I was so worried about you. Both of you." Cadence gave Jenta a wry smile from over Harley's shoulder.

"Uh huh. Cool, well, I'll pass on the rib crushing hug for my part if that's good."

Jenta's tone was her usual sardonic one, but with an edge of sadness. Harley appeared healthy and hale. Jenta looked okay, but tired.

Cadence grinned, and Chris turned to Jenta. "What happened? Where did you go?"

"Were Aoife and Leif with you guys?" Cadence asked.

Jenta and Harley glanced at each other, then shook their heads. Harley said "No, we woke up in a clearing by ourselves."

Yiannis spoke as he approached, flanked by the riders. "Perhaps these questions may wait. I am told that baths are waiting for us, after which we are expected by Grandame Oddyn Gal. It has been my experience that it is ill luck to leave a queen waiting."

Harlequin

While the guys took their turn in the bathhouse, Harley and Jenta went to check on their horses. The gray mare whinnied, seeming pleased to see her, and Harley patted her neck and offered her an apple provided from one of the stable lads as she checked over her things and gave the horse a well-deserved rub down. Jenta, in the next stall over, was doing the same with her buckskin, talking to him quietly as she rubbed at his coat with handfuls of straw.

Ingrid hung over the gate leading out of the stables, watching them as she asked, "Tell me, do you have claim to any of those menfolk with you?"

Harley blushed a little, and smiled to herself, but did her best to answer honestly. "Not specifically, no. Why do you ask?"

Ingrid gave her a look from beneath her brows and Harley blushed harder then heard Jenta start to laugh.

"Don't mind Harley, Ingrid. She and Cay are... complicated would be the best word for it." Jenta said, even as Harley glared daggers at her. "Oh, Harley. Don't pretend it isn't true. At the very least, you have the hots for him, but you, of all people, were never the type to *just* anything for anyone, but especially Cay."

"And Christian? Is he your betrothed, Jenta? He is quite handsome, if you do not mind my saying so. He would look quite fine, with belled braids, I think." Ingrid clapped a hand over her mouth, her face turning a lovely shade of pink, and Harley's scowl became a grin that she shared with Jenta. Ingrid stammered and ducked her head. "My apologies. That was forward of me!"

"No apologies needed, Ingrid. I've no claim on him, no." Jenta said, her voice gentle.

Harley studied Jenta who met her gaze squarely. "No, no claim, but you and I both know he wishes you did." Harley said.

"Yeah, well, that's not what she asked though, is it?" Jenta responded, though her tone didn't match the chiding words.

"Oh, how romantic!" Ingrid said, and Harley wondered just how old the elven maid actually was. "To have a companion so devoted! Unrequited love, truly, is there anything so... so..." Ingrid grasped for a word.

"Inconvenient." Jenta said, laughing. Ingrid huffed at her, and Jenta laughed harder.

Harley dropped the last of the straw and patted her mare then made her way out of the stall. She stepped up to the gate where Ingrid leaned and met her gaze. "It's a long story, Ingrid. Jenta doesn't mean any harm, and the truth is, no, none of us have any claim to each other, other than the claim of friendship."

"For now." Jenta said, as she joined them, dusting off her hands.

Harley inclined her head and gave a little shrug. "For now."

Ingrid flicked her gaze back and forth at them, then stepped away from the gate to let them come through. As they left the stables walking back toward the cottages, she asked "Are all humans this... what was the word you used, Jenta? Complicated?"

Harley and Jenta shared another glance, but both answered at the same time. "Yes."

Extra tubs had been taken into the bathhouse, so that all the members of their party could clean up more quickly, and apparently, Yiannis, and Ximeno worked together to heat some water while Faustus and Dia moved rocks in and out of the fire and dropped them into the great metal cauldrons to heat more.

Harley saw none of it, but Gildred was more than happy to tell her about it while they waited for everyone to come trooping out, washed and scrubbed.

Cadence and Chris were in their own clothes, which had been freshly laundered along with Harley's and Jenta's, while the guys bathed.

As they exited the bathhouse, Cadence offered Harley his arm, and Chris watched them, then turned to Jenta.

There was a silent moment of Jenta and Chris considering each other, but then to Harley's surprise, Jenta shook her head, though her laugh wasn't mocking so much as tired. "I can escort myself. But thanks, though."

Jenta patted Chris's offered arm gently.

Harley took Cadence's arm while Jenta moved past them to take the lead down the path. As Chris moved up beside her, Harley took his arm as well. When he gave her surprised eyes, she gave him back a smile, and patted his forearm. His expression softened, and Harley bumped his shoulder with hers as they made their way down the path.

Jenta walked just ahead of them, deeper into the valley and past the watchtower where the path sloped down gently into a great shallow bowl ringed with lush trees full of flitting birds and bright foliage. The branches stretched out and up, but still ended far short of the center of the clearing to reveal a vast circle of darkening sky above them, already thick with stars.

To the right was a small pond ringed by river rock and a wall of stone that rose up out of the ground near the trees. A natural spring trickled and gurgled along the rocks down into the water, and the pond itself was dotted with water lilies and great green leaf pads on which sat a multitude of winged fae. Some of them were so tiny they were barely larger than moths, but some of them were nearly a foot tall with enormous butter- and dragon-fly wings, all lending their voices to the happy song of the water on rocks.

The grass in the center of the bowl was short-cropped, and the ground beyond where the path ended was soft under foot. Harley pointed toward the very back of the bowl, at a tall willow with draping vines. The tree was dappled with lights that hung like jewels and lit the whole thing from high up in the branches all the way down to where the roots tangled themselves into the grass. When she saw both the guys gaping, she couldn't help but grin.

Harley let go of their arms and urged them forward, then went around to one side of Oddyn Gal, to watch from beside her as Cadence and Chris stopped at the edge of the wall of willow vines and dropped to one knee, pressing their closed hands into the soft ground, and bowing their heads.

Oddyn Gal gave her a look out of one large eye, and Harley felt a brush of thought. *This one is yours? He is handsome, for a human.* Harley clapped her hand over her mouth while the unicorn gave a whinny that was almost a laugh, then tossed her head and stepped forward on silent hooves, stopping in front of Cadence. Oddyn Gal dropped her head to snuffle at the guys' hair, her chin-beard mingling with first Cadence's bright red, then Chris's dark blond.

Harley waited until the unicorn returned to her position at the base of the tree, standing between Jenta and herself, before introducing them out loud.

"Grandame Oddyn Gal, this is Cadence, and this is Christian." Harley tried to stifle the laughter, but it crept into her voice. Cadence, coming to his feet, gave her a look, then his face split into a broad grin. She wondered if it was for the same reason as hers.

Yiannis stepped forward as Cadence and Chris came to stand beside her and Jenta. Behind him, Ximeno and Faustus stood to either side of him, but Dia was only just approaching from up the slope near the outpost. He gave a deep bow, mirrored by the brothers, and spoke as he straightened.

"Grandame Oddyn Gal, well met. You are a joy to my eyes and heart. I will admit, I was not expecting to see you this close to the Wildes. Are those of your blessing well?"

The unicorn regarded him, but Frode spoke, stepping forward so everyone could hear her words. "Grandame Oddyn Gal says she is pleased to see you as well, Yiannis Tide-Borne. She thanks you for asking and confirms that yes, her children and grandchildren reside in safety, well and hale and far from this place. She says she was beseeched to intercede by those who learned you had been denied safe harbor and safe passage."

Yiannis inclined his head again but not before Harley caught a flair of anger in his expression. "I did not know there were any who would have spoken on our behalf, but I am grateful, nonetheless." Dia just reached them as he finished what he was saying, and a disgruntled look crossed her face.

Oddyn Gal made a soft chuffing noise and tossed her head. Frode spoke again, "She was moved to grant the boon as she has seen the dimming of the stars and the turning of hearts to face the darkness. She worries that soon the hunters will come again, as in times before. Even so, she was also approached by one of the denizens of the Wildes and not even one of greater standing. A brave thing for one of those considered the least among us to seek aid."

Yiannis looked a question at Frode, but the elf just shrugged. "I've no idea of what she speaks."

Harley spoke, adjusting her shoulders as she felt all eyes turn to her. "When we woke up in the Wildes, there was a little rat-man." Cadence startled, and Harley waved him off. "He was tiny, and way more scared of us than we were of him, and we had no reason to keep him or hurt him, so we let him go, and asked just that he ask the forest to let us go, if he could."

Frode inclined his head. "It is a rare kindness in the Wildes. It is no wonder he sought to aid you in return." The elf bowed to Oddyn Gal, then smiled at Yiannis.

"She bids you and yours to rest this night under her aegis. The lands have shifted, and much of them past the bounds of our outpost have been claimed by allies of the dark. As for we elves, we will ensure you are well provisioned, and a guide will be sent with you."

Yiannis scanned the clearing, then returned his attention to the unicorn.

"Our last night of respite, I will happily receive under the protection of your grace. You honor us, both with your intercession, and with your presence." He stepped forward, and as Cadence and Chris had both done, he dropped elegantly to one knee, one forearm resting on his other knee, the other hand folded so his curled fingers pressed into the soft ground. Behind him, the other warriors did the same, all of them bowing their heads in what Harley took to be a grave sign of respect.

Yiannis held himself there for a long moment. Oddyn Gal stepped forward, dropping her horn to lay the length of its rapier-thin spiral against the back of his head. His body shuddered with a deep inhale of breath, and she stepped back, throwing her head to the sky and letting out a high, keening trumpet.

"The honor is hers to know again the sight of her great friend, Hianius. Grandame says it is good to see you." Frode's face lit with a broad grin. "Though it has taken you long enough to earn Danann's grace, 'young upstart'."

Yiannis' head came up and he goggled at the unicorn for a moment, then threw his head back and laughed, the sound full of true joy. The other warriors shared a glance, but soon they were grinning, too, as the valley rang with the sound of Yiannis's laughter.

When his laughter subsided, he inclined his head, again, but the smile didn't fade. "Fair enough, Grandmare. Fair enough. Come, everyone. One last night of safe rest, we shall not waste it. Tomorrow starts the hardest portion of our journey, but hopefully the shortest."

Yiannis came smoothly to his feet, bowing again at the waist and receiving a whinny that sounded very much like laughter.

Chapter Thirty-Five

Christian

They sat on soft blankets, dining on a hearty grain and nut porridge that was both spicy and sweet, topped with a sharp crumbly cheese cut with veins of green and blue and served with thick, fluffy bread. Wilhelm, Frode, and Arne sat with them, surrounded by blankets full of other elves. Chris initially thought that the sidhe *were* elves, but as they interacted, he saw that past the basic similarities, they were quite different.

Yiannis and Dia, Faustus, and Ximeno absolutely towered among the much shorter elves, who, in some cases barely came up to even Jenta's shoulders. The three riders were some of the tallest, standing about as tall as he was. Whereas the sidhe back at the palace all dressed in seemingly endless finery, all of the elves were dressed in simple garments in various shades of green and brown, though occasionally there was a splash of color in a bright blue shirt or a vibrant red apron. Their hair was waist-length almost to a person, none with hair shorter than their shoulders, and all wore their hair in at least one braid down their back. Many, like Frode and Arne, had things woven into their braids like beads or bone jewelry, or even just a long piece of fabric.

While they ate, the three riders informed them that the territories hadn't only shifted but that the land itself had changed drastically in the last hundred years or so. Swamps previously far to the north moved south, and much of the river lands originally home to the naiads receded north into where the swamps had been, leaving a great canyon in its wake, surrounded by a swath of scrub desert. Yiannis worried at how much the land had changed, but Wilhelm and Arne were excited at the opportunity for more exploration, having mapped much of the new territories while scouting.

As full night fell, the bowls were cleared away and the conversation drifted to their journey thus far. Chris, still not sure how to feel about the last two days, sat back on his blanket while the winged fae came from the pond carrying all manner of instruments. They were already playing, and started dancing in the air and spinning among the branches of the trees like acrobats. Harley drew Cadence away to meet some of the elves, leaving Chris sitting on the blanket with Dia and Yiannis, watching the festivities. Even Ximeno and Faustus allowed themselves to be pulled into the dancing, their broad forms clearly visible among the smaller elves.

Chris's gaze was drawn time and again to Jenta. There was something different, something that hadn't been there before they were all separated. A shadow lay on her, some darkness that he didn't like. She was sitting on a blanket near the grandame in the grass below the limbs of the willow. His heart swelled up when the small fae went to dance among them, and Jenta started laughing, and clapping. Then he had to quash a pang of jealousy as she accepted the hand of one of the elven men and went to join the dancing.

A hand was extended to him, and he stared up into the eyes of the young elven maiden who smiled at him when they arrived.

"Will you dance, my lord?" She asked a bit shyly.

Chris looked around, nervous. Jenta was already being spun and handed off as if she had known the steps of the dance her whole life, and Chris started to shake his head, with the intention to politely decline. Dia, sitting beside him, leaned over when he hesitated.

"It is the way of our magic, Christian. Allow yourself the joy of this night. Fear not; you will not falter." She nudged him with her shoulder and gave him a warm smile, pushing at him while the elven maiden grabbed him by both hands and pulled him, laughing, to his feet.

The steps were quick, and the circle became two, then three, then four, and then back to one. The dancers spun and leapt and whooped, the music pulling them across the ground and guiding their feet, and Chris suddenly grasped why Jenta danced like she already knew the steps: The magic pulled and pushed at him; the music plucked at him, and his body just *knew*. Instead of making him tired, the dancing filled him with energy, his heart singing in his chest as he moved through the circles, face after face passing him as he reeled and spun and whooped. At last, the music drew to a close and his hand touched the hand of his last partner. He blinked. Of course, it was Jenta.

His heart lurched to a stop, and his chest heaved as he tried to catch his breath. Her face was alight with mirth, her eyes sparkling. His fingers tingled where their hands touched. Of course it was Jenta. The magic of fairy tales, the wonder of the world around them full of myths and legends walking and talking and existing, and here in front of him was Jenta. The smile was slowly fading from her face, and he couldn't bear it. His hands raised and sunk deeply into her hair, her scalp warm and her hair silken soft. He drew her face close, and met her eyes, searching them, knowing his own screamed with hope and need and some unknown emotion.

They stood there forever, and for no time at all. Her eyes slid closed, and her arms wrapped around him.

They kissed. He thought his chest would explode. Her lips were soft, so soft. The kiss was gentle. Tender. Perfect.

A loud, joyous cry broke out in the crowd, raising and spinning up into the sky, as many voices joined in. Jenta and Chris came back, blinking and laughing as the music spun up again, drawing them into another dance. The air glittered and sparkled. Chris felt as if he could fly, his feet light as he leapt and whooped, and his eyes never left Jenta.

Chapter Thirty-Six

Harlequin

Harley's pillow was moving, and panic rose up in her chest. Had the last two days all just been a dream? Something swam in her mind: large liquid eyes, and the sound of singing like an echo from far away, or underwater. It tugged at her memory, but when she grasped for it, the images fled through her fingers like smoke on sand. She took a deep breath and let it out and tried to focus. She didn't hear any rasping breaths. No putrid smell of rotten meat and dung. She took another deep breath, coming more awake.

The air was full of the smells of sun warmed grass, and the rich scent of flowers. It made her think of the massive lilac tree in her backyard at home, and she finally made herself open her eyes. She was lying on her side on a thick blanket, and her pillow was someone's arm, sun darkened, and dusted with fine, gold-red hair. She shifted a little and found Cadence looking down at her with a grin.

"Morning. Sorry. I was trying not to wake you. You fell asleep on my shoulder last night, and I didn't want to move you." Harley's eyes widened, and she started blushing. She pushed herself up into a sitting position and scrubbed her face with both hands. The blanket that had been covering them both puddled down to her lap.

"Oh, oh my God, Cay, I'm sorry. Were you stuck there all night?" She peered at him, reclined on his arm next to her.

"I wasn't 'stuck.'" He grinned wider. "It was actually really nice."

Harley gawked at him, then laughed and slapped him gently on the chest. "Jerk. You should have woken me up. I would have moved."

She pushed the blanket off her legs and surveyed the clearing. Two more blanket-covered bodies lay near them. Only two. Yiannis was standing over by the willow, speaking quietly with one of the elven men. Arne? Harley thought that was his name. There was no sign of Grandame Oddyn Gal, and Harley felt a pang of disappointment, wishing she'd had a chance to say goodbye.

Nearby, a small wooden table was laden with a cloth covered basket and two clay pitchers, surrounded by a grouping of clay mugs. Harley pointed to the table. "When did that get there?"

Cadence followed her pointing finger. "Arne and one of the other elves brought it down a little while ago. Do you want some?"

"I can get it. I need to stand up, anyway." Cadence made a disappointed sound but laughed as Harley got up and dusted herself off.

She still wore the clothes she'd been gifted when she and Jenta arrived from the Wildes. The pants were billowy around her legs, tied by a surprisingly complicated knot pattern of lacings down the back of the calves, and the tunic was loose and soft. It made her think of the outfit Dia was wearing when they first met her, except that these were all a mix of various greens. Over the top of it, she wore her sidhe-crafted red belt, Fire's Bite, and felt a bit like a Christmas tree, but the clothing was comfortable, and blessedly wrinkle free.

Harley went to the table and pulled back the linen from the basket to reveal a pile of rolls, still steamy and dotted with fruit. The pitchers held something that smelled like apple cider. She poured a mug for herself and, after a moment, another for Cay, balancing a warm roll on top of each mug. She walked back to the blanket where he still sat, legs now crisscrossed in front of him and his forearms resting on his knees as Yiannis and the elven man approached.

They stopped by the two other blanket-wrapped sleepers, waking first Jenta, then Chris who both rose, gathered their blankets, and followed after.

"Arne and I have worked out what we believe will be the best path through to Dark's doorstep. It is time we got going for the day."

Cadence scanned the clearing, then brought his attention back to Yiannis. "Are we down more escorts?"

"Faustus and Ximeno left with a group of fae who came seeking aid, this morning." Yiannis said, not sounding exactly happy.

"Doesn't that seem a little risky? You said, yourself last night that we're headed into the most dangerous part of the journey, today." Harley asked, not able to hide her worry.

"I agree, Harlequin. I was loath to part with them. I know that Dia mentioned to you that we sidhe are stewards, the Seelie doubly so. Our first role is to aid those who come seeking it. Ximeno and Faustus are capable fighters, and were sent with a contingent of elven scouts, and Arne, Frode, and Wilhelm will be traveling with us as guides." Yiannis clapped Arne's shoulder and gave him a nod. "We could not have better to accompany us."

"And Dia? Where's she?" Jenta asked while folding her blankets.

"Dia is already up with the horses, packing provisions for us."

Chris shook his head. "That seems weirdly convenient timing, for a group to just randomly show up asking for help. Especially after two of our escorts already vanished into the Wildes, and no one has seen or heard from them in days. Did they say *why* they needed help?"

"Their townlet was attacked by a band of gobkin. They were able to escape and come to the outpost for help, but the rest of their families were being held up in their homes. It is the first time in a long while that something so... overt... has occurred between clans." Yiannis glanced at Arne. Harley and Cadence met eyes, him returning the concern she knew was in her own expression.

"I must go check on the horses. I bid you break your fasts quickly and join us once you are finished." Yiannis headed up the slope toward the outpost, Arne walking behind him like a willowy shadow.

The four of them shared a moment of quiet fear. Harley envisioned the brothers and how they'd changed over the last few days, or maybe just finally felt able to be themselves, once out from under their father's thumb.

"Danann, please be with your children." She said quietly, and the other three just nodded.

Christian

Something had changed between Chris and Jenta. They headed to the path behind Cadence and Harley, and he wracked his brain for something to say; something light and silly and simple—some joke or sarcastic remark about sleeping on the ground—but his head was filled with the music from the night before, and all he could remember was the feel of her lips and dancing and the heady magic of the fae circle. He felt strange and detached but also free and clearheaded in a way he hadn't since he woke up from that first nightmare, bruised and terrified.

Jenta walked beside him, her eyes focused up the slope. Again, she appeared like she hadn't really slept, but she moved as if she were as well rested as he was, despite their night of dancing among the elves. As if she sensed his eyes on her, she gave him a slight smile.

"Did you sleep okay? I think I found all the rocks under my blanket." She laughed a little, and Chris tried to laugh with her, but it was awkward.

He opened his mouth to say something, then closed it, swallowing the words. He tried again. "Yeah, I slept okay. I don't think you found *all* the rocks. I may have kept one or two for my pillow."

"Oh, well. That's as good as a luxury massage, so I've heard." She smirked, and he really laughed, some tension easing out of his shoulders.

Deeper words hung on the tip of his tongue, words he couldn't bring himself to say, so he spoke around them. "Who needs a memory foam mattress when you've got soft grass and hard rocks, right?"

"And now, we head for another day in the saddle. It's practically a spa trip!"

Harley and Cadence, walking in front of them, shared a look and rolled their eyes, laughing.

As they topped the rise and entered the stable yard, the looks on the faces around them sobered him quickly. Many of the elves were already up and at morning chores. Dia was standing with Wilhelm, Frode, Wilhelm's wife Bodil, and Frode's partner, Bo, who they'd met the night before. Bodil was delicate, nearly frail, one of the only elves Chris had seen with hair that wasn't a rich chestnut brown or similar. Hers instead was a nearly white blond, and her eyes were a blue so pale they were almost white. *Like a husky's eyes*, he thought. Standing beside Wilhelm, her coloring was that much more obvious next to his sun-darkened skin and thick brown braids hanging over either shoulder.

Bo on the other hand was a study in brown hues. His hair was nearly black, like strong coffee, and skin the color of honey. He had high, strong cheekbones, and large, hazel eyes that nearly glowed out from the hollows below his brow ridge. His clothes were all some shade between the honey brown of his skin and the coffee brown of his hair, except for a solid white belt of cured leather on which hung a staff made of bone, tied at one end with a thick black braided cord. Chris wasn't sure what it meant, but Bo was the only elf he'd seen who had one.

The elves were saying their goodbyes, Wilhelm holding Bodil close, and whispering something into her hair that made her shake her head as she gripped his shirt. Bo, a little taller than Frode, beheld the smaller man's face as if he would memorize every inch of it. The roll Chris had eaten started twisting and churning in his stomach. It was one thing to offer himself to this mission—he had nothing to lose. He tried to remind himself that the others were choosing this, too. Of everyone, it seemed the sidhe were the only ones who'd had no choice.

Jenta was embracing some of the elven women, Harley at her side. The elves all understood that this leg of their journey was the most dangerous. There was no question in the stoic faces that studied them as they mounted and made their way out of the stable yard toward the track that would take them deeper into the hill country.

Chapter Thirty-Seven

Cadence

T he tension had been growing all morning. Cadence ached, his muscles tight as they rode as silent as the shadows that dragged behind their horse's hooves. The track Arne led them to was barely more than trampled grass that wound through the gullies between hills.

The morning was warm, even among the hill shadows, and the only thing keeping the sweat out of his eyes was a wind cutting down the path toward them, kicking up dust and throwing around the errant leaf or blade of grass.

Wilhelm and Arne were riding close at the front, their heads bowed together in discussion when another gust pushed around a turn of the hill. It carried with it the tinkling sound of tack and a rancid, sour smell. Arne's head came up, followed quickly by his hand.

Cadence, riding third back behind Yiannis, felt a wash of fear run through him as Arne slipped from the saddle, making no noise, and handed off his reins to Wilhelm. He dropped into a crouch and made his way up the side of the slope to their right. The crouch became a belly crawl as he gained the top of the rise, and Cadence only knew where he was by watching the shifting of the tall grass.

A long silence followed, and Cadence held his breath, barely daring to blink. A sudden confusion of scattering rocks became Arne backtracking down the slope and throwing himself up onto his horse. He dragged at the reins of his mount, the horse nearly turning on one hoof as Arne urged them to turn back the way they'd come. The horses panicked in the moment, legs almost tangling and hooves sliding among the talus on the track. After what felt like an eternity, they were starting to progress back down the path.

Then they heard the first horn.

It blared, long and discordant, bouncing down the valley from behind them. It was echoed by another and then another, all coming from different tracks among the hills. Bellows and howls filled the air, and hooves pounded the earth, causing the rocks beneath them to bounce and clatter.

Frode took the lead and drove his mount ahead, drawing them off the main path and down a narrow pass at the bottom of a deep gully that was just wide enough for one horse at a time. They raced through the passage, Cadence watching the sides of the steep slopes, waiting to see nightmares come pouring over the ridges. On the far side, the valley opened up to a plateau stubbled with scrub grass and spindly, wind-twisted trees. The riders ahead of him let their horses have their heads as soon as they cleared the pass, necks stretching and bodies flying across the open ground.

Cadence cleared the gully and looked over his shoulder, immediately wishing he hadn't. The nightmare he'd feared would pour down the slopes in the pass was rushing up over the crests of the hills behind them. Three enormous, tusked goblins rode boars nearly as big as his horse with burning red eyes and their own huge tusks capped with metal spikes. The goblins were flanked by a pack of wolves—at least twenty of them, some as large as the boars, all with dirty black shaggy coats and mouths open to show sharp, snapping teeth.

He made himself turn to face forward so he could watch the ground and his fellow riders, spotting Harley on her dappled gray and praying that the week of riding would be enough to help her keep her seat. Jenta rode just ahead of them, her buckskin showing no signs of tiring as his legs churned, driving him forward with Jenta hugged close to his shoulders as if she were a part of her horse. Chris' black mare was a bullet, neck nearly straight and mane streaming back. Cadence's own blood bay was running with all the strength and speed his sleek body implied, Cadence gripping the reins hard and letting himself lean into his horse's lunging strides.

Ahead of them, Dia and Frode split off in two directions. Tracks they passed led back into the hills, and he could still hear other horns blaring, calling back and forth, but it sounded like they were dropping behind. He debated and ultimately peeled off behind Frode. Harley, Jenta, and Wilhelm drew with him, but Chris, Yiannis, and Arne all drew off to follow Dia. He swore but knew it was too late to change any of it now. He hoped that having their party split nearly in half would cause the goblins to pause, since they wouldn't know which to follow.

Frode led them through another narrow passage and down a slope into a winding, mazelike canyon. They were able to slow their horses, but Frode wouldn't let them stop, guiding them along a path that doubled back on itself more than once. Cadence's blood rushed in his ears, his skin jumping with nerves at every turn among the confusion of pillars and rock walls.

The horns behind them grew ever more distant. The howling echoed through the canyon, but it sounded like what it was: far away and fading. The path finally began to climb back upward until the canyon walls around them became the steep, then more gently graded sides of hills. They eventually cleared the top of the rise and exited the canyon, and Cadence was greeted by the shine of the afternoon sun, sitting only a short distance from the horizon.

They rounded a tall hillock that blocked sight from the maze, then down into a small sunken valley where Frode allowed them to stop and dismount. Harley nearly collapsed as she dismounted, and Cadence dropped from his saddle, only a little more stable. He moved over to her and gripped her arm, while she steadied herself.

"Are you okay?" He asked, then immediately wished he had the words back. Of course she wasn't okay. They'd just spent who knew how long riding hell bent for leather, and then weaving themselves into a great big knot through that damned canyon. Though distant, the sound of horns still blared from the way they'd come, and Harley flinched a little every time one bellowed its low, mournful call. Too often, still, a first would be answered by others around it.

Even so, she met his eyes and tried her best to give him a smile. "Yeah. I mean, no, but yeah."

Jenta stood next to her horse, her forehead resting on his sweaty shoulder.

Frode and Wilhelm stood next to their mounts, talking urgently, but with their tones low while Cadence, Jenta, and Harley caught their breath.

Frode came over to them. "We will wait here for a short time. I have a hope that the others will catch up with us. It will also allow the horses a rest, and for us to refresh ourselves a moment. The grass here is good, and the water is safe for the horses to drink."

Cadence surveyed the little valley. In retrospect, it was probably less of a *valley*, and more of a small bowl between the slopes of two hills, though one of those hills was nearly a fifty-degree slope. Would that be more of a cliff, at that point, he wondered? The grass was a bit greener down in the shadow of the hill, but the water Frode referred to was a muddy pond, barely a puddle in a ring of dry clay.

"Where is the water from?" Harley asked.

"There was once a great river that ran all through this basin." Frode answered. "The spring deep below the ground is still there, but the water this far above has long since dried up due to the change of the clans."

"Wait, so this was where that clan of naiads lived?" Harley asked. Cadence caught Jenta shifting, behind her. He raised his eyebrows at her, but Jenta met the look and shook her head.

"Yes. They have moved some distance north, due to the encroaching of another clan of gobkin." Frode said. Cadence couldn't help but notice how different this conversation was from when they'd first tried to ask Cristobal questions in the map room. So much had happened since then, and yet he still felt a flair of anger for the pompous ass. This time, though, it was followed by a pang of worry for Faustus and Ximeno.

Harley led her horse to the edge of the little pond and let her start drinking then asked, "Okay, I thought I remembered what a 'gobkin' is, but I don't. Are they like goblins?"

Frode nodded. "Just so. The ones you saw riding the war-boars, are hobgobs. They are big strong brutes, who lead mainly by force. They aren't particularly smart, but they're very clever, and it has been my experience that what they lack in speed, they make up for in determination."

"Huh. I guess I just thought all gobkin are just all called goblins." Jenta said, shrugging a little as she ran fingers through her buckskin's mane while he nipped at grass by her feet.

Frode shrugged a little. "True but also untrue. In their mounds, all gobkin answer to their king. Though I suppose 'king' is not the right term. They call their leader 'king', whether they are male or female or somewhere in between. But even among themselves, they have hierarchies." He moved to his saddle bags and pulled out some cloth-wrapped packages, handing one to each of them.

"So, are the hobgobs the top tier or highest class or whatever?" Cadence asked, as Jenta and Harley started opening their bundles to reveal more rolls like the ones they'd eaten for breakfast.

"No. That would be the bogies and just below them, the redcaps. The Bogies are both clever *and* smart, and also incredibly monstrous. Many of them are not able to leave the mound, as they cannot stand the light. When they do leave the mound, it is almost always under cover of nightfall. Some bogies also become water dwellers, since it allows them to be out in the day for better hunting."

Beside him, Harley shuddered and stopped mid-bite, her face going white. She swallowed hard and took a long deep trembling breath and let it out slow. "I remember them." She met Cadence's worried look, and he saw the tamped down fear in her gaze. "The Dark Queen has at least two down in the dungeons."

Cadence started to reach for her, but then let his hand drop to his side. "I'm sorry," was all he could think so say.

Harley shook her head, but the smile she gave was pained and a little bitter. "Don't be. You saved me from one of them."

347

"I did?" Cadence asked, honestly confused.

Harley laughed a little. "Yeah. You told him you'd rip him to shreds with your bare hands, I think."

Cadence gaped at her, wide eyed. "You... you remembered that?"

Wilhelm cleared his throat a little, and Cadence and Harley turned their attention to him. "It is my suggestion that if she has any in the dungeons, you avoid that area if you can."

"And the redcaps?" Jenta asked.

"More vicious than goblins, more intelligent than hobgobs. They are named such as they like to dip their head coverings in the blood of their victims. The fresher the blood, the higher up in the clan that redcap resides." Wilhelm said.

None of them knew what to say to that.

They ate in silence, and Cadence studied their surroundings. He could just make out a distant mountain range far to the east. The horns hadn't grown any further distant though they'd slacked off. Cadence wasn't entirely certain how to feel about that.

Not more than a handful of minutes later, they heard the quiet echo of slow hoofbeats approaching the shadowed bowl. Cadence, Wilhelm, and Frode made Jenta and Harley press themselves as close as they could to the base of the steep slope, and moved in front of them, bows nocked and ready. Cadence hoped they would just look like more shadows among the scrub, though the horses were easily spotted if whoever it was happened to look their way.

The head and neck of a chestnut bay horse bearing elegant sidhe-crafted tack moved carefully around the side of the hill, announcing the first of the approaching riders. The breath Cadence was holding whooshed out of him, and he lowered his bow and moved out into the open. His movement drew Yiannis to look downslope.

"Thank Danann." Yiannis let out his own breath and shifted in his saddle to wave the rest of his group forward. The other half of their group came in a rush down the slope on the far side, settling their mounts amid a rattle of pebbles and dust.

They took a moment to stop and catch their breath, though that calm evaporated when the long, deep sound of another horn ricocheted along the canyon walls.

"They're not going to give up, are they?" Jenta asked, plaintively.

"Not unless we give them a reason to, no." Arne said. He was just dismounting, turning his horse out to the little muddy pond and the grass surrounding it.

Dia peered up the slope to the ridge line of the hillock blocking their view of the canyon.

"Then let us give them a reason to." She pulled off her riding gloves and tucked them into her belt. It seemed like a million years ago that Cadence first saw those red inked markings of swirls and wavy lines that covered her hands. Now, they appeared to pulse in time with her heartbeat as she started working her way up toward the ridge.

Chapter Thirty-Eight

Harlequin

Dia scrabbled up the hill, using scrub and jutting rocks as handholds. The moment she'd pulled off her gloves, there was that same
neck-ruffling tingle of magic, but instead of a wall Harley walked through,
it was more like standing near a heater, warmth radiating from its surface.
She moved to follow Dia up the slope. Cadence put a hand on her shoulder,
stopping her.

"Harley, don't—"

"Cadence Murphy, you will not stop me from seeing this. You can come,
or you can stay down here, but I'm going."

"Harley, you've seen magic, already! You don't need to endanger yourself
for this!" He glared at her.

She met his look, unflinching.

Cadence let out a sigh and shrugged. "Damn it. Fine. If you're going,
I'm going."

She fought not to give him a pleased grin. She knew this was serious,
but a part of her hummed with excitement, and her fingers tingled as she
reached for the first bits of scrub.

The climb was awkward, partly done in a crouching scuttle, and partially like climbing an angled ladder. The handholds were plentiful, but gripping the roots and rocks tore up her hands and left little bloody patches on the ground behind her in a couple places. Arne and Wilhelm made their way up as graceful and easy as mountain goats.

Dia lay on her belly, looking out over the canyon maze when Harley cleared the ridge, so she did the same, dropping to her stomach with her arms crossed in front of her so she could rest her chin on her hands.

"Keep your head low. With the sun behind us, we may give ourselves away if we are not careful." Dia said without looking at her.

Harley nodded, then realized Dia wouldn't see it, so she said, "Okay."

Dia extended one arm out in front of her, pointing nearly straight ahead of them. Harley followed the gesture, but all she saw at first was a confusion of shadows and stratified stone pillars and walls that seemed to go on forever. Then she spotted a couple huge dust clouds still well within the bounds of the canyon maze.

"Are those them?" The wolves looked to be leading them in circles, and Harley thought back to Frode guiding them through the maze.

"Yes," was all the answer she got, then Dia went silent.

Harley's whole body raised in gooseflesh, and a wave of heat washed over her. Dia cleared the space in front of her of rocks and scree, lay her hands palm down on it, and closed her eyes. The ground beneath them thrummed like a struck tuning fork, and some of the loose rocks clattered down the slope. Harley scanned the valley below. For a long time, nothing happened. She snuck another glance at Dia, but the warrior still lay with her eyes closed and hands flat on the dirt. The waves and swirls on the backs of her hands glowed and shifted, and her hair had taken on the look of a forge fire, glowing red in the light of the setting sun.

In the canyon, the wolf pack was milling in a circle, kicking up a giant dust cloud. No, not just milling around, they were attacking each other, spinning and snapping at themselves and those around them. Some of the smaller beasts started running off back the way they'd come, but the larger wolves were in a frenzy.

"Holy shit." Cadence uttered next to her.

"No kidding." Harley said, not taking her eyes from the canyon.

The huge hobgob brutes tried to urge their boars among the wolves, but the boars refused, balking, rearing and bellowing. Two of the riders were thrown off, the now riderless boars trampling hobgobs and wolves alike as they bolted toward the far ridge of the canyon. One of the riders lay unmoving. The other pushed itself to its feet, attempting to wade in among the wolves but getting bitten and clawed for its efforts.

"Well. That would certainly do it." Arne said, wonder and awe in his voice.

"Yes, but not long enough, I fear." Dia let out a breath, sounding frustrated. The whirling lines on her hands had stilled but continued to glow like her hair. "Their mounts and hounds will not be inclined to try to pass through the maze again, but that may not stop them from bringing through a full patrol of their own troops."

"Yes, but it will take them some time to gather those troops, and still more time to navigate the canyon again." Yiannis said on Dia's far side, but Dia was already shaking her head.

"You should go. I will stay. I can at least slow them down."

"You will do no such thing. I keep my word—especially to my queen—and I will not leave you here." Yiannis said heatedly.

"Yiannis, we do not have time for this argument. I have never hesitated to do what needs doing, and I will not stop now."

They continued to argue, but Harley went back to assessing the canyon. She studied the path of the walls and pillars. The striations in the rock showed a history of erosion. Frode had confirmed that this was the land where the naiads previously dwelled, and that meant not all that water would have left.

Harley interrupted their argument to ask, "Yiannis, how big is the spring that feeds the pond below us?"

"What?" Dia stopped mid-sentence, that one word filled with incredulity.

Yiannis, his face angry, glared past Dia to her, but answered her question. "I would say it is perhaps more a lake than a spring, fed by a large underground river. Why?"

"Are you able to access it but just bring it to the surface and let it pour? Like, instead of turning it into a bubble, let it flow down the slope and into the canyon?"

"Yes... I believe I would be able to do that, but why?" Yiannis was studying her, but it was Cadence who spoke.

"Shit. Harley, you're talking about creating a flash flood." He addressed Yiannis as he continued. "If you pull as much of the water up as you can and dump it down the slope and into the valley, it will wash out the canyon and make it impassable until the water drains back down into the ground."

"Better, Cay." Harley looked at Yiannis. "You would really only need to pull enough to start a siphon effect. Basically, instead of a bubble, create a tube that pulls the water, and it will use its own suction once it starts to run up and out, then down the hill."

Yiannis was already nodding.

"Yes, I think I understand. Similar to the storms on the sea when the wind draws the water up into the maelstrom. Yes." He grinned and reached over, clapping Harley on the shoulder. "I will need to work from down below. Come. We must move the horses, and you all will need to get to higher ground."

Getting down the slope was really just a matter of sliding down amid loose rocks that clattered along with them to the bottom of the hill. Once back on the valley floor, they gave a quick sketch of the situation and the plan. The horses were moved, and everyone not casting massive amounts of magic was moved to high ground up on the plateau to the far side away from the canyon. Unfortunately, that meant none of them had a view of what Yiannis did, but that didn't stop them from feeling it.

The ground beneath them rumbled and groaned. The rumbling became a pounding and then an explosion of pressure as a plume of water burst from the valley, and up into the sky like it was being sucked up through an invisible straw.

The waterspout towered above them, showering them with spray—a river wide fountain that bent, looping over itself like a hose. It held that irregular position for a moment, and then it was roaring and tumbling out of sight down the hill toward the canyon.

Arne, who volunteered to stay on the slope to watch, came barreling down toward them, running full out and grinning like a madman. Harley couldn't help but cheer, the others raising their voices with hers as Cadence and Chris both pumped their fists in the air, and she and Jenta grinned and high fived. Shortly after Arne stumbled his way to a stop, Yiannis made his way up the hill out of the basin. His hair was wet and dripping around his face, but his clothing was dry, and he had a broad, boyish grin on his face.

Wilhelm laughed and clapped Yiannis on the shoulder. Frode smiled and gave a nod, but his gaze drifted past them back toward the hidden canyon.

Yiannis caught the look, and the smile faded a little. "Yes. You're right, my friend." He gestured for them all to mount. "Come, we should be away from this place. That will definitely win us time and distance, but we have far to travel, and we know not what the night will bring."

Christian

The land beyond the valley leveled out into a broad plateau covered in more scrub grass. It made travel both easy and anxiety-inducing since they had nowhere to hide, if any pursuers caught up with them. Arne took lead of the group, with Frode bringing up the rear.

For a time, they traveled along a narrow creek with a rocky bed, their horses splashing through ankle-deep water that was otherwise surprisingly clear amid the desiccated landscape.

Out among the scrub, he saw what he thought at first were something like great big sticks or dead tree stumps, but as they drew up close past one, he spotted a skull, long-nosed and full of teeth.

"Frode?" Chris said quietly. Frode rode forward a little so Chris could ask, "What is that?"

Frode glanced at the skeleton, and then further out to the jutting rib bones of more dead creatures.

"This was part of the naiads' land, so was once under a lake." Frode said, as if that answered the question. It didn't.

"Okay, but those things are huge. Like, some of those bones are bigger than whale bones I've seen back home." Chris responded.

Frode scanned the landscape again, then back at him. "It was a big lake." Frode grinned at him. Chris just shook his head and couldn't help but chuckle.

Thankfully, the scrubland started sprouting sizeable spiky bushes among the rough grass, and the air, though hot and dry, was blissfully empty of the calling horns as they sought a camp for the night.

Chapter Thirty-Nine

Jenta

J enta was looking up into a face so white it might have been carved from marble. The woman's full, red lips made Jenta think of some horrifying parody of Snow White, and dark eyes like drops of mad black ink studied her as if she were a fly caught in a spider's web. Those eyes crackled with far away lightning, giving glimpses of roiling clouds in their depths. Black hair, slick and shiny as raven's feathers, tumbled down around pale shoulders and melded with a dress made of shadows and smoke. Jenta staggered back, her butt hitting the table that took up the middle of the room. She heard the clatter of things on the table moving around but didn't dare take her eyes off the woman—no, creature—in front of her.

"You need not fear me, Jenta."

"You say that like you think I'll believe you." Jenta's bravado was only a little marred by the tremble in her voice.

The woman tilted her head to one side. "I say it because it is true."

A slim, long-fingered hand reached out and caressed Jenta's cheek. Jenta tried to flinch away, but the hand followed her, then was suddenly gripping a handful of her hair. Not exactly painful, but definitely startling. Jenta's body reacted to the grip. Her eyes slid closed almost immediately, a sigh shuddering from her slightly parted lips. Her breathing sped, but more in anticipation than in fear. The response was automatic, and she tried to fight it. Tried not to enjoy the feel of giving up control to the hand that gripped her hair. The hand slowly released her head, the tips of fingers just brushing her cheek as the touch withdrew. She opened her eyes slowly and stared at the Dark Queen.

"There. You see. I know the rules, and I follow them."

"You're murdering people. That's pretty far from following the rules." Jenta tried for her usual snark, but her voice was breathy and low.

The Dark Queen continued to study her. Her voice was soft, almost dreamy as she spoke. "They call to me. Sweet nothings whispered to the darkness. Poor souls, so full of hurt, of fear. Have you not felt it?"

Jenta shook her head. "I don't understand. Felt what?"

The queen smiled. "The deep, dark wishes of your secret heart. I hear them. I hear the prayers you whisper in the shadows of your mind." The voice was smooth and silken, pulsing through Jenta's head and leaving her dizzy. That gentle caress of fingers touched her cheek again, and she made herself step away.

Jenta struggled to speak, even as her body tried to betray her. She wanted the hand back in her hair. She wanted to let go, to not have to make all these hard choices. She was so tired. Tired of fighting. Tired of hurting. She longed for the silence. She ached for the quiet, floating emptiness the Dark Queen was offering. The exact things she wished Jonathon would have given her but had only dangled in front of her to get what he wanted.

She shook her head, trying to clear it. It didn't seem to help, but she spoke through her fog. "You're torturing people. I've seen it. Hell, I've been one of those tied up on your wall. You can't tell me every single person you've dragged here has wanted to die."

The Dark Queen studied her for a long while, her expression unreadable. She gave that same strange head tilt, and another of those slow blinks. It was like being scrutinized by a particularly smart crow. Some of the madness cleared her eyes, but in its wake came a different darkness, like blood spilled on black carpet. Her voice changed, the dreaminess replaced by something low and growling, and the anticipation and desire of a moment ago transformed immediately to fear, cold sweat popping out on Jenta's skin.

"I see. I had hoped that you would understand. I have seen the dark wish you hide in your heart, Jenta. Even now, I see it on you, laid over you like a burial shroud."

Jenta flinched and wanted to look away. "I don't know what you're talking about."

"Let us not lie to each other, you and I. Your desire is laid like spiced honey on my tongue. You wish for an end. Are you not tired? Do you not feel the pull in your mind, your heart, your very *bones*, to return to the earth? To rest? I see it behind your eyes. I feel it, drawing me to you, calling out to me." The Dark Queen took a step toward her, but Jenta didn't move.

"No." It came out as a bare whisper, as she tried to shake her head, tried not to look into those mad black eyes.

"Yes, Jenta. What you call torture, I call a means to an end." The Dark Queen's voice coated her like a silk sheet, the words wrapping around her as unbreakable as chains. "There are some who come to me with the wish so close it falls from their lips, but some still keep their desire buried so deeply they themselves do not know of its presence. It is the greatest kindness I can offer—to help them find this wish, to embrace it."

As the Dark Queen spoke, she pressed close, stopping with only a breath between them. She raised her hand, and again, touched Jenta's cheek, drew her face up so that they gazed at each other from only inches away.

Jenta fought herself. The hand on her cheek was gentle, a delicate brush of skin on skin, and a small sob bubbled up in her throat. God, but she was so tired. *God, Danann, whoever... please, give me strength. I don't know what I'm doing.* Jenta held the thought in her mind. Then, there was an answering thought, one that wasn't hers.

I am with you. You see her madness. She, too, longs for freedom. Help my daughter.

The Dark Queen's whisper melted over her skin and raised goosebumps. Her voice had regained that dreamy quality, her eyes filling back in with those roiling inky clouds. "Come to me, Jenta. Come and help me to bring the gift of peace. With you by my side, they will feel no pain, only sweet release. Come to me. Help me save them as you wished to be saved after the loss of your father."

Help my daughter. Go to her. I am with you. Have faith.

Jenta searched the Dark Queen's eyes. The queen smiled gently, that same soft sadness still in her features. Jenta swallowed hard, and her heart pounded in her chest, fear and desire mingling in her and leaving her breathless as the queen slowly leaned forward. Jenta's eyes slid closed as the queen spoke, her mouth hovering just above Jenta's.

"Come to me. Come, and find peace."

Have faith.

Hot breath blew across Jenta's face, smelling sweet and dark. Then blood-red lips were pressing against her own. Gentle. Trembling. Perfect.

Chapter Forty

Christian

C hris pulled himself free of his nightmare and sat up, his sweat soaked blanket falling away from him in the chilly night air. *It's just fear. She's going to be okay. You'll get there in time.*

"Stay strong, kiddo. I'm coming. I promise." He repeated the words uttered in his dream. *I promise.* Those words seemed to have more power, in the land of the fae, and he gripped them now, like a talisman.

He drew his knees up to his chest and looked around. The moon was fully set, and the only light was a sky full of faraway stars. The place where they'd camped was tucked in the middle of a ring of thorny scrub trees, and the ground under his blanket was hard-packed and parched. He remembered pictures of Africa he'd seen in those old Nat Geos in the library. He wondered if there were lions here, like there were, there.

He spotted Frode's slight frame coalescing out of the darkness. The elf crouched beside Chris but continued to scan the night's shadows. "I thought that I heard you cry out. Are you well?" Frode asked, his voice only just above a whisper. Chris could just make out the shadowed profile of Frode's face. A sharp nose and pointed jaw made all the elves appear made of angles, but Frode was so rail thin as to seem fragile.

Chris scrubbed at his face with both hands, as he tried to think of how to answer. Finally, he shrugged. "I mean, no, but yeah. I just had a nightmare."

"A what?" Frode asked.

"A nightmare. It's like a dream, but, well, bad, you know?"

Frode stopped scanning the horizon to look fully at Chris. Even in the dark, Chris got the strong feeling that the elf was studying him, curious and worried. "I find it fascinating that you are able to touch the Void here. I wonder if it is to do with your being human or something more sinister."

Chris shrugged again and ducked his head. "Never mind. I'll try to go back to sleep."

Frode shook his head. "I do not mean to dismiss your troubles. My apologies. Do you wish to speak of this nightmare?"

Chris started to give an immediate "no," but then let himself really think about it. Coming to save Sara had been his whole reason for coming, hadn't it? Hadn't it?

Unbidden, his gaze was drawn to the blanket covered bodies. Among them was Jenta. Jenta, who made him crazy and confused and hopeful, and so many other feelings he couldn't describe. Jenta, who he'd kissed, but since then, he hadn't had time to process what that meant. If they were still back home, would he have ever talked to her, or would he still be doing the whole pining-from-afar thing?

"She has my sister." He'd hoped saying it fast would make it hurt less, but the words dragged his heart with them, and he swallowed hard to push the well of panic back down into his stomach, where it settled like an anchor in his gut.

"Ah." Just that one word, then Frode asked, "Does Yiannis know?"

"Yeah, and Dia."

"And you are having nightmares about her, while you strive to save her. Is it your fear she is already beyond saving?"

Chris rolled his shoulders, trying to release the ever-present tension in them. "All I can do is hold my breath and wait and hope she survives and that she doesn't hate me at the end of it."

"Hate you? Why?" Frode sounded genuinely curious. Chris wouldn't normally have answered, but the darkness gave him anonymity, and the elf's voice in the night was kind and free of judgment.

"For abandoning her. Sara's just a baby, but everybody in her life—hell, both of our lives—has left us. My dad took off when I was young and died not long after, taking even that hope of escape. My mother sent me off to live with my grandparents for a while, while she dated around, and somewhere in there, she started drinking a lot more. She brought me back home when Sara was two. I think mostly she was bored of taking care of her, and I was old enough to babysit by then. My mother started spending a lot of time at bars after that, bringing home random guys and kicking me out of the house with my baby sister in my arms."

Frode made an angry noise. "That is no way to raise a child. We do not treat our children thus, here. They are rare among us and always cherished. I am sorry you have had this experience."

Chris gave a Gallic shrug. "Thing is, for a long time, I hated my mother. Hated what she did to me and my sister. But now I mostly just feel bad for her. She was young and poor and had all her big dreams torn away from her when I was born. My dad tried to make it work with her, tried to do right by us, but he was young, too. Sara... She just deserves so much better. She's great, smart, and funny. She's this sweet little innocent doll, and I've spent every waking hour trying to keep her safe, and now here I am, sitting in the dark, not knowing what she's going through but knowing that whatever it is, she's going through it alone."

Chris swallowed and went quiet. He was staring out into the night, but in his mind, all he could see was her silent, accusing, tear-filled eyes. Her, turning away from him to take the hand of a shadow wrapped creature.

Frode's voice was soft, but it pulled him out of his fear and back into the night-shrouded camp. "She is *not* alone. You may not be with her physically, but you have not abandoned her, Christian. She is surrounded by the love of her brother, and love is a form of magic."

Chris nodded, holding back tears. Frode patted his shoulder gently. "Try to get some rest. We draw close, and tomorrow is a new day."

Chris laid back against his blankets though he wasn't certain if he'd be able to fall back to sleep. Pulling his blanket around him, he curled on his side. Surprisingly, the moment he closed his eyes he was pulled into a blessedly dreamless void.

Chapter Forty-One

Harlequin

Wilhelm and Arne woke them well before sunrise. Yiannis handed out a breakfast of chew bread—Harley wondered if this batch was part rubber—and more of the blue-veined, hard, crumbly cheese the sidhe seemed to favor. She had to admit, the salty cheese and thick, hearty bread were filling, if not the most exciting thing to eat. Certainly preferable to going hungry.

This close to what the elves called Dark's Doorstep, none of them rested well. Harley ached from sleeping on the ground, and she did her best to stretch out the worst of the knots before she clambered up into her saddle and followed the group away from the campsite. They stopped a little distance away, and Dia pivoted in her saddle, raising up one gloved hand. The ground rumbled as if it were sitting on a giant speaker, but when she was done, the signs of their passing had been largely erased.

They'd only ridden another half mile away from the campsite, when Arne signaled a stop. Harley was fascinated by how even the fae, if they'd done any fighting at all, used hand signals in place of words in cases that called for stealth just like she'd seen in movies. Not the exact *same* hand signals, but close enough that the four of them intuited the meaning without needing to talk about it.

That thought didn't stop her heart from thumping in her ears, though, so close after yesterday's madcap chase through the canyon. She noticed she was holding her breath and tried to let it out slow. Arne and Wilhelm dismounted and crouched together a short distance from where they sat on their horses. The pair had a short discussion comprised of whispered words and hand gestures until Arne said something and pointed, so far as Harley could discern, southeast. Wilhelm followed the gesture with his eyes and sat that way for a moment while he crouched there beneath the already baking sun.

Arne's hand went from a pointed finger to a questioning gesture, and Wilhelm gave a nod then they both returned to their horses.

Harley wasn't sure what had just happened and knew she most likely wouldn't get an answer if she asked, but as she heeled her horse forward, she peered at the ground beneath their horses' hooves to see if she could spot whatever they'd been looking at.

She apparently needn't have worried. The ground they crossed was more dry, dusty earth, hard packed and studded with that same course scrub that they'd been passing through. A broad swath of it had been trampled and was covered in split hoofprints, claw marks, and heel dents from thick humanoid feet.

Boars, wolves, and goblins. Oh my. Harley knew that thought should have been funny, but it was hard to bring herself to laugh, as they rode over the tracks and on toward a slope that led down among trees.

Christian

Chris lay on his belly in tall grass, his skin tingling and his fingers gripping the roots as he forced himself not to draw his sword and see how many goblins he could slaughter in the valley below before they ripped him a part.

They milled about in a great mass, many geared up in leather armor and carrying at least a spear, or sometimes a spear and buckler. Others were naked except for long tattered trousers or loincloths, their greenish gray skin making them look sickly in the sunlight, though Chris knew better. Zombies in horror movies also looked sickly, but they could still kill you, and the goblins had proven themselves far heartier than zombies.

Arne, Cadence, Yiannis, and Dia lay in the grass near him. Yiannis caught his eye and pointed down the hill the way they'd come. Chris gave him a nod, and used the roots he was gripping to push himself back down the slope hand-under-hand until he could raise himself up to his hands and knees and crouch walk back to where the rest of the group waited with the horses.

"That is many more than we can fight." Dia said, sounding almost disappointed.

"Not more than we *can* fight, simply more than it would be *prudent* to fight. Not without bringing more down on our heads." Yiannis responded.

Cadence shrugged and grumbled, "Same difference." Chris got the impression the other guy, despite not previously seeming like the violent type, had maybe struggled almost as much as he had, not to go see how many of those gray-skinned goons he could take out.

Arne let Wilhelm know what they'd seen, and Yiannis deferred to the smaller man. "We go around, I assume?"

Wilhelm grudgingly agreed. "Yes, though it will be difficult. The land here has remained swamp, but the redcaps let their... *pets* loose to claim the waters, and some of the bogies have opted to become bog dwellers. We cannot ride the ridges, but nor do we dare ride close to the water."

Arne was nodding agreement. "I believe I know a path we can take. Wilhelm, how would you feel about a bit of stow and seek, with some hobgobs?"

Wilhelm stared at him then broke into a grin. "Arne, my friend, I thought you would never ask."

Stow and seek was exactly what Chris thought: hide and seek, but with bands of goblins and hobgobs, and the possibility that they might wound or be wounded. Wilhelm and Frode took off on their sure-footed, agile mounts around the far side of the slope to the east, while Arne led the rest of them back the way they'd come, to loop around the other side of the hill and head south.

Not long after the two elven riders vanished, the horns started sounding, bellows and shouts filling the air as what they hoped would be most of the force waiting in the valley harried off to chase Wilhelm and Frode.

Arne led them between two slopes, the grass here lush and green, studded with wildflowers and the shoots of trees. It probably would have been beautiful if Chris's heart wasn't in his throat as he listened to the blaring of horns back and forth and far too close for comfort.

The path spilled out onto the side of a steep hill, across a ledge onto which Arne guided his horse. It was barely more than a goat path that ran along the side of the hill under full sun. There was a slope at their right that pressed close, grass covered but impossible for a horse to climb, and downhill on their left, the grass leveled out a little but was immediately subsumed into the swampy, tree-shaded recesses of a gobkin bog.

The water's edge was only maybe thirty feet from them, and as they rode, little rocks clattered down into the water. Chris could just see tiny ripples among the reed shoots, making their slow way out onto the surface. Two thick bubbles of something viscous came to the surface and floated there for a moment, then popped, releasing a smell like rancid milk and rotting meat that wafted toward them in a nearly visible cloud of stink. Chris gagged and retched, leaning over to vomit and heard those around him doing the same.

The group of goblins picked that exact moment to come barreling up and over the hill, charging down the embankment to launch themselves at the party. Chris caught sight of a hobgob standing at the top of the incline, raising a horn to his lipless mouth just as goblin practically flew at Chris, arms and legs akimbo. He had just enough time to draw his sword, but not enough time to bring it on guard properly. He slashed wildly at the thing and pushed it behind him even as it knocked him out of the saddle and sent him rolling down the slope toward the water.

Chris swore and threw his left arm out in the hopes of slowing himself down. His fingers sunk deep into the muddy bank as he started to roll again, and his vision was filled with a closeup of another gray-skinned, bug-eyed face coming up out of the water in front of him.

"Fuck!" already on his side, he used the momentum to let his arm fall forward, the blade burying itself deep into the thing's neck, nearly decapitating it as he came to a stop. He pushed with hands and feet, dragging the blade with him so that it pulled loose from the creature's neck in a spray of viscera and ichor.

The monstrosity lunged at him, and Chris saw thick skinned, flippered feet and long fin-like arms on its torso beneath those reaching for him.

An arrow whistled just past his head to puncture one of those black, fathomless eyes. The thing dropped like a rock at his feet and didn't move again.

Chris scrambled to his feet and spun, nearly falling again as his foot squelched among the muddy grass. Their party was fully entrenched, all their focus on fending off the group of goblins. It appeared Cadence had been knocked off his horse, too. He was covered in mud and blood from a wound in his side—a gnarly gash Chris could see through the cut in the other guy's shirt. He'd somehow gotten a hold of his bow and found solid footing up on the path where he stood, firing arrows in quick succession.

Jenta was moving with quick efficiency, and it took Chris a moment to realize she was wielding the little cat dagger. A goblin came in low, trying to grab for her legs, and Jenta, for all the world as if she was simply bending over to tie her shoe, folded herself in half, her arm coming down like a hammer to stab into the back of the goblin's head so that it crumpled to the ground, one hand just touching the toe of her black combat boot. Jenta kicked out, hitting the thing in the shoulder and sending it rolling back down the hill. Her head came up and she met his gaze for a moment, then she was turning to swing at another goblin trying to dart past her at Dia.

Chris threw himself forward and up the hill, struggling to gain purchase. Behind him, something snarled, then claws were sinking into his back and dragging him back down the incline toward the water. Chris yelled and swung but couldn't seem to reach whatever had grabbed him from behind.

He tried to pull himself free but saw with panic that he'd lost all the ground he'd originally made and was nearly back at the edge of the bog, his feet squishing and slipping in the mud.

"No, no, no! Damn it, you piece of shit. *Fuck Off!*" Chris spun the blade in his hand and gripped hard on the hilt, thrusting his arm hard behind him. He thought at first that he'd missed, but then he met resistance as the blade sank into something solid, and the thing screamed and released him, throwing him face down into the muck.

Chris sputtered and finally got his hands under him. Pain shot through his back as he pushed himself back up onto all fours. The whole time, he waited for another attack. His ears rang, and his eyes were partially stuck shut from the mud. He knew his sword was somewhere to his right, but he didn't dare grab for it on the chance that he'd grab the blade and cut his hand.

"Chris?" Harley's hesitant voice spoke above and in front of him.

"Yeah." Chris sounded exhausted, even to himself. His whole body was one big bruise, and his back…

"I'm going to come help you, okay? It's me touching you." Harley said from a little closer.

Chris just nodded. Gentle hands touched his shoulders, and Harley helped him sit back on his heels.

"Yiannis is coming. We need to get mounted as soon as we can, though." She seemed to be talking more to herself than to him. He felt what had to be a wet rag against his cheek as she started to wash the mud off his face, until he was able to blink and look up at her.

"Is everybody else okay?" Chris asked. His voice was ragged with pain, and he almost laughed when Harley gave him an incredulous look.

"I don't think anyone got as hurt as you did. Cay was knocked off his horse but landed on the path. Jenta was able to keep her seat, even though one of the smaller goblins landed on her shoulder. That buckskin she's riding..." Harley glanced back over her shoulder toward the path where the other riders were already making their way back to their horses. Cadence caught her look and started making his careful way down the slope toward them.

"Jenta's horse stomped one of the goblins into the ground. It was pretty damned impressive." Cadence said as he approached. "Need help standing?"

Chris allowed himself a moment to assess his wounds, then answered honestly. "I don't think I can."

Cadence's expression grew panicked. "What do you mean? Did you lose feeling in your legs or something?"

"No, but that thing shredded the fuck out of my back." Chris said, gesturing vaguely behind himself then wincing at even that little movement.

Cadence exhaled, relieved. "Okay. Okay. Yiannis is coming."

"Who else was hurt?" Chris asked, again. He knew he couldn't have been the only one injured, or Yiannis would already have been there, sending his breath stealing, goose-bump making magic through him.

Harley and Cadence shared a look, and Cadence answered. "Dia got one of her hands bitten off. They had to catch and gut the goblin to get it back."

"Fuck me running... Bitten *off*?" Chris stammered, and suddenly the world grew hot. The mud on him stank and his stomach twisted, and then he was back on his hands and knees, vomiting. His back burned like fire, as his muscles heaved.

The sour smell of bile filled his nostrils, but weirdly, it was an improvement compared to the mud.

"Cay, help me stand. I don't care how much it hurts." Chris said it through gritted teeth, then did his best to breathe through his mouth while Cadence stood behind him, hands going under his arms.

"Give me something to bite. I don't want to yell and bring more attention." Chris was already trying not to whimper as Harley pulled another scrap of fabric from a pouch he hadn't noticed. She started to hand it to him, but he just opened his mouth, and she gingerly stuffed the rag into it. It tasted of the crumbly cheese, and he realized it must have been from breakfast.

"On the count of three." Cadence said, and Chris gave a nod of agreement.

"One. Two." Cadence grunted and dragged Chris to his feet. Chris bit down hard on the rag and let himself groan into it.

He didn't even have time to catch his breath before the magic hit him, and only Cadence standing behind him and Harley standing in front of him, gripping him at his shoulders and hands respectively, kept him on his feet as Yiannis's power swept through him, healing his back and bruises, and exiting by way of the mud that dried and crumbled from his cloths. The cloth in his mouth captured his curses, then dusted the last of the mud off his hands so he could pull it back out, flexing his jaw and moving his tongue around in his mouth.

Chris peered up the slope to see Yiannis standing by his horse.

"A little warning next time would be nice." Chris said grumpily.

"It would not have helped." Yiannis said, then mounted.

"Lousy Kung-Fu old guy." Chris grumbled under his breath as he retrieved his sword and let Harley and Cadence help him back up the slope to where their horses waited.

Jenta

They rode in silence for what felt like hours, skirting along below the ridge lines and occasionally dipping down when the track took them along a valley floor then back up but never cresting any of the hills.

They had to ride close alongside the bog twice more. The first time, a creature that appeared to be a fish who'd grown arms and legs—but still had that quintessential fish head and a back ridge and tail fin flopping behind it—trundled out from among the trees as if to attack them. Instead, it stopped at the edge of the grass where the sun broke through the branches above, then waved one webbed hand at them in greeting. It made no noise but waddled off back into the trees, slowly slipping below the surface of the water with barely a splash.

The second, closer toward sunset, was less pleasant. Wilhelm and Frode joined back up with them, after taking the gobkin on a merry chase, and all three of them now rode with their bows strung and ready. A good thing, since two bogies erupted from the water to their right as they were hugging the line of another steep ridge with nowhere to go except forward or back the way they'd come. The fetid water was nearly lapping at their horses' hooves as they rode.

The sudden appearance of two towering serpentine creatures thrusting themselves from among the rocks and dead trees laying across the water caused their mounts to startle, Dia's horse rearing and almost falling into the water before she could settle him and urge him forward to a wider portion of the path.

Wilhelm and Frode both got shots off at each of the creatures though that didn't seem to slow them. Behind her, Jenta heard another bow twang, and an arrow with a red ribbon suddenly blossomed from what was probably the chest of one of the towering monstrosities.

Jenta looked back to find Cadence dismounted standing next to his horse with another red ribboned arrow already drawn as he aimed then released.

Both bogies dropped back into the water without another twitch, the only sign they'd been there being the ripples bouncing back and forth across the surface.

Chapter Forty-Two

Harlequin

Harley almost cried when, as the sun sat low on the horizon behind them, the swamp drained out to a lowland full of lush green grass dotted with trees. The fields in front of them stretched out and out, and behind her, Harley heard a hiss and a horse's frightened whinny. She twisted in her saddle to see Cadence's horse kick hard at something green and slithering, sending it flying out into the field to their left. The grass came alive with hisses and inhuman screams as whatever else was out there attacked the injured creature.

Arne led them to a raised road flanked to either side by the vibrant grass. The road wound around and up onto a promontory, ringed with trees. The grass was shorter there, flattened and rock strewn, and the trees sat down slope in a horseshoe, creating a natural barrier for the wind that blew almost non-stop across the grassland.

Wilhelm dismounted and signaled for Arne and Frode to make a circuit of the hilltop while the rest of them dismounted. Harley noted a bit of relief in his voice as he addressed the rest of them.

"We are close now. Nightfall Glade is only perhaps an hour's ride from Dark's doorstep. Tomorrow morning, we will need the sun, so we will not need to start so early. Tonight, we will light a fire, and have a hot meal." He started to say more but closed his mouth without continuing.

Harley helped Dia to hobble and curry the horses, then rubbed down her own mare with handfuls of pulled up grass and let her drink from a waxed leather bucket that Yiannis filled with water.

Once she was done, she came and sat with Jenta, Cadence, and Chris, while Arne, Wilhelm and Frode set up a ring of stones around a fire pit over which they erected a three-legged metal rack with a hook-ended chain. A pot was hung from the hook and filled with more of Yiannis' water, some grain, and a small portion of dried meat. Arne even tossed in a small sachet of herbs he gathered during their trek through the hills. How he'd had any time while they dodged patrols, Harley had no idea. Lastly, Arne and Wilhelm asked Cadence and Chris to help locate a couple of logs to bring back for seating around the fire.

Dinner was eaten out of shallow wooden bowls, scooped up alternately with some of the chew bread or with their own fingers. Yiannis also gave each of them another piece of the sharp, crumbly cheese but instead of water, Harley was overjoyed to see Arne used another sachet of herbs to make a fragrant tea.

The night was quiet save for the sound of insects, and the occasional bird. It seemed like even the animals felt the weight of what was coming.

As they sat watching the fire and sipping their tea, Yiannis broke the silence. "In the morning, we will escort you to the boundaries of her territory. There, we will wait until... Until you return."

Cadence startled. "What do you mean? You're not going in with us?"

Yiannis shook his head, but not like he was happy. "You know we cannot."

There was a long, heavy silence.

Harley scanned their faces around the fire, then turned her gaze up to the night dark sky. The stars hadn't come out yet, and the moon hadn't yet risen. Very on the nose.

"Hey Cay?" Chris said into the waiting quiet.

"Yeah?"

"What was with those arrows with the red ribbons?"

"They had my blood on them."

Harley shuddered. Mortal blood, indeed.

Christian

Chris lay under his blankets, staring up into the night sky. The darkness of the night was complete except for the immense, unblinking eye of the baleful moon and the softly glowing embers from the fire. He lay awake, unable to face what he feared waited in his dreams.

A soft rustling to his right drew his attention. They'd been traveling hard, their path irregular and stilted, and he'd figured everyone else would be asleep by now, knowing they wouldn't have to worry about patrols tonight. His heart sped and he turned his head slowly, trying not to draw any attention.

His heart went from speeding to a dead stop.

Jenta was crouched over her gear, her shape mostly lost among the tree shadows. He saw her head turn toward where he, Cadence, and Harley had set their blankets. She rose slowly, bringing up her saddlebags with her. Chris wondered if he should say something. His heart pounded and his breath rasped in his throat. He waited for her to turn and look at him, to realize he was awake, but she didn't, after that first glance back at them. Very slowly, her movements careful, she crept down the hill toward the horses.

Chris pulled his blanket off and got to his feet as quietly as possible, then headed straight for the horses. He reached the picket line quickly, the only sound the scraping of his boots on the rocky ground. He made his way to Jenta's horse, crouched down low. The buckskin stood a little to one side of the picket line, his head down and drowsing, but Chris didn't see Jenta.

Something sharp touched the side of his neck.

"Don't shout." Jenta's voice was barely a whisper, her breath hot on his ear. She had one arm wound around him with her dagger drawn and pressed to his throat. His pulse jumped and threw itself at the edge of the blade.

"Jenta, don't do this." Chris' voice was quiet, and pain filled.

"Do what? Leave? You won't talk me out of this, Chris, so don't try."

"Jenta... Why?" Chris tried to keep the despair out of his voice. He wasn't sure he succeeded.

"We all have our paths to walk, Chris. This one is mine."

"Then let me go with you."

"No." The word was immediate. Hard. Cold.

"What do I tell Harley and Cadence? That you just left? That you ran away?" The blade pressed a little harder into Chris's neck, and hot blood ran down his skin.

"Tell them... Tell them not to waste their time trying to miss me."

"What does that even mean? Jenta—" Chris tried to turn, but Jenta's arms tightened around him, the blade biting into his skin. He swallowed hard and tried to draw his neck back and away from the pressure.

"I only ever said that the blades weren't for me, Chris. I never said I didn't know how to use them. Don't come after me, and don't wake the others. I won't betray you, so don't betray me." There was a moment of silence, and then, "I'm sorry."

With that, the blade was gone from his neck, and the weight of her at his back as well. She moved past him, a shadow among shadows, and threw her pack over the back of the buckskin, followed by the saddle and blanket. She didn't bother taking the time to strap down the saddle, instead just pulling loose the hobble and leading the horse quietly off into the night.

She never looked back at him.

Chris watched her leave, and almost wished she'd gone ahead and slit his throat. He wanted to scream, to run after her, but instead, he froze as if his feet had grown roots and scanned the darkness where she'd disappeared into the tree line.

When he finally circled back to his blankets, Yiannis was standing up slope, his features lost in the darkness, face silhouetted only by the glow of the banked fire.

Chris hurried up to him, rigid with fury. The words came out as a hiss. Even now, he couldn't bring himself to betray her. "Why didn't you stop her? You could have! Wrapped her in magic or—"

"It was her choice. It has to be her choice, as it has to be yours."

"You're supposed to be here to protect us!"

Yiannis gave Chris a look he didn't need to see to understand. "Christian, I will spend every drop of immortal blood in my body to protect all of you from any and every fae weapon aimed against you, but I cannot protect you from your own decisions."

381

"Fuck, Yiannis. Why? Did she tell you anything? Did you talk to her? Do you know where she's going?"

Yiannis held up a hand, but his voice was sad. "No, I do not know where she is going. I could posit any number of guesses, but in the end, she is mortal, and mortal choices were never the purview of immortal hearts. We will keep her secret, Christian, and we will hope that in the keeping of a secret, a promise will be kept as well." Yiannis rested the raised hand on Chris' shoulder.

"As for why, I can only tell you what I have learned from seeing so many mortal lifetimes: Life is made up of choices. Some easy, some exceedingly difficult, and some in between. Easy, hard, and in between, the choices you make will guide the path you walk. No two paths are the same, just as no two hearts are the same. There will be times where you walk with friends and times when you may walk with only Danann to guide and comfort you. At those times, have faith. Trust Danann to guide you, and that when the time comes, your choice will lead you to a path that converges again with those you love."

Chris stared out into the darkness to the east. The direction Jenta had gone. The direction of the Dark Queen, and the court of the Unseelie.

Chapter Forty-Three

Harlequin

Harley peered over the edge of a sheer cliff. It was as if the land had been ripped apart, leaving a tear in the ground that dropped off to a river made of shadows and fog.

"Well, Fuck. How are we supposed to get across *this*?" Cadence made no effort to hide his exasperation, but Harley couldn't blame him. There was no conveniently placed rope bridge. No rock promontory that they could use to race their horses pell mell to a long, hail Mary leap across. There was just the chasm and the path on the far side.

The path to the Bastion of Night, that, due to the chasm, might as well have been on the other side of the world.

Behind them, Yiannis and the elves were discussing their options. Harley couldn't make out what they were saying. She was still reeling from the morning's news. Jenta was gone. Up and vanished in the night, so Chris said. Did she stand here last night? How had she crossed? Or *had* she? Was her body down there among the shadows? Harley swallowed hard and dragged herself away from the cliff's edge.

Cadence and Chris joined the conversation with the other men, and Harley made herself try to pay attention to what they were saying.

"—Was not here when last I came. This looks very new, and I am afraid to think it was done by the Dark Queen herself as that would imply that she has come into much more power than I remember her having. It also does not smell of her magic." Yiannis glowered toward the ravine and the path on the other side, but not as if he saw them. His head was tilted up slightly, as if he were more scenting the air than looking toward the rift.

"Can we go around it, do you think?" Cadence scanned the horizon to north and south.

"To the north, there are only mountains coated heavily in ice and snow. We will have no luck traversing them. Even so, they do not pass through to her lands but only further north into the lands of the Titans."

"What about south? Could we follow the chasm and see if it closes back up or if there's a way to cross? It looks like the land slopes off down that way." Chris was looking south, one hand raised up to shade his eyes.

Harley studied the lands to the south. The ground swooped downward to a low, wide prairie filled with the same vibrant green grass that surrounded them the day before. Far away on the horizon a band of black mountains stabbed into the sky like the teeth of a sawblade. She couldn't tell from her current vantage point whether the ravine ended, but it couldn't go on forever, right? Even the Grand Canyon had end points. Dia stepped up next to her. She pointed at the line of towering black peaks in the distance.

"Those are called the Keeper's Teeth. If we reach those without finding a way across, we will have to come back north and try again, but Christian has a fair point. If this gap is new, perhaps it does not go all the way to the southern range, and Danann will grant us a way through." Dia patted

Harley's shoulder. Her next words were quiet, spoken only between the two of them.

"I do not believe she is down there. I have hope and faith."

"I almost wish she *was*. If not, the only other option is that she really did make it to the Dark Queen. If she—" Harley stopped, and took a breath, letting it out. "I think I would rather she be dead, than think she's evil." Without letting Dia respond, Harley made her way back to her horse.

The land sloped down and down until the pressure in her ears shifted. The spiked mountains grew closer, looming up over them, black and menacing. She knew that even when mountains seemed close, they could still be miles and miles distant. The Keeper's Teeth? She hoped they found a path across the ravine before they needed to worry about it.

She was pulled out of her thoughts by Yiannis drawing all of them to a halt. The sun was just hitting its zenith, the heat of the day beating down between her shoulders and the back of her head. Yiannis, Dia, and the three elven riders appeared unphased by the wavering heat, but Yiannis had a wariness around his eyes as he told the rest of them to hang back. He and Arne rode up over the rise to look down at whatever lay beyond. When they turned back to the group, Yiannis looked angry, but Arne looked pale.

"What now?" Cadence said in irritation, and Harley shot him a look for it. He just glared at her before turning back to their escorts.

"There are... fae in the field ahead. Many of them. We will have to pass amidst them in order to continue south. I—" Yiannis started to say something more but cut himself off.

"What, like just a big group of them?" Cadence asked, the irritation giving way to confusion.

My children suffer.

Harley glanced around. None of the party was looking at her, all the rest of them focused on Yiannis and Arne.

Arne lowered his eyes and shook his head, but Yiannis just answered, his voice flat. "No. For as much as a fae cannot die, they are as close as one of us may come to it."

Harlequin. Daughter.

Harley froze. She closed her eyes, and behind her eyelids, a warm light shone just out of sight, as if, if she opened her eyes, someone would be standing beside her.

"Harley? Are you okay?" Cadence's voice beside her made her open her eyes and meet his worried gaze.

"What?" she asked, a little dreamily.

"I said, are you okay?" Cadence said.

"If you wish not to see, we can blindfold you and lead your horses behind ours. You are not warriors, and you need not have these images stain you." Arne's voice was earnest, as if he wished he too had not seen what lay beyond.

Danann? Harley thought the name, and even to her, the thought was incredulous.

Cadence answered Arne's offer though for a moment, he continued to study her. "No. I hate to say this, but I think we need to see." He brought his attention back to the elf. "We aren't just here for us, we're here for you, too. Queen Estian told us fae can't die by normal means, and Aoife mentioned previously that severing can only happen using human blood. That means whatever happened to these fae was because of humans."

Yes, Harlequin. My children—all my children—have suffered.

Harley could hear the pain in those words, the sadness of a parent, grieving for their children.

Will you permit me your vessel that I may grant them rest?

Harley's eyes went wide. She peered at the group around her again. This couldn't be real, right?

Cadence was still speaking. "I won't claim to answer for Harley or Chris, but for me, I'll go in with my eyes open." He spoke firmly.

Chris gave the barest nod of his head in agreement.

Please, daughter. Grant me your vessel.

Harley closed her eyes and bowed her head. The world around her stilled and narrowed down to the pale glow behind her eyelids.

What will happen to me?

You will not be harmed. You shall know all I do, and I will be with you.

Will...Will it hurt?

The warm light around her pulsed, and a gentle pressure touched her shoulders like someone set their hands there.

No. It will not hurt.

Harley opened her eyes and raised her head, meeting Yiannis's sad gaze. She said, "They will be seen and remembered." Chris and Cadence regarded her, sitting her horse a little behind them.

Yes. I grant you the use of my vessel, Danann. Please use me to put your children to rest.

387

Harley's head swam, and she gripped her reins then steadied herself. The air was alight with rainbows as if she was surrounded by prisms hanging in the air.

She tried to swallow and felt a pressure in her throat.

Halos and light bursts shone in her vision as everything and everyone took on an aura.

Thank you.

Words flowed from her lips unbidden in a voice that both was and wasn't hers.

"*For those lost, may we now bear witness. May we be Danann's hands and feet, to carry peace and respite to the fallen.*"

The words rang through the hills, tolling in the air like great bells. The feel of magic on her skin grew and built into an almost electric crackle like the air during a thunderstorm. Her body felt light and strange, and she heard a soft whispering inside her head.

"Harley?" Cadence said beside her. *He's scared.*

All will be well. The voice was inside her head and all around, the feeling of Danann suffused every cell of her. Harley gave him a smile, but his look became, if possible, more worried.

"I'm okay, Cadence. All is well, and all will be well." Cadence didn't look convinced.

Harley urged her horse forward. A wind started to swirl around her, picking at her hair and dancing through her horse's mane as she rode up and over the slope.

Cadence

Harley spoke, and her voice boomed across the landscape, resonant and profound. Bands wrapped around Cadence's heart and squeezed. Harley guided her mare past them, and when he closed his eyes, she shone like a sun behind his eyelids. A wind that wasn't there danced around her.

Cadence rode behind her as she led them down the trail, but he stopped next to Yiannis who still sat his horse at the crest of the hill. Chris drew up a little behind them, and they watched as she started down the path ahead of them.

"Yiannis..." Cadence said, unable to keep the fear out of his voice.

"She is God-ridden." Was the answer he got.

"What does that even *mean*?" Cadence asked and could tell Chris was close enough to hear the answer.

"I've not seen it in... far too long. Danann has requested a vessel, and Harlequin has agreed to provide it." Yiannis said, as if it were the most natural thing in the world.

Cadence gaped at him then brought his gaze to look at Harley, making her way on horseback through the field beyond.

The grass to either side of the road was crushed and trampled under piles of slaughtered fae, and the burnt remnants of buildings. Many of the victims had been cut down where they stood, as if they'd waited in place for the butcher's axe. Some had tried to run, their bodies thrown across the scorched ground, arms outstretched and beseeching. About halfway into the field was a row of towering pikes sticking up out of the ground, skewering two armored bodies, one to either side of the road, with a large horse staked up beside each. Cadence couldn't help but think those mounts were familiar.

As Harley's horse picked a path among the bodies strewn across the road, the wind that surrounded her pushed out, sweeping across the field, washing the bodies in bright light. Cadence closed his eyes again, seeing the spirits of the fallen dancing and spinning in place, hovering above their mutilated bodies. They glowed like stars to Harley's sun; their hands raised and faces resplendent. He opened his eyes, and Harley continued to shine like a beacon, even in midday.

"Is she... Will this hurt her?" Cadence asked, plaintively.

Yiannis gripped his shoulder without answering the question. His eyes burned, and the bands around his heart squeezed a little tighter. "Come. We must stay with her."

With every step the dappled gray mare took, the bodies Harley passed slowly sank down into the soil, disappearing from sight. The group caught up as she approached the pikes in the middle of the field, and behind them, the grass filled in over the rubble, lush and new, a riot of wildflowers turning their heads to the sky, and the air was filled with a shower of petals.

As they reached the pikes, all of them drew to a stop as if on cue. Cadence couldn't bring himself to look fully at the warriors at first. He scanned the rest of their group, feeling cowardly.

"Holy shit." Chris uttered. Cadence could hear him gulping convulsively, as if trying to keep from throwing up.

Yiannis was frozen, his face a mask of horror. The three elven riders sat their horses a little behind, their heads bowed. Cadence finally forced himself to face forward, to see what was there.

"Oh my God." He said and tried to swallow past the lump in his throat. Tears welled and fell, and he didn't bother to stop them as he stared up in horror at the warriors hanging from the bloody stakes on which they'd been mounted.

Dia let out a sound that was part keening wail, part pained moan. She rode up past Harley to look up at one of the figures.

They moved their head, struggling to look down at her. The figure's armor was coated in blood, dried nearly black. Dia stood in her stirrups to reach the helmet and pull it off so the warrior could look down at them with pain-filled eyes.

"I... tried. I am sorry. It was... an ambush..." Faustus coughed. Blood bubbled up on his lips. He swallowed convulsively before continuing. "Do not trust... the twins..." His eyes fluttered and closed. Beside him, his mount hung suspended above the ground, but like its rider, it breathed still, though bloody mucus bubbled with every breath and coated its muzzle.

The other warrior had to be Ximeno.

Sidhe warriors, two of the strongest fighters and magic users of the Seelie court, yet here they hung, impaled and abandoned in a forgotten field far from home. What had they gotten themselves into? *Don't trust the twins.* Had they done this? If not, where were they? And if so... This was death for all of them.

Cadence opened his mouth to say just that only to notice Harley standing in her stirrups.

She leaned forward and lay a chaste kiss on Faustus' cheek, and the wind wrapped around him. The warrior blinked eyes now glowing with blue fire. His body rose off the pike and into the air. He didn't make a sound as he was laid gently on the ground like a sleeper, then drawn down into the earth.

Ximeno's body followed. He'd never moved, but Cadence saw his eyes as he was lifted into the air. A blue like his brother's, glowing like trapped stars in his serene face as his body was laid on and then embraced by the soil. The two great chargers followed, freed from their pikes and laid to rest where they, too, vanished into the earth.

Harley settled back into her saddle and guided her mare past Dia at a sedate pace, the earth rippling in her wake to embrace the bodies that lay atop it. When they reached the far ridge, Cadence surveyed the field. The only thing remaining to indicate that something happened in the field was the empty spikes with their gore and viscera. Carrion birds were already landing on and around them, but the ground was clean, covered in fresh grass and wildflowers.

The top of the ridge revealed a long descent on the other side from the field. The path wove back and forth in a switchback, before being swallowed up by a thick black forest of dead trees.

"What the hell is that?" Chris rode up next to Cadence, looking down at the trees.

Behind them, Yiannis sighed. He moved his mount up beside them and peered down the slope. "The Guardian's Sepulcher."

Chapter Forty-Four

Christian

C hris saw real fear on Dia's face as she and Yiannis rode forward to where Harley sat her horse facing down the slope. Neither of them appeared inclined to move their mounts between Harley and the path leading into the dead forest.

Cadence and Chris shared a long look. Chris asked, "Are you okay with this?" Even to him, the question seemed insufficient to what was happening.

"Which part? My best friend being possessed by a capital G God? Knowing that we just saw two of what are supposed to be the most powerful fae in the realm skewered on pikes like sidhe-kabobs, at the center of a field that might as well have been a butcher's workshop? Or do you mean that regardless of what we may face if we actually *reach* the castle, that presumes we don't get killed trying to pass through a place even Yiannis is terrified of?" The words were said with quiet heat, as if Cadence was afraid Harley would hear him.

Chris didn't really blame him. Whatever was going on with Harley was, if not exactly *scary*, definitely fucking weird. "I don't really know what to say to that." He finally said.

Cadence sighed and shook his head. "I don't think there's much *to* say. If it's where she's going, I'm going there, too."

They turned together and watched as Yiannis dismounted and approached Harley on foot, laying one hand gently on the neck of her mare as he addressed her, his voice pleading. "Goddess, please. We must not. You may protect this mortal vessel, but two more we have, and I dare not lead them into that place."

Harley smiled kindly down at Yiannis, but Chris knew it wasn't really Harley behind those rainbow-faceted eyes. Her movements were strange. Not so much stilted, but more controlled, as if every tilt of her head, every shift of a finger was perfectly and elegantly calculated. The voice was like the feeling of warm blankets on a cold night, and as she spoke, the air was filled with the scent of flowers and new grass, and the soft breath of the divine.

Harley leaned down in her saddle to touch Yiannis' face tenderly, like a mother offering comfort. "Hianius, my sweet child. Your faith in me is not unfounded. All is well, and all will be well. Return to the Nightfall Glade. For good or ill, you will know when all is done."

She turned to Chris and Cadence. Cadence shuddered as he gazed into Harley's God-flecked gaze.

If she saw the shudder, she ignored it. She merely considered them for a moment then said, "Come. We must hurry. More dreams will soon turn to nightmares if the Keeper is not freed."

She drew her mare around and heeled it forward, driving the animal down the steep slope across the switchback path in a skidding trot. Chris and Cadence both looked to Yiannis and Dia. Yiannis met their nervous expressions and gave them a nod, his own expression resolute. Dia frowned after Harley as if she would follow regardless, but sat her horse unmoving.

Yiannis raised a hand to them. "Go. We will be here, as she says, for good or ill. Fair well, and Danann bless you both."

Chris and Cadence drove their own horses forward to slide and skid down the steepest part of the hill until it leveled out and the horses were able to catch their balance.

By the time they reached the edge of the forest, Harley was already dismounting. She took the reins of their horses while they also dismounted, holding them while Chris waited, and Cadence went to retrieve his weapons. Once Cadence returned, Harley touched the horses one at a time. Each mount wended its way unerringly back up the slope to the waiting fae. Meanwhile, Harley led them under the first dead branches of the trees, never hesitating.

Spindly stick arms reached for each other over the road and wove back and forth, blocking out the sun. The path around them became darker and darker until no sky was visible among the branches, and the trunks of the trees grew so closely together that the path in front of them was the only way forward. It made Chris think of the forest from the *Wizard of Oz*, and he had to stop himself from whistling the Wicked Witch's song.

The forest seemed to go on forever. After so long in the saddle, Chris' legs were starting to ache as they walked out onto a small ledge overlooking a valley covered in fog. The sky beyond the trees was gray and overcast, the clouds above rushing by in a high wind, though the air around them was stale with a smell that made him think of snakes.

Again, Harley never hesitated. She went to the ledge and stepped down into open air.

Cadence lurched forward, one arm extended. "Harley!"

She stopped and faced them, her feet a little lower than the edge.

Chris stepped forward cautiously, only to find a narrow stairway winding down into the fog below, invisible from where they'd been standing.

Chris and Cadence stared at each other.

"You wanna go first?" Cadence said, his voice a little shaky. Harley was already making her way down the stairs ahead of them without comment.

Chris shrugged. "Not really, no." Regardless, he found himself stepping off down the stairs after her. The treads were worn with age, and the stairs dropped off to either side with not even a railing to stop a fall down into clouds and darkness. A couple rocks tumbled down into those clouds, which swirled and ebbed, but other than the clatter of them falling down the rock face, he didn't hear them land.

Cadence was swearing under his breath. "Shitshitshitshitshitshit."

"You okay?" Chris asked, looking back.

Cadence gave him wide, scared eyes. "Not really, no."

"Trust your feet and focus on my back. I'll worry about the stairs. Got it?" Chris waited a beat, then focused his attention on the stairs.

He heard a rustling, then a mumbled "Got it." from Cadence, then the crunch of steps on stairs.

Cliff walls rose up tall and gray and dead around them as they made their way down the winding stairs. Along the cliffs, dotted like holes in Swiss cheese, were cave openings. Each ledge held a creature straight out of legend.

Dragons of various colors were curled, wings folded along their backs and thick, iridescent scales glinting even under the racing clouds. Asleep.

Griffons were huddled, great eagle's heads tucked under one large feathered wing. Asleep.

Chris saw what he thought might be a sphinx, with a huge cat-like body of tawny brown fur, and great coppery wings, with a serenely beautiful woman's face in closed-eyed repose. Asleep.

More and more creatures, and the further down they went, the more terrifying the beasts were. Some Chris didn't even have a name for, covered in midnight black scales with teeth that jutted from closed mouths like the mountains that towered above them.

They sleep because he sleeps. He wasn't sure if the thought was his, or, maybe more frighteningly, *not* his.

Then the fog engulfed him, and Cadence's hand reached out to grab his shoulder.

"It's okay. I'm here. Trust your feet and hold on to my shoulder." Chris moved slowly, one tread at a time, waiting for Cadence to take each step behind him before he moved forward. As they cleared the fog above, he could see Harley standing at the bottom of the stairs, waiting for them. Unmitigated blackness surrounded them, but he could see Harley clearly. Looking around, he noticed that he could see himself and Cadence clearly, too. They reached the last stair, stepping down into the middle of a giant three-dimensional sheet of black paper, though the ground beneath their feet was solid enough.

"You must wake the Keeper. It is his power the Darkness uses to maintain her gate. Once he is awakened, the gate will close, and her power will diminish. I will now release this vessel. She will remember, but she will not be harmed."

Not-Harley studied them, her eyes shining with prismatic light. "You have done well. Know that I am with you. You are already on the path. Your task now is to walk and trust."

Harley blinked, and the strange light faded to leave her eyes their normal rich brown. Cadence just caught her as she stumbled forward.

"Are you—?" He asked, worry plain on his face and in his voice.

"I'm fine. I'm okay." She met his eyes and smiled, then laughed. "That's twice, now."

Cadence tilted his head and furrowed his brows, confused.

She shook her head. "Never mind." The laughter faded, but the twinkle in her eyes remained. "Come on. We need to find the Keeper."

Harlequin

Harley walked through the darkness, her steps unfaltering. Her mind still tingled and hummed, and behind her eyelids, she could see flashes and starbursts.

Despite the unrelenting blackness around them, the path glowed under her feet as if it were made of individual stars, lighting a trail in the vastness of the Void.

"Do you hear that?" Chris said into the silence.

"Hear what?" Cadence asked behind her.

"It sounds like snoring." Chris's sounded confused, as if he didn't believe his own words.

Harley, walking just ahead of them, saw the creature first. Her throat closed in fear.

"Holy shit." Cadence's voice was barely a whisper.

Before them lay a great beast, legs curled up under it for all the world like an enormous dog or cat, giant furry head resting on huge forepaws that could have doubled as a pair of overstuffed ottomans. The head was somewhere between a dog and bear, the body covered by a thick coat of shaggy black fur only just visible among the black of the Void. A long, thin whip of a tail curled around the back legs and up along the side of the beast's body, the tip of the tail curled out to point toward them. Thick, gleaming canines stuck down over the lower jaw like a sabertoothed tiger.

She stopped just within arms' reach of the big, long-muzzled head, studying the massive beast. She'd never had a pet of her own, though she'd always wanted one. Her fingers tingled and itched with the desire to bury her hands in that soft fur, to snuggle against the slow rise and fall of the ribs.

She turned to Chris and Cadence, her voice unintentionally hushed. "We need to wake him, but I'm afraid if we touch him, it will startle him, and he might lash out or think we're part of his dream."

"What if we try to call his name to wake him? I remember a bunch of the books talked about the importance that the fae give to names." Cadence said, one brow raised in question.

Harley tapped her chin with the tip of her index finger, thinking. "I really like that idea, and I think you're definitely on the right track. The only problem is I also remember Yiannis saying that the Keeper doesn't have a name, as far as anyone knows. If we need his name to call him, but he doesn't have a name, how do we call him?"

"That's easy. We name him." Chris said.

Harley and Cadence both eyed him curiously.

Chris shrugged awkwardly but answered their silent questions. "What? It makes sense, doesn't it? If he doesn't have a name, and we need to use a name to call him, then let's name him. At best, it wakes him, at worst, it doesn't work, and we're no worse off than we were."

Harley grinned. "I love that idea, and you're right. Even if it doesn't work, the worst case is that we're right where we already are."

"Okay, so what do we name him?" Cadence asked. They all studied the Keeper.

After a moment, Chris spoke again, his voice a little sad. Harley peered over at him, but he was focused on the sleeping beast. "About a year ago, Sara came home from playing in the park, and she had this tiny little scraggly black kitten she'd found in a bush. He was scruffy and skinny and followed her everywhere. We named him Shadow, and they were best friends."

Cadence's voice was soft when he asked, "What happened to him?"

Chris barely spared him a glance, his attention focused on the sleeping form as he spoke. "My mother hit Sara one day. Smacked her so hard Sara fell down. Shadow launched himself at her, scratched the hell out of her. The next day we came home, and he was gone."

"He sounds like he was very brave." Harley said, matching Cadence's tone.

"He was a really amazing cat. I miss him."

Harley let the silence be for a moment, then gave a resolute nod. "I think Shadow is a perfect name."

"I think Shadow's a great name for him." Cadence said.

Chris smiled a little.

They all took a deep breath, blowing out the air through their mouths in unison. Though the action was unintentional, the great black nose twitched, scenting the air. Then they started calling to him. Their voices were gentle, soothing, cooing, coaxing. Chris even crouched and patted his legs a little before he grasped what he was doing, blushed, and straightened.

The thick, rounded ears twitched, and as they grew quiet, they saw the body take a long, heavy breath that huffed out. They waited, and the silence stretched out.

Chris tried one more time. His voice was quiet, questioning, and hopeful. "Shadow? Buddy, you have to get up now."

One heartbeat, then two, then three. The eyes came open, great black orbs that sparkled with a sourceless light. The head raised and those great black eyes studied them. A rumble started deep down in his belly, rhythmic and thrumming through the air around them. Beside Harley, Cadence got a strange look on his face and reached for her, but Chris started to laugh, a low, happy chuckle. "He's purring."

The thrum grew louder and more insistent. It vibrated through Harley's chest like she was sitting on the engine of a Mack truck.

"You *are* purring, aren't you Shadow?" Chris stepped forward and raised a hand to scratch at the great black head just behind one ear. His hand and part of his forearm were lost in the fur, and the eyes slid closed as the purring continued.

When Chris stopped and took a step back, the beast's eyes opened and focused on Harley as if waiting for her to say something. She cleared her throat and met that expectant gaze.

"Shadow, you've been under a spell, and the Darkness has been using your power to capture and kill dreamers. Can you take us to the fae side of

401

the Void bridge she opened and then close it?" The purring turned sinister. The eyes narrowed and one lip curled to expose a muzzle full of large, sharp teeth. Shadow swung his head to look out into the Void, drawing another deep breath as if sniffing the air.

He pushed himself to his feet and gave a shake that started from his head and went all the way to the tip of his tail, then a long stretch that bowed his front down over his paws, his hind legs pressed up into the air and his tail stretching back behind him. He held the crouch, and moved his head to look behind himself, then at Harley.

"Is he telling us to get on?" Cadence asked, baffled. Shadow huffed, and his head moved in an almost-nod.

"I think so?" Harley didn't wait, stepping forward to place a hand on one huge, furred shoulder. When he didn't move, she placed one foot on his foreleg, and pulled herself up to straddle just behind his shoulders. Cadence followed, then pivoted enough to offer Chris a hand up. Harley saw Chris give him a skeptical look, one brow raised, and the corners of his mouth pulled down. Cadence laughed.

"Hey, don't make it weird, dude. Get up here and hug me." All three of them laughed and Chris accepted the offered hand, climbing up on the great furry foreleg and onto the huge back. Harley patted Shadow's furred neck to let him know they were ready, and then the big beast was launching himself into the darkness, muscles churning beneath them though without surroundings to look at, they just as easily could have been sitting absolutely still.

Seconds—or maybe hours—later, a pinprick of light appeared far ahead of them that grew into a tall opening out of the darkness into a natural cave filled with the echoing sound of dripping water. Torches lit the space at irregular intervals, but after the darkness of the Void, it was almost blindingly bright.

Shadow drew to a stop, lowering himself carefully to the ground so they could climb down. Harley slid down to the ground, and threw her arms around Shadow's neck, her face buried in his thick fur.

"Thank you. Be safe, okay? You'll see us again, I promise." She whispered the words against that great head, then pulled back, her hands still lost in his softer-than-soft fur. A gentle rumble vibrated through the Keeper as he nuzzled the side of her face. She stepped back and Shadow was just suddenly gone. Cadence and Chris startled, but Harley just laughed.

"Remember what Yiannis said, at the inn? He's the Void's Keeper, but he also *is* the Void. Come on. We need to get through before he closes it." They hurried to clear the gate, stepping down out of the darkness onto the pitted and uneven ground of the cave.

Chapter Forty-Five

Christian

The cave was, kind of surprisingly, completely empty. Chris drew his blade and led them to a set of stairs carved into the far wall which appeared to be the only way out besides the gate into the Void. Cadence took the cue, readied his bow, and nocked an arrow. Chris took lead up the stairs with Harley right behind him then Cadence in the rear.

The stairs ended at a closed door. Chris pressed on it with his off hand, hoping for greased hinges. The door swung in silently, and even better, the room on the other side was empty except for a rough-hewn table surrounded by a few three-legged stools. One guttering torch hung on the far wall, stuck through a ring next to another door. Chris shook out his left hand and tried to relax his shoulders.

He moved into the room, blade held in front of him. Harley followed, her small dagger in one hand, the long leather strap of her belt wound around the other so that the dragon's head would crack out like a whip. When she met his eyes nervously, he nodded in approval. Cadence stopped just inside the doorway.

Chris led Harley across the room, skirting the table and stools, trying to make as little noise as possible. The light of the torch bounced off hinges sticking out of the wall. That meant the inner door would open toward them. He gestured for Harley to put herself against the wall behind him and pressed himself flat to the wall next to the door then grabbed the big wrought iron handle and pulled as hard as he could.

As the door swung open, he heard startled grunts and the scraping of feet on stone. A head poked through the opening, and the moment it laid eyes on Cadence standing just inside the far doorway, it startled. A heartbeat later, an arrow was buried deep into one of its eyes just as Chris's arm dropped like an executioner's blade. The goblin gurgled and dropped to the ground, unmoving.

A second face appeared, and before either Chris or Cadence could respond, Harley lashed out, the belt buckle making full contact with the goblin's face. There was a flash and a wave of heat as the dragon head buckle flared and set the goblin on fire. The creature stumbled back into the other room, and they followed it, Cadence side-stepping to clear his aim, then letting off another arrow that found its target in the goblin's chest.

The creature crumpled to the ground, and they had a moment to look at what they'd just done. The one Chris and Cadence took down lay partially beheaded, measuring its own length into the room behind them. Long gangly arms and legs twitched, but its chest was still. The other goblin, still smoldering in the middle of this new room, stared blankly at the ceiling out of a charred mask, its mouth open in a silent scream.

"Well, that was much easier than I was expecting," Cadence said, looking around the room.

"Harley, did you know that belt would set things on fire?" Chris gawked at Harley who was staring down at the burnt goblin, goggle-eyed. She held up the belt to study it. The red leather was pristine, the buckle shiny as if it had been polished. She gaped at Chris, startled.

"I definitely did *not* know it would do that. If I had, I would have used it sooner." She stammered, but Cadence put a hand on her shoulder.

"Hey. You did good. The important thing is, we know, now." He gave her an encouraging nod, and then another nod to Chris.

The room they'd entered was long and narrow. Against the wall to his right, a set of stone stairs led up to a landing and another door across from the one they'd entered. To his left, a set of grated doors set into the stones led off into darkness. Chris tried one of the grated doors, but the lock—a huge panel of metal with a keyhole at the center of the bottom edge—was engaged. The hallway beyond was heavily shadowed and there was a strong stench of mildew coming from that direction.

"Dungeons, maybe?" Cadence asked.

Chris shrugged. None of them had ever seen much of the castle in their dreams *besides* the dungeons, but those moments were all chaotic and terror filled. He doubted he would have been able to point at any one spot and say he definitely remembered it.

"Not sure. Maybe?" Chris swiveled away from the grated doors and made his way to the base of the stairs. He squinted at the wooden door on the upper landing, and again hoped for silent hinges.

He was halfway up the stairs when the door opened, revealing the silhouette of a hobgob stepping onto the landing. The creature spotted them and bellowed, pointing a spear down toward Chris as it lumbered to the steps and started down. An arrow blossomed from its chest, a red ribbon dancing and mingling with the blood that sprouted behind the sharp point. The giant became a rolling boulder headed straight toward them.

As if they'd planned it, all three of them pressed themselves against the wall along the stairs, letting the body tumble past. Chris kicked out, and the prone form fell off the side of the stairs and down to the room below while he spun to face a goblin rushing him. It was small and fast with long, reaching arms. It swung a nasty, hooked dagger at his head, and he nearly fell down the stairs trying to dodge.

He threw up his left arm to block the beast's swing as it tried to double back, feeling the hot sear as the dagger grazed his forearm. He buried his blade into the thick meat of its belly.

It cried out and wheeled back, ripping itself open on the hooked spine of his sword and landing on its butt on the stairs. He spun the hilt in his hand and drove it down, planting the full length of the blade into the goblin's chest. The goblin screamed and flailed, then stilled.

Chris planted his foot on the goblin's torso and pulled, dragging the sword back out of the now-still body, and kicking it, too, over the side of the stairs and down into the room below. He turned back to the door, expecting to see more goblins coming at them, but instead he saw a pile of bodies pin-cushioned with arrows and still smoldering. Apparently, while he'd been fighting his one, Harley and Cadence had made neat work of four more.

They cleared the landing, dragging the bodies free of the door. As they entered the room beyond, Chris spotted another goblin trying to drag itself across the floor away from the doorway, its legs a burnt ruin. It stared at them wide-eyed and started keening, waving its hands in front of its face. In one, swift motion, Cadence nocked, drew, and released an arrow that punched the goblin right between its wide, frightened eyes. Its expression blanked and it fell back to the ground, its fear gone.

"Shut up." Cadence said into the silence.

Harley gaped at him, horrified. "Are you okay?"

Cadence met her gaze, squarely. "No. I don't know which ones of these might have helped torture me, or you, or anyone else we know. I'm sorry Harley, but I can't help but hate them." His tone was hard, with an edge of anger to it.

Chris stepped to one side, trying to give them a moment of privacy while he ripped a strip from the bottom of his shirt to wind around his arm. The slice wasn't bad, but blood welled steadily to the surface. He pulled a rag out of his back pocket and wiped what he could of the goblin blood off his blade then ran his fingers along his arm under the cut, rubbing the fresh blood into his blade. He wasn't sure if a blooded blade needed refreshing, but better safe than sorry, he thought.

Cadence and Harley were talking quietly, and Chris took the moment to look around. This was less of a room, and more like a big underground foyer with doors leading off in nearly every direction. The walls to either side were flanked by stairs leading up to a balcony where he could see three more archways leading in even more directions.

In the center of the room was an old fountain, broken and crumbling, the statue at the center long since reduced to rubble. Whatever water had originally run through the fountain was long since dried up, and from the smell, the goblins had been using the basin at the bottom as a toilet. Piles of bedding and broken furniture strewn around told him there would definitely be more than just the ones they'd already killed around. Potentially, lots more.

"So, which way do we go?" Chris asked. He would have left the two of them to talk out whatever they were discussing, but the air pressed on him, making him feel anxious and like he needed to be moving.

Cadence and Harley stopped their hushed conversation. Harley peered around the room, while Cadence regarded Chris. "We do seem to have a lot of options, huh?"

"Well, let's logic this out." Harley said, gesturing back to Cadence. "What do we know so far?"

"Right, we came in by a cave. We came up one set of stairs to get up to the first room, and then another set of stairs to get up here, and yet I still haven't seen a single set of windows, or anything that implies venting, but wouldn't we see at least something?" Cadence asked.

"Hey, don't look at me. I'm just the hired muscle." Chris shrugged.

"Maybe..." Harley said, and there was the sound of rocks scraping. Chris and Cadence scanned the room, but Harley murmured, "Guys, don't look now but we have company."

Chris and Cadence followed her look up to the landing, where a face was peering at them from a gap in the balustrade. The eyes bored into him. In the shadows, he couldn't make out much else except that the features didn't appear to be gobkin.

Chris couldn't move. Then the figure was standing up. It appeared to be about human height, based on the balustrade, and placed two five-fingered hands on the top rail as it stared down at them... *Jenta?* His heart pounded.

The figure hesitated, then spoke, the voice soft, barely above a whisper. "Chrissy? Is that you?"

"Sara?" Chris said her name in disbelief. *That can't be her. This can't be. Danann, what did you do to my sister?*

They heard the pounding of multiple pairs of bare and booted feet, coming from the doorways to their left and right. The figure on the balcony waved at them to follow, then darted through one of the archways.

"Do we follow?" Cadence asked.

"I don't think we have much choice." Harley said.

They followed.

Harlequin

They made a run for the stairs, and out through the archway, following the scuttling figure ahead of them who darted in and out of alcoves, glancing back periodically to make sure they were following.

Behind them, the room erupted with the sounds of shouts and some guttural language as whoever entered through those other doorways found the bodies they'd left. Harley tried to swallow past the fear, knowing it would only be a matter of time before someone checked this hallway, and she hoped they'd be out of it by then.

She wanted to look at Chris, to see his face, but the light here was minimal with long stretches of shadowed hall between low burning braziers that only just took the chill out of the air. They hugged the wall, trying to utilize the alcoves like the figure leading them, but there was simply no way Cadence's shoulders were going to disappear into the tiny spaces just big enough for the occasional vase or statuette. The stone walls were otherwise bare, and the hallway itself felt largely forgotten, rubble strewn and dusty.

They made at least three different turns, coming to four-way halls where the figure darted off ahead of them, letting herself be seen just enough for them to know which turn she took. The turns seemed random, and Harley quickly lost track of where they were and started to worry about the sense in continuing to follow the darting form ahead of them.

The figure led them to another intersection where she stopped, under the light of a guttering torch to look at them, and Harley finally got a clear look at her in return. Serious blue eyes shone out of an unwashed face, and other than the vaguely hollow expression, they were the match for her brother's. She had the same dirty blond hair, and Harley let herself take a surreptitious glance at Chris. He had the expression of someone who'd just taken a two-by-four to the face, bafflement and confusion filling his eyes.

"No time. Follow." Sara said in that same whisper-speech then led them to the right and down another bare, shadowed hallway until she reached a wooden door that looked exactly like other doors they'd passed.

Harley glanced around. This hall was slightly cleaner than the ones they'd just been in, but cobwebs still hung like streamers from the arched stone ceiling and the dust coated almost every surface.

Sara crouched and pried up a small stone in the floor, pulled out a key, and then placed the stone back. She worked quickly, opening the door and ushering them in before closing it again.

The moment the door was closed, the space was pitch black. Harley heard the scratch and click of what she figured must be Sara locking the door from the inside.

"Sara..." Chris said into the darkness.

"Shh." There was the soft slap of bare feet. Then another door in the opposite wall came open, shedding scant light into the space, and Sara waved them through, pushing the door closed behind them.

"Okay, seriously, if your goal was to get us lost, you've done it. You can tell us who you are, now." Cadence said, anger and frustration mixing in his tone as he glared at the girl.

"Cay, look. Look at this place." Harley said. Cadence turned the glare on her, and Sara took the moment to dash to one wall, fussing with something Harley couldn't see. Suddenly light blossomed, filling the room with a surprisingly warm glow.

The room was small, probably not more than eight feet by eight feet. In one corner was a pile of bedding, blankets and pillows stacked on top of a matt stuffed with straw. Next to the bed sat a small, rickety table, bearing a book, a candle in a clay candleholder, and a plate holding the remains of a meal. A couple bones and a scrap of bread. High up in the wall, over the bed, a tiny window, let in scant, weak light from outside.

Sara flung herself at Chris, her narrow shoulders racking with silent sobs. She was whispering something under her breath. Harley realized she was just whispering, "Chrissy," and, "I knew you'd come," over and over.

Chris held her, arms wrapped tightly around his sister as she clung to him, but he stared at them over her shoulder, his expression haunted.

It took them some time to get Sara calmed down, and even then, she couldn't seem to bring herself to let go of Chris's hand. They ended up all sitting on the floor in her room, her huddled on her makeshift bed with blankets pulled around her, one thin arm stuck out of the blanket so she could grip Chris's hand in her small grimy fingers.

She was definitely older, but a lack of proper nutrition and light had stunted her growth, so that she appeared small and frail. All her movements were quick and jerky, as if she was more used to having to watch all directions at once.

"Sara..." Chris started, then paused. He looked to Harley, and his expression screamed, "help me."

Harley inspected Sara who couldn't seem to meet her eyes for longer than a moment at a time. "Sara, can you tell us what happened?"

"You mean, 'Why are you old,', don't you. Or, 'How do we know you're really Sara?' I know. She's really good at tricks. I'm not sure how to prove myself since you might think I'm lying, and I don't think we have much time. You guys need to get to the throne room." Sara sat for a moment in thought, then shoved the blankets off her shoulders and thrust her arm forward for them all to see. A long, jagged scar ran down her bicep. It was pale and shiny with age, and Chris reached out gingerly, as if to touch it.

Sara sat quietly under his hand, as he pressed the scar, then met her gaze with his searching one.

"A week before I was taken, I was playing outside of our house. The neighbor, Mrs. Fulmer, let out that stupid dog, the one that always liked to chase me. Marmalade. Do you remember?"

Chris gave a silent nod.

"I ran away, and tripped, and slid with my arms in front of me, and my underarm was cut up on Mr. Harris' broken sprinkler, the one that sticks up out of the ground. You ran outside when I started screaming, picked me up, and rushed me to the urgent care, and you paid for everything out of the money you'd saved from work because Mama used up the last of her most recent paycheck to buy alcohol."

Chris sucked in a breath, and Harley saw tears spring out from the corners of his eyes. He tried to blink them away, but his expression was horror filled. "I'm so sorry, Sara. What the hell happened?"

"*She* happened. She said it was to punish you, but Miss Geldith once said that the years fly like days, here, and that it had been that way before I came." Sara said sadly. "Poor Miss Geldith. She was just trying to get me new clothes."

Harley shook her head, confused. "I don't understand. What do you mean?"

Sara swallowed hard and met her eyes. "I'm fifteen, now."

Harley gaped. "Are you telling me that—"

"I've been here for seven years." Sara said.

"But... how?" Cadence said, unbelieving.

Sara shrugged uncomfortably under the scrutiny. She didn't seem to like having all their eyes on her. Harley couldn't exactly blame her. "I don't really know. Time just moves different, here. Mr. Silas said the same thing when he came. But the point is, I need to tell you some stuff before I can take you to the throne room." Sara squeezed Chris's hand and covered their held hands with her other hand.

"Sara, you don't have to do this. You can just take us there. We'll get you out of here, okay?" Chris said earnestly, but Sara shook her head.

"No, Chrissy. She said you'd need to hear."

"She?" Harley asked, but thought she already knew the answer.

Sara shot her an indecipherable look. "About eight months ago now, another human showed up. She's... strange."

Harley's stomach dropped. "What do you mean, strange?"

"She's... nice. She came and found me. I was afraid the queen sent her, that she was finally going to..." Sara gulped audibly, then continued. "She told me you guys would be coming. She said she'd come to help the queen, but if the queen asked, not to mention you guys, and that her name was Jenta. She said you'd know her. But... she goes down into the dungeon with the queen."

Oh Jenta... What have you done? Harley swallowed back bile.

Cadence furrowed his brows. He said, "What does that mean?" but after a moment, his eyes widened, his mouth opening in horror. "No..."

Sara just nodded, her expression sad.

Chris sat stoically, his expression guarded as he stared down at his sister's diminutive hand.

Harley tried to focus on the present, asking "Why the throne room? Do you know something we don't?"

Sara gave a half-hearted smile. "Jenta told me that's where you'd have to go, but I know it's because that's where all show downs with the bad guy are supposed to happen. I don't remember much from back home, but I remember that."

"Showdowns." Chris said, his voice as empty as his expression.

"Do we have much other choice?" Cadence asked.

"Are you saying you've changed your mind?" Harley asked in return. "When we first started this, you seemed to want to find a way to resolve this without one."

"That wasn't what I meant." Cadence shot back.

"Then what *did* you mean?" Chris asked, anger edging his words.

Cadence started to get angry back, then let it out with a whoosh of exhaled breath. "What else did we come all this way for, except to fight and try to stop her? Sara has a point. I've tried not to think about it because it's fucking weird to let myself dwell, but the truth is, we're in the place where fairytales were born. And what do most fairy tales have in common? Winning the day means defeating the bad guy. And as far as I can see, there's no bigger bad guy than the Dark Queen who has literally been torturing and killing people."

"You know we can't kill her, though." Harley insisted.

"No, we can't. But you know what we *can* do?" Cadence responded.

"What?" Sara asked, seeming honestly curious.

Cadence dropped the words into the waiting silence. "We sever her."

Chapter Forty-Six

Harlequin

The conversation after that was mostly taken up with planning. Trying to figure out the best next steps and what to do once they got to the throne room. They knew the plans were shaky at best, but as Cadence pointed out, better shaky plans than none at all.

Sara led them back out of her room, and they listened at the outer door, breaths held while they waited for the sound of feet to pass.

When the hall outside the door was no longer rebounding with the echoed footfalls of a patrol, they exited quickly, Sara locking the door and stowing the key under another loose flagstone in the floor. She pressed a finger to her lips, then led them away into a warren of halls and stairs that wove itself among, around, and under the main halls. The occasional doorway was visible covered by a tattered tapestry so that, presumably this back hall wouldn't be visible from the main hall into which it entered.

Sara brought them to a halt near one of those tapestry-covered arches.

Cadence started to walk forward but Sara shot a hand out, grabbing his forearm. He stopped, which Harley assumed was her intention, and opened his mouth to say something when they heard people speaking, approaching from their left. Cadence moved carefully back away from the tapestry, and they huddled to either side of it in the shadows. The tapestry hung nearly to the floor, giving a bare edge of flickering light, just enough that they could meet each other's scared eyes.

"...got here, now we're leaving. Which is it, Aoife?"

"It *is* what I say it is, and right now, it *is* that we are leaving."

Aoife?! Harley mouthed the name at Chris who huddled with Sara across the doorway from her. Chris shrugged as if to say, "I don't know either", then tapped his ear. They were talking again.

"You do this every time. We *abandoned* the job the queen gave us to come here which means we may not be able to show our faces again at our *own* court. Then you make me attack warriors I've traveled and fought with. Hell, Ximeno and I..."

"They are *nothing*, Leif. Probably already severed and rotting on those pikes where I left them."

"It is a disgrace, sister, and I am getting tired of it." Leif's voice was growling and furious, but Aoife's response was flippant.

"You've followed me this far. If you did not like it, you could have left any time." There was a long silence and then her laughter rang through the halls, and Harley flinched. "Yes, that is what I thought. You are pathetic, brother. You have followed me and will *continue* to follow me and do as I say because anything else would see you in chains. So, when I say we are *leaving,* that means *we* are leaving."

Their voices were already fading, but Harley just caught Leif say, "I hate you, Aoife."

Another round of laughter bounced down the hall. "I know. But you love me, too."

If they said anything more, Harley didn't catch it. Their footfalls faded into the distance, and finally all was silent.

Sara held a finger up to her lips and then crouched, darting out from their hiding place and leaving them in the relative darkness. Forever—but probably not more than a couple seconds—later she pulled the tapestry aside so they could walk out into yet another long hallway. *This place is an absolute labyrinth!* Harley thought to herself. There was no way they would have figured out how to get anywhere, let alone the throne room, by themselves.

Ahead of them, the hall met at a T with a much wider one. A long runner of motheaten, threadbare carpet was laid down the center of both the side hall, and the one it led into. Other than the carpet and the torches along the walls, both appeared empty. They made their way down to the T, and Sara steered them to the right.

Chris whispered, "How many more halls?" at Sara.

Sara's expression was serious, and she whispered back, "Just this one. But it's long."

She led them along the carpeted floor which muffled their steps a little. The passage curved to the right, and it felt as if they were walking up a very gently inclined ramp with the occasional offshoot hall to their left or right looking nearly identical to the one through which they'd come. Harley wasn't entirely certain how some of the halls on the right could exist. The further they went, the less sense the intersections made.

As they walked, figures started dotting the sides of the wide hall.

At first, Harley thought they must be statues, but as they drew closer, she slowed. If they *were* statues, they were the finest craftsmanship she'd ever seen. One was a hulking bear-man, his fur real-looking, and his eyes bright with intelligence. His clothing looked real, too, if aged and tattered.

Just down from him was a fox-man, his tunic and pants faded to various shades of dingy gray, thread-bare rags.

"They aren't statues." Sara whispered from just beside her, and Harley Jumped. She'd stopped walking, and Sara had apparently doubled back to stand beside her. Harley tried to remind herself that it wasn't Sara's fault that Harley was creeped out in all kinds of ways to know that the eight-year-old child who'd been taken was now a fifteen-year-old young lady, guiding them through the Dark Queen's palace. Sara could almost be Chris' twin instead of his baby half-sister.

"What are they?" Cadence asked from behind them.

Sara studied the figures lining the hall. "Dreamers."

Harley's brows furrowed in confusion. "What do you mean? Fae can't dream."

Sara regarded one of the statues sadly. "Exactly why they're stuck like that. They're trapped."

Harley shook her head. "I still don't understand. Do you mean, that they," she pointed toward the statues, "are living, breathing fae who are, what, stuck in their own dreams? But they *can't* dream. They can't even get into the Void from this side..." She trailed off as it clicked. They *could* reach the Void from this side. What was downstairs wasn't the right kind of Void bridge. It wasn't open on both ends like it should be, blocking travelers from accessing the Void. It led straight into a world not meant to be entered while awake.

"The queen takes them in there and does something with them, and when she leads them back out, they're like that." Sara said, looking sadly at the figures. "Miss Geldith was punished for bringing me my lamp and a new dress. Silas used to bring me toys and taught me to read." She pointed at a tiny, pinch-faced elderly looking fae with thick black hair in a braid pulled over one shoulder, and a stout man beside her who wore deep brown trousers and a pale cream shirt with a broad white beard that made her think of Miles.

Christian

They continued on, seeing more and more statues as the hall spiraled upward. Sidhe, goblins, demi-fae, a smattering of elves. They were all lined up along the edges of the carpet as if they'd been placed. In the distance, Chris finally spotted a set of great double doors.

Dreamers. They not only won't *attack, I don't think they* can *attack.*

He made himself walk, steadily, evenly, fighting not to start running. Eyes here and there followed them, but none of the figures moved, otherwise.

The distance to the door seemed to stretch. The closer they got toward it, the darker the space became, like walking into a cave. The doors gaped open into blackness, yawning in ominous promise.

Then the doors were behind them, and they were standing in a throne room. It was all dark marble veined with white and a deep, saturated garnet red. Torchlight danced off gold filigree and warmly polished wood furniture placed along the walls. The carpet that ran the length of the great hall was richly woven in shades of wine red and grape purple and went all the way to the foot of a wide, low dais.

"Holy shit." Chris said with feeling.

"What the actual fuck?" Cadence said, spinning on his heel then continuing in a fast circle.

"I'm starting to really dislike magic..." Harley muttered.

"No kidding." Sara responded, earnestly.

In front of them, the ornate throne sat empty at the top of the deep steps, carved of some rich, oily black wood draped in colorful fabrics that matched the pillows strewn about the floor. The air was warm and smelled of beeswax. Tall, multi-armed candelabras had been placed throughout the room, filled with creamy white candles all alight with flames that danced in the fragrant air. It appeared to be the luscious, opulent opposite of the austere beauty of the Seelie court. And it was empty.

Chris peered back through the door behind them to find that the hall was also empty. Moreover, the same rich red and purple carpet stretched out from the wide double doors down past more black marble pillars along the torch-lit corridor. He blinked and turned back to the dais.

Jenta stood at the top step of the dais, looking down at them.

Chapter Forty-Seven

Harlequin

"Neat trick, isn't it?" Jenta said, for all the world as if she was showing them some slight-of-hand in the hallway at school, except that her expression was completely empty.

Harley felt like she'd been slapped. All the words she'd wanted to say to her friend were gone. Chris, beside her, had that same heartsick look he'd had when he'd told them of Jenta's leaving—when he'd repeated back what she'd said. Despite everything, Harley missed her even more, seeing her standing there.

Jenta was no longer wearing the clothing the elves had given them. Instead, she was in a flowing black dress that hung around her in satiny folds like a carefully draped robe. She regarded them, her expression haughty—one eyebrow raised, the corners of her mouth drawn down in disapproval, as cold and distant as the moon.

The neckline of her dress was modest, but her arms were bare. Harley thought at first that Jenta wore gloves of a similar dark red to the carpets under their feet, but as she shifted, Harley saw that they weren't gloves—Jenta's arms were covered up to the elbow, as if they'd been dipped in paint. *It's paint. It has to be paint. Please, let it be paint...*

"Sara told us you've been here awhile." Harley spoke quietly, not really sure what else to say.

Despite it not really being a question, Jenta spoke as if it was. "Yes. You could say that." She raised the bottom hem of her robes, showing bloodstained feet. "In the fae realm, time runs as the ruler wills it, and the Dark Queen wishes all the time in the world to indulge in playing with her toys." Jenta slowly descended the stairs, and Cadence came to stand beside Harley, raising his bow to point it straight at the other girl.

"Don't come any closer," he said. His voice shook, but the bow was steady.

Jenta raised her hands up in surrender, but she continued to look at Harley. "Do you really think I would hurt you after all we've been through?"

"You're wearing blood on your hands like gloves, Jenta. You tell me." Harley said. Her heart lurched in her chest. She didn't dare look at Chris again but wondered if he was struggling as much as she was, to see their friend like this.

"I wear what my Queen bids." Jenta said.

"And how well it suits you, my love." The voice cooed through the room and raised gooseflesh on Harley's arms, as if someone had run fingers along her skin, a butterfly's wing of touch.

The Dark Queen stepped from the shadows behind the throne, tall and elegant with hair like black water trailing down around her to mingle among the swirling shadows that formed her gown. Her face was as pale and clear as a marble statue, her lips the color of fresh blood. Her eyes were black on black, though even from across the room, Harley could swear she saw lightning crackling in their depths.

The Dark Queen moved forward and placed one alabaster hand on Jenta's shoulder as she studied them.

"Come now, Cadence. Will you not wait to see my gifts for you all?" The Dark Queen made a gesture, and the bow was ripped from Cadence's hands and sent clattering to one side of the room.

Harley swallowed hard. "What do you want from us?"

The queen gazed at her for a long moment, and Harley had the distinct impression that she was being laughed at. "Harlequin Swanson. Truly, you were the hardest to select a proper gift for. I feel I may owe you an apology for my inability to locate just the right one." The queen was poised at the edge of the dais, talking to them as if they were all old friends.

"I don't understand what you mean." Harley said, though she was afraid they were about to learn the answer.

Instead of speaking, the queen gestured again. Along the wall behind and to the left of the throne, thick draperies were pulled aside, revealing three prisoners hanging by their arms, their bare feet just barely touching the ground. The moment the curtain opened, one of them started screaming.

"Cay! Cay, oh my god, Cay, get me down from here! Cay, help me!"

"Shhhh...." The queen raised a finger to her lips and tilted her head slightly toward the screaming prisoner. That screaming mouth kept moving, but Harley could no longer hear any sound coming from her.

"Becky..." Cadence took a step forward, and Harley wasn't certain whether to stop him.

"Ah, good! You begin to understand." The queen said, her lips turning up just a little.

"No, I don't begin to understand, you bitch. What the fuck are you doing? Why do you have Becky?"

The queen *tsk*ed and waggled one finger back and forth. "Now, now. It is my host gift. They wish to die, and have already wrested control of their spirits to me. All that awaits them is the final blow, which I offer to you."

"What does that have to do with Harley?" Cadence asked, angrily.

The Dark Queen raised one eyebrow, the corner of her mouth pulling up in a condescending smile. "Cadence. Sweet child. Do you not see? I was unable to provide a host gift for her, because I could not string her up to kill *herself*, and even if I did, she is too afraid to wield the blade." She gave Harley a knowing look, and Cadence turned to gape at her.

"Harley... That's not true, is it?" The concern in Cadence's voice seared through her heart.

She raised her head and straightened her shoulders but wasn't able to meet his searching eyes. She almost found it easier, or at least less painful, to meet the Dark Queen's smug gaze. "My mother is dead, and my father can't help himself, but he was also never a creative. I bet he just never dreamed closely enough for you to reach him."

"Harley..." Cadence reached out his hand to touch her, and she flinched, taking a step away from him. His hand hung in the air for a moment, then dropped to his side.

Harley sighed, but still couldn't bring herself to look at him as she answered. "Cay. All of us were in the dungeon. I know you probably heard the same offer of release that I did. Who wouldn't want relief?"

"Jesus, Harley... Why didn't you tell me?" Cadence sounded so disappointed. Harley couldn't stand it.

She used the wave of fury and glared at him, her words coming out heated. "I *tried*, Cay. You and I met only days after I'd found Jenta in the school bathroom, covered in blood. I ran away from what I'd seen, but not because I was afraid of her." Harley turned to look at Jenta, meeting the other girl's sad stare. "I was jealous of how close she'd come."

Jenta

She swallowed back bile as they entered the throne room. *Danann, please be with me. Help me. I need them to survive this.* She did her best to hold onto the emotionless mask she'd been cultivating since she arrived at the doors of the castle as she met Harley's stare.

Jenta had a moment to remember what, within the castle's bounds, had been months ago, now. *She'd ridden straight east from the camp site, across a crumbling stone bridge over a ravine and up the path to the gates of the Bastion of Night where she'd been greeted with obsequious bows and a disturbing level of pomp. She'd been led directly to the throne room to find the Dark Queen waiting for her and found exactly what she'd expected. The queen was mad. Crazy as a June bug in July, her grandmother would have said. The storm that filled the queen's eyes was shot with lightning that flashed and lit up her cheeks as if she were wearing reverse sunglasses, but through those roiling black-on-black clouds, Jenta saw something surface. Something* desperate.

"Yes. You could say that." *You've been here for a while.* Harley had no idea. Every minute was a day, every hour a month, every day a year. It all ran together for her. Nearly eight months had passed since she'd snuck off in the middle of the night, breaking not only Chris' heart but her own as she held a blade to his throat and bade him not to miss her. *Danann, please let Cadence have understood my message.*

Eight months of trying to find that part of the queen she'd seen—the part that screamed for help. Eight months of seeing the madness grow with every mortal death. Eight months of sneaking down into the dungeons when she could, and killing or freeing whoever she could, to remove them from the queen's grasp in the hopes it would be enough.

Eight months. And now, the madness was growing in her, too.

One path. One choice. One chance. Please, Danann. Please.

The thought that wasn't hers came again.

I am with you, child. Have faith.

Christian

He was staring toward the wall of prisoners, his chest heaving as if he'd been running. He swallowed convulsively and finally made himself ask, "That's mom, isn't it?"

Sara nodded, tears running unbidden down her dirty cheeks. Her face was a mask of pain and despair. "Yes." she choked out. "She's been here with me the whole time."

"Sara, child, did I not promise you that I would ensure you were reunited with your brother? You see? I keep my promises." The queen's voice was soft, but with a sharp edge of malice. "You may despise me, child, but I have been good to you. *Fair* to you. Do not confuse my kindness for weakness. You may still join your mother, yet." Sara dropped to the ground, prostrating herself and mumbled something. The queen stamped one bare, bloodstained foot. "Say it louder."

Sara shook like a leaf in strong wind, and raised her head just enough to say, "I'm sorry, my Queen."

Chris couldn't seem to take his eyes off his mother. Tonya. Toni, to her friends. She hung from the wall by her wrists, naked but for the blood that coated her, but all he could see was her eyes. Eyes that screamed at him, begged, cried, pleaded.

"Do you wish to approach your mother, Christian? I know she wishes you would draw close. One last look at her beloved son. Would you not grant her this?" The queen said, as if it were the simplest question in the world, which, Chris supposed, it might as well be.

He walked wide around the dais as if in a trance and approached his mother, where she hung on the wall.

"Ma." That one word made her grunt like she'd been stabbed.

"Chris..." Her voice was raw, full of so many emotions, and yet he felt nothing.

"What did you do?" The words fell from him, but he knew he wouldn't take them back, even if he could. She gave a sharp sob, her body trembling as she hung suspended. She was covered in cuts, claw marks, and weeping lashes. Her eyes shone, wide and fearful, out of a tear-stained, and blood-smeared face.

"P-p-please, C-c-chrissy... P-please, help me." She whispered it, spittle forming at the corners of her mouth.

"I never hated you, *Tonya*. Not once. No matter what you did to *me*, I let it go. But you gave her *Sara*. Of all the things you could have done. You gave her *your own daughter*. I may not hate you, but I'll never forgive you." Chris clenched his teeth around anything further, then turned and went back to where Sara was huddled on the ground.

As he walked away, his mother started screaming. "Christian Alexander Johnson, you get back here! You will *not* turn your back on your *mother!* *How DARE you!*" Chris ignored her as he crouched and wrapped one arm around his sister's shoulders, raising her to her feet and hugging her to him as he glared at the queen.

"Kill her or don't, but don't claim that offering me the knife is a gift to *me*."

The queen considered him, and then moved to stand in front of his mother, her back to them. Tonya grunted, and the Dark Queen stepped away, revealing a black handled blade about the size of Chris's own jutting out from just below his mother's ribs. Chris made himself watch as her face drained of life, even as more tears ran down his cheeks.

Becky started screaming again, her mouth wide and her eyes huge in her bloody face, though they still couldn't hear her. The queen came to stand in front of her, running one bloody finger down her cheek. She pressed the finger against Becky's lips, shushing her. Becky's eyes bulged, but she closed her mouth, her body shuddering as she tried to still herself.

The queen turned to Cadence. "And you? Would you also spurn my gift?"

Cadence shook his head. "Like Chris said, don't call it a gift. I can't make you not kill her, but I also won't kill her *for* you."

The queen gave a genuine smile. "Oh, goody."

The queen flexed her hand, her fingers becoming thick black talons. She drove those talons in and up into Becky's chest.

Chris flinched and pressed Sara's face into his chest. This vision, he could save her from.

Cadence

The room filled with the sound of Becky's shrieks, as if whatever silencing magic on her was undone the moment the queen started her gruesome work. Along with the screams came the wet squelching of whatever the queen was doing. Cadence tried to tell himself he was grateful to be positioned so he couldn't see anything besides Becky's writhing body, her head tossing back and forth—first vigorously, then more slowly as her chin dipped. The queen pivoted to better focus on her work, giving her back to the room as she became fully engrossed in what she was doing. Becky's shrieks dropped away to whimpered pleading and then to silence.

With the queen's back turned, Cadence took the chance. He swallowed back his horror and moved as quietly as he could to where his bow lay. Finally, he was close enough that he could have bent down and grabbed it, just as the queen whirled to smile triumphantly at them.

Harley turned away from the scene, retching.

The queen extended her blood-soaked hand to Jenta. "Come, my love. Come and accept my gift."

Jenta shot a quick look at Cadence, and there was something in her expression. Something he wasn't expecting. Fear, and hope, mingled. He realized she'd seen him moving but had remained silent. *What was it she said to tell us?* That they shouldn't waste their time trying to miss her. *This can't be what she meant... Can it?*

Then she was turning back to face the queen, taking her hand, their fingers entwining as she drew her small cat dagger from her belt and approached the third prisoner.

"Jonathon, I offer you the final release. Will you accept?" Jenta's voice was clear, and it was only then that Cadence grasped who it was hanging on the wall in the third spot. *Holy fuck, she's going to kill him...* What he wasn't expecting was the answer.

"Please... Please release me. I wish to be free." The words were pain-filled, but his eyes were clear as he gazed down at her.

Jenta didn't hesitate. The point of the blade went up under Jonathon's chin, and she used both hands to shove the blade up, fast and hard. Fresh blood ran over her hands in a wash.

There was no sound, and then there was only the ringing in his ears. The Dark Queen took Jenta's hand and led her to the dais, then moved to stand behind her and wrapped her long arms around Jenta's smaller shoulders.

The ringing stretched as he dropped to one knee, picked up his bow, drew the arrow, and fired.

Don't bother trying to miss me.

Cadence didn't miss.

Chapter Forty-Eight

Harlequin

A shockwave shook the castle, and the world went white. Harley couldn't see anything, including herself, and the only thing she could hear was the pounding of her heart in her ears.

Just as she started to wonder if she'd died, or lost all her senses completely, sound started returning. Chris's ragged breathing to her right and Sara's quiet sobs. The scrape of shoes. A muffled curse, which must have been Cay.

A hard gasp in front of her, where the dais would be. *No...*

Harley blinked, and vision returned in reverse starbursts. There, the throne, empty save for a bloody arrow. There, the wall, empty of the bodies. There...

"Jenta!" Harley ran forward, stumbling as her vision flashed in and out until her shins smacked into the first step of the dais, and she dropped hard to her knees.

Jenta lay on her back on the top step, her head lolled to one side and her eyes fluttering open and closed. Chris was close behind Harley, and he rushed past her to kneel next to Jenta on her other side, pushing Jenta's hands out of the way so he could find and put pressure on the wound where the arrow had pierced her.

Jenta's dress puddled down the stairs like a black satin waterfall, but beneath it, Harley saw the unmistakable glint of liquid, just barely visible against the black marble floor. She reached fingers down and touched the already cooling fluid, raising it up to see deep dark red blood.

She raised her gaze to look past her hand at Jenta who met her gaze, a small smile on her face.

"You were never jealous of me." The words came out strained. She reached out a hand, still coated in the glove of blood, but Harley took it without flinching.

"Not jealous, no." Harley said. "Just sad." A tear started down her cheek. "Why, Jen? We could have found another way."

Jenta tried to shake her head, but it ended up more of a weak wobble. Chris was pressing on her torso, and Harley could see he had his own tears streaking down his face.

"Danann. Will and choice. She..."Jenta winced, and her eyes slid closed.

"Jenta? Jenta..." Harley wasn't sure what to do. She rubbed the back of Jenta's hand and looked up at Chris who stared back at her, his face a broken mask of pain.

"You told me not to waste my time missing you. I didn't understand what you meant, at first. Did I get it right?" Cadence came to stand behind Harley, and she didn't dare let him see her expression, since she wasn't sure she'd be able to keep the fury out of it. His voice sounded sad and hollow, though that hadn't stopped him from taking the shot.

Jenta moved her head slightly, and she seemed to have a hard time focusing on him. "Yes." She said, her voice now a bare whisper.

"Jen... I still don't understand...why?" Harley couldn't seem to keep the tears out of her voice, no matter how hard she choked them back.

"Ask... Sara... Storm. Mad." Jenta said, and Harley had to lean over her to hear as she continued. Jenta's hand convulsed in Harley's, and she made a pained noise.

"Shh... Jenta, it's okay... We'll get Yiannis, and you'll be all better. It's gonna be okay." Harley brushed tendrils of hair from her friend's face with gentle fingers, but the skin was already pale and clammy. Jenta gave her a slow blink, and the corners of her mouth pulled up in a beatific smile.

"I welcome the dawn."

Chapter Forty-Nine

Cadence

The smoke-black glass windows shattered, blasting across the throne room, and slicing through fabric and furniture. *I welcome the dawn.* Jenta's voice rang through his head and against the walls of the castle like the toll of a bell.

Cadence threw himself over Harley as the glass blew over them, shards slicing through his back and arms. In front of him, Chris was bent over Jenta's still form.

He'd seen the storm in the queen's eyes—the roiling clouds and flashes of red and purple lightning. He'd also seen Jenta's face. The fear and sadness and then the determination and hope. He'd watched the arrow pierce Jenta, and through her the Dark Queen. He'd practically felt the blow as if it had pierced his own torso. In the moment before the shockwave, he'd seen the storm clear from the queen's eyes before they'd closed, her face going slack.

Was that the storm Jenta had meant?

As the glass settled, Cadence pushed himself to his feet, drawing Harley up with him. He glanced behind to find Sara huddled on the floor. Her arms, crisscrossed with cuts, were still held over her head. The throne room was in shambles, furniture shoved and smashed against the far walls away from the windows or crumbled to dust in place. Some of the candles still guttered in their overturned stands, but otherwise the only light in the throne room was the rays of the rising sun shining in through the shattered windows. It poured in and over them, bringing with it that tingling wash of magic.

Cadence turned toward the door to find that whatever spell keeping them from seeing the dreamers in the hallway was gone. He wasn't sure if it had been the shockwave or something else, but many of the fae still lay on the floor, or were just sitting up, while others were already standing, the latter looking at each other or toward the throne room.

He snatched up his bow, trying not to take his eyes off them, just as the weight in the room shifted. It felt for all the world like a wave breaking over him. Harley shuddered beside him, and he immediately knew she'd felt it too. The fae in the hall parted and Yiannis strode past them, Dia, Arne, Wilhelm, and Frode close on his heels. The three elven riders had their short swords drawn, watching those in the hall even after the five of them cleared the doors. Cadence watched as they passed through the wavering surface of one of Yiannis' bubble shields, now wrapped around the throne room.

Yiannis stood tall and resplendent, his armor shining and pristine in the morning sun. His eyes practically sparkled with magic and behind him, Dia glowed like a flame. They looked like what they were; elemental powers, full to bursting with the magic of their kind. Behind them, the elves positioned themselves so that they faced the door and the crowd of fae beyond.

"How did you get here?" Cadence asked, honestly perplexed.

Yiannis studied him, the magic in his eyes dimming. "You are all well? You have won? The ravine is gone."

"What?" Cadence stammered.

"I am not certain. We returned and thought to check it on our way back to the Nightfall Glade, and it was already... Narrower, I suppose. So, we camped beside it, and the moment it closed completely, we rode as quickly as we could." Yiannis peered past him, and his face fell. "Ah. Ah, Christian."

Cadence finally made himself see the scene behind him. At the top of the dais, Chris had pulled Jenta's form into his lap. He was carefully brushing hair out of her face, and when he lifted his head, Cadence flinched at the pain and fury that screamed out from him. Worse, it wasn't aimed at Cadence.

"Sara, what did she mean?" Chris's voice was low and growling, and Sara huddled around herself on the floor where she'd dropped when the windows had blown in.

"I don't..." Sara started.

"*Don't lie to me!*" Chris's voice cracked like a whip through the room.

"Chris!" Harley stepped toward Sara as if to guard her, but Sara just shook her head.

"No." She made herself meet his eyes, and Cadence had to admit, it was impressive to watch the steel resolve build itself up in the straightening of her spine and squaring of her shoulders. Sara met Chris's eyes and spoke clearly. "I told you she found me. She wanted to make sure I knew her plans, in case it came down to... This one."

Harley crouched next to her, putting a hand on the younger girl's shoulder. "It's okay, Sara. It's over, now. Just tell us."

Sara met Harley's concerned expression; sadness clear in her own features. Cadence still felt hollow. It was *his* arrow that... And yet, Sara was taking the brunt of Chris's ire.

"She told me the queen had been coming to her in her dreams. She said she'd been shown that the queen was mad. She wasn't sure how, but that the storms in her eyes worsened every time Jenta saw her."

"Worsened how?" Harley asked, coaxing.

Sara shrugged. "Bigger. Stronger. Closer to the surface of her. Jenta wasn't sure what would happen if the storm... If it *left* the queen."

"Okay. Jenta saw the queen's madness, and came to...what? Stop her, herself?" Cadence said doubtfully.

"No. She said she came to see if there was anything left to save, and if there wasn't, to be a distraction so you could do what you needed to." Sara said, lowering her head so that the last words were spoken more toward the floor than to any of them.

Chris rose to his feet, Jenta's body cradled in his arms. Her head rested against his shoulder, as if she was sleeping. Chris made his way down the dais and past his sister without looking at her. He started to walk past the rest of them and toward the hallway doors, but Yiannis reached out a hand and placed it on Chris's shoulder. Chris allowed himself to be stopped and turned his head slowly to regard Yiannis as if the movement hurt.

Yiannis responded to the look in those eyes, his tone sad and sincere. "She chose, Christian. Chose, and chose again. Do not discount her decision."

"She chose, Yiannis. Danann's will, Mortal's choice. Well, this decision is mine. If you're going to ask me not to make it, you can fuck off, because it will be the first time you've given me that option."

They stared at each other in the weighted silence. Cadence thought Chris would be the one to give in and speak first, but it was Harley who asked the question.

"Where are you taking her?" She asked, still crouched beside Sara, arms wrapped around the younger girl who held her hands to her face, her shoulders shaking with silent sobs.

Chris looked back at her but gave his answer to Yiannis. "The one place I know of where I've seen the dead come back." He rolled his shoulder, and Yiannis removed his hand. Chris continued on past them and through the doors where the fae parted for him without comment.

"Why the fuck didn't you stop him? Where is he going? Chris!" Cadence tried to push past Yiannis, who instead took him by the shoulders to keep him from following as Chris disappeared down the hall and out of view.

Harlequin

Harley straightened and rested a hand on Cadence's arm. When he wouldn't look at her, she reached up and grabbed a fistful of his hair, dragging his head around to look at her. He tried to fight her at first, tried to yank his head free but finally turned the full force of his fury on her. His face was red, and spittle sat on his lip. He was panting from his efforts to pull free of both her and Yiannis. Once he was looking at her, she released his hair so she could grip his forearm.

"Cay, let him go." She couldn't keep the anger out of her tone, and he opened his mouth to argue.

"Harlequin is right, Cadence. You must have faith, now." Cadence shifted his gaze back and forth between Harley and Yiannis, then shook his head hard.

"Have faith. Have faith. I *had* faith, Yiannis. I had faith in a God who loves and forgives and *saves* people, a God of wonders and miracles. Danann created all this, or so you keep trying to remind us, so where are they? Where is all this wondrous creation? Where are the miracles? Jenta could have used the blade to kill the queen, right after she killed Jonathon, but she didn't. She made me kill the queen and her both! Why did she do that?" Cadence's face crumpled, the rage fleeing in a wash of pain. "Why did she do that?" The words ripped from his mouth, a mournful cry as his knees sagged.

Yiannis lowered him slowly to the floor and let go of his arms as Harley came to stand in front of him. His arms wrapped around her waist; his face pressed into her stomach as he sobbed. She held him, petting his head gently and whispering soft words as tears ran silent down her own cheeks. She followed Yiannis with her gaze as he moved around them and up the dais. The fallen Fae King stared down at the empty throne and bloody arrow, and Harley saw true sorrow in his eyes.

After what felt like an eternity, Yiannis stepped down and sat on the lower step. Sara, who had been kneeling on the floor near the dais, scooted away from him, terror written on her face, but Yiannis ignored her.

"And you, Cadence? Why did you not use your bow sooner? Why did you hesitate? If Jenta had an opportunity where the Dark Queen was distracted and did not use it, was it for the same reason that you did not use your own chance?" His face was not exactly happy as he spoke, but his tone was still gentle, rational.

Harley glared at him, her heart wrenched and twisted in knots.

"We stopped her, Yiannis. We closed the gate. Everything Estian tasked us with. That was supposed to fix things, but this doesn't look *fixed*." She gestured around them with one hand, her other still subconsciously holding Cadence to her, even has he hugged her waist like a child seeking solace. "You've said time and again that Danann is in this, but all I see right now is death and destruction. I see pain and suffering just as much as if we'd never stopped the Dark Queen, so what now?"

Behind her eyes, Harley felt that pulsing warmth she now associated with Danann's presence, but instead of feeling soothed, it made her feel, if possible, angrier.

Frode stepped forward, drawing everyone's attention to him as he cleared his throat. "Yiannis, some of the Unseelie would like to speak with you."

Epilogue

Estian

E stian sat at her vanity. It was another gift—this one from Faylin for her coronation as queen, and still one of her favorite pieces. The surface was well polished wood, smooth and clean. She studied herself in the mirror, her eyes tired, as her hands moved back and forth across the scroll worked edges of the table's surface.

It had been over two weeks since the departure of the four and their escort. She'd received sporadic messages back for the first few days as they passed through the Seelie lands, but when there should have been a message from Comhaontu, there was only silence. She'd ultimately given in and sent a rider only to learn that Comhaontu was no more. Accord was ended. Yiannis must have a good reason for his decision, surely, but that kind of power was not something she'd expected from him. Moreover, she wasn't exactly happy it had been done without her knowledge or approval beforehand.

And then there was the message she'd received from the steward of the catacombs.

That maze of halls and rooms beneath the castle that held their healing and resting ancestors and forebears, a place that was built by the first king,

443

using Danann's own power of creation. The steward wrote to let her know an entirely new hall had appeared unbidden. The steward investigated and found a large group of fae in need to healing, including Faustus and Ximeno, whose bodies were so thoroughly damaged she had gone to detach their spirits for healing, herself.

No new halls had been created within the catacombs since before she was born, and many of those among the fae sent to her owed no fealty to either Seelie or Unseelie. Even so, Estian approved healing for all, and to provide living quarters for those who requested it. At least until such time as they were well enough to depart for their homes.

Then, seven days past, a powerful force blasted through the castle just a little after dawn, leaving damage to the buildings and her people shaken. She'd already set masons to repair the sections of the wall that received the brunt of the damage, and some of the windows needed replacing, but fixing the nervous hum of conjecture and uncertainty was not nearly so simple.

An attack? A sign of success? Or of failure? Fear gripped Estian's heart, and she could do nothing but wait and pray to Danann for strength and patience.

A soft scratch at the door startled her. She gripped her nerves tightly and shook herself. She was the queen, and she had to be better than this.

"Come."

One of her ladies stepped in quickly, closing the door and leaning against it as she studied Estian.

"Your Majesty, a delegation just arrived, under the sign of truce. They claim to be from the Unseelie court, and bring tidings from His Royal Highness, King-Steward Yiannis Tide-Borne."

End of Book One, The Mortal Scales Trilogy

Acknowledgements

In a world full of interesting stories, I never anticipated that getting to share mine would matter to other people. It is because of their passion and support that I was able to open the door and let my story out. I owe so much to so many, but especially, I want to thank the following people:

To Ryan: My love, my heart, the Guardian at the gate to keep me safe. You've shown me that 'happily ever after' isn't just a fairy tale, and that true love exists.

To Leighann, thank you for being excited with me, for me, and sometimes, even in spite of my fear. Thank you for being the one who finally threw the door wide, when it had been so long shut and barred against the words that wanted to be told.

To E., I honestly never would have guessed that reaching out to you about editing would turn into a friendship that spans the miles, and now the increasing years. Without your encouragement and feedback, I don't know that the unpolished gem that I started with could have become the diamond that shines in my heart, and off the page.

To my family, thank you for introducing me to the worlds in which I walked as a child. The verdant fields of whimsy and fantasy, and even the darker passages, where I learned to fight for the things and people I care most about.

Last, to Shadow. Keeper of Dreams, traveler of the void. May you always dwell in my heart, my brave boy.

www.ingramcontent.com/pod-product-compliance
Lightning Source LLC
Chambersburg PA
CBHW030756260626
47169CB00001B/74